A Defense of Honor

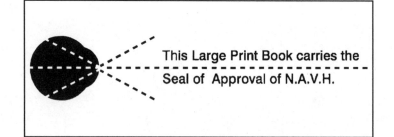

This Large Print Book carries the
Seal of Approval of N.A.V.H.

HAVEN MANOR, BOOK 1

A DEFENSE OF HONOR

KRISTI ANN HUNTER

THORNDIKE PRESS
A part of Gale, a Cengage Company

Farmington Hills, Mich • San Francisco • New York • Waterville, Maine
Meriden, Conn • Mason, Ohio • Chicago

LIBRARY OF CONGRESS CIP DATA ON FILE.
CATALOGUING IN PUBLICATION FOR THIS BOOK
IS AVAILABLE FROM THE LIBRARY OF CONGRESS

ISBN-13: 978-1-4328-5559-8 (hardcover)

Published in 2018 by arrangement with Bethany House Publishers, a division of Baker Publishing Group

Printed in the United States of America
1 2 3 4 5 6 7 22 21 20 19 18

To the Ultimate Owner of Justice
Romans 12:17–19

And to Jacob,
for always making me feel like
I have a place to belong.

CHAPTER ONE

London
1816

Graham, the Viscount Wharton, heir to the earldom of Grableton, pride of the Cambridge fencing team, coveted party guest, and generally well-liked member of both Brooke's and White's, was bored.

While the ball swirling around him held as much sparkle and elegance as ever, a dullness had taken the sheen off everything lately. The years he'd spent traveling the world after school had shown him the brilliance and variety of life, but since he'd been back in England, there'd been nothing but routine.

How long since he'd seen something new? Someone new? Three years? Four?

It wasn't so much that he wanted to chase adventure as he had in his youth — at a year past thirty he was more than ready to stay home — but was it too much to ask that his days have a little variety to them?

Everything and everyone simply looked the same.

"This year's young ladies seem to be lovelier than past years," Mr. Crispin Sherrington said, drawing Graham's thoughts away from his maudlin wanderings and back to the conversation he was having with two old acquaintances from school.

Lord Maddingly jabbed Mr. Sherrington with his elbow and chuckled. "The lighter your pockets, the prettier the partridges."

Even the conversations were the same, and they weren't any more interesting on their forty-second iteration than they were on their first. Different players and occasionally different motives, but Graham could say his lines by rote. "Are you looking to marry this year, Sherrington?"

Sherrington, a second son with limited prospects, slid a finger beneath his cravat and stretched his neck. "I don't have a choice. Pa's been ill, and when he's in the ground I'll have nothing. My brother Seymour is a little too thrilled at the idea of cutting me off when he inherits."

Maddingly grimaced. "At least your father didn't gamble it all away. You should see the mess I'm left with. I've got to build up the coffers if I hope to keep the roof over my head."

Graham resisted the urge to sigh. There were better ways for a man to further his fortune, but that opinion wasn't very popular among his peers. Instead of suggesting either man learn how to invest what funds they had or possibly even endeavor to save a bit, he continued on the conversation's normal course. "Who has the deepest dowry?"

Past experience told him that question was all that was required for him to seem like he cared. The others could hold a passionate debate about it without Graham's participation. Which was good, because he simply couldn't get excited about discussing how much money a man was willing to pay to get another man to marry his daughter.

It was all well and good to have a bit of support when starting a life together, but shouldn't the lady herself be a bit more of the enticement? She was, after all, the one a man was actually going to have to see for the rest of his life.

How had he ended up in a conversation with these two anyway? Graham's gaze wandered across the ballroom once more. Where were his friends? Granted, Mr. Aaron Whitworth probably wasn't in attendance, as he found socializing endlessly awkward, but Oliver, Lord Farnsworth, should be around somewhere.

The room fell into an unfocused blur until a flash of green near the terrace doors caught Graham's attention, making him blink furiously to bring everything into focus.

When he finally got the terrace doors to settle into their crisp lines of windowpanes and heavy drapery, no one was there. At least, no one wearing the shade of green he knew he'd seen a moment earlier.

The doors were closed, keeping the revelers sheltered from the unseasonably cold night, so where had the person come from? Had she gone outside? Was she coming back in?

"What is your opinion of her, Wharton?"

Graham pulled his gaze from the windowed doors lining the far wall and glanced at Sherrington's raised eyebrows. With a tilt of his head, Graham tried to appear deep in thought. And he was. Only he was trying to come up with a statement that wouldn't reveal he'd been ignoring the other two men, not considering the merits of any particular girl.

"Her family is good enough," he finally said. That should apply to every girl in the room. "She isn't likely to cause you much grief."

Unfortunately, there weren't many girls that second sentence didn't apply to either. Most of the gently bred women had been raised to smile and simper and act like nothing was ever wrong. It was part of what made them remarkably interchangeable. Which was probably why Graham was no closer to marriage at thirty-one than he'd been at twenty-one. He didn't want to lose track of his wife in the melee because he couldn't distinguish her from someone else.

Maddingly nodded in agreement with Graham's vague statement. "She might even be willing to live in the country while you stay in the city."

Sherrington scoffed. "Can't afford that nonsense." He frowned. "Think she'll expect such a thing, Wharton?"

How should he know? His parents enjoyed eating breakfast together every morning and talking in their private parlor into the night. He wasn't exactly the person to ask about distant marriages. Still, he didn't want his companions to know that he couldn't hold up his end of the conversation even if they'd given him a bucket to put it in. "Many matrons find a quiet life within the city, so she'll have no problem being more settled and less sociable."

Unless, of course, the woman was a har-

11

ridan or bluestocking, but by the time Sherrington discovered that, he'd have bigger problems than Graham's poor advice. Of course, the chances of Sherrington considering such a woman were nonexistent. He wasn't looking for distinct and memorable.

Unlike Graham. Who had apparently imagined a splash of bright green in the shape of a dress because he was that desperate to meet someone who didn't bore him. A woman he could even begin to consider making a life with.

Sherrington and Maddingly continued their discussion, debating whether or not the girl's father would be amenable to Sherrington's suit. Graham made sure to pay a token of attention to the conversation so as not to be caught off guard again. Most of his attention was on the women dancing by, though. One wore a blue dress, the color distinct enough to stand out in a crowd. It wasn't as bold as a bright green, but it was at least unusual. The girl was probably less inane than the rest of them.

"I'd best move into position if I want to ask her for the next set of dances." Sherrington straightened his coat and nodded to his companions. "To the gallows, gentlemen."

Graham grinned. "Rather confident, isn't he?"

Maddingly laughed and wished his friend luck.

"Charville's girl won't be enough for me, I'm afraid." Maddingly adjusted his coat. "Only the biggest catch of the season will do for me."

Maddingly's difficulties weren't as bad as he made them seem, so Graham left him to his self-sacrificing monologue. The girl in green was more intriguing, even if she were only in his imagination. He turned his attention to the more deeply colored gowns of the matrons and spinsters. Still no vibrant spring green.

When Maddingly stopped talking, Graham continued the conversation, more out of habit than actual curiosity. "Who have you settled on, then?"

Whatever name Maddingly responded with didn't matter, because there, barely visible through the limbs of a cluster of potted trees along the far wall, was a patch of green. How had she gotten all the way over there without him seeing her?

"Yes," Maddingly continued, "I think Lady Thalia will be delighted by my intention to court her."

Graham actually knew who the mildly

popular Lady Thalia was, and that far better matches than Maddingly were taking her for a turn around the floor, but he wasn't about to contradict the man. Especially not now that he knew the woman in green wasn't imaginary. Though why would a woman wear such an eye-catching color if she intended to plant herself behind the potted shrubbery all evening?

Plant herself behind the shrubbery.

A grin crossed Graham's face as he chuckled at his own cleverness.

Now that he'd found the woman, he had a desperate need to meet her, but first he had to get away from Maddingly. "Why don't you start by asking her to dance?"

The branches parted slightly, and a hand reached through and plucked a *petite duchesse* pastry off the tray of a passing servant.

Was she hiding? Well, obviously she was hiding, but was it from a persistent suitor or an overbearing mother?

With a grim but determined look, Maddingly nodded and made his way around the edge of the ballroom. Graham wished him well and meant it, but he was more interested in watching another servant carry a tray loaded with food past the grouping of trees. Again the hand reached through and grabbed a morsel as the footman passed.

Why didn't she simply go to the refreshment table and get a plate of food?

His palms began to itch with the same excitement he'd had every time he boarded a ship bound for a new part of the world. It was the itch of curiosity, of questions that needed answers. At last, here was something new and unusual.

And if she turned out to be nothing special? Well, at least he'd have filled one evening with something other than tedium.

He kept his eye on the cluster of greenery as he wound his way through the room. She was not slipping away from him again. A blond head popped out from behind the trees and glanced out the window before disappearing again. What could possibly interest her in the gardens she'd only recently left? Was she running from someone? A gentleman who had tried to take advantage of her?

An unbidden and unfathomable desire to defend the unknown woman's honor rose up in him. For all he knew, she might not have any honor to save. She was hiding behind a potted tree, after all.

Accomplished excuses tripped off his tongue without a great deal of thought as he dodged through the crowd of greetings and attempted conversations. He snagged two glasses of lemonade from the refreshment table as he passed.

If he was going to commit a major breach of etiquette, he should bring a peace offering. Besides, she must be thirsty. A tray of drinks hadn't passed by yet.

He slipped behind the trees, ducking his head a bit. He wasn't overly tall, but neither were the trees, and he'd worked too hard to slip back here and meet the mystery woman only to have someone notice him and ruin the moment.

"Good evening."

She jumped and spun toward him, clutching a bundle of dark grey fabric to her chest.

Up close, the dress was even more unusual. Bold and confident without appearing garish or tawdry. It lacked the abundance of jewels and trim other ladies were wearing. In fact, it looked nothing like what the other women in the ballroom were wearing. He'd never claimed to hold any excessive knowledge of women's fashions, but this dress looked . . . old.

That was the only word for it.

As they stood there, quietly staring at each other, he noticed that the glorious green satin had been altered, adjusted. More than one seam showed wear, and the hem was frayed in a couple places. Where had she come from?

She recovered her composure before he did, erasing the surprise from her face and giving him a regal nod. "Good evening."

Her voice was calm, quiet. It didn't hold the grating, overzealous brightness that so many of the other women in the ballroom used. He liked it. His smile widened as he extended one of the glasses. "Lemonade?"

Pale blue eyes stared at the glass for a moment before rising to meet his. Not a flicker of expression crossed her features, which weren't as young as he'd first expected them to be. Fine lines appeared at the corners of her eyes and mouth, a maturity that she wore easily. She was well past the age of the simpering beauties filling the dance floor. A widow, perhaps? An older sister of a family racked with genteel poverty? Perhaps even someone's companion or a governess?

They looked at each other until the moment grew awkward, but still she didn't take the glass. Did she think he would do something to her in the middle of the ball? Very well, it wasn't the middle. They were off to the edge, but more than a hundred people milled nearby.

"I assure you it's harmless." Graham took a sip of the offered drink. "See?"

A small smile tilted one side of her lips as

she finally took the glass. "I see."

He leaned one shoulder against the wall. "I know I'm being abominably rude by introducing myself, but your friend here" — he nodded to the shield of greenery — "doesn't seem too talkative."

"No, he isn't." She took a sip. "And you still haven't introduced yourself."

He felt like a lad just out of school, pinned by her laughing blue eyes and small, pink smile. "My mistake. Lord Wharton, at your service."

"A pleasure, Lord Wharton. I've never heard of you, which I can assure you is to your credit." She took another sip of lemonade and peered around the edge of the tree.

Was he being dismissed? The possibility was both uncomfortable and unpleasant. He'd never had to fight for a woman's attention before. "Would you care to dance?"

She looked back at him with a sly grin and patted the sculpted tree. "Sadly, I've committed the next two to our friend here."

He was being passed over for a bush? "I'm sure he won't mind if I cut in."

"I believe in honoring my commitments, Lord Wharton. I'm afraid I would have to protest such an action on your part."

This was what he'd been looking for without even knowing it. Spirit. Freshness.

And all wrapped in a strikingly beautiful package. Her blond hair was piled on her head in a simple style and she wore no jewelry. Graham's brow furrowed. No jewelry? At a *ton* ball? London's elite socialized a mere five feet from their current position, and she wore no jewelry?

"I suppose I'll dance with his companion, then." He gestured to the tree on the other side of the cluster. He nodded to the two in the middle. "They can partner each other. Should be the oddest quadrille I've ever danced."

The woman sputtered a short giggle. "Particularly as there are only three couples involved."

"Indeed."

Silence stretched as Graham took the smallest sips of lemonade possible, allowing the tart liquid to rest on his tongue before swallowing it. Somehow he knew that once his drink was gone, she would expect him to leave. He closed his lips on the glass and allowed the liquid to touch his upper lip without actually drinking any.

"Why are you here, Lord Wharton?" She held out her empty glass, forcing him to take it from her in order to remain a gentleman. Apparently she felt no need to prolong the encounter with extended sipping.

"I like the company and activity. There's a bit of social expectation —"

"No, *here,* Lord Wharton. Dancing with a bush."

"I'm dancing with a bush because you declined my invitation."

She raised an eyebrow. Again he was transported back to his school days, getting reprimanded for his poor Latin conjugations. "I saw your dress," he admitted.

Surprise lit her features as she glanced down at her skirt. "My dress?"

He shrugged. "It's green. I like green."

She looked skeptical but said nothing. The Mozart piece lulled to a quiet finish. By silent agreement, they waited until the music swelled once more before speaking again.

"You haven't told me your name." Graham looked directly into her eyes, willing them to stay on his own so he could try to guess what she was thinking and feeling. At a glance, she seemed simple and straightforward, but her eyes hid things. They were tight around the edges, as if she couldn't quite completely relax.

Her gaze kept his but remained shuttered, granting him nothing. "No, I haven't."

No name, then. "Are you new to London?"

Her gaze dropped from his to the wall on his right. "No."

She was lying. This got more interesting by the minute. She kept staring at the wall, though, tilting her head as if the blank expanse were fascinating. "Do you like green?"

"I beg your pardon?" Her gaze snapped back to his.

Graham wanted to grin at catching her by surprise but nodded to her dress instead. "Your dress. Do you like green?"

"Oh. I suppose." She slid a section of skirt between her fingers. For the first time, a bit of hesitancy flitted across her face. "It reminds me who I am."

Someone beyond the trees laughed loudly. The woman in green pressed herself against the wall, dropping her skirt so that she could wrap both arms around the grey bundle and hold it tightly.

Graham drained his lemonade in frustration. They were sure to be discovered at any moment. Her skirt might be easily looked over, blending in somewhat with the color of the trees. His black trousers, however, would soon be noticed in the small gap between the pot and the bottom branches of the shrub.

"May I call on you?" When was the last

21

time he'd asked permission to call on a woman? Years, if ever. The question always raised impossible expectations.

She didn't answer. Simply stared at him, mouth slightly agape.

"Graham, there you are!"

Graham looked over his shoulder to see a man in pristine evening black strolling around the edge of the trees. *Now* Oliver decided to make an appearance? Where was the man when Graham was drowning in boring conversation about dowries and marriage settlements? Honestly, if Oliver weren't one of Graham's closest friends, he'd push him into one of the potted trees.

Oliver's brows drew together. "What are you doing back here? Didn't you know you're supposed to be on the other side of the trees, where you can be found by all the people who need you to inject levity and hope into their miserable lives?"

The reference to an old love letter Graham had received while attending Cambridge made him groan even as he smiled. He should never have shown that letter to Oliver. "If you must know, I'm replenishing my well of levity by talking with —"

His words trailed off as he turned to find the space beside him empty. The woman had vanished once more.

Chapter Two

Kit, buried in the memories of some people in the ballroom as The Honorable Katherine FitzGilbert, took a deep breath in the hopes that it would somehow calm the heart stuttering in her chest. Emotions she couldn't even begin to name pounded through her so fast and with such variety that all she could do was close her eyes and hope the whirling in her head didn't make her ill.

This had been a night for firsts. Or at least a night for things she hadn't done in so long they felt like firsts.

Things she thought she'd never do again.

She leaned against the wall in the dark and focused on breathing. In. Out. Repeat.

This night was supposed to have been so simple. Come into London, frighten a man into signing away a portion of his fortune for the next twelve years, then go home. On the surface it probably wasn't the most noble way to provide a living for those she cared about, but then again, she'd lost hope for most things considered noble more than a decade ago.

After all, it was the nobility that she was protecting innocent children from, the nobility who didn't mind their own secret, dark, and vile behavior, the nobility who would gleefully cast one of their own onto the mercies of the street if it meant another day's worth of gossip.

She should know. She'd been one of them. The Honorable Katherine FitzGilbert. Until she'd fallen from honor in their eyes — condemned, ruined, and suddenly worthless to her own noble father. No, worse than worthless. She'd been a detriment.

So, after cleaning up after the nobility for a dozen years, not being considered noble was practically a compliment.

Still . . .

She rolled her head to the side and allowed her eyes to fall open, looking through the darkness as if her gaze could pierce through the wall and see the dancers beyond. See him.

He was noble. And he'd seemed nice. But then again, they all knew how to put up a pretty front.

His humor and ability to mock himself,

however, were something she didn't remember ever encountering before.

One hand groped along the wall until she found the edge of the hidden door she'd eased through. It blended with the ballroom wall, leaving only the faintest outline for Kit to notice while avoiding the man's golden-brown gaze. It had made the perfect escape. Obviously, the host hadn't intended for people to use it, given the dark corridor beyond and the tree barricade, but that was all the more reason for Kit to seek her escape through it.

She eased the door open the slightest bit and pressed her face tightly to the wall while squeezing her left eye shut. Nothing but light and trees. The man was gone.

With any luck, she would never see him again. She didn't want to discover that a man who brought lemonade and a charming smile to women hiding behind ballroom decorations was also the type of man who would dally with a woman and then leave her to deal with the consequences. She didn't want to one day have to accost him in his own home and demand he take care of a life he had carelessly and thoughtlessly created.

A slight nudge of her hand slid the door closed once more, leaving her in near total darkness. She didn't mind the darkness. It was easier to hide in the dark.

Which was why she'd run for the lights of the ballroom in the first place. The two thugs chasing her had been as comfortable running down a dark alley as she'd been, probably more so. Her only defense had been to find as many people as possible. Important people. Ones the thugs' employer wouldn't want them disturbing.

It had been a good idea, actually, right up until she'd lingered. She'd let the music and candlelight overwhelm her with memories, leaving her frozen in her hiding place, unable to work her way quietly to the nearest door. She shouldn't have given in to her desire to see if the cream-filled, chocolate-glazed confections were as good as she remembered.

She shouldn't have let herself remember in the first place.

But nostalgia had caught her by surprise, smothering the urgency to escape, and she'd stayed, unable to stop the visions of a happier time.

A time before she knew how cruel the people smiling on the dance floor could be. A time before she knew the secrets everyone tried to hide and pretended to ignore.

A time when being approached by a

charming gentleman would have been welcome.

What had his name been? Wharton? It wasn't a title she knew, nor had she recognized the man. Of course, thirteen long years had passed since her days in society. Even then, her one and only Season had been cut short.

Oh, how she missed the dancing. And the food. She pressed a hand to her midsection, which felt odd and sort of swirly. It had to be the rich food, though the luxurious explosion of sugar and chocolate had been worth it.

Yes, it was the food. She could not have actually enjoyed the attentions of the gentleman, could not be relishing that moment of feeling pretty and interesting again, could not be missing the naïve, carefree girl she'd once been.

Her arm squeezed the bundled cloak tighter and her other hand buried itself in the green satin skirt. The crinkling sound of papers in her cloak pocket chased out the lingering melodies of a string quartet. This was her life now. It didn't include pastries and dancing, but long days of hard work sprinkled with occasional visits to horrible men like she'd had to do tonight.

Kit walked carefully down the dark passage. Moonlight from a nearby window cut across the floor, giving her just enough light to make her way without stumbling. She paused at the window, looked down at London. A pit of greed and lies covered in the mask of false smiles and frivolity. Did those people in the ballroom behind her really think the lavish gowns and the ostentatious promenading would protect them from the ugliness in life?

No, they only hid it. In this world, proof mattered little, and truth mattered even less. Appearance was the true ruler of London's elite. As long as they sparkled in all the right places, no one bothered to look beneath the surface.

Until it cracked. Then they picked and prodded, painted it with whatever color they wished before discarding it like last week's rubbish.

This was the danger of awakening memories. The bad ones slept right beside the good.

No matter how enticing the man with the gentle smile and wit had been, it would be better for everyone if Kit did what she did best and disappeared.

She walked down the passage, away from the window. Away from the scents of smoke and perfume, away from the overused platitudes and rehearsed conversations. Away from the pleasant tang of lemonade.

Life in the shadows might be lonely and scary compared with the popular existence she'd led before, but at least in her new world people were honest about what they were doing to each other.

Well. Most of the time.

She shook her head. Philosophical musings weren't going to get her safely out of London with the packet of papers intact. And she needed to get home. They were supposed to sow carrots tomorrow, and if Kit wasn't there to make sure the lines were straight, Daphne would let them be planted in swirls and whorls because it made the garden prettier. And Jess would let her, just to see Kit get irritated.

What she needed to do was get out of this house, find the nearest inn, and take the first stage out of town. It didn't matter where it was going as long as it was out of London.

Were the thugs waiting in the garden, thinking she'd go out the way she came? Had they circled around to the front of the house? It would be nice if they'd simply given up and gone home, but Kit didn't think she'd have that kind of luck.

The passage gave way to a dimly lit parlor.

Three closed doors broke up the two side walls, and a large arch across from Kit opened into the large landing at the top of the wide, curving staircase. She'd climbed that staircase once before. A lifetime ago.

And now, she would go down those stairs. She would lose herself in whatever crowd of people departed next, slip through the carriages waiting out front, and disappear into the night.

With a deep breath that she hoped would convince her heart to stop crashing against her ribs, she stepped into the parlor.

She had made it halfway across the room when one of the closed doors opened and a lone man emerged, adjusting his waistcoat over a slight paunch.

No. Her luck couldn't possibly be that bad, could it? But as the man stepped into a circle of light cast by a nearby candle, Kit's heart nearly stopped, because yes, she was indeed that unlucky. Even though the face wore a decade's worth of additional age and the hair sported considerably more grey, she knew that man. She knew him well.

And she really, really didn't want to talk to him.

She dropped her gaze to her toes and willed herself to keep walking. Her father had yet to see her, hadn't even acknowledged that he wasn't alone in the parlor. But her feet refused to move, gripping the rug through the soles of her boots. Apparently she was going to be attempting the statue method of concealment. She held her breath and made herself as small as possible, inching her heels sideways until her hip pressed against a decorative table.

While she was usually very good at not being seen when she didn't want to be, an empty room didn't leave her many places to hide.

The man passed her, head down as he focused on straightening his waistcoat. His foot bumped into a chair and his head popped up. "Pardon me."

A gust of momentary laughter rushed from him as he realized he'd apologized to a chair, but then his gaze swung sideways and connected with Kit's. The small, self-deprecating smile fell from his face to be replaced by the thunderous frown that hadn't aged a bit. "Katherine."

"Father." She tilted her head sideways in a gesture that fell somewhere between acknowledgment and respect.

Then there was silence. Long, heavy silence. After all these years, did they have nothing to say to each other? Even in the absence of onlookers? Kit swallowed. Had he cried for the lost years as she had? The midnight book discussions? Their long walks through the parks?

Perhaps he hadn't. It had been at least five years since Kit had acknowledged feeling any sort of loss. She'd thought herself well and truly done with those thoughts, so the spark of hope that flared in her heart surprised her even as she chided herself for allowing it. No good could come of it, just as the desire to throw herself into his arms was ridiculous and futile. It didn't matter how badly she simply wanted to breathe, to be held by someone who cared, to be innocent and naïve.

Those luxuries were lost to her, and the hard look on her father's face proved they weren't coming back.

That sad truth freed her feet from their strange emotional mire. She stepped forward, intent on leaving the room and the house.

"You'll not get any more money from me." His voice smashed the silence with the force of a hammer.

Anger welled within her, an emotion she hadn't even felt when he'd cast her out all those years ago. She'd understood, made excuses, rationalized it all from his point of view. But now to deny a monetary request she had never made? She wanted to lash out. Make him guilty. If it worked, they could use the money.

"Why not?" She took her sternest pose. The one she used when staring down irresponsible young men, careless young women, and neglectful fathers. "I've asked nothing from you in thirteen years. Why shouldn't you be called on to support me, your own flesh and blood?"

Thirteen years. One year more than the amount of time she forced other men to take care of the children they didn't want. And yet it had never occurred to her to force her father to do the same.

He huffed. "We made an agreement."

"And I have kept it," Kit bit out.

"Yet here you are."

That was a statement she couldn't argue with. She had agreed not to return to London. "I had business."

He scoffed. His tone was ugly. "Business. What business could you have at a society ball?"

"I had to make my way in this world. Did you think my dowry large enough to live on forever? It wasn't that big, Papa."

He growled. He actually growled at her. The childhood name she'd used for him must have struck a chord. Tears threatened.

Had it really come to this? An ugly estrangement from her father? Suddenly she couldn't do it anymore. She couldn't manipulate her father the way she did the unscrupulous cads she forced into supporting their children.

"You should have found some hapless country *cit* to marry you. You were pretty enough when you were younger. He would have overlooked a scandal then."

Was he saying she looked old now? She certainly felt it. Still, perhaps she had it in her to manipulate him, after all. At least enough to make him sleep a little bit worse tonight.

It took Graham a full five minutes to extricate himself from Oliver and his relentless teasing about Graham's new imaginary friend. He'd finally mumbled his excuses and simply walked away while Oliver tried to control his laughter enough to avoid the censure of society's matrons.

Graham couldn't care less about society's matrons at the moment or what they might be whispering behind their fans. He wanted to find the woman in green.

He rubbed his hands together as he stepped out of the ballroom. The white evening gloves pulled against his fingers as the fabric caught itself, and he resisted the urge to tug them off and stuff them in his pocket. One last glance over his shoulder confirmed there was no bold slash of green in the ballroom. So where had she gone?

The house was large, built before Mayfair had become crowded with terraced housing. That meant it had a ballroom large enough to fit the entire party and plenty of unused rooms where someone could hide if they were so inclined.

And since Graham wasn't quite willing to wander aimlessly around his host's home, he was left with nothing to do but make his way toward the door and try to convince himself she hadn't actually been imaginary.

If he'd made her up, wouldn't he have at least given her a name? What would it say about him if his mind invented a woman who then soundly rejected him?

"Get out."

The angry voice had Graham stumbling to a halt and looking around to take his bearings. He was near the retiring rooms, just around the corner from a parlor that had been lit and prepared for guests needing a moment of respite.

Or apparently guests needing to have a semi-public confrontation.

"Get out," the man repeated, "and stay

out. Stay out of London. We had an agreement, and I expect you to at least have enough honor left to keep it."

Graham frowned and leaned around the edge of the open archway. He recognized the man standing near a cluster of chairs. The tension rising from Lord FitzGilbert's shoulders rolled across the room in waves until even Graham felt the need to adjust his cravat. The baron was blocking Graham's view of whoever was making him angry, which actually wasn't that hard to do. The man's temper was rather notorious. But to make a man agree to leave London?

"And if I don't?"

Right, then. Not a man. Graham nearly tumbled headfirst through the archway as the feminine voice sank into his brain. It was familiar. He knew the woman.

Graham's attention snapped to the floor where the lines of a brilliant green skirt were visible.

Lord FitzGilbert growled. "If Hamilton has brought you here to befoul my plans, so help me, I'll —"

"You'll what?" She stepped around him and unbundled her cloak. "What could you possibly do to hurt me now?"

The baron sputtered, trying to mention something about Australia, but the mystery woman simply walked away without a second glance, draping her cloak across her shoulders as she went.

"You aren't worth my time," she said over her shoulder.

Once through the archway, she lifted her eyebrows as her blue gaze connected with Graham's, but she didn't pause, didn't even slow down. A moment later, she was disappearing down the stairs.

Graham followed her, trying to see the dark cloak among the clusters of people in the hall below. Servants ran to and fro, fetching cloaks and wraps to keep people warm on the short walk to their waiting carriages. Finally he found her amid a group near the door. She flipped her hood over her head and followed them out into the night.

It took him longer than he'd hoped to wade through the people and convince the servants he really did intend to leave without waiting for his greatcoat. Yes, it would be embarrassing to come back for it later, but if he lost the only thread he had on the enigmatic lady in green, he had a feeling he'd regret it for the rest of his life.

He almost lost it anyway. Shadows stretched across the street outside, providing numerous places for a woman wrapped in dark grey velvet to hide.

But God was of a mood to bless Graham tonight, because he saw a flutter of green in the light of one of the carriage lanterns as the lady he was searching for crossed the street.

Graham walked quickly in that direction. She was rather good at slipping away, which sent a spear of worry into the middle of his obsessive fascination. Something new didn't necessarily mean something better.

He followed her down the street and into a square. He didn't even know which square, since he hadn't paid that much attention to where tonight's ball had been and simply gave the direction to his coachman.

What did he think he was doing? He knew nothing about this woman — well, nearly nothing. Didn't know where she was going or even really where they were. What little he did know about her didn't point to her being someone he could really build a relationship and a life with, so why was he chasing her?

Was he truly so bored that he would tangle his life with that of a woman who could be involved in all sorts of unpleasant endeavors?

"We'll be having your valuables now. Don't think to run from us again."

Graham sighed and looked toward the sky. Perhaps God wasn't in such a blessing mood this evening, but it was Graham's own fault. If he'd stayed where he was expected to be, he'd still be mired in idle conversation, not hearing angry men throwing threats around in the shadows. What was it with men being so aggressive tonight?

He'd been robbed by thugs of this ilk before — who in London hadn't? A flicker of sympathy for tonight's unfortunate victim warred with a gratefulness that it wasn't him.

"If we have to catch ye a third time, we'll not ask so nicely."

Graham frowned. That sounded a bit more persistent than the average park footpad.

"As you can see, gentlemen, I've no baubles to give you. Not even a reticule at my disposal."

He knew that voice. It had never graced his ears before tonight, but he'd heard it quite a bit over the past hour. And it was a common factor in all the situations with angry men he'd come across. It would seem he really should let the woman run out of his life the way she wanted to.

But not before he made sure she could do so safely. He moved quietly toward the voices, tucked in a small copse of trees at the corner of the park.

"I'm afraid I have nothing for you." The woman's voice had grown grim now, dangerous. Gone was the teasing lilt he'd heard behind the trees in the ballroom, gone was the haughty disdain from the parlor. In its place was a voice cold and hard enough to send chills down Graham's spine. And he wasn't even the target.

"Oh, I think you do." One of the thugs laughed in that creepy manner that Graham had never understood. He'd always imagined the villains in gothic romances laughing like that.

"No, I really don't."

Graham was close enough to make out the outlines of three people now, and one of them, the one with skirt and cloak billowing about her knees, had just pulled a knife.

CHAPTER THREE

Kit's mouth dried up as her fingers curled tighter around the handle of the knife. A few years ago, a woman named Jess had joined their household. She'd insisted on training everyone to protect themselves, but to date the only person Kit had ever actually cut was herself.

But if getting home safely meant creating a slash or two in the flesh of one of these men, well, this had already been a night of firsts. What was one more?

The angry swirl of nausea in the pit of her stomach disagreed with her attempted nonchalance. She tried to swallow, but there wasn't a drop of liquid to be found in her mouth.

If she was forced to draw blood, there wouldn't be anything left in her stomach either.

One by one, she forced her fingers to relax their grip until she was holding the knife more loosely. Throwing had been the only part of knife training that she'd excelled at. Although *excelled* might be a bit of an exaggeration. It had been the only part she enjoyed. There was something cathartic about throwing knife after knife into a tree. If she threw this knife, though, she'd only have one more at her disposal and that one was strapped high on her leg. Not really something she wanted to retrieve in front of Lord Charles Tromboll's two thuggish footmen.

"Hullo there!"

The voice from the open area of the park distracted the men enough for Kit to shift sideways a bit so that at least she didn't have trees to her back. Jess would skewer Kit to the knife-throwing tree if she learned Kit had run herself into a corner trying to hide. Her cloak snagged on one of the tree branches, bringing her sidling escape to a halt. A swift tug broke the small limb the fabric had snagged on, bringing the branch banging into her arm as the cloak resettled around her shoulders.

A man appeared, his face shadowed by the moon behind him. He strolled toward their little gathering with his hands clasped behind his back. "What seems to be the problem?"

Kit almost laughed at what this must look like, her standing ready with a knife in her hand and the other men seemingly unarmed. She took another glance at the newcomer and realized she knew him. It was shrubbery man. What was his name? Wharton.

Was he following her? Her mouth pressed into a grim line. She'd known he couldn't be as perfect as he'd seemed. No one was. She'd have to shake him loose, but she could only deal with one problem at a time. "These men were just leaving. They have an urgent message to carry across town."

The presence of a young, sober man made her attackers much more cautious. "Of course," the one with teeth, and apparently a few wits, said. "If you'll just give us the papers with that message on it, we'll be on our way."

What had Jess said about bravado? It was practically as good as actual bravery? Kit pictured pushing all of her rioting emotions down into her feet. Cool, calculating, and untouchable were what she needed now. "The message isn't written."

With a slow arch of her eyebrow, she snagged the limb at the edge of her cloak. She gripped it tightly to keep from trembling. A single tug released the branch, the first blessing Kit had received all day. She switched the knife to her left hand and held the limb in her right. Would it throw the same as a knife?

A flick of her wrist sent the limb flinging forward to plant itself between the feet of one of the hired men. She'd been aiming for the other one's chest.

No one needed to know that.

"Next time," Kit said, in the same voice that sent the children in her household scurrying to do their chores, "I'll use the knife. And I'll aim a bit higher."

How she hoped that sounded menacing to ears other than her own. In her head she sounded like a child playing pirate.

Still, she moved the knife back to her right hand and stood ready. As much as she enjoyed knife-throwing, she couldn't really aim for anything other than a general area. A man's body was a fairly large general area, though. Sinking the knife anywhere would probably buy her enough time to run away, though she'd hate to lose the knife, and it really only guaranteed she'd slow one of them down.

Brazening it out was still her best plan.

Of course, none of her other plans had gone well today, so perhaps she should go with the worst plan she could think of and just run into the night, screaming like a banshee.

Several moments of silence weighed heavily. A carriage rolled down the street, wheels clattering and horses snorting, but no one in the small copse of trees paid it any attention.

The man she'd thrown the stick at — the one she'd actually almost hit, not the one she aimed for — took a step forward, knocking the stick aside.

Kit flipped the knife in the air and caught it, pinching the blade between her fingers while trying to look haughty and confident. She couldn't throw with the blade for anything, but Jess always looked impressive doing it, and right now, Kit needed to look more impressive than she actually was.

"Our master will be wanting those papers." One of them growled. "Soon."

Then they started sidling away, looking from the knife to Lord Wharton and back again. Roughing up someone like herself with no real connections and a bit of a shady reputation was one thing, but it was obvious that Lord Wharton was someone important. They might even know who he was. Kit wasn't even going to pretend that it was her amazing display of stick-throwing that had finally scared them off, but she was proud that she hadn't stood by helpless.

Jess would be proud as well. At least, she'd be proud of Kit in the version of the event that Kit would tell at home.

Now she just had to get rid of Lord Wharton.

And then get out of town.

She slid the knife back into her cloak pocket. "Are you following me, Lord Wharton?"

"Yes. No." He rubbed the back of his neck. "In a manner of speaking."

The picture he made was so charmingly boyish that Kit couldn't stay mad. "I suppose I can overlook it, seeing as your presence made a difference tonight. This, however, is where we part ways."

"Can I walk you home? They might return." He offered his elbow.

Part of her wanted to slip her hand into his offered arm. But those days were long past. They belonged in a different life. London was dangerous in more ways than one. She couldn't afford to dream of that old life. She had no right to it anymore.

"I think it best if we part here. Should someone recognize me, I wouldn't want your reputation harmed." With a quick nod, she hurried across the park. Maybe the incongruity of her statement would keep him befuddled long enough for her to escape the public area. Once on a side street, she could lose him easily.

"Please," he called after her. "A name. Your street. Your town. Perhaps the breed of dog that you walk in Hyde Park."

Kit stopped, the weight of the loaded-down cloak pockets feeling more like a burden than it ever had before. One hand groped through the folds until she could wrap her fingers around the edge of a sheaf of papers. Papers that would ensure the support of an innocent life. These were why she was in London. To get these papers signed and nothing else. This was her life now — these papers and everything they represented.

She couldn't let him find her.

Ever.

For all of his pursuing, he'd been nothing but nice. Kit desperately wanted to believe, just for a moment, that nice, honest people actually existed among the upper echelons of British society. And if he were one of those rare people, he didn't deserve to be overwhelmed by curiosity about her. Better for both of them if he forgot this entire night.

There had to be something she could give him to break his fascination, to save the hor-

47

rid nights of asking himself *what if.* She knew all too well how exhausting such nights were.

She turned to face him. His features were highlighted by the moon now, and a light breeze whisked his dark brown hair into a frolicking dance. "You seem to be a good man, Lord Wharton, and as much as I hate to admit it, I am in your debt for your timely presence this evening."

"Then grant me a boon. I ask for your name." He stopped a good five paces away. Had he come any closer, she'd have run. How had he known?

Words flitted through her mind. She could give him a fake name. A lie that could be as comfortable for him to cling to as her real name.

Would he know who she was if she told him she was The Governess? She hated the name she'd claimed in a desperate attempt to sound more authoritative and imposing. Like the men who oversaw the Foundling Hospital called themselves governors. Hated or not, she was grateful that its murky fame amongst less honorable men expedited explanations a bit.

If Wharton was a good man, though, he wouldn't know that name. And she wanted to leave here still thinking he was a good man.

"Kit."

Well, then. Apparently she was going to leave him with her real name. An interesting choice she couldn't remember making.

With a tight smile and a nod of acknowledgment, she turned and walked away, straining her ears to hear if he would indeed let her leave on her own this time. There was nothing. She was free to go home. Why wasn't she happy about that? Did she want the man to chase her all over London?

Four turns later she took her first deep breath of the evening. She was finally confident that she was completely alone.

One more turn brought her to the inn, but she'd already missed that day's post headed west. The delay of dealing with, well, men, had meant that she'd more than used up her narrow allotment of time. She'd either have to spend the extra money and take the long way home or hide for most of tomorrow while she waited for the next mail coach.

Money was tight, so there really wasn't an option, now that she was out of danger, at least for the most part. Wrapped tightly in her grey cloak, she waited until no one was looking and then settled against the outside wall of the stable. In the morning she'd go into the inn, buy a meal, and wait for the stage, but she couldn't afford to let a room. Her head dropped forward onto her knees, the large hood of the cloak settling her in a shroud of darkness. Then she tried to sleep.

Graham blinked his dry, tired eyes in an effort to focus on the plate in front of him. He'd stayed awake most of the night, alternating between wondering about the woman named Kit in a brilliant green dress who was clearly nothing but trouble and analyzing his apparently desperate need for a break in the monotony that was his life.

All that either had given him was an aching head.

He shoved a bite of food into his mouth, not even sure what it was, putting all his energy into chewing and swallowing and not becoming irritated by the scrape of fork against plate or the rustling sound of his father turning the page of his newspaper.

"Are you feeling well this morning, Wharton? You've hardly touched your food." The concerned voice of his mother didn't quite match the disapproval on her face as she looked pointedly at Graham's plate.

"Stop badgering the boy, Lady Grableton, or he'll do like his friends and take up some horrid bachelor residence." Graham's father folded one corner of the paper down and winked at his son.

"Why would he want to do that?" the countess mumbled. "It's not as if I asked him why he stepped out of the ball early last night without even collecting his great-coat — we brought it home for you, by the way. I'm not even asking where he went afterward, since he wasn't yet home when we arrived back." She sniffed. "I'm simply trying to see to his sustenance and well-being."

His father sighed. "If he can't take care of that at the age of one and thirty, I'm not sure there's much we can do about it now."

Graham hid his smile behind a serviette. His parents were certainly entertaining in the mornings. Perhaps that was why break-fast had become such a tradition for his family. Maybe even why he still lived at home.

Because one day *he* would be Lord Grableton, and he'd miss these moments.

He tried to stifle a yawn. Maybe he should have skipped this morning, though. Ignoring his mother's frown, Graham excused himself from the table. Normally he lin-gered, enjoying the fact that his family actu-ally liked each other, a rarity among his friends, but this morning that likability was going to have to extend a bit of forgiveness.

Perhaps he should simply go back to bed. The fear that he might lie there, head awash with questions he could never answer — instead of going to sleep — kept him from indulging the idea very long.

Instead, he made his way to the billiard room and proceeded to knock the balls around, his mind still on the woman more than on the game. What sort of a name was Kit for a woman? Had she gotten home safely? Where was home anyway? Could she actually have hit anything with that knife she'd been brandishing about? The ludicrousness of it all left him praying for some form of distraction. A big one.

The door to the billiard room slammed against the wall, mak ing Graham jerk his mace against the ball and send it careening across the green baize.

Mr. Aaron Whitworth, the man who rounded out Graham and Oliver's trio of friends, strode into the room looking polished and professional. The man he was dragging behind him looked anything but. Oliver was still in the clothes he'd worn to the ball the night before, though *disheveled* would be a compliment to their current state. Aaron's fist wrapped in Oliver's jacket collar wasn't helping.

With a fling and push, Aaron sent Oliver into the room. Oliver didn't stop moving once he regained his balance, though. He simply started pacing, agitation in every line and feature. He walked right past Graham and kept walking until he'd crossed the room and it was either turn around or hit the wall. Oliver chose to turn around, but that didn't still his feet. He paced the entire room, obviously upset and clearly in need of assistance — from a good valet, if nothing else.

Graham watched him, frozen in his position crouched over the billiard table. *Thank you, God.* Ask and ye shall receive. It looked like a distraction had just landed in his lap.

Aaron crossed his arms and glared at the pacing Oliver.

"What's going on?" Graham asked, straightening.

"He" — Aaron jabbed one blunt finger in Oliver's direction — "showed up at my door this morning, ranting and rambling until my brain's gone scrambled. I can't make sense of it, so I brought him to you."

Graham looked from Aaron to Oliver and back again. Oliver hadn't ever been what one might consider clever, but he'd always seemed quite rational. "Rambling?"

Aaron shrugged and crossed his arms over his chest.

Finally, Oliver stopped moving and placed both hands on the edge of the billiard table, staring at Graham with eyes rimmed in red. "Lady Anne Brigston is in France."

Graham blinked. What was he supposed to do with that information? He looked to Aaron, who simply waved his hand as if this was all the evidence Graham needed to know that their friend had gone a bit crazy.

"Who's Lady Anne Brigston?" Graham whispered to Aaron. He had a vague notion of who she might be, but he couldn't come up with a single reason he should care about her whereabouts.

Aaron shook his head and shrugged again.

"Didn't you hear me?" Oliver frowned. "Lady Anne is in France."

"That's all he's said for the last twenty minutes," Aaron said, leaning against the wall.

Graham slid the billiard mace through his fingers, using the tip of the handle to line up properly to the ball. He gave the billiard ball a satisfying thwack and sent it careening into two rails before it tripped into the pocket. "I hope she enjoys her trip? It should be safe enough now. The war is over, after all."

Aaron chuckled as Oliver growled and pounded the table in frustration.

The action did nothing but confuse Graham. He considered himself a fairly intelligent man, though he'd been more known for his athletic prowess at Cambridge than his distinction in the schoolroom. Aaron, however, had taken more than his share of academic accolades. Yet neither one of them had any idea why they should be alarmed that a fresh-faced young girl had taken a trip abroad.

Oliver smacked the wood of the table, then began pacing again.

Graham slid a hand back and forth along the smooth wood of his mace. Obviously he'd missed something. Something important. He slid the mace into the rack and leaned against the wall, shoulder to shoulder with Aaron, while they waited for Oliver to get to the point. Given his current state, that could be hours.

"Don't you see?" Oliver shoved his hand through his hair, making it stick up in little light-brown horns.

Graham smothered a grin. "I'm afraid I don't."

Another muffled snicker came from his left.

"He wasn't courting Lady Anne, was he?"

Graham whispered to Aaron. It was the only reasonable explanation he could come up with for Oliver's agitation.

"Not that I know of," Aaron whispered back.

Oliver paced the length of the room once more, mumbling. Finally he threw himself into a leather chair, sending it rocking back on two legs. An impressive feat given the bulk of the piece of furniture.

"If Lady Anne is in France, then Priscilla can't be visiting her."

Graham schooled his features to prevent his shock from showing. Oliver's younger sister Priscilla was friends with Lady Anne? The only thing Graham knew about Lady Anne was that she was the epitome of refinement, poise, and grace, and Priscilla, well, wasn't.

"Her little winter season didn't go well," Oliver said.

Aaron succumbed to a series of violent coughs as he dropped his head forward to stare at the ground. Graham couldn't really blame him. *Didn't go well* was an understatement. Lady Priscilla Kingsley's last appearance in society had included an unfortunate incident involving the host's pet mink and an ornamental fish pond.

"Father said she went to visit Lady Anne.

Intended to spend the whole spring with her and start fresh next year."

Graham winced. "There might be some merit to that."

Oliver waved a hand in the air. "Of course there is. Prissy is most assuredly lacking in the social graces needed to make a splash in London."

Graham bit his lip to keep from laughing. There'd been quite a bit of splashing in the fish pond. "Lady Anne is actually a brilliant choice of companion. The lady has an impeccable reputation. If Priscilla can learn to be like her, even a little bit, she'll be better situated."

"Of course she is. But didn't you hear me earlier?" Oliver leaned forward, bracing his elbows on his knees. "She's. In. France."

"And Priscilla isn't?" Aaron asked.

"Prissy detests boats. Won't step foot on one even to row across the lake back home."

The idea of Priscilla loose somewhere in England without anyone looking after her was enough to make Graham uneasy. No wonder Oliver was pacing a hole in the floor. When their mother had died, Oliver's father hadn't quite known what to do with Priscilla. Oliver had tried to step between them, but there was only so much he could do while away at school. By the time he'd gotten home, her unusual tendencies had become set. "When did you last see her?"

"Two weeks ago. I was away when she left. Didn't find out she'd gone until I got home from Sussex two days ago."

"Maybe Lady Anne returned early. Or maybe Priscilla went with them."

Oliver shook his head and resumed his pacing. "Lady Anne left for the continent a month ago."

Graham rubbed one hand along the back of his neck and looked at Aaron, who was still looking more curious than concerned. "How did you find out about Lady Anne's departure?"

Oliver dropped his head back and closed his eyes. "Last night after you left, I danced with Miss Albany, who mentioned what a shame it was there wasn't going to be a garden party in the fabulous Brigston House conservatory this year. I wondered if they weren't doing the party because of Priscilla."

That didn't make a whole lot of sense, since the point of sponsoring young women for the season was to help them socialize, but it also wasn't the point of the story, so Graham stayed quiet. Oliver was too easily distracted.

"I started looking around for Lady Anne

but didn't see her or her parents in attendance," Oliver continued. "So I danced with Miss Carmichael, who didn't know anything about Lady Anne. But when I was taking her back to her mother, I heard a lady I'd never met talking about how much she liked living in Portman Square. I know that's where Lady Anne lives, so I got an introduction only to find out the woman's family isn't living on Lady Anne's street but is renting Lady Anne's house for the Season."

Graham exchanged wide-eyed looks with Aaron. This was a rather convoluted story. Even for Oliver.

"This concerned me since I don't want Prissy to miss the Season completely, so I asked another young lady." Oliver's head snapped up. "Her name is Miss Emily Feltstone and her father is a baron, but he's the heir presumptive to a viscountcy. He's likely to inherit any day now."

"Oliver," Aaron said. "Lady Anne?"

Oliver nodded. "Yes, I know, I'm getting there."

"By pony cart," Aaron grumbled under his breath.

Graham slapped a hand over his own mouth to soften the chuckle that escaped.

Oliver wasn't paying them any attention,

though. "So I asked Miss Feltstone if she knew where Lady Anne's country estate was. Well, not Lady Anne's but rather Lady Anne's family's. She didn't know, but she did know that the family was in France."

"And how do you know Priscilla didn't go with them?" Graham asked, starting to get just the slightest bit worried.

"Because I went to the docks this morning and bribed three different clerks to show me passenger lists for ships bound for France." Oliver braced himself against the table, staring down his two friends. "And one month ago, Lady Anne left for France, and Priscilla was not on any of the lists."

No one said a word. They simply stared at each other. Finally Graham spoke. "Have you asked your father?"

Oliver tilted his head and frowned at Graham.

Right. Oliver didn't have the same relationship with his father that Graham did. It was quite a shame, that.

"Could she —" Graham rubbed a hand through his own hair. He really hated to ask this question, but Priscilla was so . . . unpredictable. "Could she have run off with someone, and your father is attempting to cover it?"

Oliver shook his head. "She hasn't been

taken with any one gent since she started going out in society. I've scoured all her letters to me. She never mentions anyone twice."

Graham sighed. Did he want to get himself involved in Oliver's family affairs? He'd never hesitated to do anything for Oliver, but coming between family members could be disastrous. He picked up one of the billiard balls and rolled it from hand to hand. The white ivory caught the sunlight, reflecting it onto the green baize. Like the moon had shone on the park last night while Kit held off her attackers with a stick and a knife.

He slammed the ball against the table and gave it a push, rolling it across the felt surface with enough force to crack loudly against one of the other balls. He'd asked for a distraction, and he apparently needed one more than even he had realized. He looked from Aaron to Oliver. "Very well, let's find Priscilla. What do we know thus far?"

Chapter Four

Approximately twenty laps around the billiard room later, Graham and Aaron determined that Oliver really didn't know anything. He had, however, managed to make his hair stick up in so many directions that it looked almost blond in the morning light streaming through the window.

He'd stopped even acknowledging that Graham and Aaron were in the room, instead mumbling to himself. "I didn't think much of it when she got quiet and stopped going out. It was February. No one socializes in February. But I should have known something was wrong. Priscilla was never quiet. She never particularly cared for London, you know, so I thought that was it. I thought she was bored."

And on he went, alternating between declaring Priscilla unfathomable and chastising himself for not knowing something was apparently wrong.

Aaron sighed. "We need to go to his house."

"And question his father?" Graham asked.

"I was more thinking the man needs a good dousing of cold water, and he might as well be near a dry change of clothes when we do it." Aaron grinned. "But we could talk to the earl while we're there."

Graham nodded and caught Oliver on his next trip around the billiard table, throwing an arm around his shoulders and redirecting him toward the door. "Let's get you home, shall we?"

Oliver, Graham, and Aaron were always a rather odd combination of looks and reputations, but Oliver's state of dishevelment wasn't helping matters this morning. Fortunately, most of the people who cared were still inside, if not still in bed.

"Is it possible she was worried about the upcoming Season?" Graham asked as they walked down the street.

"Why?" Oliver's eyebrows drew together.

Graham winced. "Those months leading up to Christmas had been rather disastrous. I know you couldn't be here for most of it, but trust me when I say she has reason to be concerned. She went to a musicale and tried to convince the hostess to let her rearrange the room to achieve better acoustics."

Aaron coughed, but he was grinning too hard to convince anyone it was natural.

Oliver didn't seem to notice, though. He just let his shoulders slump farther. "I know. She wrote me about it. Perhaps we kept her home too long, but we thought an extra year or two would make it easier. She reached the age of two and twenty months ago. Shouldn't she know how to simply smile and nod and get through a social engagement by now?"

She should. Whereas Oliver always struggled a bit when it came to thinking through overly complex ideas, Priscilla's mind was faster than the racehorses her family raised. Graham cleared his throat. "Maybe she doesn't want to."

"She should know she has to. How else would she find a husband? Send one of her crawling vines after him?" Oliver shook his head vehemently and started walking faster. "No, she's been excited about being out in society for years, couldn't say enough about it in her letters last December. Then this year, the invitations finally started coming and she simply chucked them in the rubbish bin."

Aaron stumbled. "And your father let her?"

"I should have known something was wrong when he sent me back to Winterberry so soon after my arrival in London. He needed me out of the way while he . . . did whatever he did. When I came back, Prissy was gone."

Graham had to admit it sounded suspicious. For all of Lady Priscilla's oddities, timidity had never been one of them. A strange fascination with very obscure sciences, yes, but never a sign of bashfulness. And while Oliver's father had never been a particularly warm fellow, he'd never struck Graham as violent. The man was an earl, after all; he'd been raised a complete gentleman. "Where do you think she went?"

"I don't know." Oliver stopped on the pavement, looking up at his house. "Father must, though. He's been acting strange almost as long as Priscilla has."

"And since she left?" Aaron asked.

Oliver shrugged. "Almost normal."

Graham placed his hand between Oliver's shoulder blades and gave a push. "Let's get you cleaned up and see what we can find out, then."

With Oliver once again looking like a polished and distinguished future earl, the three men walked toward the current earl's study. It was going to be difficult for this to look like anything but an interrogation, but Graham wasn't about to leave Oliver to do this alone. Aaron apparently felt the same way.

The study door was open, so the trio strolled in, Oliver leading the way.

Only the earl wasn't there.

Oliver dropped into a chair in front of the cold fireplace and ran his hands through his recently styled hair. "What do I do now?"

Graham sat next to him. "You said he'd been acting strange. What exactly has he done?"

"He bought a chess piece."

Aaron and Graham looked at each other, equally unsure what they were supposed to do with that information. Who bought a chess *piece*?

Graham cleared his throat. "You mean a chess set?"

"No, a piece." Oliver gestured to a bookshelf behind the desk. There, beside a decanter of brandy, sat a lone chess pawn, beautifully carved in a simple but unique shape and polished until it was as smooth as glass. "It was delivered three days ago, the day after I returned to London. It was in a velvet pouch with a few papers. I thought Father was going to chuck the thing in the fire, which is ridiculous considering how much he paid for it."

Another curious look passed between Aaron and Graham. This time it was Aaron who asked the obvious question. "How much did he pay?"

Oliver stated a sum that sent Graham groping for a chair so that he, too, could sit down. The elaborate ivory chess set Graham's father had commissioned last year only cost three times the price of that small wooden pawn. And that had included a custom table with elaborate inlaid board. There was certainly something suspicious.

Graham crossed the room to pick up the chess piece. It was remarkable craftsmanship, but nothing worth what the earl had apparently paid. "And you think this has something to do with Priscilla?"

"It's all I've got." Oliver dropped his head into his hands.

"What about the papers that came with the piece? What did they say?" Graham asked, running a thumb along the smooth surface of the pawn.

Oliver lifted his head, eyes wide. He blinked a few times, glancing from Aaron to Graham and back again before a slight flush crept up his neck. "It was a contract."

"For what?" Graham asked.

"More chess pieces. One delivered every six months as long as he keeps making the payments."

The smooth pawn nearly slipped from Graham's suddenly limp fingers. The man was going to buy more ridiculously expensive chess pieces? Every six months? Who would agree to such a thing? "Why . . ." Graham swallowed. Oliver wouldn't know why. Even if he'd thought to ask, the earl wouldn't have told him. "Who is the contract with?"

"I don't know." Oliver dropped his gaze to the carpet. "I only had a chance to glance at the contract before I heard a noise and threw it back in the drawer."

Aaron strode to the desk, opening the first drawer on the right. "Let's figure it out, then."

While Graham had to admit he was impressed Oliver had found the gumption to pry into his father's business, he wasn't sure it was something they should all do. "We can't go through the earl's desk."

"Why not?" Aaron paused, one hand already riffling through the drawer's contents. "Even if that pawn has nothing to do with Priscilla, this is Oliver's future the man is signing away on mysterious contracts. What if he's lost his mind? What if he's making other business deals like this one? He'll sink the earldom before Oliver even buys his court robes."

Aaron had a point. Still, it made Graham feel better when Oliver crossed the room to do the actual searching. In moments he was pulling out a small sheaf of papers. "Here it is."

The three men leaned over the desk, heads almost touching as they looked through the document. It was a well-written contract, covering all the details and leaving no one in question of the agreement. The earl would make payments twice a year in return for a single chess piece each time. The agreement was to continue until he received the chessboard.

"That's oddly worded," Graham muttered. Why not say until the completion of the set? Considering the tight but straightforward language in the rest of the document, there had to be a reason it was written that way.

"His connection is a solicitor in Marlborough," Oliver said, running a finger along the names at the bottom of the final page.

A glimmer of excitement sparked in Graham's middle. After they'd all finished school, the three of them had set off to see the world, traveling with little baggage and no servants, hiring people along the way when needed, and absorbing everything they could. Their last adventure had been nearly five years ago, before wars and maturity had driven them home and they'd all grown up and taken on a bit more responsibility in their lives.

Marlborough wasn't as exotic as the Caribbean, but the idea of the three of them setting off once more melted a bit of the frustrating boredom he'd been battling.

"I know that look," Aaron said with a sigh, "but you're going to have to do this one without me."

Graham frowned as his excitement inside fizzled like a Chinese firecracker. "Why?"

Aaron stood and adjusted the sleeves of his coat. "Because unlike you two titled gentlemen with nothing to do but wait for your fathers to pop off, I have a job."

As the acknowledged illegitimate son of the Marquis of Lindbury, Aaron dwelled on the edges of polite society and knew that his future was his own to carve out. Oliver and Graham knew what lay ahead for them with their estates and titles. It was a good thing that the three of them had met as boys who cared more about who was growing out of their boots the fastest than inheritances and allowances, because as men they'd probably have barely crossed paths.

By choice, though, they'd made sure their adult lives stayed intertwined.

"Don't you work for Oliver? I think he'd approve your absence," Graham said with a grin.

"Technically," Aaron said, crossing his arms over his chest, "I work for Oliver's father through his solicitor, but regardless of who oversees my work, if Oliver wants his horses ready for this year's races, I have to go see to a problem at the stable in Sussex. My bags are already packed and ready for me to leave on tonight's stage."

And it would seem that once more, being adults was going to inhibit the gallivanting of the traveling trio. It was only fitting, Graham supposed, seeing as how their problems weren't as simple as they'd been when they were youths.

Graham sighed. "I suppose it's you and me then, Oliver. Pack your bags. We're going to the fascinating location of Marlborough."

The ragged and overgrown trees lining the rutted drive would have made most people cringe and turn back, but they brought

71

nothing but a sigh to Kit because they meant she was almost home.

Nash Banfield chuckled as he shifted the reins in his hand, directing the plain, sturdy wagon through the woods. "You haven't been gone long enough to miss the place."

"A single day in London feels like an eternity," Kit muttered. And she'd been gone for two. The truth was, even a quick visit to the city left her head swimming with *what if* questions inspired by all the smells, sounds, and sights of her old life. No matter how easy the visit — and this one had been anything but easy — the peace she'd fought long and hard to find became riddled with holes.

This trip had left a ragged gash running through her, nearly as painful as the first time she'd left London, when a single decision had ripped her future from her hands.

Patching herself up wasn't going to be simple.

But now she was home. As the donkey pulling the wagon plodded out of the tree line, the morning sun danced across the Palladian-style manor house, lighting the columned portico and heavy roof balustrade in a happy greeting.

The simple, strong façade never ceased to encourage her. It was like a reminder from

God that she could atone for the mistakes of her past, even if it took her a lifetime.

The rutted, overgrown path turned into a pressed-gravel drive that curved gracefully across the sprawling front lawn of the house.

The first time Nash had brought Kit and Daphne to the house, they'd stopped at the front steps and walked up them in awe, nothing but dreams and conviction motivating them to attempt the impossible. But now, Nash didn't even pause the wagon, simply kept driving until he could turn off on the path that led around to the servants' entrance on the lower level.

Children's laughter drifted out of the open barn door to frolic with the sounds of birds in the morning air. A small smile touched Kit's lips as she heard it. What had once seemed impossible had become a reality. This home was a safe haven for the innocent children created by the indulgences of the aristocracy. It was a way to save the futures of women who would otherwise be trampled under the feet of the greedy.

A burning sensation crept up Kit's chest at the reminder of the man she'd gone to visit in London. His disdain for the consequences of his actions made her want to —

"You'll find a few bolts of fabric in the back." Nash's voice cut through the steam building up in Kit's throat.

She looked over at the solicitor and had to blink a few times to bring herself back into the moment. "Fabric?"

Excitement and trepidation collided, leaving her dizzy at the whirl of emotions the last five minutes had thrown at her. While some of the children were in rather desperate need of new clothing, their finances were strained due to the amount of coal they'd had to purchase this year as the temperature remained cold far longer than anyone could have expected. "Nash, we can't —"

"It wasn't me." He held the reins in one hand and lifted the other in a vow of innocence. "It was Mrs. Lancaster."

Kit bit her cheek to keep from smiling. The old shopkeeper from town was the sweetest lady Kit had ever met. Without her, she and Daphne would never have come through that trying period more than a dozen years ago as well as they had. "Let me guess, she's tired of dusting it?"

With a smirk, Nash pulled the wagon to a halt. "No. Her customers are complaining it's too ugly for her to keep."

Laughter sputtered through her lips, despite Kit's trying to keep them pressed together. No matter what she did, Mrs. Lancaster always found a way to add one or two items to their monthly supply order. Each excuse was more creative than the last as to why they absolutely had to take something or another off the shopkeeper's hands.

Fabric being too ugly to keep on the shelf was quite a new one, though.

"I suppose if we're doing her a favor . . ." Kit said with a smile and a sigh.

The truth was, they needed the fabric. Kit and Daphne had run out of dresses from their old lives that could be remade as the oldest girls grew. Finding clothes for the boys was even more difficult. Besides, it would let the girls learn another skill. Sewing from clean fabric was a bit different than remaking an already-cut garment.

"If it helps," Nash said as he jumped down and offered a hand to help Kit climb to the ground, "the fabric actually is rather ugly."

Kit laughed and pulled a small crate draped in linen from the back of the wagon. She couldn't help but notice that the rough linen had been cut a great deal larger than was needed to protect the contents of the crate. Probably large enough to cut out half the pieces needed for a little boy's shirt. She shook her head. "It helps."

The door to the kitchen area opened, and three children spilled out, fighting to be the first to feed Nash's donkey a piece of carrot or apple.

"Hands flat," Kit called as she hauled her crate to the kitchen. "We don't want Balaam to get a finger along with his treat."

The children giggled as the donkey snuffled at the treats, standing obediently still while little hands patted wherever they could reach.

Inside, Kit blinked to adjust to the dimmer basement kitchen. Small square windows high in the ceiling let in some light, but it never quite seemed to reach down far enough. She plunked the crate onto the thick wooden worktable.

A woman knelt near the fireplace, using a poker to reposition a pot hanging from one of the high hooks. She glanced at Kit over her shoulder, her porcelain complexion tinted with red from the heat of the fire. Her eyes narrowed as she looked at Kit's face, and she replaced the poker on the rack without shifting her gaze.

Straightening to her slight but still somehow intimidating height, Jess crossed her arms over her chest. "How was your trip?"

Disturbing, frustrating, and more than a little terrifying, but none of that mattered. She reached into her cloak pocket and pulled out a thin set of papers, careful to leave the thicker set tied with a piece of string nestled in the cloak's large pocket. Holding the first set of papers aloft, Kit made herself wear a carefree smile. "Successful, if a bit longer than anticipated."

Nash set a crate on the table beside Kit's and reached for the papers. As the solicitor in charge of their contracts and financials, he knew everything there was to know about the contract, but he still looked it over closely, checking for the proper signatures.

Jess narrowed her sharp gaze in Kit's direction, not even sparing a glance at the contract.

Kit fought the urge to squirm. How did Jess always seem to know when something was wrong? Did Kit walk differently? Frown even though she tried not to?

"What happened?" Jess asked.

With a shrug, Kit busied herself removing the linen from the crate and folding it. "He signed the papers."

Of course he'd signed the papers. Kit had twelve years experience getting men like him to sign the papers. Greedy men who thought nothing of letting a young girl suffer the consequences of a mutual decision alone as long as his reputation remained untarnished. Insufferable men who turned their backs on daughters who had made a mistake that money and lies couldn't cover up. Dishonorable men who thought nothing of bending and discarding the laws of society and country if it was to their benefit.

Jess cleared her throat, and Kit looked up from the cloth she'd been folding. Or rather thought she'd been folding. A pointed look from Jess and Nash's wide-eyed wonderment made Kit look down and realize she'd been grinding the poor linen into the table with angry twists.

She cleared her throat and gently smoothed the fabric before folding it with care. Then she grabbed the uncovered crate of dry goods and hauled it into the storage room.

Jess followed right behind her.

Kit was going to have to tell her something, but what? She certainly wasn't about to say anything about the charming man with the lemonade. Jess would assume the man had nefarious intentions, and Daphne would dream up ten romantic scenarios before she could even blink.

The threatening footmen should probably be mentioned, though. They'd been a first. Had Lord Charles known she was coming? The same murky reputation that had the blackguards of London trembling when The Governess announced she was there to make them pay for their sins — quite literally — may have grown to the point that her arrival was anticipated.

But to be prepared enough to send miscreants after her before she'd even gotten around the corner? It wasn't as if Kit was descending upon negligent fathers and vile philanderers every other night. They took in a woman to help once, maybe twice a year.

Yes, Jess and Daphne needed to know about the prepared attack, but how to tell the story without including Lord Wharton?

"Kit?" Jess lifted the lid on the flour box and began refilling it.

"What else do you want to know?" Kit kept her back turned, busying herself with placing items on the shelves with care. "Nash should have the first payment by next week, and Priscilla is safely tucked away with a wonderful family in Yatesbury where no one will ever think to look."

Though how sweet, strange Priscilla had ever ended up in the arms of a cad like Lord Charles, Kit would never understand.

Jess coughed. "That's because no one goes to Yatesbury. I'm not even certain the people who live there know it's a village."

"Which makes it the perfect place for a young woman who doesn't want to be found."

The lid to the flour box shut with a clang, but Jess didn't move. Finally Kit had nothing left to unpack and was forced to turn around.

"What was he like?" Jess asked.

An image of Lord Wharton's grin as he handed her a glass of lemonade flashed through Kit's mind. She shook her head to clear it. "Lord Charles Tromboll?"

One thin golden eyebrow rose slightly above Jess's shrewd gaze. "Is there another *he* involved in this scenario?"

Kit tried to pass it off with a shrug. "Priscilla's father. But he signed his contract weeks ago."

That actually had been one of the easiest negotiations Kit had ever done. He'd been almost happy to have a solution that allowed Priscilla to safely have the baby but still have some way of creating a future for herself.

"Then obviously I'm not talking about him," Jess said.

"Lord Charles was reluctant, of course," Kit said. The putative fathers were always reluctant. It was so easy for them to walk away, to retain their prospects and reputations. "I was able to persuade him, though."

"With logic and compassion?" Jess's voice dripped with disbelief.

"No." Kit drew her shoulders back and

turned toward the door. "The law plainly states that men have to provide for their offspring, legitimate or not. Reminding them that they can quietly support the child and save the reputations of both parents instead of forcing the desperate mother to drag his name down along with her own is all it takes."

Well, that and Kit's threatening to expose whatever other ugly secrets she'd dug up about them. Yes, she'd been yelled at, spit on, and called a blackmailer, and she hadn't even been able to argue that point, since she was, in effect, blackmailing them. But she was blackmailing them into doing what was right, so it wasn't really a bad thing.

She just didn't want Jess and Daphne to know about that part of it.

Jess placed an arm on Kit's shoulder, keeping her from retreating back to the kitchen. "I know I've only been here two and a half years, but I've seen you return from these trips enough to know there's something you aren't telling me."

Kit tightened her grip on the empty crate. "I suppose I could mention that the mail stage I took last night had a wobbly wheel and I spent the entire ride terrified we'd end up in a ditch."

One side of Jess's mouth kicked up in a

knowing grin. "You could mention that. But I don't think it's worth it. Obviously you made it home in one piece."

"I'm sure anything you're noticing is simply the remains of my fear on my ride home." Never mind that she'd been so consumed with memories of the strange man and the hired thugs that she'd only noticed the wobbly wheel in the vaguest of ways.

Jess pushed past Kit to exit the storage room. "I'll just tell Daphne that you can't make these trips anymore. They're obviously wearing on you."

Kit chased Jess into the kitchen, dropped the crate onto the table, and braced herself on it as she leaned over the table, staring Jess down with the sort of bravery only friendship could allow. "You wouldn't."

"Wouldn't I?" Jess placed a hand on the table and leaned in as well, lifting her other hand to point a finger in Kit's direction. "You're as pale as that linen, doing your best not to look me in the eye, and you've licked your lips twenty-three times since you came in the door. You can't tell me that something didn't happen."

"Twenty-three times?" Kit asked with a bit of awe in her voice, her hand flying up to see if she had indeed been licking her lips without noticing. "You actually counted?"

Jess didn't answer, just stared at Kit. It was times like this when Kit was forced to remember that Jess hadn't been with them forever, that her past was a large block of unknown, but at some point she'd been a spy. Fortunately she'd been on England's side, despite the lilt of a French accent that occasionally flitted through her words when she was especially tired.

Kit swallowed hard and licked her lips and then had to restrain the urge to again give in to what was, apparently, a nervous habit of hers. She'd never be a match for Jess, but that wasn't going to stop her from trying.

The deep sound of a throat clearing broke the stalemate first, and both women swung around to see Nash standing in the doorway with a paper-wrapped bundle. "Should I come back later?"

Chapter Five

Nash's interruption provided the perfect opportunity for Kit to slip out of the house and retreat to the barn under the guise of sending the children to assist with the unloading of the wagon. Plenty of hands were already helping, but it was the fastest way to escape from Jess's knowing smirk.

It also let her relieve the weight of the cloak still draped across her shoulders. Every time she moved, her hip bumped the thick stack of papers still tucked in the depths of the cloak's pocket, a reminder of the necessary but unpleasant side of providing a life for these children and a future for their mothers.

The chickens clucked at the children as they raced out of the barn and up the slight hill to the house. A goat bleated in the remaining silence, but otherwise the barn soon grew still. Satisfied that she was alone for the moment, Kit slid the bound sheaf of papers from her cloak pocket and entered the empty stall at the end, the one they milked the goats in when it was raining.

She reached into the unused feed bin and felt around for the short iron bar hidden in the crevices of the worn boards. With practiced efficiency, she pried up the loose floorboard beneath the feed bin, revealing an old wooden chest. The lid didn't have to be opened far for her to slide the papers inside, hiding away the proof of Lord Charles's dealings with smugglers. They would remain hidden as long as the agreed-upon payments kept coming, just like all the other secrets she'd dug up over the years. Men who were dishonorable in one area of their lives were just as willing to break the rules in other areas.

The lid fell closed faster than she'd intended, sending a sharp crack through the quiet barn. But Kit didn't want to see the contents of the box, didn't want to think about why they were there. If she dwelled on it, she'd become angry all over again. Angry that people who did those things, who had every intention of abandoning those who couldn't care for themselves, still lived lives of elegance and ease.

It wasn't fair, but it was life. And if she could bury the ugly side of life under the floorboard in the barn, then it didn't have to touch those she cared about, living a few hundred feet away in a manor home that had been all but abandoned. Just like her. Just like the children. Just like all of them.

Kit slid the floorboard back into place and stomped on it for good measure. The deed was done, another child's future secure. The pull of the cloak on her shoulders felt lighter as she returned to the house to change out of the ball gown she'd been wearing for two days.

Once simple muslin floated around her body once more, she drew the first full, deep breath she'd drawn since departing London.

As she left her room, she glanced at the tall clock that sat in the saloon that they'd converted to a large dining hall. Thin strips of coiled paper covered the inlay of the clock cabinet, decorative swirls pressed together in a colorful pattern, a project from their early days in the manor house, when Kit and Daphne had only one child to watch and plenty of time in the evenings to indulge in the sorts of activities they'd done when they'd lived genteel lives in the city.

Now with a dozen children in the house, a garden, and a business making goods to sell at market, there wasn't time for such indulgences.

Nor was there time to sit around staring at them.

In half an hour, Kit would need to gather the children in the library for their lessons.

She bit her lip and looked warily at the door leading down to the kitchen. Leading down to Jess. Who had certainly not forgotten she had suspicions still to voice. It wouldn't hurt to start lessons early today. After all, there wasn't really anything useful Kit could do in a mere half an hour.

And if the time she spent with the children allowed Jess to forget a thing or two she wanted to say, well, that was all the better.

If the multiple excuses Jess found to walk through the library during the children's lessons were anything to go by, she hadn't forgotten a thing and had perhaps added a statement or two to the list. Every time she passed through the room, or simply found a reason to stick her head in the door, she glared at Kit.

Given the way the library was situated at the side of the house in its own private wing, there was little doubt that her visits and her glares were quite intentional.

Kit ignored her. At least, she tried to. She gave all her focus to little Sophie, wrapping her hand around the child's small chalk-wielding fingers and moving their joined hands in a fluid motion over the slate. "There's two humps in an *M*, Sophie. Not one."

"I don't think this is right, Mama Kit," six-year-old Henry said, kicking his feet back and forth underneath the table the younger children used for lessons. "Because if three away from seven is four, that means John stole one of my marbles yesterday."

Kit looked up from the wobbly *M* on Sophie's slate to the youngest boy in the cluster of older children studying books they'd found in the house's extensive library. The subjects covered everything from farming to philosophy, and at that moment, John had a book of advanced mathematics propped open on his chest.

He slid down a bit lower in his chair but grinned at Kit over the top of the book. "You're always telling us that real-life lessons teach more than books. Now he'll know to always do the math himself, right?"

Kit left Sophie's side and crossed the room to lower herself down to John's eye level. She ran a hand lightly through his light brown hair. "I think we can make our real-life lessons effective without scarring anyone or stealing anyone's marbles, don't you think?"

"But he won't forget it!"

"And neither will I." Kit bit her lip to keep from smiling at the adorable conniver. "You'll be cleaning out the goat shed this week."

John groaned while five-year-old Arthur cheered. It had been his week to clean out the goat shed and she'd just given the task away. He gave her a wide grin. "Eggs?"

Kit bit her lip, knowing the quiet younger boy was asking if he could take John's job of collecting the eggs. But Arthur wasn't ready to collect eggs on his own, was he? Wasn't he too young? There were so many children in her life that sometimes it was hard to know when each one was ready for something new, for more responsibility. They depended greatly on those eggs. What would happen if they ended up in a heap on the ground?

"Yes," Kit finally decided. After all, what were broken eggs compared to a little boy taking one step further in becoming a man? "You can collect the eggs. Sarah can help you."

Perhaps she wasn't quite ready to let Arthur grow into a man on his own yet, and Sarah was good with the children. She would make an excellent governess one day. Or she would have, if she'd been able to grow up with respectable parents and connections. As it was, she'd be fortunate to find a life in service, working her way up to the position of parlor maid, and one day possibly a housekeeper. She was already eleven. In a few years, they would have to start looking for that first position for her, to help her get started in a job that would allow her to support herself.

That had always been the plan — to raise and educate them until they were old enough to work and then make way for more children — but now that the oldest children were reaching that age, it was hard to imagine actually sending them out into the world.

Jess slid back into the room, but instead of passing through or performing some imaginary errand, she simply stood and gave Kit an expectant look. "Sarah, could you help the younger ones with their work for a while? I need to speak with Mama Kit for a moment."

"Of course, Mama Jess," Sarah said as she rose from where she'd been burying her small, pointed nose in a biography of Mozart.

A brief wince flashed across Jess's face, and it almost made Kit smile. She'd never quite felt comfortable being called Mama

Jess, having tried to stay away from the children when she first arrived, trying to create a role somewhere between servant and friend. But Haven Manor wasn't just a refuge, it was a family, and the children hadn't allowed her to lurk on the fringes.

The first time one of the children had called her Mama Jess, the normally unflappable woman had paled and nearly passed out in the middle of the kitchen.

What Kit wouldn't give for one of those spells of weakness right now.

Jess stared at Kit across the library, eyebrows raised in an unspoken threat that if Kit didn't come now she'd be removed from the room by force. Kit held no illusions that the four inches of height she had on the other woman would keep Jess from hauling Kit anywhere.

With a sigh, Kit followed Jess through the short passage that connected library to the parlor in the main block of the house. Then Jess kept going, leading Kit through the front hall, past the stairs to the upper floor, and on through the dining hall, all the way into Kit's room.

Daphne, who'd run away from London with Kit all those years ago, sat on the bed, blue eyes wide in her round, gentle face.

"What has happened?" A thread of worry

but also relief coursed through Kit. Perhaps this had nothing to do with her trip to London, after all.

Jess crossed her arms over her chest and leaned one shoulder against the doorframe, trapping Kit in the room. "This way you only have to tell us the story once. Since it's obvious you don't want to talk about it, I thought I'd save you the trouble of telling us separately."

Kit swung her gaze to Daphne, who still looked fresh and young as if the past thirteen years of learning how to work for a living hadn't changed her at all. She shrugged. "Jess told me to sit here, so I sat."

"Kit is going to tell us what happened in London," Jess said. "And she's going to do it while there's still time for someone to catch the mail coach back to London if we need to."

Even though it was futile, Kit gave evasion one more effort. "Lord Charles signed the papers."

"And?"

There was nothing for it. She was going to have to tell them about the men who'd chased her. It was probably necessary, since it would remind them all to be a bit more careful for a while in case Lord Charles decided to pursue her beyond London.

Nash's office in Marlborough wasn't that far from Haven Manor, and while no one had ever found the house, aside from the handful of trusted men who occasionally helped with maintenance around the house, that possibility always existed.

"And . . ." Kit drew the word out, hoping to make it sound like it wasn't a big deal. If the other two women dug too deeply into why Lord Charles was having her chased, they'd find out that her persuasive skills relied more on extortion than any sort of convincing logic. And while Jess probably wouldn't care, Kit wanted to protect what remained of Daphne's naïveté and innocence. "He tried to get the papers back by having two footpads chase me through London."

"What?" Daphne shrieked as she surged to her feet.

Jess simply raised her blond eyebrows into two perfect arches.

"I managed to evade them once, but they caught up with me again, so I threatened to throw a knife at them if they didn't leave me alone." Kit almost smiled. Apparently it wasn't going to be as difficult to leave Lord Wharton out of her story as she'd thought.

Jess snorted. "You can barely aim at the side of the barn. You certainly couldn't throw with enough accuracy to take down a grown man."

"Yes, but they didn't know that." Kit crossed her arms over her chest and pulled herself up to her tallest height, trying to look confident and imposing. "I threw a stick at them first to show them I knew what I was doing."

"How much did that miss by?" Jess asked with a grin, all traces of alarm cleared from her features while Daphne continued to fret on the bed, chewing on her bottom lip as she twined her fingers together.

Kit blushed but forced herself to keep her chin up. "I aimed for the chest of one and instead hit the ground between the feet of the other, but again, they didn't know I'd missed."

"And that's all that happened?" Jess paused before narrowing her eyes. "Nothing else?"

Had Jess somehow spied on Kit while she was in London, or was there really something different about her? "Yes," Kit said with as much calm as she could muster, "that's the only thing of note that happened."

Because meeting a charming, handsome gentleman had no bearing on her life whatsoever. It really wasn't worth discussing. Kit tried to smile in Jess's direction. "You've already said you don't care about the wobbly coach wheel."

There was silence for a few moments as Jess and Kit stared at each other. Finally Daphne spoke up. "We should warn Nash."

Kit shook her head. "Nash is always careful, especially during the weeks after new contracts are signed. Most of the men send someone to visit him at least once."

"We could spread more brush at the road, though, disguise the entrance better," Jess said.

Kit nodded, more because doing so would get her away from Jess than because she thought the entrance to the manor was in any real danger of discovery. "The children should be finished with their lessons. Why don't you take the boys and cover the entrance? Daphne, the girls, and I can go see about the garden."

Jess looked like she wanted to say something, but instead, she nodded and abandoned her post at Kit's door, only to stop and poke her head back inside. "Oh, and Kit?"

"Yes?"

"Knife practice. This afternoon. If you insist on continuing to handle the contracts this way, I want you prepared. Next time you might not be able to bluff your way out of it."

Kit's throat tightened as Jess disappeared to collect the boys. What if there *was* a next time? She'd considered this encounter an exception, an oddity, but what if more men decided to try it?

What would happen if she didn't make it back from London next time? What would happen to Daphne? To the children? To the women like Priscilla who wouldn't know the first thing about surviving on their own? Didn't have the ability or skill to do so? Haven Manor was too much work for Daphne to handle alone, and there was no guarantee that Jess intended to stay forever.

Without Haven Manor, the children would be forced to work in the poorhouse, destined for a life of poverty without any hope of finding respectable work. Half of them wouldn't survive a year in those conditions.

It was enough to make Kit's stomach roll but also to shore up her resolve.

Her hand fumbled on the door latch as she pulled it closed, the mental image of young Sophie's hands wrapped around a loom instead of a piece of chalk enough to make Kit shake. She'd never known fear like she knew the other night, running through

London's streets to save her very life.

She'd thought she was prepared for anything, but maybe Jess was right. Maybe it was time to rethink things.

CHAPTER SIX

Graham had, of course, been to Marlborough before. Everyone had been to Marlborough. It was a convenient and easy stop on the way from London to practically anywhere to the west.

He just couldn't remember hearing of anyone going there with the intention of staying more than a single night.

It felt odd to be riding into a town with just Oliver. Normally Aaron would be on his right, reminding them all to take proper care of their horses when riding them long distances.

His admonishments were ingrained in their brains, though, so Oliver and Graham spread the relatively easy distance to Marlborough from London over three days in the saddle. Now Graham was more than ready to relax in an inn's public rooms.

They plodded down the abnormally wide cobbled expanse of High Street. Several inns off the main road were bustling with people in fine traveling clothes and stacks of luggage. In silent agreement, Oliver and Graham rode right past. Oliver's problem was a family matter, so the last thing they wanted to do was bump into someone they knew who'd want to know why on earth they were staying in Marlborough instead of simply passing through it.

A bit farther down on a side street, they found a clean and respectable-looking inn that appeared to cater to a more middle-class clientele. Graham's stomach grumbled as the smell of food drifted over the inn's courtyard. He was more than happy to turn over Dogberry's reins to a waiting stable-boy. The fact that the horse nearly pulled the lad into the stable instead of the other way around was a sure sign that he was as ready to be done traveling as Graham.

With the horses cared for and rooms secured, the men settled into the inn's tavern area with fragrant bowls of hearty stew.

"Is it too late to pay a visit to Mr. Banfield, do you think?" Oliver asked as he pushed a bit of carrot around with his spoon.

Graham paused, his bowl of stew not even half empty. "I should think so. It won't hurt anything to wait until morning. She's not in any danger."

"That we know of," Oliver grumbled.

"You know she's not. If either one of us thought there was a chance of that, we'd have thrown discretion to the wind and come in a carriage. We'd have been here two days ago." They'd discussed it at length, debating the merits of having their own horses available versus the speed of taking a stage. In the end, they'd decided that discretion was more important. For all of Lord Trenting's gruffness, Oliver's father would have been distraught if Priscilla had actually come to physical harm.

"I know." Oliver chopped a carrot in half with his spoon. "But now I'm reconsidering."

"You're simply anxious now that you don't have traveling to occupy your mind." Graham pushed his bowl away. "We can walk down that way and see if he's in his office."

Oliver shoveled a few more bites of stew into his mouth and dropped a coin on the table for the serving lass before heading for the door. Now that Graham had been off his horse for a while, he was actually glad for the excuse to stretch his legs a bit before bed.

The town looked different in the early evening, the street quiet but still interesting. They'd seen Mr. Banfield's office sign on the way into town, so they knew where they were going, even if the chances of the man being in his office were somewhere between unlikely and nonexistent.

As they passed a store bearing the name *Lancaster's,* Graham paused to look over the odd assortment of items in the window display. An array of food items sat side by side with, well, stuff. What sort of grocer also sold decoratively tooled saddlebags and rag dolls?

"Look at that." Graham pointed to a box covered in rolled paper filigree. He'd seen similar ones in some of the homes he'd been in for soirees and dinners. His mother had once deliberated for days on end whether or not to purchase a table covered in the paper curls, but then her friend Lady Mitchum had beaten her to it. This box was exceptionally detailed. Maybe he'd buy it and take it home to his mother. It wasn't a table, but it was pretty.

Several shadows passed by the window, proving the store was still open for business. Graham took a step toward the door.

Oliver frowned. "The solicitor."

Graham nodded and started walking

toward the solicitor's again. They'd be in town for a while yet. He'd stop into the store on another day.

If he were honest, Graham would have to admit that Oliver's single-minded fixation on finding his sister was stirring up a bit of jealousy. Aside from his parents, Graham didn't really have anyone in his life whom he cared about like Oliver cared for Priscilla. Oh, he supposed he'd go to great lengths if Oliver or Aaron needed something, but that was rather different. He couldn't see either of them needing him to ride across the country following slim clues about small-town solicitors.

The jealous feeling didn't sit well with Graham, like a coat that had been retailored an inch too small for his shoulders.

It was impossible to miss the solicitor's office, with its large, multi-paned window overlooking High Street.

It was also impossible to miss the rather startling mess inside. Newspapers and books covered nearly every available surface. It didn't look dirty so much as it looked full. Well, full of everything except an actual solicitor.

"The door's locked." Oliver ran a hand over his face and looked out across the town. "We'll have to wait until morning."

Graham threw an arm across Oliver's shoulders and directed him back down the pavement toward the inn. "Remember what we discussed on the way here, Oliver. Your father would not do anything to put his daughter or the earldom in danger. There is an explanation he simply didn't want to give to you."

Beneath Graham's arm, Oliver's shoulders slumped. "Prissy has never been what he wanted her to be."

It was true. But then again, Oliver hadn't ever been quite what the earl wanted either. There wasn't a man with a finer heart than Oliver's, but Graham knew the earl would have preferred a son with a bit more gumption. Perhaps, if Graham were being brutally honest, a son with a few more brains. How to remind Oliver of that without making him feel worse, though?

"Prissy may not be everything an earl's daughter should be," Graham said slowly, "but she's not the one who had a row with him in the middle of a dinner party."

As intended, the memory made Oliver grin. He was oddly proud of that moment, when he'd shown his father that he could actually stand up to someone if the matter was personal enough. It had resulted in Aaron being allowed to make several changes to the family's stable of racehorses, but not before the earl had turned nearly purple in shame.

Oliver straightened his shoulders and nodded. "I suppose it's entirely possible Father cares more for her well-being than for mine."

Graham's mouth dropped open but he snapped it shut. That hadn't been the conclusion he'd thought Oliver would make, but it served the purpose of easing his fears for a while, so Graham would let it be. "And yet, here you are, alive and healthy."

With the urgency of finding the solicitor set temporarily aside, Oliver deflated. "I think I'll retire. It's been a long week."

The last thing Graham felt like doing at that moment was returning to the inn. What would he do there? Sit in his room and listen for Oliver to fall back into fretting about his sister? They were far enough from London that Graham wasn't worried the man would lose his grip on sanity and threaten to knock his father over the head with his brass bust of Henry V, and there really wasn't anything he could do.

So he bid his friend a good evening and went in the direction of the interesting little grocer.

The inside was as equally charming as the

outside. Near the front of the store stood bins of foodstuffs and shelves of herbs and tins of candy. The normal items to be found in any small grocer.

The back of the store, however, was a veritable treasure trove of odds and ends, waiting to marvel a potential buyer.

At the front counter, a short, older woman with a round face and a wide smile helped a dark-haired woman and a young girl.

Neither the women nor the items behind the counter were of much interest to Graham, but the assortment of goods in the back was fascinating. He wandered through the shelves until he stumbled upon an assortment of wooden toys on a low shelf in the very back.

A soft laugh escaped as he lowered himself to one knee and looked at the toys. Who sold such a thing at a food store?

He slid a Shut the Box game forward and flicked numbered panels back and forth, recalling the game he hadn't played in years.

"Are you going to buy that?"

Graham looked up to see a little boy standing next to him with wide blue eyes and dark hair that stuck up in a strange tuft on the back of his head. One front tooth was larger than the rest of his teeth, so the boy couldn't be that young. When had Graham started getting new teeth in? Six? Seven? How did parents not constantly go a bit touched in the head trying to remember details like that?

With a shake of his head, Graham angled the box so the boy could see it better. "No, I was simply remembering playing the game as a child."

The little boy nodded earnestly. "Good. I like to play with my friend Henry when he comes to visit Mrs. Lancaster. She's the shop owner. When I come to visit her, she gives me peppermints, which I like, but she always hands them over with this funny little laugh saying that my father met my mother over a tin of peppermints. I don't particularly like that part."

The boy's face held such sincerity that Graham had to bite his cheek to keep from smiling too broadly. He'd never had much to do with children, assuming they were annoying and messy, but this precocious little boy was rather entertaining.

Especially when he kept talking after barely taking a breath. "It's not that I'm not happy my mother and father met, you understand, but more that I'd rather not have to hear the story every time she sneaks me a free peppermint."

Graham released the grin. He couldn't

help it. He was definitely going to have to start giving more attention to his friends' children. Were all children this adorable? "You'd rather get your free candy and run, hmm?"

"Yes!" The boy's eyes widened. "Do you want to play?"

Without waiting for an answer, the boy plopped himself on the floor between two rows of shelves and set the box down in front of him. He fished a pair of dice from the bottom of the box and set all of the numbers to one side so they could be flipped. Then he rolled the dice.

Fascinated, Graham lowered himself to the floor. Apparently the people who came to the store were just as eclectic as the items inside. The boy had said he was visiting Mrs. Lancaster, not shopping or coming to the store. Was the old woman the child's grandmother? He certainly looked comfortable playing with the merchandise.

As the little boy rolled the dice and flicked the number panels accordingly, he talked. "Mother always says she's only stopping in to pick up a few things, but if no one else is here she ends up talking for hours. It's not so bad when Henry is here, but he doesn't come into town very often."

Graham raised one knee and propped his

arm on it, trying to settle himself between the shelves. He was a good bit larger than his companion and didn't fit quite as easily. "Where does Henry live?"

"Out in the trees." The little boy rolled an eight and flipped the tabs on the seven and the one before looking up at Graham with an earnest gaze. "No, really. We have to go through so many trees to get there. Papa takes me with him sometimes when he goes, and I have to help push the limbs away from the wagon. That's fun. Not as fun as playing with Henry, though. Sometimes Papa lets me drop sticks on one side of the bridge and then watch them come out the other side. We can only do it when we go over the north bridge. There's too much traffic on the London Road bridge."

Graham felt out of breath just listening to the boy. How did he possibly have that much air?

The boy sighed and slumped his shoulders as he rolled a number he couldn't play. He flipped all the tabs back to their starting position and passed Graham the dice.

Was he really about to play Shut the Box on the floor of a grocer in Marlborough? With a shrug, Graham cast his dice and flipped his first numbers. If he were honest, this conversation was more interesting than most of the ones he'd had in the past few months, even if he didn't know the script. Perhaps that was what made it interesting. He latched on to the last thing the boy had said. "You like the bridge?"

The boy popped up on his knees and leaned over so he could see which numbers Graham was playing. "Yes. We have to be careful when we go, though, because when it rains a lot the river floods the bridge. Henry likes coming over the bridge, too, but he doesn't get to do it very often. I wish we could play more together, but Father says that if you visit hidden treasure too often it doesn't stay hidden. So I play with the boys in town. I like them, but Henry's more fun."

Graham's turn finished so he passed the dice back to the boy. Was there some sort of trick to understanding the speech of children? Half of what the boy was saying didn't make any sense. Perhaps his friend was imaginary. That was something children did, wasn't it? His father might take him for walks in the woods to visit this imaginary friend. Graham couldn't blame a man for not wanting to do that too often. "Why don't you like playing with the boys in town?"

The little boy tossed the dice from hand

to hand. "They think I talk too much. Henry is used to it because he said there's always someone talking in his house because there's so many children there. Sometimes we both talk at the same time to see which of us can tell a story faster than the other."

Graham bit his cheek again to keep from smiling. He hated that the little boy was having trouble with the other children, but they might have a point about the amount of talking he did. His little mouth hadn't stopped moving the entire time Graham had known him, which, granted, was only about ten minutes, but it was more than he'd heard some of his acquaintances say in ten years.

"I think it's going to rain tonight," the boy continued as he rolled the dice. "It's rained every day for three days. That's why Mother brought us to visit Mrs. Lancaster today. She said we had to get out of the house before she sewed us all up into the bedsheets just to get a little peace. Have you had to sit inside because of the rain? Father's still gone to work, so I don't think men have to worry about the rain as much as women and children do."

"I came in from London today. We didn't get any rain on our trip," Graham said with a smile, reaching over to point out a number combination the boy had missed.

But the boy wasn't interested in the game right then. His mouth dropped open a bit as he looked up at Graham. "You mean it doesn't rain everywhere at the same time?"

There was no more keeping it in. Graham chuckled. The whole of London had it wrong, shutting their children away in the nurseries. They should be trotted out as the evening's entertainment, along with tables full of childhood games.

"Daniel!"

Man and boy looked up to see the dark-haired woman with her fists propped on her hips. She looked vaguely familiar, but Graham couldn't place her. A tired sigh sifted through her lips. "What are you doing, Daniel?"

The boy glanced at Graham, then tilted his head back until he was looking at his mother upside down. "Playing Shut the Box with my new friend."

One side of the woman's mouth kicked up in a grin she couldn't seem to help. "New friend? Did you remember to introduce yourself this time?"

The boy froze and very carefully placed the dice on the floor beside the box before standing to his feet and straightening his clothes. He pushed his shoulders back and cleared his throat before looking back at Graham.

From his position on the ground, Graham was eye to eye with the little boy. He took a deep breath himself and schooled his features to look as serious as the little boy.

The boy stuck his hand forward. "My name is Mr. Daniel Banfield. Pleased to meet you."

Graham blinked and was very glad that he'd already cleared the smile from his face. Wasn't the solicitor's name Banfield? Graham cleared his throat and shook the boy's hand. "Graham, Viscount of Wharton."

The boy's eyes widened, and beyond his shoulder Graham could see the woman stiffen. She'd had no problem with his presence until she'd learned his title. Did she know him? Or was it that he had a title at all? Assuming she was the boy's mother and assuming the boy's father was the solicitor Oliver had come to meet . . . well, Graham couldn't imagine why she'd be bothered by his name. He wasn't connected to anyone who'd had dealings with Mr. Banfield. At least, not that he knew of.

"A real viscount?" Daniel asked.

"No," Graham couldn't help but say teasingly. "A fake one."

The boy crossed his arms and frowned

while the small smile returned to his mother's lips. "You can be arrested for impersonating a peer. I know. My father's a solster."

A solster? Graham grinned. It probably was rather difficult for little mouths to learn to say the word *solicitor.* "My father is an earl, so I think he'll vouch for me."

The boy considered this for a moment. "Probably. Father says that the aristocracy gets away with —"

"And I think it's time we were going." The mother surged forward and wrapped an arm around Daniel, covering his mouth with one of her hands. "Please allow me to apologize. I had no idea anyone else was in the store or I wouldn't have let him wander around."

Graham pushed himself to his feet and brushed off his breeches. "Please don't apologize. It's been a pleasure." He leaned down. "Mr. Banfield, thank you for making my first evening in Marlborough an enjoyable one."

The boy pulled his mother's hand away from his mouth and grinned. "You're welcome!"

Graham found himself smiling as he slid the game back into its position on the lowest shelf, pushing it all the way back so that it was harder to see. He had a feeling the game wasn't truly for sale if the little boy came in and played it often.

When he stood back up, the mother and son had been replaced by a smiling old woman. "Welcome to Marlborough." She held out a tin. "Would you like a peppermint?"

As he took the candy, Graham couldn't help but send a little prayer of gratitude up to God for bringing him on this trip. Tomorrow he would help Oliver get his answers and make sure Priscilla was safe, but for today at least, Graham had been reminded that life was a rather wonderful thing.

CHAPTER SEVEN

They'd done it again. The thrill of imminent success wove through Kit's tired muscles, giving her the strength to toss Lady Elizabeth's valise into the back of the wagon. Nash slid the larger, heavier trunk in beside it.

It wasn't a massive trunk by aristocracy standards, and Lady Elizabeth was probably convinced that she'd spent the past several months living in near squalor, but the sad yet hopeful smile that offset the sheen of tears in her eyes said it was all worth it.

"What will you do now?" Kit asked. She always asked because she needed the hope as badly as the women did. They were why she was doing this, the women robbed of innocence and opportunity. And after today, she'd never see or hear from Lady Elizabeth again. That was part of the agreement. It was Kit's job to make everything disappear.

Lady Elizabeth glanced back at the small

house she'd lived in for nearly seven months. "I'm hoping to marry. Start a family." She smiled at Kit. "Father said he would take me to Edinburgh when I'm ready. Let me have a Season there. I . . . I told him I didn't want to have anything to do with London. I didn't want to have to see . . . certain people."

They all knew there was only one person Lady Elizabeth wanted to avoid. One man. Kit didn't blame her. She didn't want to ever see that man again either, and she'd only had to talk to him one night. She hadn't spent months being lied to and promised love and a future only to have the man walk away when a larger dowry showed interest in him. By then it had been too late for Lady Elizabeth.

"I can't thank you enough, Kit." Lady Elizabeth ran a hand down her skirt, a simple muslin she probably wouldn't have dreamed of wearing before finding herself with child. "Mrs. Foster and I would take food to the workhouse sometimes."

Kit didn't know what to say to that. It was good for Lady Elizabeth to see the fate that could easily have been hers, wasn't it? A little perspective was always a good thing. Perhaps, once she married and had a house-hold and means of her own, she would still reach out and help those trapped in forlorn situations.

"There was a girl there when we first went," Lady Elizabeth said. "She wasn't there last time."

A tightness gripped Kit's throat. She knew all too well what happened to young girls in those workhouses. The illness. The poor conditions. It could easily have been Kit or Daphne who encountered such a fate, but for Kit's sheer stubbornness and the kindness of a few strangers they'd stumbled across.

Lady Elizabeth glanced back at the house once more. "You won't let that happen to her, will you? She won't be one of those girls?"

"No," Kit said firmly. "She'll likely never know luxury, but she'll get an education, learn the skills needed to support herself. Probably go into service somewhere, but that's not a bad lot in life."

The other woman's mouth opened, but then she pressed her lips into a thin line and let Nash hand her up into the wagon seat.

"We need to be going if we're going to have Lady Elizabeth on the next stage," Nash said as he untied Balaam from the post.

Kit nodded. "I'll go get Daphne."

As Kit approached the house, she heard a low singing and shook her head. While Kit did this for the women, there was no question that Daphne loved the children. Oh, she cared about the women, too, related to them more than Kit ever could, but the babies really made her smile.

Inside the house, Daphne was pacing the floor, staring down into a bundled grey blanket as she sang. In a chair to the side sat another woman, older and with a few more lines on her face, with another baby pressed to her chest.

"I believe Luke is finished. I can feed little Olivia now," Mrs. Foster said, leaning to the side to lay her baby in a wooden cradle.

Daphne looked up at Kit and sighed. "We have to leave anyway, don't we?"

Kit nodded.

After a light kiss on the top of the baby's head, Daphne passed the baby off to Mrs. Foster. "If you need anything, let us know. Otherwise, I'll be back to visit the baby in a month or so."

As they stepped out of the house, Kit whispered, "Why do you come visit the babies? In a little more than a year she'll be weaned and come live at Haven Manor with us."

The frown that creased Daphne's face was such a foreign expression that Kit had to blink. "If the baby knows me she won't be as scared when the time comes for her to move." A serene smile took the place of the frown. "Besides, that baby is a gift from God. She deserves to know that."

There was a time when Kit would have challenged Daphne's statement, saying that God wouldn't have given a gift that destroyed lives in the process, but she couldn't imagine a world without the children she cared for, couldn't imagine trading their lives for the potential future their arrival had interrupted.

"That may be," Kit said as she tugged Daphne toward the wagon, "but we've twelve other children who need to know that as well, and right now the only person watching over them is Jess."

Who was likely doing a fine job of things. Jess could probably manage the entire manor and the neighboring town of Marlborough without breaking a sweat.

"It wouldn't hurt you to come along with me on more of those visits, you know," Daphne said as she climbed into the back of the wagon. "It takes a good year for the children to warm up to you once they move into the house."

Kit climbed in beside Daphne and signaled to Nash that they were ready to go. "I don't know what to do with them those first few years," she said. "I'm only just now making progress with Sophie. The younger two . . ." Kit shrugged. "They just seem to toddle around and run into things."

Daphne laughed. "Pheobe is barely two years old. What do you expect?"

"Not a thing," Kit said honestly. With the first five or six children, she'd hoped for an absolution, a relief of the guilt she felt every time Daphne got a wistful look on her face. Whether or not Daphne was actually pining for what she'd lost didn't matter. Kit felt the guilt down to her toenails, and it was becoming apparent that no matter how many children they gave a home to, no matter how many women she saved from having the same fate as Daphne, there wasn't a way to change the past.

Which meant Kit would always have to live with what she'd done.

They left Lady Elizabeth and her luggage at an out-of-the-way posting inn. The stage would be by in less than an hour, and she'd be on her way to meet her father and try to find a new path forward. It wouldn't be the one she'd originally planned — no one could go through this experience and simply go back to the way she'd been — but at least it had the potential to be a good future, free of disease and despair.

Nash then drove the wagon back to Haven Manor, getting Kit and Daphne home in time to help with the final dinner preparations.

Daphne was quiet as they carried the dishes up to the dining hall. Much quieter than normal. Had it all been too much? They'd brought Priscilla into the fold, dealt with the two required contracts, and sent another woman home after the birth of her child, all within a matter of weeks. What sorts of memories had it pulled forth?

Twelve little faces frowned at the bowl of boiled turnips Kit set on the table followed by Jess's pot of broth. None of them said a word, but they didn't have to. Everyone knew that turnips were easy to grow and plenty filling.

When Daphne came in with a tray of apricot cakes and marmalade, though, even Kit had to admit it was fun to watch the faces light up in smiles.

On the heels of enjoyment came another wave of guilt and a hot flash of anger. It blurred together into the threatening burn of tears. These children shouldn't be marveling over apricot cakes. Had life been kinder, they'd eat like this every day. Marmalade wouldn't be a cause for celebration. They deserved to know whether or not they liked white soup or venison. They should have their pick of puddings and fruit compotes.

But they wouldn't have that, because other people had made decisions that robbed them of that chance.

Twelve years ago, Kit and Daphne had vowed to try to give a little bit back, preserve just a bit of that innocence and opportunity.

Giving them apricot cakes didn't feel like enough.

Was it enough for Daphne? She looked happy, helping the youngest children hold their forks properly. Was Daphne ever sad that Kit hadn't managed to save her from this? Hadn't been able to send her off the way they'd done Lady Elizabeth? The way they'd done eleven other women?

"She doesn't miss it," Jess said quietly in Kit's ear.

Kit cleared her throat and tried to look confused. "Miss what?"

"London. The parties. The gowns. All of it. She doesn't miss it."

The bottom of Kit's stomach lurched. Did Jess and Daphne talk about this when Kit wasn't around? While Jess had become a close friend very quickly, Kit and Daphne had been friends for nearly twenty years. They'd shared everything since they were children.

But they didn't talk about London. They didn't talk about the incident. Not once since they'd started Haven Manor in the old, nearly abandoned estate had Daphne engaged in a single conversation about their past life.

It was like London was a distant fairy tale for her.

Kit dropped her gaze to the floor. "Has she said anything?"

"No," Jess said softly. "But she doesn't cry about it in the middle of the night either."

A fine tremble started in Kit's fingers and worked its way up her arms. She didn't want to ask the obvious question, but she refused to be a coward. "Do I?" She swallowed. "Do I cry at night?"

Jess's face was blank as she looked into Kit's. "I'm glad it's my room that shares a wall with yours and not the children's." She paused for a moment and then spoke again. "It's always worse when you come back from London."

Kit was still having the dreams, still waking up in a cold sweat having dreamed about a life where she'd abandoned Daphne just like everyone else had, where she still swirled through ballrooms in jewels and satins, indulging in as many exquisite dishes as she wished.

What she hadn't known was that she'd been crying out. What did she say? Had she mentioned the blackmail? Or Lord Wharton? Was that why Jess had been making small, pointed comments for the past three days, poking and prodding away at Kit's sanity?

Jess knew Kit was holding something back, and trying to remember not to say anything was exhausting. Perhaps Kit should tell her friends a bit more. She could tell them about seeing her father. That would surely explain a great deal of her added distress.

If at all possible, she didn't want to tell them about Lord Wharton. She didn't want to have to examine everything that came along with him, the pangs of longing that, for all that she hated about London society, revealed what she still missed. She missed dancing and pretty dresses. And good food. She missed the city. As much as she loved the beautiful forest that surrounded their new home, she sometimes missed the noise and life of London.

But she could never tell anyone that. She

could never let Daphne know that Kit had a sliver of regret about running away with her all those years ago.

Because Kit didn't regret that. Even knowing what she knew now, she'd still have made the same decision.

"I know guilt, Kit," Jess said quietly, "and I know regret. But I also know, whatever it is you're beating yourself up with, don't let it be Daphne. She's happy."

Jess gave Kit's shoulder a single pat and then moved to the table to keep the boys from playing marbles with their turnips.

Kit looked over at the woman who had been her dearest friend for as long as she could remember. Daphne's round cheeks were creased with a smile as she rolled a turnip around on the youngest child's plate, encouraging the child to view the simple food as fun and exciting. Was Jess right? Was Daphne happy?

Kit hoped so. She really did. So she would keep the man she'd met to herself. No one needed to know about him or how he'd made Kit feel. Because everyone in this house had been knocked around enough by life and deserved a little happiness.

And as Kit stepped forward to join in the laughter around the large table, she thought maybe, just maybe, that might even include her.

CHAPTER EIGHT

The meeting with the solicitor wasn't going well.

Then again, any man of the law who was writing up a contract that sold a man a chess set piece by piece over the course of several years wasn't likely to be a delicate sort of fellow.

"Mr. Banfield," Oliver said, arms crossed over his chest, "let me be honest with you."

Graham sat up a little straighter in his chair in the corner. Mr. Banfield was a man with thick, dark hair shot through with grey at the temples that stuck out in messy spikes, proving the little boy from the store the day before was definitely this man's son. He and Oliver had been going back and forth about the chess set contract for nearly twenty minutes.

After listening to it all, Graham had to agree with the solicitor on one thing, ridiculous though it may be. The contract was solid. And legal. And signed by the man who actually controlled the purse strings. So there really wasn't anything Oliver could do about it. Unless, of course, Oliver wanted to challenge his father's mental capabilities and fight for control of the earldom and the estates.

The solicitor had even offered to help start the paperwork.

Oliver had obviously declined. Now, apparently, he was changing tactics.

The man sitting behind the desk strewn with books, papers, and other assorted office accoutrements leaned his elbow on the arm of his chair and dropped his forehead into his palm. "By all means, Lord Farnsworth. Please be honest."

Oliver took a shaky breath and leaned forward in his own chair, propping his elbows on his knees. "I'm looking for my sister."

The solicitor froze for a moment, and his whole demeanor shifted as he slowly lifted his head from his hand. "Your sister?"

All of the fight seemed to drain from Oliver's body. "Yes. She's disappeared, and I'm worried about her. My father isn't, which means he knows something he isn't telling me, and this strange chess purchase is the only abnormal thing I know of that he's done since my sister disappeared."

Mr. Banfield reached for a quill and began sliding the feather through his fingers. "And you think one had something to do with the other?"

Graham dropped his head back and stared at the ceiling. If the chess set had anything to do with Priscilla, this was, indeed, an extremely convoluted situation. Beyond comprehension. Did Oliver truly believe the two connected?

And if they were, would Mr. Banfield actually admit it?

"I was hoping you would tell me," Oliver said in a quiet, steady voice.

"Lord Farnsworth, I'm afraid missing young ladies are outside my expertise. I'd be happy to recommend —"

"Whomever you send me to will just end up right back in this office if they're worth their salt, because the only thing to go on is this chess set," Oliver growled. "My sister is very important to me, Mr. Banfield, and she has always counted on me to be there for her."

"I understand," the solicitor said softly. "I'm sure a missing family member can be quite distressing, but there's nothing I can tell you about your sister."

Mr. Banfield leaned forward, his mouth

drawn in what might have been sympathy. "If your father believes her to be safe, perhaps you should trust him. I consider my wife and daughter a treasure as well. But sometimes treasure needs to be hidden for a while in order to reach its full value. Perhaps he knows something about your sister that you don't."

Something about the way the solicitor phrased his advice niggled at Graham's brain. It was a strange wording to have come from nowhere. It was almost as if the man had spoken something similar enough times that he'd really given thought to how best to view such a situation. But the phrasing . . .

Oliver stood, breaking into Graham's ponderings. "I'm not leaving Marlborough, Mr. Banfield. And I will be watching you."

All ease left the solicitor as he, too, rose to his feet. "Are you threatening me?"

Oliver blinked, and it was all Graham could do not to laugh at the incredulity on Oliver's face. For all of his tough talk over the past few days, when actually challenged with whether or not he was going to do anything, he looked aghast. Oliver didn't even care that much for the violence level of fencing. "Of course not!"

It was the solicitor's turn to blink in

surprise and pause for a moment. Truly, if Priscilla's well-being hadn't been a factor, the whole exchange would have been highly entertaining.

Mr. Banfield cleared his throat. "Well then, I hope you enjoy your stay in Marlborough. Be sure to visit the white horse."

Oliver prowled straight out to the white horse, a depiction of a running animal carved into the chalk hill outside of town. "Do you think it was a clue?"

Graham looked from his friend to the carving. "A clue?"

"Yes." Oliver nodded enthusiastically. "A direction of sorts for searching for Priscilla."

"No," Graham said slowly. "I rather think he just wanted us out of his office."

On their way back into town, they made it a point to chat with any locals they passed. They didn't learn anything except that the townspeople were all rather proud of their market.

Back at the Bear Inn, where they'd taken rooms, Oliver collapsed on his bed, staring at the ceiling. "I want to go to the market."

Market day was only a few days away. It wouldn't be too difficult to stay around that long.

"Twice," Oliver added.

Oliver wanted to stay in Marlborough for more than a week? Doing what?

Graham didn't say anything, though, just sat and let his mind churn. There was something he was missing, something that part of his mind was trying to latch on to. Something important.

"There are other white horses, you know."

"What?" Graham blinked at Oliver.

"Like the one outside town. There are more of them. All around Wiltshire."

Did Oliver mean to visit all of them? "I really don't think Mr. Banfield was sending you a secret message."

"Have you got a better idea?" Oliver sat up in the bed. "I want to be at the market. If she is in this town, that's where she's likely to show up. In the meantime, I've got to look somewhere."

Graham didn't have a good argument for that, but he didn't relish sitting around the Bear Inn's public rooms for a week and a half.

"We could split up," Oliver said, "see what there is to be found around the carvings. Maybe even explore the area around Marlborough a bit more." He fell back on the bed, his voice dropping to a hoarse whisper. "It's better than doing nothing."

There was no answer Graham could give,

nothing he could say. He didn't agree with Oliver, but he didn't really know why. Until he managed to put a finger on what was bothering him in the solicitor's office this afternoon, he might as well go along with the white horse theory.

Graham sat in silence, staring out the window. When soft snores indicated Oliver had given in to his emotional exhaustion, Graham couldn't help but smile. Sometimes a person just had to hide away from the world.

The churning thought that had been dangling just out of reach suddenly slammed into place, nearly sending Graham out of his chair.

"Father says that if you visit hidden treasure too often it doesn't stay hidden."

Graham had been right. The solicitor had said those words before. Enough that his son had learned them as well.

What if the boy's tree-living friend wasn't imaginary?

It still didn't tell them anything about where Priscilla was, but to be honest, it was more of a lead than chasing after horses carved into hillsides.

Oliver's mention of Priscilla had at least made the solicitor think about hidden treasure, so perhaps there was something to be found on the north side of town.

It shouldn't take him much time to ride out there and find out. He left a note in case Oliver woke before Graham returned.

Collecting Dogberry from the stables didn't take long, and soon Graham was heading north. The redbrick buildings became smaller, plainer, until they gave way entirely to a narrow, tree-lined road. Eventually even the modern pavement turned into the packed pebbles and dirt of a common country lane. Occasionally he spotted a tile-covered house, surrounded by small gardens and clusters of chickens, but the hustle and bustle of the small market town fell behind him faster than he had anticipated.

He closed his eyes, trying to listen for the sounds of the town's main area, the bark of the stage drivers, the rattle of deliveries. But there was nothing but the peace of the countryside. A bird chirp. A breeze flitting through the tree leaves. The rush of the nearby river.

Graham paused as he approached the river.

He'd seen bridges such as these before, had gone over them as a kid and remembered the way his steps echoed on the exposed stone arch.

Well, the stone arch that was probably

exposed on a regular day. Today what was likely little more than a large stream had swollen far beyond its normal bounds. It gurgled against the side of the stone bridge, swelling over the edge and sending rivulets of water streaming across the top of the bridge, tracing grooves in the dusty path before tumbling over the far side of the bridge and joining the water gushing through the arched opening.

Farther upstream, the River Og swirled around tree bases and seeped into grassy patches, indicating that all the rain the little boy had mentioned hadn't finished taking its toll on the land.

Even as his horse plodded forward, splashing through the water across the bridge, Graham reconsidered chasing this crazy notion. What was he doing? Riding off into the countryside because of a child's imaginary friend?

Graham pulled Dogberry to a stop on the other side of the bridge and glanced up again. More rain might make this bridge impassable, and there hadn't been a lot of other roads leading out to the north side of town. In fact, he'd seen none.

Would he be able to make it back? The sky wasn't showing signs of imminent rain, but it wasn't an exceptionally sunny day either.

If he didn't investigate the trees, though, he'd always wonder.

And besides, it had to be more interesting than searching the countryside for white horses.

The solicitor knew more than he was sharing.

Graham knew it.

Oliver knew it.

The solicitor likely knew that they knew it.

But there was no way of making him talk unless they learned something more. At the very least, the fellow was guarding human treasure while making contracts no sane man would agree to. Was it blackmail? Was he threatening the earl to the point that the man had taken time to make sure his daughter was safely out of the way?

Unless Priscilla wasn't safely out of the way. What if the solicitor stole people away and made their families pay for their return? Graham shook his head at the fanciful turn of his thoughts. If that had been the case, Priscilla would have been returned when Lord Trenting signed the contract, the longevity of which wouldn't make a lick of sense.

Not that much about this situation made sense.

Graham had gotten to the point of chasing down imaginary little boys, after all.

Was he really so desperate to escape the boredom of London that it had come down to this?

Apparently. Graham nudged Dogberry forward. He couldn't return without at least looking for Daniel's strange friend. While it wouldn't seem that a boy living in trees, a missing aristocrat's daughter, and an obscenely expensive chess set had anything in common, it was obvious that something wasn't quite as it should be in Marlborough, and Graham had a burning desire to find out what.

Past the bridge, the lane continued, meandering its way between hedges, beside pastures, and through shadowed areas caused by dense patches of trees. In one such area, another rutted and less traveled path, wide enough only for a single wagon to pass through, jutted off through the trees. It didn't look at all appealing.

Which probably made it an excellent place for someone to hide.

Graham turned his horse and gave him free rein to pick his way along the road, avoiding the hoof-sucking mud on the darkened parts of the wooded lane.

The trees to his right gave way to fields and farms while the woods grew deeper and denser on his left, the scraggly trees from the main road turning into a thick, substantial wall of greenery. In some areas, the undergrowth thinned, revealing patches of bluebells and delicate moss draped from the sprawling limbs of mighty oaks.

Graham had never seen anything like it. In his vast travels he'd seen the grandeur of the mountains and the glory of the ocean. He'd even seen the beauty to be found in the barrenness of a desert, but never had he seen anything like the woods outside of Marlborough.

Entranced, he reined Dogberry in and nudged him closer. This part of the country had always just been a stopping point on his way to somewhere else. What else had he missed in life because he was too focused on where he was going?

Graham sent his horse off the path and into the woods, where he was swallowed up by breathtaking beauty. Scraggly pale green plants were crushed beneath Dogberry's hooves as they wandered under tree branches that were as big around as Graham's waist. Overhead, the limbs of the giant trees twined together, forming a roof that blocked out what little sun had managed to break through the clouds. Graham shivered at the drop in temperature and paused to pull his cloak from the saddlebag.

As he was wrapping it around himself, he heard voices.

"You're going too high!"

"No, I'm not. You're being a milksop. John said he climbed up here to see the bird nest last week, and I want to see it, too!"

"But what if you fall? I can't carry you back to the manor. We're already going to be in trouble because we were only supposed to go as far as the blackberries!"

There was a pause in which Graham could almost picture the owner of the young male voice making a face at the worried little girl he was with. It made Graham smile. He remembered taunting his cousins with his own daring exploits.

"Henry!"

The little girl's shriek wiped the smile from Graham's face. Yes, Henry was a common name, and there were probably hundreds in Wiltshire, possibly even a dozen or so in Marlborough alone. But a little boy named Henry in the depths of the woods? Stuck up in a tree? It was too much of a coincidence for Graham to leave alone.

He tied his horse to a tree branch and set

off on foot, not wanting to scare the children away with his approach.

"Alice!"

Graham had to pause and contain his laughter at the boy's mocking impression of the little girl. It was nice to know that some things never changed.

The voices stopped, but Graham could still easily follow the loud rustling of leaves. Apparently Henry wasn't the smoothest of climbers. That, or Alice was frantically pacing beneath the tree and sending the rustling noise echoing through the woods. She seemed like the pacing type, most likely with her hands fretting about the entire time Henry was aloft.

A sharp crack followed by two screams spurred Graham to proceed with a bit more speed and a lot less caution.

"Henry! Henry!"

"Don't worry, Alice." The voice was tiny now. Young. And trembling. All of the confidence was gone, though it sounded like he was trying to be brave. It was the false bravery more than anything that sent Graham crashing into the small clearing. He'd seen a lot of idiots hurt themselves in the name of proving something.

The little girl shrieked again as Graham cleared the trees bordering the open area.

He held up both hands in an attempt to show her he only wanted to help.

"Who are you?"

The girl was small, though Graham hadn't spent nearly enough time around children to be able to guess her age. Dark brown hair rolled in long curls down her back, and her mouth was set in a firm, mutinous expression. Only the slight trembling of her chin showed that she wasn't as brave as she wanted him to think.

"My name is Lord Wharton," Graham said carefully, easing forward at a slower pace now that he'd found the children and knew Henry was still up in the tree somewhere and not broken on the forest floor. "I heard you scream and wanted to help."

Why didn't the child instantly accept his offer of help? Wasn't that what children were supposed to do?

Instead, she bit her lip and looked at a break in the woods, probably the path the children had come down to get to the clearing. Then her eyes lifted to the tree. What type of life made a child consider running away instead of helping?

Perhaps the hidden treasure sort of life?

"Can you get Henry down?" she finally asked in a very small voice. "I think he's stuck."

"I'm not stuck," the boy said with belligerence, obviously moving past the fear of whatever had caused the loud cracking noise earlier. "I just can't go anywhere."

Her two small fists found their way to the little girl's hips as she glared into the tree. "And what exactly do you think *stuck* means, Henry Cotter? That you're meeting the queen for tea?"

Graham lifted one gloved hand to his mouth until he managed to contain his smile. "Perhaps," he said, clearing his throat to stop the laugh that threatened to emerge. "Perhaps I should go up and see what I can do? I was quite the tree climber myself in my boyhood."

Without waiting for Alice's agreement, Graham took off his cloak and jacket and folded them into a neat pile on the ground. Then he grasped one of the wide, low branches and hauled himself up. He could certainly see why little boys wanted to climb this tree. The lower branches were nearly begging for it, creating a perfect combination of ladder and staircase at least twelve feet into the air. Beyond that he could see that the limbs started stretching upward instead of out, creating a tangle of footholds and thinner limbs that made climbing to the top a treacherous challenge.

He climbed high enough to get a clearer view of Henry, and it made his heart pause and his stomach threaten to jump through his throat. One wrong move and the little boy would indeed be in a great deal of trouble.

The *V* of limbs he was currently nestled in looked secure enough, but the thick branch that had caused the loud cracking sound was perilously close to trapping his legs. Two skinny branches that were already bowing under the weight were all that kept the limb from crushing the boy and breaking his legs.

Or worse.

Graham had climbed trickier places before, though none were quickly coming to mind at the moment. Perhaps the mountains he'd scaled in Switzerland or the jungle tree he'd scaled on a dare from Aaron. Just because there was a scared little boy involved this time didn't change the process. Place one foot carefully, test the hold before shifting weight, repeat.

"Good afternoon," Graham said in his best society drawing-room voice once his face was even with Henry's. Tears streaked the boy's cheeks, and Graham made a point of not looking at them.

The long gash at his hairline slowly oozing blood was a bit more difficult to ignore.

"Who are you?" the boy asked with only a small hiccup.

These children were certainly concerned with knowing who he was. "Lord Wharton. What do you say we get you down out of this tree?"

"I can't," the little boy whispered. "My leg."

Graham flattened himself against the branch composing one side of Henry's impromptu chair and eased over to look at the boy's leg. It was bent at an odd angle and hooked against his other skinny limb. It didn't appear broken, thank goodness, but the boy certainly didn't have the leverage to get his foot free, not without knocking into the larger limb hanging over him, waiting to crush him.

That threat needed to be taken care of first.

Bracing a foot against the other side of the *V,* Graham leaned out and gave the loose limb a shove. Another crack echoed through the woods as it broke the rest of the way and tumbled into the limbs below, but not onto the little boy.

Alice set to shrieking again. "Henry! Henry! Oh dear, Mama Jess is gonna scowl something fierce if I bring you home dead!"

Graham ducked his head to hide a smile. Whoever Mama Jess was, she must have some powerful facial expressions. "Everything is fine, Alice," he called toward the ground. "We're just moving some limbs around."

He turned back to the boy. "Henry, isn't it? What do you say we get down out of this tree?"

Wide blue eyes peered at Graham from a very pale face. Blood trickled down Henry's temple, but Graham resolutely refused to frown. There'd be plenty of time for worry once they got on the ground.

One booted foot slipped as Graham tried to scoot around enough to ease his way in front of Henry. His arm shot out to wrap around a limb, but it made the whole tree shake, and the boy sucked in a great breath of air before catching his lower lip between two huge front teeth. Air whistled through the gap between the teeth, and the tears that had dried while the boy watched Graham started flowing again.

Maybe talking would distract him.

"You live around here, Henry?"

Graham leaned over, keeping one arm securely anchored, and worked to free Henry's trapped leg. The branch gave way and the leg swung free, causing another sharp inhale from the boy. "I live in London," Graham said, as if the boy had answered the initial question. "But I travel a lot. Have you ever traveled?"

Out of the corner of his eye, Graham saw Henry shake his head.

"Think you can hold on to my neck?" Graham leaned over and Henry's little arms clamped around, nearly choking Graham with the strength of their grip. "I'll take that as a yes." Graham coughed as he eased one arm beneath the boy, lifting him toward his chest.

He was lighter than Graham had expected, but the responsibility of carrying him down the tree was weighty indeed. Right at the moment, the boy was almost completely dependent upon Graham. The idea turned him into a bit of a boggler.

He'd had more interaction with children in the past day than he'd had his entire adult life. Of course, he'd always assumed that one day he'd have children — he was the heir to an earldom, after all — but they had seemed vague, nebulous things. A duty. Much like having a social presence or being a member of a certain club to secure political advancement.

The shuddering chest pressed to his, though, was very, very real.

"Hang on tight," Graham said, even though the boy was nearly choking him as it was. "This could be a bumpy ride."

Normally Graham would have jumped and swung his way to the bottom, but scraggly blond hair impeded his vision and the weight clinging to the front of him encumbered his movements.

Feeling with his left foot, Graham blindly kicked around until he found a good foothold and then started making his way down the tree. Every time he brushed against the boy's injured leg, a sharp hiss would puff against his throat.

Finally they'd gotten low enough that the little girl could see them clearly, and she accompanied their final descent with helpful phrases such as, "Please don't drop him," "Be careful with your footing," and "Don't fall." Graham had to bite his tongue to keep from thanking her with enough sarcasm to knock the leaves off the tree.

He jumped the last five feet to the ground, wrapping his arms around the boy to keep from jarring him too much. With the security of solid earth under his feet, tension Graham hadn't even realized he'd been holding unwound from his muscles.

Alice pranced around them, her little hands fluttering and occasionally reaching for Henry but not actually touching him.

Graham knelt so the boy's feet could touch the ground. "How's the leg, lad?"

Little arms slipped from Graham's neck as the boy tested his ability to hold himself up. He immediately cried out and crumpled to the ground.

Alice's hands fluttered faster before she fell on the ground next to the boy. "Oh, Henry, what are we going to do?"

Graham stood and straightened his waistcoat and cravat before retrieving his jacket. He wrapped the cloak around the duo of children. "Wait here. I've a horse just in the trees there. I'll be glad to take you home."

Two pairs of wide eyes looked up at him before their gazes locked with each other. Alice's chin trembled again before she set her mouth in that mutinous line of strength once more. "Yes. We will let you take us home."

"Alice, we can't!" Henry snuck a quick glance at Graham before looking back at the little girl. "You go get help and I'll wait here."

She shook her head, sending her hair flying. "You're hurt. And it might rain. Mama Kit says that rules are only useful when they solve a problem."

Henry's brows lowered. "She does not."

"Does so. I heard her telling Mama Daphne that in the library a few weeks ago."

"We're not supposed to go in the library when they're talking," Henry whispered.

Alice frowned. "I didn't go in the library. I was in the garden under the window. Now hush. We're going to get to ride a horse."

That notion seemed to perk the little boy up, and Graham set off to retrieve his horse. His mind whirled with the barrage of information and ideas. So many *mamas*. And when had women being called Kit become such a popular thing?

Whether or not these children had anything to do with Priscilla's disappearance, one thing was certain. Whatever he had just stumbled his way into certainly wasn't boring.

CHAPTER NINE

Alice's eyes were wide enough to show the white around the pale green middles as she looked up at Dogberry. Graham chuckled as he guided her limp hand to the horse's shoulder. The muscle quivered beneath her hand, but the well-trained horse didn't move.

"He's big," the little girl whispered.

Dogberry wasn't all that large of a horse, but to a little girl he was probably giant. Particularly if she didn't spend a lot of time around horses. "Have you ridden a horse before?"

Alice shook her head. "I've ridden in the wagon when Mr. Ban —" She clamped her lips shut so tightly they turned white around the edges.

Graham continued as if he hadn't noticed, even though his curiosity was riding him with a fierceness he hadn't felt in a very long time. These children were obviously part of

Mr. Banfield's "hidden treasure," but that didn't tell Graham whether or not their hiding was a good thing. Alice's comment had sounded like that man was a friend, but then she was young enough that she might not know any better.

"I'm afraid your first ride won't be a proper one," Graham said with an exaggerated sigh. "I haven't the proper saddle for a young lady such as yourself."

Her thin shoulders lifted and fell. "I won't know the difference."

Another chuckle rose in Graham's throat as he lifted her onto the back of the horse, right behind the saddle. It took her a few moments to adjust her skirts to her liking, but she was soon settled and clutching the back of the saddle as he instructed.

Graham turned his attention to the now-sniffling Henry. Blood was smeared across his cheek, mingling with the unchecked tears and snot. Graham never knew children could be so . . . disgusting. He might have to revise his opinion on whether or not keeping them hidden away in the nursery was a good idea.

Arranging Henry on top of the horse was a bit more difficult, given that every bump made him whimper, and he refused to let loose of Graham's cloak even though the fabric could wrap around the boy twice with some to spare.

Once the boy was perched on the front of the saddle and draped over the horse's neck, Graham faced yet another difficult mounting: his own. He'd have to lift himself up and then slide one leg between the children. More than once, Graham thought he was about to tumble back into the bluebells he'd been admiring earlier, but he didn't. He settled into the saddle with his cloak bunched between him and the boy and Alice's thin fingers buried in his jacket.

"Off we go, then. Alice, you'll have to show me the way."

She was silent so long that he twisted around to look at her. One lip was snagged in her tiny teeth as she looked up at him. Finally she nodded and pointed toward a break in the trees. "Take that path until you reach the creek."

Graham set off, keeping Dogberry to a very gentle walk. Anything above a plod made Henry moan, but the slow sway of an amble calmed him, and soon his body relaxed into a limp mass against Graham's chest. With any luck, the boy had fallen asleep and wasn't passed out from the ordeal.

By their third turn, Graham was rather

lost and could only hope that Alice actually knew where she was going — and that someone at her house would know of a simpler way for Graham to return to the road.

Finally, he saw blackberry bushes and a patch of dim grey light that indicated a break in the trees ahead. As they left the wooded area, a vast lake stretched out before him, nestled among gentle hills. A multi-arched stone bridge spanned the lake, joining its reflection to make a series of circles marching across the water. On the highest of the rolling hills perched a grand house. Smaller buildings were dotted along the lake's shoreline, and unkempt paths seemed to crisscross the entire property.

It looked like a once thriving but now neglected estate.

More questions instead of a single answer flitted through Graham's mind.

He guided Dogberry along the edge of the lake, but the closer they got to the house, the tighter Alice held him. She was trembling enough that he could feel it even through his shirt, waistcoat, and jacket.

What was at the house that frightened her so? Hidden treasure and possibly crazy solicitor aside, he wasn't leaving these two children with anyone if there was the slightest indication that they were in danger.

The grounds nearer the house had seen more attention than the lake area, though even here, certain areas, like the remains of a large hedge maze, had been left to nature's whim.

A brick wall rose up to their right, occasionally broken by a wrought-iron gate. A vast garden stretched out within the walls, showing signs of great care and tending, which the rest of the grounds were missing.

Beyond the walled garden, he could see a collection of outbuildings that seemed in good repair. The smell and sound of livestock indicated they were at least in some sort of working condition. Past that, a long lawn stretched up to the back of a glorious-looking house, with wide stairs leading up between the jutting rooms. Simple rectangular windows dotted the smooth white face of the building, and elaborate carving created what appeared to be a railing around the roof.

The door to the back of the house, however, didn't seem to match the rest of the grandeur, consisting of a rough-hewn plank attached to the intricate iron hinges.

A barn-like structure was built against one wall of the garden, though he doubted it contained any horses, considering Alice's reaction to Dogberry.

A young girl stepped out of the stable, a large bundle of dark brown hair on top of her head and her skirt about an inch higher than it should have been. Her mouth dropped open as she spied Graham and the children. The basket in her hand hit the ground before she snatched at her skirts and ran for the house.

Graham frowned. What was going on here?

He forced himself to keep the horse slow when he really wanted to rush behind the girl and get to the house at the same time she did.

She disappeared up the stairs and through the strange plank door. Moments later, another girl stepped out with her, this one with her hair twisted into a long blond braid. Were there no adults at this house?

Graham guided the horse right up to the stairs. With one arm he reached behind him to grasp Alice and lower her to the ground. She wobbled a bit as her legs adjusted to being off the horse, but then she ran up the stairs to the older girls, babbling about trees and horses and rules. Even though Graham had been part of the entire proceedings, he couldn't follow her tale.

He slid to the ground and scooped the still-limp Henry into his arms.

The tallest girl, and presumably the oldest, swallowed hard and stepped forward, laying one hand on Alice's shoulder and holding her close. "Is Henry hurt?"

Graham nodded. "I don't know how bad his leg is, and he's got a cut on his head that hasn't stopped bleeding yet."

"We'll take him to the kitchen, then." She set her shoulders and led him around the side of the house to a low wooden door.

Graham followed her, holding little Henry, still wrapped in the voluminous cloak, close to his chest. In the distance thunder rumbled. He needed to get back across the river before the rain came, but he couldn't leave just yet.

For one thing, he wasn't sure what was going on. For another, he was thoroughly and completely lost. He was fairly stuck until someone gave him directions, or until he became desperate enough to wander about the wooded trails hoping to stumble across someone who could direct him back to Marlborough.

The kitchen was large, with a thick-cut wooden worktable in the center and a fire blazing away in the cook hearth. A large bucket of water sat to one side and another table sat against the wall, covered with linen-wrapped bundles that were probably the day's bread, given the yeasty smell that lingered in the air. The floor was clean, and the smooth walls of the outside continued on the inside. He gently settled his burden onto the table.

The sound of hurried footsteps coming down the stairs pounded into the room just ahead of yet another small child, a boy this time. Two women were right behind him — finally someone who appeared to be over the age of ten. Or maybe twelve. He glanced at the girl with the braid. Possibly fifteen? Definitely not older than that, or she wouldn't still look like a child.

A look of grave concern covered the round face of the first woman as she ran into the kitchen, hands wrapped in her skirts. Behind her came a petite woman not much larger than the girl who'd brought him to the kitchen, but definitely older and wearing a maturity that marked her as an adult. Her face looked emotionless, pure as a porcelain doll's, until she set eyes on Graham.

Then her eyes narrowed, and a groove appeared along the top of her nose. Her glare was icy hard.

Graham fought the urge to squirm. He'd done nothing wrong.

Well, other than set off with the intent of uncovering the solicitor's hidden treasure, but he'd rescued two children along the way, so that had to shift his motivation to somewhere in the neutral range.

He pointed to the boy, just in case the angry woman didn't realize what he'd done. "He has a gash on his head and his leg is injured. I don't know how badly, but I don't think it's broken."

"Henry!" The concerned woman rushed forward and laid a gentle hand on Henry's cheek. With efficient movements, she unbundled him from the cloak and set about sending the various children off for clean clothes, bandages, and wood and lashings to make a splint.

Graham backed out of the woman's way until he could feel the heat of the kitchen fire through his clothing.

The shorter woman stepped to the side as the children rushed from the room on their given assignments. Once they'd left, the first woman dipped a bowl into the large bucket of water and snagged a rag from the bread-laden table before setting about cleaning the little boy's face. The boy snuffled and woke as the water hit his face, and the woman began cooing comforting noises at him.

"What happened?"

The sentence was spoken in a low voice

and very near to Graham's left ear. He jerked his attention away from the ministrations at the table to find that the smaller woman had worked her way around the room to challenge him. Her features were delicate, with pale blond hair scraped back from her face, emphasizing sharp cheekbones and a thin, straight nose. Her pale golden eyes were hard and flat.

Graham swallowed. When was the last time he felt so intimidated by a mere look? Had he ever? Certainly never from a woman. "He got himself stuck in a tree."

One golden eyebrow arched upward. "And you just happened to be nearby?"

"Yes." He felt he should give more information, but he really didn't have anything to offer.

"Who are you?"

He opened his mouth to answer, but the room was invaded once more with children talking and asking questions and plopping the medical supplies on the table. The woman caring for Henry wiped her hands on the wet rag she'd been using on the boy's face. Her dark blue skirt swished against the children pressed around her. She set one little boy to the side, neatly moved around one of the older girls, and set about bandaging Henry's head before moving on to his leg.

As an only child, Graham found the chaos mesmerizing.

More movement at the door of the kitchen drew his attention as a third woman stepped inside. All fear of the little woman next to him dropped away, along with his admiration of the woman juggling all the children. Every last part of him leaped for joy at the sight before him.

The sprigged muslin dress was far less fine, and the hair rolled into a simple bun had far more strands escaping, but there was no denying that he recognized the woman.

Somehow he'd managed to find his mysterious lady in green.

Kit stumbled to a halt three steps into the kitchen. She blinked. It wasn't possible. She blinked again. But the vision in front of her remained. How had he found her? *Why* had he found her?

And how was she possibly going to explain to Jess and Daphne why she hadn't mentioned meeting him in London?

Her mouth snapped open and shut a few times before she took a deep breath and steadied herself. "What are *you* doing here?"

Jess's head swung back and forth, her

sharp glance bouncing from Kit to the man and back again. "You know him?"

"I met him in London."

Daphne's head popped up, eyes wide with alarm, and Jess reached a hand toward the knife she kept in a hidden sheath sewn into the back of her spencer jacket.

"No, no," Kit rushed to say, holding up her hands, palms out toward her friends. "I didn't go there to meet *him.*"

Why oh why oh why had she thought keeping the entire story to herself was a good idea? It would be so much easier if she could just say he was the man from the ballroom. But she couldn't. And right now wasn't the time to rectify that. Right now, she needed to keep Daphne from worrying and keep Jess from threatening bodily harm.

Or worse.

Jess wasn't likely to waste her breath on threats if she thought the man was truly a danger. Not that Kit had ever seen the petite woman actually hurt anyone, but she had the confidence and skill to do so.

Jess's hand movements stalled, and the look she sent Kit promised that the knife might be coming at her later if answers weren't soon forthcoming, but then she turned her icy glare back on their unexpected visitor. "Why are you following her?"

Kit winced, knowing Jess's tone, on top of the very strange situation, would make Lord Wharton extremely suspicious. They couldn't afford not to be blunt, though. They had to know why he was there and how he'd come to be at her secret home accompanied by her children — well, the children who were in her care and the closest she was going to get to having a family of her own.

Lord Wharton spread his arms wide and gave that same charming, beguiling smile he'd sent her way when she tried to refuse his offer of lemonade. "This is simply a happy coincidence. Perhaps God rewarding my good deed of assisting a few children in need."

Kit bit her cheek to keep from smiling in return. The man seemed to bring light into the room by simply breathing, but she couldn't let herself get distracted by it. "And you just happened to be riding through the woods nearly eighty miles from London in the middle of the Season on a whim?"

He tilted his head in thought. "More the beginning than the middle, but yes. I accompanied a friend to Marlborough on, er, family business."

The careful phrasing made tension roll through the room. Daphne kept her head tucked over Henry's wound, but her hands had stilled while Jess's hand slid up her back once more, disappearing beneath the spencer and wrapping around the handle of the knife.

Was it possible that this man was friends with one of the children's fathers? He wasn't really of an age to have a connection to the fathers of the children's mothers, but perhaps he was somehow connected to one of the mothers themselves? Anything was possible. Over the years, more than one scoundrel had followed the money to Nash's office, but no one had ever ventured out into the woods before.

"And what friend would that be?" Kit asked, carefully keeping her tone as nonchalant as possible.

Lord Wharton's eyebrows climbed a notch closer to his hairline, and he slid half a step away from Jess. "Lord Farnsworth," he said slowly, "son of the Earl of Trenting."

Farnsworth was not a familiar name, but Trenting certainly was. The man's signature was barely dry on the contract for his share of the support payments. He'd made her meet him at an inn halfway between Marlborough and London to sign the papers and turn over the care of his daughter.

Kit had been hesitant to agree to taking

on a woman with a brother unless the brother was the one signing the contract, and now she knew she'd been right to be so wary. Even though the earl had assured her the brother was of no concern, there was a man in her kitchen who said differently.

And while it was certainly comforting to know that there were men growing up with more honor than their fathers, it made their current situation rather tricky.

At least they'd stopped keeping the women at the manor ten years ago. It was much easier to house them in the home of a woman who would be able to nurse the baby for a year or so after it was born. No matter what happened, this man would never know the whereabouts of Lady Priscilla.

"Trenting, you say?" Kit cleared her throat. "How nice of you."

Awkward silence fell as the children looked from one adult to another, waiting to see what would happen. They didn't get many visitors here at the manor, and the few who did come were expected and usually accompanied by Nash.

"Jess," Kit said through a dry throat, "please take the children upstairs. It's time for their afternoon lessons."

One side of Jess's mouth tilted up, causing a dimple to crease her cheek. She slid the knife back into its sheath with practiced ease. "I'll just start them on their maths, then."

Daphne coughed and lowered her head closer to the bandage she was securing around Henry's little head. Her shoulders were trembling slightly, probably from trying to hold back laughter at the thought of Jess teaching anyone maths. The girl was a fast thinker and brilliant with languages, but no one would ever consider her smart when it came to the traditional subjects of maths and science.

"Oof, Mama Daphne!" the little boy cried, swinging his arms up to his face. "You're going to smother me!"

The little boy's squirming offense sent Daphne's light giggles over the top. She got herself under control quickly and scooped Henry from the table. She looked from Kit to Lord Wharton before turning her attention back to the little boy in her arms. "Let's go bind your leg in the drawing room, shall we? That way, you can watch the birds fly around outside while you rest it."

While it was better to get everyone as far away from this man as possible, Kit had a powerful urge to stop Daphne from leaving. She didn't want to be alone with the man from London. He made her feel exposed, made her remember the ballroom and that riot of emotions that had bombarded her the entire way home.

The quiet, expectant look on his face didn't help matters any.

How was she possibly going to convince him to leave immediately and return to town without telling anyone about this place?

Then the air around them crackled, and a loud boom of thunder crashed through the sky, followed by the telltale pounding of a rainy deluge.

No matter how much she wanted him gone, she couldn't throw him out into the rain after he'd saved Henry. For the time being, she was stuck with him.

And the triumphant grin on the man's face said he knew it.

CHAPTER TEN

Graham tried not to grin — really, he did — but the frustration stamped across Kit's face was simply too fun to ignore. The woman had intrigued him in London, but this added complication made her fascinating. The last thing he wanted to do was let her shuffle him out of the house and down the road to town, which she'd obviously intended to do before the sky had opened up.

She couldn't send him out in the rain, not after he'd saved her . . . well, he wasn't sure what relation Henry was to the woman, but they were connected in some way that made her at least a little bit beholden to him.

What had the children called her? Mama Kit. And the other two women had been Mama Jess and Mama Daphne. Graham may not know a lot about children, but he knew enough to know that one couldn't actually have three mothers. Was it possible these women were nannies?

He looked Kit over once more, from her quickly tapping toe to her crossed arms to her mouth pressed tightly together in a grim line as she tried to decide what to do with him. She didn't look much like a nanny.

Neither had the other blonde. The scary little one.

He could easily believe the one with the brown hair to be a nanny. She'd had kind eyes and gentle hands as she'd tended Henry's wounds.

Graham waved a hand at the kitchen door. "I'll just go see to my horse then, get him settled. Is there room in your barn?"

Her cheeks sucked in as she pressed her lips together hard enough to turn them into thin, white stripes. It made her cheekbones stand out even more in her heart-shaped face. "Yes. But not near the chickens. He might" — she waved a hand toward the ground — "step on them or something."

Graham had never seen Dogberry, or any other horse for that matter, trample a chicken for the fun of it, but he wasn't about to argue.

His cloak had been left on the table, so he scooped it up and tossed it around his shoulders. Hopefully it would be enough to keep the clothing beneath mostly dry. He'd seen no sign of anyone other than women and children in this house. There probably weren't many extra linen shirts lying around, at least not any large enough for an adult.

The rain pelted his face as he jogged around the corner of the house only to stumble to a halt in the middle of a puddle. His horse wasn't where he'd left him.

Graham stood in the rain, looking back and forth across the land. It wasn't surprising that the animal had chosen to get out of the rain, but where had he gone?

The door to the barn was open. It was the most stable-like building in the area, so he could only hope Dogberry had chosen to be smart today.

Once he was out of the pounding rain, voices could be heard from deeper in the barn, which did appear to also be a stable of sorts with several stalls lining one of the walls.

"Do you think we're supposed to brush the horse like we brush the donkey?" A young male voice floated across the building's musty air.

The responding voice was also young, though it was deeper and more masculine than the first. "I think so. The saddle was sort of like the wagon harness, so I would think the coats would be the same." There was a pause, and then the older boy continued with a bit of awe lacing his tone. "Though this beast's coat is ever so much softer than Balaam's."

"Horse," said a third voice, definitely the youngest of the three and possessing a slight lisp at the end of the word.

Graham chuckled as he followed the voices deeper into the building. A gangly boy, with reddish-brown hair and spectacles sliding down a nose that was a bit too large for his face, was draping Graham's saddle over a low wall. The bridle lay next to it. Beside him a little boy stood in front of Dogberry, head leaned back so he could look up into the horse's face. The horse was looking down at the boy, occasionally lowering his head to snuffle at the little boy's hair and make him giggle.

A rough brush appeared over Dogberry's back, held by two hands that obviously didn't know what they were doing. The brush dug into Dogberry's back with enough force to draw a wince from Graham, but the horse didn't even shift his weight.

"Hullo, there." Graham stepped out of the shadows of the entryway and crossed to the small group.

Graham patted Dogberry on the neck, and the animal butted his brown head into Graham's chest before returning his attention to the little boy's hair, apparently as grateful to the boys for getting the horse out of the rain as Graham was.

Over the horse's back, Graham's gaze connected with dark eyes under a shock of straight dark hair.

The hair was longer than was fashionable, falling off the boy's head like a sleek cap of black. His hand froze on the horse's back and he lifted his chin a notch. "This your horse, my lord?"

"Yes," Graham answered, swinging his gaze to look at the boy at his feet. He looked to be about the same age as Henry and the solicitor's son, Daniel. Perhaps a bit younger. Or maybe a bit older. The boy's upturned face was bordered by shags of light brown hair, and caramel-colored eyes stared out over a thin, straight nose. Graham had yet to see a bit of similarity among all the children running around the estate. Where had they all come from?

He cleared his throat and looked back at the boy brushing the horse. "I'm Lord Wharton."

The boy didn't say anything for a moment as his dark gaze searched Graham. What the boy was looking for was anyone's guess, and Graham couldn't tell whether or not he'd found it when he broke the connection and turned his attention back to the horse. "I'm Blake." He jerked his head toward the boy with the spectacles. "That's Reuben. And down there's Arthur."

Graham blinked at the informality of the introductions. No surnames?

"Thank you for taking care of Dogberry." Graham saw another rough-looking brush on the low wall near the saddle and took it in his hand. He began smoothing Dogberry's other side in a brisk circular motion, hoping that Blake would pick up the correct method by example.

"Couldn't just leave him in the rain," Blake murmured.

"We've got some grain we feed the goats sometimes. I could get your horse some of that." Reuben shifted from foot to foot.

Graham nodded his thanks, and the boy took off down the short stable aisle, arms and legs flapping awkwardly.

Arthur didn't say anything, just stared up, alternating between looking at Graham and the horse. Apparently all children were not as open and chatty as young Daniel had been or as accepting as Henry and Alice. How was anyone supposed to know how to act around children if they all behaved so differently? With every moment he spent near one of the tiny human beings, he grew more unsure of the proper response.

For a man who was adept at always reacting properly even without having to think about it, the sensation was more than a bit disconcerting.

A little thrill of triumph ran through him, though, when Blake began to copy Graham's circular motions with the brush. Dogberry grunted and sighed.

He'd managed to do something right there. Perhaps he could engage the littlest boy as well. "Arthur, was it?" Graham leaned around the horse's shoulder to look into the little boy's freckled face. "Do you think you could find a spare pail around here? Perhaps get Dogberry some water?"

The boy glanced up at Graham before darting off. Hopefully to fetch a pail and not to run and tell the women in the house that he found the big man a bit scary.

Graham turned back to the horse to find Blake watching him. The dark eyes were a bit disturbing, being nearly black in color.

"You named your horse Dogberry?"

Graham fought the urge to blush. Naming a horse after a Shakespearean character wasn't the manliest thing to do, but it had seemed appropriate at the time.

Reuben returned with the grain, and there was no sign of Arthur. He was about to ask Reuben to get some water when the clank of a bucket echoed down the barn corridor.

Raising himself onto his toes, Graham peered over the stall wall. Arthur had indeed found a pail and filled it with water. A wave of liquid sloshed over the sides with every step the little boy made. Every inch of threadbare clothing was soaked and plastered to the boy's skin. His little lip was caught between his teeth as he lurched another step with the bucket, causing another small flood down his front.

Maybe Graham shouldn't have sent such a little boy off on such a task? He was managing it, though, so that was good, right? Graham should let him finish the job. At least, it seemed like he should. He knew he wouldn't want someone coming to the rescue just because he found a task a bit difficult.

When neither of the larger boys jumped forward to help Arthur, it seemed to confirm Graham's suspicion.

That or neither boy had even noticed Arthur's dilemma because they'd both returned to staring at their toes.

Finally Arthur was back in front of the

horse, plopping a half-full bucket of water in front of the animal with a triumphant smile. Dogberry lowered his head to drink, and Arthur reached out a hesitant hand to run his fingers lightly over the horse's mane.

The wonder on the boy's face was hard for Graham to fathom. Horses had been part of his life for as long as he could remember. He'd patted them, rode them, fed them since he was younger than Arthur. Well, at least shorter than Arthur.

After drinking, the horse stuck his nose in the bucket of grain and blew it around a bit. Whatever feed they had wouldn't be what Dogberry was used to, but the animal was going to have to adjust the same as Graham. He had a feeling his own meal tonight would be rather simple fare.

Blake stepped around the horse and slid his sleeves back down. Like the girl's skirt earlier, the sleeves were lacking an inch of appropriate length. Both Blake's and Reuben's trousers showed the same signs of wear that Arthur's clothing had.

He tried not to stare even as he added these facts to his growing list of things that didn't quite make sense.

Dogberry seemed settled and happy, so Graham followed the boys back into the rain. They looked from him to each other as they slowly walked up the lawn to the door he'd taken Henry through only a short time earlier.

He'd take a moment to dry off by the kitchen fire, but then Graham had every intention of locating the curious woman who he'd come on this journey to try to forget. It was time to get some answers.

Fortunately, she was still in the kitchen. Looked like he didn't have to hunt her down, after all.

Kit stirred the stew for that night's meal, forcing herself to keep her head down as the unfamiliar sounds of a grown man moving about in the kitchen surrounded her. The lighter sounds of boys shuffling across the floor were noises she knew, heard every day. Lord Wharton's heavier tread made Kit's skin shiver in a not-all-too-unpleasant manner. That scared her more than if the sensation had been terrifying and cold.

She glanced at the boys, who were dripping water onto the stone floor of the kitchen. "Go get dry. Benedict is upstairs already. He'll help you find clothing, if you need it."

"I've got another set," Blake said as he sidled toward the table to slip his hand beneath one of the linen squares and snitch a hunk of bread.

Kit pretended not to see him. Not because she didn't have a problem with the boy's constant challenging of the rules, but because she didn't want to have to turn and face the room to scold him. Once she turned, there would be no excuse for not acknowledging Lord Wharton's presence.

"If you keep stirring that, it'll turn into a pudding."

Kit sputtered out a laugh and looked over her shoulder at the man, standing far enough away that he wouldn't get her wet but close enough that he could see into the large pot bubbling gently over the fire. "You have no idea how pudding is made, do you?"

He grinned and lifted his gaze to connect with hers. "Not the first notion."

Breath slid out of Kit's lungs and she forgot to pull any back in for a moment.

He tilted his head. "But I do know that is an excessive amount of stirring you're doing."

He held Kit's gaze for a moment and then stepped away and slid his dripping cloak from his shoulders. He draped it over the back of a wooden chair and then shucked his damp coat. His hands went to his throat and began unwinding his cravat.

Kit jerked herself out of her slack-jawed

fascination. "What are you doing?"

"I doubt the aforementioned Benedict has clothing that will fit me, as I've yet to see a male taller than a wagon wheel since I got here." He dropped his hands to the buttons on his waistcoat. "I'm not keen to stay in wet clothing, though."

"Of course not," Kit mumbled. She wasn't sure what the best response was to Lord Wharton's methodical arranging of his clothing on the backs of chairs he moved closer to the fire, but standing there staring at him probably wasn't her best choice.

Particularly when he pried off his boots and arranged them on the hearth. Strange how intimate feet seemed. Kit was fascinated by how big and strong they looked. Which really didn't make much sense. Shouldn't feet seem very similar to hands? Her gaze crawled up to his hands, where she noticed they too looked broad and strong.

Kit turned back to the stew and gave it another vigorous stir.

"The bridge I came from town on was nearly covered earlier today," the man said quietly, still standing near the fire and Kit. "This rain is going to put it underwater."

"That has been known to happen," Kit said through a thick throat. It wasn't often that they got enough rain to make the bridge impassable, but it did happen at least once a year or so. "I'm afraid there's not really another way to Marlborough from here. Not one that won't take you a day or two out of the way."

"I suppose I'm rather trapped here for the night, then."

He didn't sound very upset about the prospect. But where on earth would Kit put him? She certainly couldn't put him in the room with all the boys. She didn't know the first thing about this man. Well, maybe the first thing. But certainly not a second or third thing. He would be staying as far away from her charges as she could manage. "We can make you a pallet here in the kitchen," Kit offered. "I'm sure it's not what you're accustomed to."

"I can make do. It's only for a night."

Kit swallowed. She hoped it was only for a night. After a truly long rain, they'd sometimes had to wait three days for the bridge to be safe again. He couldn't stay here that long.

Although, on the bright side, a stay of that length would probably get her to stop dredging up thoughts of the man at odd times. Days of staying in the same clothes and sleeping on a drafty floor were sure to make him a bit less of a gentleman.

It wasn't like his staying longer put them in considerably more danger. He already knew where they were, had already seen the children. The best she could do now was make his stay as unremarkable as possible so that he had no reason to mention it to anyone else.

"We eat dinner upstairs," Kit said as she used a hook to take the pot of well-stirred stew over to the worktable.

Lord Wharton laughed and looked down at his bare toes, giving them a little wiggle. "I think, for tonight, it might be best if I stayed in the kitchen. Dry out by the fire."

"Are you sure?" Kit blurted out before she could think better of it. She should be glad he'd offered to stay in the kitchen and wasn't trying to work his way into the rest of the house. But could that really be his intention? To eat a bowl of stew and then settle down for the night? He wasn't going to ask about the children? The house?

The man nodded and snagged a bowl from the shelf. "If you wouldn't mind finding me a book when you bring that pallet down, I'd appreciate it."

"A book," Kit said numbly. "We have those."

He grinned. "Good. Every child should

grow up with books."

Kit didn't say anything, simply stared into his eyes for more moments than she should have.

"Kit?" he asked quietly, holding up his empty bowl. "May I have some stew before you take it upstairs?"

"Yes. Yes, of course." Kit ladled him a bowl of stew and then poured the rest of the stew into a crockery pot that would be much easier to carry upstairs.

She glanced back at him before leaving the kitchen, but he was simply eating and staring at the fire, his feet stretched out toward the flames. He'd given her no reason to worry, no cause for suspicion. She would take the stew to the dining hall and then bring him the requested book right away. It was time to give in graciously to the fact that Haven Manor had its first-ever overnight visitor.

Chapter Eleven

Having no idea what Lord Wharton liked to read, she grabbed a novel and a collection of poetry to take down to him. He watched her cross the room and set them on the table, but neither of them said anything.

She practically ran back up the stairs.

The dining hall upstairs was as quiet as the kitchen had been, and she paused at the edge of the room. Normally, the evening meal was a boisterous affair, filled with talking, laughing, and sharing stories from that day's lessons.

Instead of the vibrant chatter, though, the children sat in wide-eyed silence. A few of the children hadn't met Lord Wharton, and they had to be itching with curiosity, but they weren't willing to be the first to ask a question. The ones who had met him were watching Jess and Daphne, and Kit now that she was in the room. They'd been raised in secret, very aware that they were hidden for protection.

A stranger made them all nervous. The fact that he was an aristocrat, a class of person they'd never been around in their life, only complicated matters.

Kit sat in front of her bowl of stew and picked up her spoon. Something had to be said, but what?

"He's really great at climbing trees," Henry said. "Scaled right up the oak in the clearing like he could fly."

That sentence was all it took. Suddenly all the children were talking.

Alice chimed in. "His horse is enormous, and its backside goes up and down when it walks." She shifted back and forth in her chair like she was back on her precarious animal perch.

"Did you see his clothes?" Sarah asked.

"I'm glad we don't have to make all the boys that many layers," Eugenia answered, flexing her fingers as if the very thought of sewing that much made her fingers cramp.

"Will Benedict need all those things when he starts working with Mr. Leighton?" one of the girls asked. Kit couldn't tell which one it was because the table had erupted in a cacophony of words.

"Do you think he'd let me ride his horse before he leaves?"

"Did you see how tall his boots were?"

"I never want to wear that cloth he had crawling up his neck."

"He knows how to dance, doesn't he?"

Kit fought back laughter. She didn't know which boy was horrified over a cravat, but that last question had absolutely been little Sophie. She was only four, but she was obsessed with anything romantic. There were paintings in the house of balls and couples courting — apparently the last occupant had been a bit of a romantic as well — and Sophie could spend hours in front of them, making up stories about the people in the paintings.

"Do you think I'll grow to be that tall?"

"Is he going to court Mama Kit? He seemed to know her."

Heat bloomed across Kit's cheeks, and she ducked her head to hide the blush. Daphne's chuckles rolled down from her position in the center of the table. Kit peeked up to glance at Jess sitting at the foot of the table. The blond woman wasn't laughing, but she was wearing a smirk, clearly happy to see what Kit intended to do about the rampant curiosity in the room.

Kit hadn't a clue.

More questions, more speculations, more observations bounced across the table until

Arthur piped up with a question that brought the entire room to a freezing halt. "Father?"

All three women snapped their heads in Arthur's direction. What to tell the children about their parents had been heavily debated when Kit and Daphne had started on this journey all those years ago. Should they know the situation? Be allowed to believe their parents were dead?

They'd gone with a simple version of the truth, because otherwise there wouldn't be a way to convince them of the importance of being cautious. The fact was, illegitimate children met an untimely fate every day. They got unexplainably ill and died or had a strange accident. If the men paying Haven Manor to care for the children decided they wanted to be free of their obligation, it could be done easily enough.

No child deserved such a fate. They hadn't asked to be born, hadn't asked their parents to throw off the acceptable conventions of society, hadn't chosen their lot in life. Kit and Daphne had decided it was their job to make up for as many of those unasked-for shortcomings as possible.

So they'd told the children a version of the truth.

Well, most of the children.

Kit's gaze skittered over Benedict, the eldest of the children, sitting in the middle of the table.

Twelve young faces looked from Kit to Daphne and back again. While they'd all accepted Jess into the fold readily, she'd kept a certain distance and they all knew she hadn't been there long. Kit and Daphne had been there from the beginning.

Kit cleared her throat. "No, Arthur, he is not your father." She glanced around the table. "Nor is he anyone else's. At least no one here or anyone we've ever met."

Daphne stood and began gathering the dishes around her. "Finish your stew. I think it's been a long day for everyone and a bit early to bed would be a good thing. Mama Jess, Mama Kit, and I will take care of the kitchen chores."

The children shuffled around, seeing to their evening chores with quiet solemnity. As embarrassing as it had been, Kit wished they could go back to the riot of questions, the speculation about his relationship to Kit. Haven Manor was usually its own little bubble of life, but for tonight, that bubble had been popped by the reminder of harsh reality, and she wasn't sure how to put it back together.

■ ■ ■ ■

The brutal bite of reality wasn't just lurking at the dining table. It was also waiting for Kit on the back porch.

Every night, once the children settled, the three women would gather outside, look down on the moon's reflection in the lake, listen to the sounds of the forest at night, or, on nights like tonight, watch the rain fall in a curtain around them, creating their own little room away from the rest of the world.

Skipping the porch meeting wasn't allowed unless illness was involved, so Kit dragged herself out there, braced for Jess to say she knew Kit had been hiding something about London.

"The bridge is going to be impassable." Jess dropped one shoulder against a column and stuck her hand out into the rain. "If it rains all night, it could be days before the water goes down."

"I'll check the conditions tomorrow," Kit said. It would likely only confirm what they all suspected, but it would get her away from the house for a few hours.

"He's going to have to stay," Daphne said quietly. "If he takes the long way back around to Marlborough, he'll have nothing

187

to do for days but wonder why we didn't want him here."

Jess sighed. "You'd want him to stay even if the sun was shining and we were in a drought. He's not a lost puppy, Daphne."

Color exploded across Daphne's cheeks, and her nose lit up bright red. Kit bit her lip to keep from rushing to Daphne's defense. Jess's particular sense of dry, brusque humor didn't seem to bother Daphne, even though it made her blush. In fact, over the past year, Daphne started trying to jibe back at Jess. The attempts were pitiful and more adorable than harsh, but Kit could also see the quiet confidence and strength growing in her friend with every attempt she made.

Perhaps Jess knew more about people than she let on.

"Perhaps not." Daphne straightened her shoulders. "But he did save Henry, and from the way Alice spoke, the boy was in a dangerous situation indeed. We owe him our hospitality — what little we have of it anyway."

Kit wanted desperately to argue. They all knew that Alice exaggerated the severity of things, tending to be one of the most serious children Kit had ever met. But the fact was, Henry had been in danger and Lord Wharton had saved him at the risk of injuring himself, and there was simply no way to repay that besides letting him stay at the manor until the road was passable.

Jess nodded. "Do we leave him in the kitchen or move him to the barn?"

"We can't put him in the barn." Daphne shuddered. "His horse is in there."

"Then he'll have company he knows," Jess said with a shrug. "Horses are good for warmth."

"So are fires," Daphne muttered. "We're not putting him outside like an animal."

As much as Kit didn't want to, she had to agree with Daphne on this one. One simply did not tell the heir to an earldom to bed down among the goats and chickens. "We don't have a good reason to send him to the stable."

Jess looked back and forth between Kit and Daphne. "Have you not considered what's going to happen if he realizes what we're doing? If he learns who these children are? We have to let him stay, but we have to keep him away from the children."

Daphne paled. "How could he possibly learn who we are and who the children are? *They* barely even know who they are."

"It would help matters," Jess said as she folded her arms across her chest and sent Kit a pointed look, "if we knew a bit more about who *he* was."

Kit sighed. Here it was. "I told you I had to hide from two thugs. Well, I took a shortcut through one of the houses." She swallowed. "He was there. He helped me find a corridor to slip through."

The sigh Daphne gave was dreamy and she looked as if she were about to melt off the porch and join the puddles on the lawn.

"What else?" Jess asked.

What else? Kit really didn't know much about him. He was an aristocrat. She didn't dally in that world any longer, only visited it occasionally to wreak havoc on those who needed it. Her world was the children, the manor, perhaps Nash and his wife Margaretta and a few of the men in Marlborough who came to the manor on occasion to help with repairs or other tasks the women couldn't handle on their own.

But those men were nothing like Lord Wharton. He'd grown up with tutors, gone to school, joined gentlemen's clubs, and rubbed shoulders with England's most elite.

Kit gasped and her eyes flew to Jess's. "He's from London," she choked out.

"Didn't we already establish that?" Daphne asked.

They had, but Kit was only now realizing what that meant. The grim look on Jess's face said she'd already put the pieces to-gether.

Their visitor probably knew many of the children's parents.

Never before had they needed to worry about that. The chances that the few country folk who met one or two of the children on their occasional ventures into town would recognize anything about the children wasn't even enough of a risk to consider. But now . . .

Jess rubbed her hand over her mouth. "The girls are likely in no danger, but the boys —"

"He absolutely can't meet John." Kit's knees were threatening to give out.

"Would one of you speak plainly?" Daphne said with a huff. "I can never fol-low these vague conversations."

Kit swallowed and reached one hand out to grasp Daphne's. "John looks exactly like his father."

"And there's a very good chance that Lord Wharton has at least a passing acquaintance with the man," Jess added. "I knew who had fathered him the first time I saw him."

Granted, Jess had trained herself to be more observant than the average person over the years, but as a maid in an aristo-cratic house in London, she would have had only the briefest of encounters with John's father. Yet it had been enough.

The aristocratic world was small. How many of the children's parents would Lord Wharton know? How much did the children look like their parents?

Jess pushed away from the column and started a slow pace around the covered area. "If it stops raining, we'll be able to manage. We can keep the children in the garden or with the animals. Maybe give Lord Wharton access to the library during the day and let him sleep in the kitchen at night." She gave Kit a hard look. "Are we in danger from this man?"

Kit hesitated before shaking her head. She didn't really trust her instincts about people, finding it safer to simply live in a cocoon of suspicion, but Lord Wharton had made attempts to rescue her both socially and physically. She had a feeling the man had been about to intervene in the discussion with her father as well before she decided to leave the premises.

He'd left London in the middle of the Season to help his friend find his sister. And he hadn't hesitated to rescue Henry from the tree. No, there was no reason to think Lord Wharton was anything other than a true gentleman, if an inconvenient one.

"No. I don't think he'd intentionally harm anyone."

Jess nodded as if Kit's assessment were gold. "Then all we have to do is keep him as ignorant as possible." She blew out a long breath. "Shouldn't be a problem at all."

There were several moments of silence as each of them contemplated what their next few days would hold. A sudden exhaustion threatened to overwhelm Kit, and she turned toward the door, intending to go to bed.

"Not so fast," Jess said, moving quickly to block Kit's path. "You have some more sharing to do."

"Start with running into a stranger's house," Daphne said. "And don't leave anything out."

Chapter Twelve

Long rectangular windows marched across the top of the kitchen wall. Graham lay on his hard pallet and stared at them, willing them to lighten from black to grey. He was awake, had been awake for a while, but he refused to rise until at least some bit of sunlight made an appearance.

Mostly because getting up in the middle of the night wouldn't make him anything but tired. Not that he'd gotten a whole lot of sleep. The pallet was hard and the kitchen had cooled as the fire died down. And he'd been alone. Probably more alone than he'd ever been in his life.

The women had bustled through the kitchen, cleaning as fast as humanly possible and saying as little as they could get away with. He tried to assist in the chores, his attempts the most laughable he'd ever seen. He hadn't a single idea how to handle the menial tasks in a kitchen. Dress himself and care completely for a horse, yes, but wash a dish? It should have been simple, yet he'd found his shirt, which he'd managed to keep dry in the rain, as soaked as the little boy with the water bucket.

After everything was clean, the women left.

And he'd been alone. Truly on his own. No Oliver, no Aaron, no servants, no family, no social acquaintances. Just him.

Now he was tired of himself. He was tired of the smooth walls of the kitchen.

It was time to explore the rest of the house.

He dressed in his now-dry clothes and took the stairs up, keeping his tread light as he rounded the curve near the top of the staircase.

The door at the top opened into a large square front hall. Paintings draped in canvas covered the wall, but the canvas itself had been painted on as well. Some of the illustrations were little more than splatters of paint and odd shapes, while others showed more inclination toward something that could actually be called art. Other than the adorned walls, the room was empty. The checkered marble floor stretched out, a large open space flanked by wide corniced doors on two sides and an enormous archway across from the main door.

A glance through the archway revealed another empty room, broken by the two graceful staircases ascending to the next floor. Looking through that room into the next revealed an enormous dining table, but no one appeared to be in there.

The bedchambers were likely up the grand split staircase, so Graham turned away from those and chose one of the side doors off the hall.

He found a music room. A large, beautiful piano sat in the center of the room, while instruments of nearly every other style he had ever heard of lined the rest of the room. Some of them he didn't even recognize. He squinted at a bundle in the corner. Was that a bagpipe?

Across the music room, another door stood open and the distant sound of voices drifted through it. Desperate for contact with people, even if they were short and confusing, Graham moved toward the voices.

Beyond the door, he found a short walkway lined with floor-to-ceiling windows that showed a rather nice view of a very overgrown front lawn, and he went into another room nearly as large as the front hall he'd just left.

It was also just as devoid of furniture.

In place of settees and tea tables, the room held toys and games. They were piled against windows and in the corners. Every style and interest he could imagine.

Faded squares on the walls showed that at some point this room had also been covered in paintings, only those had been removed instead of covered.

In the middle of the room were two children who had yet to notice his presence. One of them, a girl he'd seen flitting about in the kitchen the day before, crossed a set of sticks and balanced a hoop on them for a moment before sending the wooden ring floating through the air of the high-ceilinged room.

A boy he didn't recognize shook his dark curls out of his eyes and reached out with one hand, extending a stick similar to the ones the girl held, and speared the hoop in midair.

Then the boy crossed his sticks and sent the hoop flying back across the room.

The girl turned to run after it but stopped suddenly when she caught sight of Graham. The hoop clattered to the floor.

Graham cleared his throat. "What are you playing?"

"Graces," the girl said quietly. The boy

came to stand next to her, puffing out his chest as if he wanted to look more like a man than a boy. There was something vaguely familiar about him, but Graham didn't know what. A mere week ago, if someone had asked him if he felt he should pay more attention to the children of his various acquaintances, he'd have laughed until his side hurt, but right now he was wishing he knew a bit more about little people.

Of course, even if he had paid more attention to the children connected to his life, they would be aristocratic children. Experience with them wasn't likely to give him a whole lot of knowledge about what to do with country children.

Although, this was an awfully fine house for a country lad. It was possible Graham had circulated with whoever owned this home. Whoever the parents were, though, they were incredibly prolific, and the children all looked astonishingly different.

"You're the man who saved Henry," the boy said.

"Yes." Graham gave a little laugh. "Though I don't know that I would say I saved him —"

"Thank you." The boy stepped forward and extended his hand. When Graham didn't immediately shake it, the boy seemed to deflate a bit, revealing an insecurity Graham remembered all too well from his formative years.

Graham took a step forward and took the boy's hand in a firm grip. "You're welcome."

The boy nodded before he let go and stepped back. Manly duties now completed, he didn't seem to know what to do with himself. The moment hit Graham in a place he'd thought long hardened by the boredom and apathy of being an adult whose father was still alive and well. He could not let the memory of this moment be tarnished for this young man.

He glanced around the room until he saw a long wooden table against one wall with nine divots drilled in a grid on the surface. He'd never seen anything like it in a private home. Usually they were in taverns or public houses.

"You've a Bubble the Justice table?"

The boy nodded and ran over. "I'm the champion." He pointed to a rough wooden board with names and scores written on it. "See? I've made it all the way through the numbers and then back up to five."

Graham rubbed a hand over his mouth to hide a smile. "Well, it's been a while since I played, but I'm pretty sure I've completed the circuit twice in a row before."

The little boy's eyes widened. "Twice? In a row?"

In truth, Graham couldn't remember how well he'd done the last time he played this game, but he was sure he'd accomplished the feat at some point. Besides, all he really wanted right now was for the little boy to challenge him to a game.

It was much more fun seeing the lad be a boy than attempt to be a man. How old was he? Eight? Nine? Ten? Whatever the number, the boy was young. And apparently living in a house full of women.

The boy's face screwed up into a determined frown. He grabbed a metal ball and sent it sliding down the table until it rolled gently into the divot labeled with a one. The little girl cheered and sent the ball back down the table.

Graham took his turn and missed the number one divot, rolling past to fall into the number four.

"I'm ahead," the boy cheered, carefully lining up the ball to roll toward divot number two.

They took turns rolling the ball while the girl marked their progress on a slate. The game was simple. Roll the ball into the divots in turn, starting with one and ending with nine before starting over again. Nothing complicated. So Graham tried once more to have a conversation with a child that he had the potential of understanding.

"What's your name?" Graham asked. Simple, nonthreatening. This could actually work.

"John." He nodded to the girl with pale blond hair standing beside the game table, watching with wide eyes. "That's Eugenia."

Graham winced. Eugenia was a rather unfortunate name. At least the girl was pretty enough to overcome it. Graham picked up the metal ball. If he landed this one in the number nine slot, he would win. "Well, John, I think this turn may be the winning one for me."

"Never!" John cried, and Graham jerked in surprise, sending the ball careening clear off the table.

John grinned. "Now it's my turn to try for a win."

Over the next twenty minutes, Graham and John took turns rolling the metal ball down the board as other children trickled into the room. Alice came in holding the hands of a very little girl and the young boy he'd met in the barn. Blake entered after them, rain clinging to the slick dark hair crowning his head. Finally, an older girl entered with a small child on her hip.

"What's going on in here?"

"John's about to win against . . ." The boy with the wet curls frowned at Graham as if just now realizing he didn't know who the man was. "This old guy."

Graham choked on a laugh. Old, was he? He'd barely tipped over the age of thirty.

"That's the tree man," Alice piped up. "His name is Wharton."

Another laugh threatened to emerge at the idea of his peers in London seeing this rabble of country children using his title so casually.

"You're rather good at that game, Mr. Wharton," the young boy wrapped against Alice's side said, a slight whistle accompanying the words.

"Just Wharton will suffice," Graham said, "and thank you. I believe young Master John here has bested me, though."

The children cheered, and John beamed under the adulation.

"Now, how about a game we can all play?" Graham lowered himself to sit on his heels. He didn't know what was going on here, but as his little discussion with young Daniel in the town grocer's shop had proven, children were a fount of information that adults would rather keep hidden.

"We like to play fox-in-the-hole." A little girl with a long brown braid and enormous brown eyes popped her thumb in her mouth after making her request.

"You'll have to teach me," Graham said, even though he remembered the game well from childhood, having chased many a boyhood friend around the lawn. The more he got the children talking, the more he was likely to learn. The knowing smiles that passed among the children told him his morning was going to be interesting indeed.

The pallet was a twisted disarray of blankets. An empty, twisted disarray of blankets. Kit slid the basket of freshly collected eggs onto the table and glanced around the kitchen, as if their not-exactly-welcome guest was hiding in the larder or something.

Daphne slipped through the door on tiptoe, a half-full bucket of milk in her hand. "Is he still sleeping?" she whispered.

"He's not even in here," Kit answered, lifting her shoulder to wipe a few raindrops off her cheek. It wasn't pouring down rain anymore, but a lingering mist remained. Just enough to make a person feel like they'd walked through the rain but not enough to require a change of clothing.

After setting the bucket on the floor,

Daphne wiped her face with the corner of her apron. "Where do you think the children got off to? Benedict said no one else showed up to help with the goats this morning."

"I'm more concerned with the whereabouts of our guest." Or more importantly, if the question of where the children were and where Lord Wharton was had the same answer. Kit slid her apron off and draped it on a hook near the kitchen doorway. "Jess should be along in a moment to help with breakfast. I'm going to see if I can find out what's going on."

Daphne's apron flew across the room toward the hooks but missed and slid down the wall instead. "You're not going off without me. I'm not sure you're thinking straight when it comes to this man."

Kit rolled her eyes to the ceiling. "What is there to think? He's here. We need him elsewhere."

"Is it so very bad that he's here?" Daphne's voice was low, barely above a whisper as she picked at the edge of the worktable.

"What do you mean?" Kit fought the urge to sigh and pat Daphne on the head. Sometimes it was hard to believe that they were the same age, had been through the same turmoil, had been handed the same raw deal by life. Of course, it wasn't Daphne's fault that they'd ended up here. It was Kit's. Maybe that made all the difference in how soft her heart remained.

"I mean," Daphne said as she pushed away from the table and came to stand before Kit, "that perhaps we don't have to remain quite so isolated. What's the worst that could happen?"

A hundred horrible scenarios ran through Kit's head. If Jess were here, she could probably increase that number to a thousand. Regardless, there were plenty of reasons to keep these children safe until they could make their own way in the world. "Daph, these children are secrets. Secrets that could put very powerful people in very precarious positions. Secrets we've promised to keep. Secrets we're being paid to keep. All it takes is one person learning where these children came from and everything we've built here becomes endangered."

"That made sense twelve years ago, Kit." Daphne picked at the edge of her thumbnail. "But they're getting older. Benedict will be starting an apprenticeship soon. We can't hide them forever."

It was a truth Kit didn't want to acknowledge, hadn't wanted to think about even as she'd finalized the apprenticeship agreement with a local woodworker. Benedict could already make wonderful items out of wood, and with a little bit of guidance and instruction, he could become amazing. Even sending him to live with a woodworker in Marlborough, a man who knew about and supported Haven Manor, sent a tremor of fear through Kit. Ben would be exposed, away from the protection that secrecy provided.

But Kit had to believe that having him established, having more than a decade of years between the indiscretion that had brought him into existence and his entry into the world, would be enough to keep him safe. "We can hide them until they're ready."

Kit didn't wait for Daphne to answer. She turned and ran up the stairs as if she could leave her worries about their changing future behind with the eggs and the milk.

Loud laughter and the sounds of a jovial ruckus met her as she topped the stairs and entered the front hall. Given the number of walls between her and the old portrait room they'd emptied for the children to play in, they must be having a grand time indeed for the shrieks and cheers to be so loud.

It made Kit smile. The children had such a limited time to live a carefree life. Practically speaking, they would need to start working around the age of thirteen. And with a job came all of the worries and responsibilities of being an adult. They had so few years to truly be children that Kit couldn't quite find it in herself to be mad that they'd skipped a morning of chores.

Her smile only grew as she passed through the music room and the short corridor. The noise increased to near deafening levels as she reached the door of the old portrait gallery, which they now called the Rainy Day Room. Running children came into view. They were dodging right and left, obviously avoiding someone on the other side of the room.

The view that greeted her when she stepped fully into the room knocked her smile flat. The game was one she recognized easily, having played it herself with the children. The "fox" tried to catch the "chickens" and take them back to the den. Once there, the person who was caught turned into a fox as well. Currently, the fox wasn't Sarah or John or one of the other older children. It was Lord Wharton.

He stalked slowly across the room, letting the children run around, taunting him. His arms were raised and his hands curled into claws as he screwed up his face in a vision of comic mischief. Henry cheered from a chair on the side, his ankle still splinted, calling for his fox to bring him a chicken. The rest of the children right down to two-year-old Pheobe were scattered around the room, squealing and looking as if they were having the time of their lives. A quick count of heads in the room revealed that the only child missing was Benedict, who had been out helping with the goats earlier.

So much for keeping Lord Wharton away from John.

A loud growl ripped through the room as the man pounced on Alice and swung her high into the air. Kit's heart stopped, and behind her she heard Daphne's breath shudder until Alice was secure on Lord Wharton's back, her little hands wrapped tightly around his neck as he stalked his way back to the chair where Henry sat kicking his legs in glee. Alice dropped to the floor, and Henry performed some strange sort of knighting ceremony before the little girl joined Lord Wharton in his prowling.

He snatched up Blake next, tossing the boy even higher than he had Alice before snagging him out of the air and throwing the boy over his shoulder like a sack of flour. Alice tackled Sarah around the knees and pushed her toward Henry.

The chaos made Kit's head pound, and

she gave serious thought to just slinking back out the way she had come. The man had already encountered the children. Any display of umbrage on her part would only make him suspicious.

"See?" Daphne whispered in her ear, leaning in until her breath tickled Kit's neck in order to be heard. "He doesn't know a thing."

Lord Wharton really did seem to think them a passel of country children. While he had to consider the whole situation strange and probably had a dozen questions lurking in his mind, he didn't seem to be suspicious about the children themselves. Kit's muscles released a bit of the tension they'd been holding, and a small smile curved her lips once more.

The children were so happy. That was worth a little bit of discomfort on her part, wasn't it?

Only one "chicken" was left in the room. Little Pheobe toddling around on her chubby legs, brown curls bouncing as she jogged in a tight circle that anyone could have snagged her from. Instead, they all made a show of running into each other and missing her by mere inches. She squealed in delight and suddenly broke from the pack to dart straight toward Kit. Before Kit realized what was happening, Pheobe was buried in her skirts and a grown man and nine children of various ages were creeping steadily across the floor in her direction.

Lord Wharton grinned. "Well, well, foxes, looks like we've another chicken in the henhouse."

"Let's get her!"

Kit didn't know which child had sounded the battle cry, but suddenly she was surrounded, being hugged, pulled, and pushed, until at one point she wasn't even sure her feet were on the ground. She glanced over to see that Lord Wharton had abandoned the game entirely and was just standing in the middle of the floor, laughing until she thought he might be driven to tears.

At last she was in front of Henry and experiencing the fox knighting for herself. It didn't make any more sense at close range than it had from across the room, but it made Henry happy and let him be a part even though he couldn't run on his injured ankle. Whoever had come up with it was rather sweet. She scooped Henry into her arms. "And who made you the keeper of the fox den?"

"Wharton!" Henry smiled in triumph. "He said that becoming a fox was something special and deserved a bit of ceremony."

Kit looked over at Lord Wharton, who shrugged and folded his hands behind his back. His smile still stretched wide across his face.

What was she supposed to do with that?

Nothing. There was nothing she should do with Lord Wharton. She had children to raise. "Well. Now that we're all a passel of foxes —"

"Foxes are called a leash," Eugenia said, blue eyes wide and earnest. "I read it."

"Now that we're a leash of foxes," Kit corrected, "it's time we see to our neglected morning chores. Those bedchambers aren't going to dust themselves. Then we've a lot of boxes to make since it's still wet outside."

A few grumbles replaced the cheers and giggles from earlier, but none of the children dawdled as they left the room. Blake let Henry ride on his back with the promise that he'd set up the injured boy sorting the linens.

And then all that were left in the room were Kit, Daphne, and the increasingly mysterious Lord Wharton.

Without the children, the room seemed cavernous and empty.

And strange. This room, more than any of the others, revealed the unusual conversion they'd made to the house.

Long ago, they'd put everything of value into storage. Partly because no one wanted to take the time to clean it but also because children could be destructive without meaning to be. The last thing Kit needed was to add more guilt to her life because her charges had carved a gouge into a priceless table leg.

"Interesting group of children," Lord Wharton said, nodding to where the children had disappeared through the door.

Kit narrowed her eyes and inspected the man's words for judgment or censure. She only found curiosity. "Yes."

He lifted his brows. "Parents?"

"Irrelevant." The lie choked Kit. Their parents were probably the *most* relevant detail about these children. It was what had brought them all together under this roof.

"Hmm." He looked around the room. "I like what you've done with the place." His gaze speared back into Kit, showing the first edge of something more. "It's a nice house."

"Yes, it is." Kit swallowed. What could she tell him about the house? Certainly not the truth. It was nearly as strange a story as the children's.

She cleared her throat. "It was built by a gentleman several decades ago. He didn't have a title or anything, simply wanted a home away from everything."

That much was true. The man had a great deal of money, though Kit wasn't sure from what, and had built this house as a retreat.

"His heir didn't want to live quite such a reclusive life." Also true. To a point. Given the fact that the son had eventually lost the neglected house in a poker game, she wasn't entirely sure what the man's motives had been for living in the city instead of the country.

"So, instead of letting the house sit empty, it was placed into our care." Kit forced herself to keep her gaze steady, focusing on a single lock of curly hair just to the right of his eyes. The implications of that statement weren't exactly true. Could probably even be considered false. The man who'd won the house hadn't cared about it. It had taken three years for his secretary to find a local solicitor to arrange a caretaker of the place.

That solicitor had been Nash, who had decided that the caretaker didn't have to be a man or live in the caretaker's cottage or really even have to be a group of adults.

It was a very liberal definition of *caretaker,* but it made Haven Manor possible.

Lord Wharton said nothing, simply tilted his head back to look up at the ceiling of the tall room. It was nearly as tall as the middle portion of the house, which boasted a second floor of bedchambers and a small chapel.

"I'll put away the toys the children got out this morning, shall I?" Daphne said as she rushed across the room, head bent to avoid looking at anything or anyone.

Kit tried to act as if her friend hadn't just fled the conversation looking like a guilty criminal. "Once it stops raining, we can go out to the bridge and see what condition it's in."

They both knew — well, Kit at least knew and Lord Wharton likely suspected — that the bridge was going to be unusable, but walking out to view it would keep Lord Wharton away from the house for several hours.

He gave a huff of silent laughter as he nodded. His mouth opened as if he was about to say something, but the sound of footsteps coming through the corridor to the room stopped him.

"Mama Kit." A young male voice preceded the owner into the room. "I hate to tell you this, but we've got another leak in the roof of the boys' room." Benedict entered, pail in hand, his hair and shoulders showing a fresh coat of rain.

Another leak was hardly what they needed.

Given the busyness of spring, it would be months before one of the men who helped them maintain this place was available to come fix their roof. Then there was finding the money for the necessary supplies. The stipend Nash received to care for the house didn't cover major repairs. He would have to write and request additional funds for those, something they tried not to do, if possible, as it only served to remind the owner about the house and possibly prompt him to do something with it.

Still, she'd just told Lord Wharton that she was the caretaker of this estate, so she needed to at least appear prepared to handle such a situation. When she looked his way, though, he wasn't paying her the slightest bit of attention.

He was staring at Benedict.

And the look of stunned suspicion she'd thought they were actually going to avoid was firmly on his face.

CHAPTER THIRTEEN

Graham blinked.

Then he blinked again.

The boy before him was still there, though, like he'd stepped out of a window to the past. Graham had gone to school with a boy who looked exactly like the one standing in front of him. Exactly. Right down to the slightly uneven ears and the hitch in the left eyebrow.

"Wow," he murmured.

The tension that filled the room was as thick and obvious as the rain outside. The boy looked from one adult to another, fidgeting and curling his shoulders in. Graham knew he was making the boy uncomfortable, staring like he was, but he couldn't quite rip his gaze away.

He felt a body step closer to his. Kit, probably. "Yes," she said, confirming her identity. "I'll note it in the log. The pail should take care of it for now, but keep an eye on it and let me know if anything changes."

The boy nodded and sent Graham another questioning glance before leaving the room.

He couldn't have nearly as many questions as Graham did.

His disappearance gave back Graham's ability to move, though, and he immediately looked at Kit and at Daphne, who'd moved to stand a few feet behind her friend and looked very much as if she might cry.

On the other hand, Kit looked ready for war. Her face was set in tense lines and a bright slash of color rode her perfect cheekbones.

Daphne sniffled. "I'll —" She cut off as her voice trembled. She cleared her throat and tried again. "I'll go help Jess with breakfast, shall I?"

Kit's mouth pressed together tighter as her gaze followed the other woman out of the room. Then she smoothed her hands over her skirts, pasted a hard curve onto her lips that was probably supposed to be a smile but looked more lethal than the frown it replaced, and turned to face Graham. "Breakfast will be served in the dining room in an hour. Simply go through the main hall and past the staircases. You can't miss it."

"I know. I saw it." Graham took a few steps closer, stalking her almost like he'd stalked the children a few moments ago.

He had questions, had been gathering them ever since meeting this woman. Until that moment, though, they'd been vague, undefined. More like a prodding curiosity. But now they were shifting. Pieces of information were aligning until very small, very specific holes remained. Hazy ideas and suspicions were forming, but he couldn't quite wrap his mind around what he seemed to be learning. "I have to ask, Kit, where are the children from?"

She lifted her chin but didn't say anything.

Graham stalked a half step closer. "They're not yours. They don't look anything like you. Or Jess or Daphne either."

But he knew who one of them looked like. And it was enough to give him a theory about the rest of them. But if he was right, what in the world were they doing in the middle of nowhere?

Kit stood her ground, and Graham felt a flicker of admiration for her courage. It didn't weaken his resolve, though. While he knew his notion that the solicitor was hiding Priscilla out in these woods was incorrect — after all, she was no longer a child — the fact that Mr. Banfield was somehow involved in whatever was going on here worried Graham. Perhaps the timing of the contract and Priscilla's disappearance were a coincidence, but it was obvious that Oliver's father had entered into an agreement with a man who had his hands in some very interesting pies.

And Graham wanted answers.

Kit took a deep breath, set her shoulders, and clasped her hands in front of her stomach. "The children were born in different villages in the area. Their parents aren't — weren't — in a position to be able to provide for them. Our choice was either to help them or leave them to a life that was little more than an early death sentence."

Graham gaped at her. A death sentence? That seemed a bit of an extreme declaration. After seeing the boy, an idea had formed in his head, one that made sense the more he thought about it. Marlborough was a popular stopping place for England's elite, some of whom weren't very discretionary about how they took their entertainments. He'd never understood that. He'd kissed a girl or two and had enjoyed it immensely but hadn't particularly liked the idea that she might have kissed one of his friends the night before. It had stopped him from sowing the same wild oats other men had bragged about.

But he knew it happened, knew that it

could result in illegitimate children. Illegitimate children who would then have to be cared for somehow.

His gaze shifted to the door where the boy had disappeared. He'd looked exactly like Lord Kettlewell. Graham had gone to Harrow with him, had admired him, though their connection had always been rather superficial. He'd never seemed the type to leave offspring littered around England, though he wouldn't be the first man to make mistakes in his youth that he would never make as an adult. And Graham hadn't seen Kettlewell much during their university days. Graham had gone to Cambridge while Kettlewell had attended Oxford.

Which was less than forty miles from Marlborough.

And the resemblance was undeniable.

"How old is he?" Graham asked quietly.

He thought for a moment that Kit wasn't going to answer him, even though she'd taken a deep breath at his question, obviously having expected him to say something else.

But Graham knew how to play this game. He didn't know much about children, but one didn't get very far in society without knowing how to talk about something without actually talking about it.

"Twelve," Kit finally said. "He'll be thirteen soon."

Twelve. Kettlewell would definitely have been in the area. "Why isn't he in school, then?"

Kit's eyes widened as she dropped back a step, and her mouth gaped slightly. Yet again he'd asked something she hadn't expected. Although, truthfully, he hadn't expected to ask it either. Saying his musings out loud was letting him see her reactions, which were more informative than any sort of interrogation would be.

Her surprise dissipated quickly, though, and she was soon bristling with anger again. "Not everyone has the means or opportunity to spend years advancing his mind only to use it in pursuit of pleasure and politics. Some people have to make their way in the world."

The attack wasn't anything Graham hadn't heard before. He'd been in public houses and inns on his travels where the aristocracy weren't always welcomed with open arms. Still, had the woman seen where she was living? "You mean to tell me that a family that can afford this house and these lands — no matter their dismal upkeep — is unable to find the funds to send that boy to school?"

Her chin lifted a notch as her gaze slid away from his. "School is not the best place for everyone. We've decided the limited funds allotted to his future would be better spent on an apprenticeship."

It was Graham's turn to blink. "Is he stupid?"

"What? No!" Her arm flinched as if she'd considered slapping him for the insult laid on one of her brood, but Graham couldn't think of another reason to deny him an education.

Unless, of course, the unlikely and nearly impossible was actually true. Could Graham's memory be wrong? Had time muddled his knowledge of the boy he'd gone to school with? Kettlewell had always been a good but quiet sort. He'd never tried to make Aaron's life miserable like so many of the other boys did.

Graham glanced at Kit's hard expression. Maybe it was time he changed the direction of this conversation so she didn't completely shut him out. "What is he going to apprentice in?"

She blinked. Froze. Swallowed. Her voice was little more than a whisper when she said, "Woodworking."

"Is he any good?"

Her laugh was captivating as she looked

around the room at the many toys and games scattered about. She scooped up a doll from a nearby basket and tossed it to him. Graham looked at the face, features finely carved to the point that he could easily recognize that the doll was meant to be Kit. He nudged the arms and legs, surprised when they moved like real arms and legs, not just dowels held to the doll's body by string.

"Yes," Kit said with a smile. "He's very good."

Then she walked out, leaving Graham holding the doll, his mind swimming with more questions than ever.

For the second meal in a row, there was a tense, unnatural silence at the dining table.

This one wasn't going to be as easily broken, though, because everyone from Pheobe to Benedict to Jess, Kit, and Daphne were all too aware that there was something different this morning.

There was a man at the table.

Even when Nash or one of the other men came from town, they didn't stay for meals. But today, sitting at the end of the table where Jess normally sat, was a man. A grown man. A handsome man. A man who asked too many questions and made Kit more nervous than she'd been when she faced Lord Charles Tromboll's mercenary thugs in the park.

It was obvious he was thinking, questioning, trying to understand what was going on at Haven Manor, and there was only so much redirection she could do. If he had to spend days here, logic would lead him down the correct path and he'd know who these children were.

Jess's plan to keep him away from the children wasn't going to work, not after this morning. How long had he played with them? If she suddenly put up barriers between him and the children, it would only make him more curious. The children would ask questions, too.

They'd simply have to chaperone him instead. Never leave him alone with the children again. Never let them say anything they shouldn't. They might not know everything, but they knew enough to lead Lord Wharton farther down the road of understanding.

It would only be a matter of time before he connected that to Priscilla.

There were so many people depending on her to keep Lord Wharton in the dark that she wanted to drop her head to the table and groan.

It stopped raining while they ate, the sun spearing through the dreariness and crawling across the dining table.

"Well," Kit said with forced brightness that she could only hope sounded natural, "the sun is out. Arthur, Sophie, why don't you help me in the garden this morning?" She kept her smile plastered in place as she looked to the man at the end of the table. "Lord Wharton, you're welcome to join us."

Jess choked on her toast, but when Kit glanced her way it looked like the inhalation of food had been due to sudden laughter, not surprise.

Within moments, Kit, the two young children, and Lord Wharton were walking into the walled garden. A brisk breeze ruffled their hair and plucked at the girls' skirts and the loose sleeves of Lord Wharton's shirt. He'd left his jacket, waistcoat, and cravat off, making him look much like the boys running about in shirtsleeves and breeches. It made him seem all too approachable. Like a country gentleman instead of a London nobleman.

They went down the rows of plants, Kit instructing the children how to tell if the vegetables were ripe enough to be picked.

Arthur didn't speak much, rarely more than one word at a time, but he liked pulling weeds and was soon dragging Lord Wharton around the garden, showing him the plants that didn't belong among the neat rows of vegetables.

Before long, Lord Wharton had joined right in, gleefully digging his hands about in the dirt, laughing with the boy and throwing an occasional worm at him. Sophie hid in Kit's skirts, peeking around the folds to watch as Lord Wharton chased Arthur around the garden, a shockingly long worm in his fingers, as he threatened to drop it down the boy's shirt.

It was on the tip of Kit's tongue to berate the both of them, tell them they were being ridiculous, but Arthur's laugh stopped her. The pure glee on his face had him smiling so hard his cheeks would start hurting soon. As he looked up at their visitor, there was something in his face she'd never seen before.

The look slammed through Kit. Was it possible for three women to actually raise true gentlemen? She'd never doubted it before, but watching Arthur, it was obvious Lord Wharton brought something that Kit, Daphne, and Jess did not provide. What was going to happen when these boys left the safe, secure walls of Haven Manor? When they had to make a life with boys who had grown up with worms and school?

When Lord Wharton and Arthur ran out one of the garden gates, she let them go. Arthur wasn't about to spill secrets. That required talking. Besides, all she could hear were squeals and giggles.

As Sophie and Kit finished walking the rows, even the sound of laughter faded. Kit looped her basket over her arm and went in search of them.

They found her first, though, meeting her and Sophie at the gate and sweeping into low bows while extending bouquets of wildflowers.

Sophie melted, her little romantic heart making her cradle the flowers to her chest with wide-eyed enjoyment.

Lord Wharton extended his clutch of flowers toward her, and Kit discovered that she wasn't immune to the charm of flowers either. She hadn't gotten flowers in so long. Yes, the boys had brought her squashed and broken plants at various times over the years, but these were being held out by a man. A man who wanted to charm her.

She looked up into his eyes and felt her heart accelerate.

It was working.

What had made him pick flowers for Kit?

One moment he'd been feeling a bit sorry for the boys living in a house so full of women, and the next he'd been discussing which flowers would make the best bouquet for those ladies.

Discussion might be a bit of a strong word. Graham talked and Arthur said, "Flowers."

Graham and his father had always brought his mother flowers when they went on a walk. And while they'd never dug around in a garden, they'd certainly played their share of jokes on each other, including ones with worms. And while it was obvious the women were working hard to raise these children well, Graham couldn't help but think they had to feel the lack of a father.

Of course, there were plenty of fathers they were better off not having, but Graham's was excellent. So, for the time he was here, he'd try to mimic his own father.

As he slid Kit's vegetable basket from her arm and offered the bouquet of flowers in return, her mouth slacked open and she stared at the colorful blooms. It was the expression he'd craved when he met her in the ballroom, a mixture of adoration and fascination.

Graham liked it.

The children skipped ahead of them as they walked back to the house, but Graham made his pace deliberately slow. Kit matched it.

"I'm going to check the bridge," he said. "The boys said this morning there wasn't any way it would be usable, but I still feel like I should check."

He hoped it wasn't passable. He wanted to stay here, wanted to learn more about this strange place and what was going on. He'd never even heard about, much less seen, a place such as this, where everyone slept in a nice manor house but worked like servants all day long.

Hopefully, Oliver would simply assume that Graham had gone in search of more white chalk horses.

Kit frowned. "The boys are probably right."

"I'm happy to ride Dogberry out to check it, but I'm afraid I don't know the way." He supposed he'd have to take someone with him and walk it, which would likely take most of the day. He didn't want to lose that much time here. "Dogberry's capable of carrying two people for the short time we'd be riding."

Emotions flickered across her face so quickly that he couldn't catch them all. He could guess what she was thinking, though. If he took a child, they might tell him things.

If he took her . . . the idea of her clinging to him as they rode double through the woods made his breath a little more difficult to catch and inspired a desperate need to wipe his sweaty hands on his breeches.

"We could walk," she said softly, as if her breath had escaped her a bit as well.

Graham wouldn't mind walking so much if he were with her, but he liked the idea of riding a lot better. He squinted and looked toward the woods as he opened the latch on the kitchen door. "How far is it? Can you be away from the house that long?"

Daphne was in the kitchen, kneading some sort of bread dough with two of the older-looking girls, Sarah and Eugenia. When they'd thrown names at him in the large, toy-filled room this morning, he'd been grateful for the years of social training that made names and faces easy to remember.

He didn't know much about houses or gardens, but he liked to think he was fairly good with people, and he was very good at making any situation fun, even the sometimes tediousness of long-distance travel.

Through the window he caught sight of three boys carrying buckets toward the stable.

He'd like to bring a little bit of that fun

into their lives here. Starting with the woman next to him. He needed to get her on his horse.

"You're leaving the house?" Daphne asked, her hands buried deep in the dough.

"I want to see if the bridge is passable, but I don't know how to get back to it." Graham set the basket of vegetables on the worktable.

"Oh." Daphne's eyes were wide.

Kit walked sharply across the room and pulled a clay pitcher from a shelf. "I think it will take us a little more than an hour to walk there. I can walk all the way to town in two hours and the bridge is just over half-way."

As she dipped the pitcher in water and slid the flowers in with an almost reverent delicacy, Graham's heart turned over. He'd met so many courtable women who wanted things from him that would be all too easy to give. A walk in the park, a dance, perhaps a flower, or a visit to her drawing room. Things they enjoyed talking about but didn't really make much difference in their lives.

But he could make a difference in Kit's. He could show her how to relax. What would it take to make her laugh the way he'd made Arthur laugh earlier? Right then, more than anything in the world, Graham wanted to make that happen. "We could take Dogberry and be back in less than half that time."

The surprise slid off Daphne's face, and she grinned. Her eyes crinkled at the corners, and the smile grew until her teeth were visible. "You should do that."

"What?" Kit gasped out, looking up from the flowers.

Daphne dropped her gaze to the bread dough. "We need you here. There are boxes to be done, and the children missed lessons several times last week." Her sigh was exaggerated. "I'm afraid you'll need to ride the horse."

Sarah, the tallest, and presumably oldest, of the girls snickered and ducked her head to her shoulder to try to muffle the noise.

"I am not riding the horse," Kit said through gritted teeth.

"I guess we should start walking, then. We wouldn't want the children to miss their lessons." Graham grinned at Daphne and then offered his arm to Kit, who merely glowered.

This was going to be more fun than he'd thought.

CHAPTER FOURTEEN

She should have ridden the horse.

At least then the torture would have been shorter.

They could have gone to the bridge and been back at the house in the amount of time it was going to take them just to walk one way. Possibly even faster than that. She'd been afraid to be in such close proximity to Lord Wharton, but now she had to manage his company.

And she hadn't even managed to completely avoid his physical presence because the man was always *there.* His hand would appear, strong and steady, as she climbed over a root. His arm offered a stabilizing presence when she clambered through the undergrowth to avoid a particularly muddy patch of trail.

It was more nerve-wracking than the horse would have been. Riding together would probably have been like dancing. At least, that was what she'd been told when she'd learned to ride, to think of it as a dance with the horse. She missed dancing, but she'd done quite a bit of it before running away from London, so she was sure she could handle a horse.

She wasn't sure she could handle this urge she had to rely on Lord Wharton, to lean into him as he helped her along the wooded path. But she could not let him take her security in her ability to do this on her own. He would leave. Even if the bridge were entirely submerged, it would only be a matter of days until he was gone.

And she didn't want to feel like something precious had been ripped away from her when he left.

Worrying about what he'd do with the knowledge of their whereabouts was bad enough. She didn't need to have resurrected and crushed childhood hopes keeping her awake as well.

"I've never seen woods like these," Lord Wharton said as they passed under a sprawling oak.

"They're beautiful," Kit agreed. The trees were a safe topic. "When we first moved out here, Daphne and I spent hours walking in these woods, marveling at the peace and quiet."

"A far cry from London."

"Yes." Was he going to press? Ask questions? The anticipation, waiting for him to say or do something that would bring her world tumbling down, was making Kit ill. Not even the sweet scent of trees and moss was enough to settle her insides.

A chilled, damp breeze trickled through the trees and across her neck, making her shiver.

"I'd offer my jacket, but I left it back at the house." He sounded truly remorseful but a bit happy at the same time. "I have to admit, even though this shirt is feeling a bit stale, I'm enjoying the freedom. Even in the country I don a jacket and cravat every day. It, uh, seemed a bit pretentious here."

"We live a simple life." And it was a good life. Even if Kit needed reminding of that every now and then. It was good that she'd been given a life that allowed her to make amends for her past mistakes.

"What's the house called?"

Should she tell him? She didn't really want to, wasn't sure anyone knew but the residents. Not even Nash's paperwork held the name. She and Daphne had discovered it while going through the house. A sketch of the home had been labeled with the words *Haven Manor,* and it had felt like some sort of omen, a sign that the original owner would be happy with their intended use of the building.

"It's called Haven Manor. I think the person who built it just wanted an escape."

Graham looked around. "I can't think of a better place to escape to."

She braced herself for questions about the children, but he didn't ask them. Instead, he asked about plants. The rest of the walk to the bridge, he pilfered her limited knowledge of the flora they passed.

There were botany books in the library, and she'd read them all, occasionally taking the children out to the woods with the books so they could try to identify some of the plants. She didn't know the answers to half of his questions, though, so he spent several minutes speculating on whether or not sweeter-smelling flowers helped bees make sweeter honey.

How did a man of means and position develop such a unique outlook on life? He seemed truly happy to observe what was around him, soak in the atmosphere. By the time they reached the bridge, Kit's emotions were a churning mess.

Much like the river water that had overtaken the bridge and road around it.

The bridge flooded often in the spring,

but it hadn't been changed or fixed because hardly anyone used this road on a regular basis. Over the years, the stone had been extended up the road a ways to prevent the swollen river from washing away the path, but that was the most anyone cared to do. It was part of the reason Haven Manor had felt securely hidden for so long.

She'd never seen the water this high before, though.

The surface of the stone bridge wasn't even visible. Water rushed over the top and surged high up the surrounding banks, past the stones in the road, until she could see it wearing away some of the surrounding gravel and dirt.

There would probably be repair work needed after the water receded. How much was anyone's guess. But one thing was certain. Lord Wharton wasn't going anywhere.

Graham bit his cheek to keep from smiling in triumph over the state of the bridge. It was even better than he'd hoped. If he were desperate enough, he could take Dogberry and walk along the river until they found a place to cross. It would mean riding through farmland and across the countryside, but it wasn't all that daunting.

Except that if he was desperate for any-thing, it was for a reason to stay.

Kit didn't say a word. She simply whirled around and started back the way they'd come, her pace quicker than it had been on the walk to the bridge.

Graham jogged a bit to catch up to her. "How long until the water goes down?"

She sighed. "Two days. Maybe three. It happens a few times every spring, and it's usually passable by the next day." She glanced over her shoulder. "That's a lot of water, though."

Two days. He could learn a lot in two days.

Questions burned in his mind. Questions about Kit, about the children and Daphne and Jess. But the stiffness of Kit's shoulders and the way she dug her heel into the ground with every step was a clear indica-tion that she was on guard right now. She was probably expecting him to voice some of those questions.

Stiff shoulders and a guarded mind weren't very fun, though, and Graham was determined to bring a little bit of levity into her world.

He bent to scoop a small limb off the ground as they walked back into the woods. "Were you really going to throw a knife at that man in the park?"

She stumbled a bit but righted herself before he could take her elbow. "If I had to."

"Would you have hit him?"

The look she sent him was drawn in confusion. "Hardly. Did you see the size of him? My fist wouldn't have been anything but a pesky fly to him."

Graham grinned at the picture of her swinging her fists and screaming. "I meant with the knife. If you'd thrown it, would it have hit him?"

Confusion cleared and a splash of red touched her cheekbones. "Probably. Possibly. I'm fairly good at hitting a tree."

Graham extended the limb toward her. "Hit that tree."

Her pace slowed as she took the limb, holding it delicately as if she thought it would turn into a snake. "Which tree?"

"Any tree. Your choice."

She stopped walking, slid her grip to the end of the stick, and launched it. It crashed against a tree several paces in front of them, sending bits of limb and bark flying through the air. "I choose that one."

The impish grin she threw him brought Graham stumbling to a halt. Then he started laughing. Keeping the conversation away from the children while they walked might have been his best idea ever.

He kept at it all the way back to the house. The conversation would naturally lull, and he'd wait for her to start tensing up again, obviously expecting him to finally ask more about Benedict or the other children. But he didn't. Instead, he pulled the most ridiculous questions he could think of from the depths of his brain. He was actually glad when the house came back into view because he'd resorted to asking if she thought beef or rabbit made a better cottage pie, and there really wasn't anywhere else to go from there. As far as conversation topics went, that was scraping pretty close to the bottom of the barrel.

Kit obviously shared his relief at returning to the house, though probably for a very different reason, as she took off running as soon as they cleared the lake, leaving him standing alone on the lawn.

He let her go. He knew he had been flustered enough by the walk to need space, so she probably needed it even more. She was the one with secrets, after all, and he'd poked at her walls until she'd finally relaxed enough to laugh. Had that left her feeling vulnerable?

He rather hoped so. It would make it easier to peel back the layers and learn the truth, though it was debatable which truth he wanted to know more, Kit's or the children's.

They were likely tied together, so Graham might as well attack from all sides, and one truth he'd learned in his hours this morning was that it was going to be a lot easier to inject a bit of fun into the house through the children. And when people were laughing and having fun, they relaxed. And it was ever so much easier to get to know a relaxed person.

Kit had run to the house, so Graham wandered toward the barn. Off to the side, three boys were standing in the goat paddock.

When he was close enough, he saw they were milking the goats. He'd never seen the process, so he leaned against the barn wall and watched, asking questions and making comments about the funny way the one goat's hair stuck out around her ears.

"It's like a crown. Only a small one. Sort of like a goat earring," Graham said with his head tilted to the side as if he were giving very serious consideration to the tufts of wayward fur.

John laughed and aimed a stream of milk toward Graham's boot.

Graham jumped out of the way with an

exaggerated yelp, but what he really wanted to do was cheer in victory. Fun was the siren call of the young, but he had a feeling that the women would follow where the children led when it came to personal involvement.

"What do you do after this?" Graham asked as the boys untied the ropes holding the goats in place.

"We do lessons in the afternoon," Henry said, flipping his blond hair out of his eyes with the back of his wrist.

"Lessons?" Graham asked. Daphne had mentioned lessons earlier, implying that Kit needed to be present for them. Had the women taken on the role of tutor as well?

He cast a glance at the house, as if he could see through the smooth stone sides to the women working within. How was it possible that three women managed the upkeep of a place this large? The children were lending a hand, of course, but how much help could twelve youths be?

"Where do you do your lessons?"

"In the library," Henry said.

"Stuffy," Arthur grumbled.

Graham was growing to really like Arthur and his short sentences. The boy managed to convey quite a bit while saying practically nothing. He'd have done well in London.

Henry shrugged. "It can get a bit crowded

with all of us in there, but Mama Kit says if she had to teach us in shifts she wouldn't get anything else done."

Was there anything that woman didn't do? "Don't Daph— er, Mama Daphne and Mama Jess teach you anything?"

"Sure," Henry said, standing and attempting to pick up his full milk pail. Arthur tried to do the same, but remembering the disaster the water pail had been, Graham stepped forward and picked up the younger boys' pails.

The boys grinned at him, and Arthur skipped ahead, leading the way back to the house.

John took his own pail and fell in step beside Graham. Henry came along Graham's other side, limping a bit as he favored his ankle. At least he was walking on it.

Walking well enough to kick at a loose pebble on the path, anyway. "Mama Daphne teaches us music and sewing," he said with the bored disdain only young boys can muster. "She doesn't make the boys sew much but said we didn't know where life was taking us and there might not always be someone to fix a seam."

Music and sewing. Skills a woman raised in a genteel setting would have in spades. Had both she and Kit fled from London?

"And Mama Jess?"

Henry and John both grinned. Arthur spun around and walked backward a few steps. "Fighting."

"And cooking," John added.

Henry nodded, making his hair flop into his eyes. "She's even more adamant that boys learn alongside the girls than Mama Daphne is. Says she knows plenty of men who would have starved if they hadn't known how to make their own food."

"Is she a good cook?" Graham asked, though he was really more curious to know if she was any good at the fighting. There was something about her that made him feel like he should walk a little more carefully. And someone had to have taught Kit how to throw a knife, even if the lesson hadn't fully taken.

He had a feeling that someone had been Jess and that the little blond woman wouldn't have had any trouble hitting the footpads with the knife if she'd been the one cornered in the park.

The boys made noises of affirmation, but Henry, of course, had more to add. "I think it's because it involves knives. Mama Jess really likes her knives."

Graham rolled his shoulders in reflex at the thought of Jess having an affinity for sharp cutting tools. The feel of his open shirt collar rolling against his neck was strange. He supposed dressing simply, as the boys did, was something he would become accustomed to, but while he enjoyed the freedom of an open collar, there was something uncomfortable about the unfamiliarity.

Probably not as much discomfort as the boys would experience when they had to add cravats and waistcoats to their adulthood wardrobes, though.

The steady sound of metal on wood greeted them as they entered the kitchen. Jess stood at the worktable, cutting vegetables with an efficiency that gave credence to Henry's knife theory.

John stepped forward to show Graham where to put the pails, and Graham was a little glad it was on the other side of the room from Jess and her knife.

She glanced at the pails and nodded in his direction but didn't say anything. What was she thinking? How did she feel about having him here? Was she happy about it the way Daphne seemed to be, or was she thinking of ways to replace those vegetables with his fingers?

As far as he could tell, her only goal was to ignore him as politely as possible.

Her gaze flitted to the children, the knife not stopping while she looked up. "Lessons in the library in half an hour."

"Globe!" Arthur cried and grabbed Graham's hand to drag him toward the stairs.

Henry seemed just as excited about the prospect of looking at a globe. John rolled his eyes and sighed, but he headed toward the stairs as well.

Graham followed because the alternative was to rip his hand away from the little fingers clasped around it. The sensation of that little hand grabbing his left him a bit wobbly in the knees. It was so small. It couldn't even grab his hand correctly, instead wrapping itself around two of Graham's fingers.

Henry's hand curled into Graham's free one, and the sensation hit him in the gut all over again.

Graham was happy to head up into the main part of the house again. That was where Kit was, after all, and she was the one he really wanted to learn more about, to the point that it was becoming a bit of an obsession.

Who was he trying to fool? He'd been obsessed when she'd been dressed in silk and hiding in a London ballroom. Now that she'd taken on the additional persona of country maiden happily ensconced in her unreachable house, he was even more intrigued.

Why had she been in London in the first place?

It had to have something to do with the children because everything she did seemed to revolve around them. But why London? What could she possibly need to do in London on behalf of twelve tiny country people?

Benedict was already in the library, book open on his lap, one foot propped on a footstool while his knee jiggled back and forth. Exactly the same as how Kettlewell would lounge around the common room reading. The similarity set Graham's wits to woolgathering once more. Perhaps the tiny people weren't all country folk.

Arthur pulled him over to the globe. It was large, resting on an elaborately carved three-legged base. The piece reminded him of the globe in his father's study in Grandridge Hall, his Staffordshire estate.

In fact, everything in this room looked like something he could find at Grandridge Hall. What he'd seen of the rest of the house was simple, even a bit rough, but in here, the furniture was of a high quality. Walls of floor-to-ceiling shelves were filled with books, and above the double-glass doors leading out to the lawn, a stained-glass scene of cherubs danced.

"Look at all the ocean," Henry said as he spun the globe gently and with a measure of awe in his tone. "I wonder why God made so much water."

"Noah," Arthur grunted, softly running his own fingers across the surface.

Graham bit back a chuckle, but another one sounded from across the room. Benedict rose from the sofa and crossed the room to join the group at the globe. "You were listening to the story last night, Arthur. Good for you."

Benedict, who was tall enough that his head nearly reached Graham's shoulder, ruffled the little boy's hair. Arthur beamed up at him before turning his attention back to the globe.

Graham made himself look at the globe since he assumed staring at Benedict for too long would make the boy nervous. India swung slowly by as the boys turned the wooden orb. Graham reached out his hand and planted a finger in the middle of the country. "I've been there."

Three sets of wide eyes swung his way. "You have?"

Graham nodded. "Shall I tell you about

the time I witnessed two elephants fighting?"

The boys all nodded, and soon Graham was telling story after story of the places he'd been, making sure to point out every location on the globe. The group around him grew until he was fairly certain he had the entire household of children at his feet, listening to him talk about the icy expanses of the Canadian tundra.

"I apologize for my delay, children, I —" Kit said as she entered the room, only to be shushed to silence by several of the children.

Graham didn't miss a word of the story he was telling, but he couldn't prevent a smile from curving his lips as he met Kit's surprised gaze.

She sank into a chair that was situated a little bit behind the children and listened as he finished his story about fishing through a hole in the ice.

"D'you get sick on the boats?" asked Geoffrey, a very little boy with dark hair and round cheeks. "Sometimes Benedict swings me round p'tending I'm a boat, and it makes my stomach feel funny."

A swirl of pride brought a grin to Graham's face as he realized the child's strange shortening of words was becoming easier to understand. "I've never gotten sick on the boat, but my horse was never exceedingly happy about riding on one."

Graham had never been sure if the horse actually disliked riding on boats or if Dogberry knew that huffing and snorting got him coaxed onboard with a lump of sugar or whatever fruit happened to be close at hand.

That single question, though, opened the floodgates, and soon Graham was digging around in his brain for facts about ships that he wasn't sure he even knew.

He hadn't a clue how they spliced the ropes together because he'd never needed to care, but he had watched them hoist the sails several times and was able to give an accurate accounting of the practice that seemed to satisfy the children.

He talked so much that his throat began to itch, and his mouth felt thick and dry.

After he'd had to clear his throat three times in one sentence, Kit stood and clapped her hands. "I think Lord Wharton has taught us enough for one day."

"So we don't have to do lessons?" one of the girls asked.

Kit shook her head. "No. But Mama Daphne still wants to have music after dinner."

The children ran from the room as if their

shoes were on fire, and it drew a chuckle from Graham's scratchy throat. Rich or poor, it seemed there were some traits all children had in common. Graham could remember escaping before his nanny could change her mind about something.

With all the children departed, however, it left Graham and Kit alone in the library. The warm and rich atmosphere of books and comfortable furniture made it feel more intimate than their walk through the woods.

She must have felt the same way, because she couldn't seem to stop smoothing her hands over her skirts. Why didn't she bolt the way the children had? Did she not trust him in the room that seemed to contain the only riches in the house?

Whatever it was, Graham wasn't about to let this moment go to waste. For all her apparent nerves, she seemed softer than she had on their walk, more open. And he wasn't above taking advantage of it. As much as he wanted to learn information as they felt comfortable telling him, he did only have a few days. At some point, he was going to have to push a little if he actually wanted his curiosity satisfied.

He rose from the chair he'd pulled over to the globe at some point in his story-telling extravaganza and propped himself on the back of the sofa Kit was standing beside.

He swallowed, trying to generate enough moisture in his mouth to talk without choking or coughing, holding her in place by holding her gaze. "I think it's time you tell me who they are."

CHAPTER FIFTEEN

She wanted to say no, wanted to tell him he had no right to ask anything about the children. But he'd been so gentle with them, so willing to share and teach and interact, that she couldn't seem to find the strength to deny him.

Whereas he looked strong enough to demand an answer.

Oh, not physically. She had no fear for herself or anyone's well-being, but he looked ready to follow her around, wear her down. And she didn't really blame him. She'd been nothing but a mystery since they'd met, and now here he was in a house that couldn't possibly make any sense to him.

Half the time it didn't even make sense to her, and she was running the place.

She could leave. She could tear her gaze away from his golden-brown eyes and follow the children to wherever they'd gone.

Usually after lessons she spent time on the household accounts, but those were in the desk in the corner and she wasn't about to pull those out with Lord Wharton in the room.

Yes, she could leave.

In theory.

Her feet seemed sewn to the rug beneath her, though, and her eyes refused to shift away from his. Maybe if she gave him a little bit of information, it would be enough to convince him of the importance of keeping their secret once he returned to his normal life.

"Kit?" he asked, his voice rough from the amount of talking he'd just done.

"They're children," she murmured. "Children who needed to be forgotten."

The truth was, she could have called them a lot of things and none of those would have been as accurate. The people — the women — whom Kit and Daphne had started Haven Manor to help needed the children to disappear from their lives as if they'd never been born. If anyone knew about them, if anyone ever found out, those women would be cast aside, dropped into a harsh world with no skills, no way to make a living, and no sense of what it took to survive.

They'd have resorted to trying to work in a poorhouse where likely one, if not both mother and child, wouldn't survive more than a year or two.

Kit knew. She knew all too well. Because when she and Daphne had left London all those years ago, they'd been in those shoes. If it hadn't been for the aid of people like Mrs. Lancaster and Nash Banfield and his wife Margaretta, she didn't know what would have happened to them.

But they had survived, and Kit was now paying her penance by making sure other women didn't have to suffer as Daphne had.

It was the least she could do. And even then it didn't feel like enough because there were only so many women they could help at a time. While so many others . . . so many others had to find another way. And while Haven Manor was far from a perfect solution, it was the best they'd been able to come up with.

"Illegitimate?" Lord Wharton asked.

How much could Kit tell without telling him too much? How much was needed to satisfy his curiosity? She knew she had to give him answers before he left here or he'd seek them elsewhere and cause them more problems. But she was only going to give him the answers he sought. "Yes."

"Aristocratic by-blows?"

Her eyes widened, likely confirming his guess. "Why would you guess such a thing?"

His eyes flicked around them at the lush furniture filling the library. "Call it intuition."

Kit felt heat rising to her ears. She'd stopped viewing the house as a manor a long time ago, focusing more on the fact that the large building allowed them plenty of space to house the children. But to an outsider, the house probably seemed an extravagance for a group of illegitimates. "I told you the truth about the house. We're simply taking care of it. The grounds had already been left to grow at will when we moved in here, so the agreement is only for the house and the immediate outbuildings."

Lord Wharton shifted more of his weight onto the back of the sofa and extended his legs in front of him to cross his booted ankles. "And you do this, manage this by yourself?"

"Yes." She had to put some distance between herself and the earnest glow in his eyes. Where had this serious man come from? When she'd met him in the ballroom, he'd been all jokes and smiles. Even when facing down thugs in the park, he'd done so with wit and charm. Telling stories to the children, he'd captivated everyone with his self-deprecating humor.

But now there was no levity in his tone, no crinkle to his eyes.

And it made it difficult for her to slough him off. She'd left carefree joviality so far behind her that she could barely remember living with it and could easily keep herself away from it now. But honest concern had been the one thing to seep through the cracks in her armor in the past few years, and his was hitting her harder than normal considering he was the last person she'd expected to extend it.

She dropped her gaze and picked at the rough, broken skin of a callus on the side of her thumb. "It was harder when the children were small. It was just me and Daphne then. Now we have Jess, and the children are old enough to help."

"Until Benedict leaves you to learn woodworking."

Did the man remember every little detail? "Yes. But then the others will be older and new young ones will be coming in. And Ben's apprenticeship is local, so I'm sure he'll be home to help when he can."

"Is he Kettlewell's?"

Kit's gaze flew up to meet his. "Who?"

"Benedict. Is he Kettlewell's son?"

Who was Kettlewell? It was probably a title, though Kit had no idea which one. It wasn't one she remembered from her time in London, but names had never been her strongest talent. Especially names of people she hadn't met. She did, however, clearly remember the names of every person who had parented one of her children.

Especially the man who'd fathered Benedict.

The man who'd tried to ruin Kit's life, only to damage Daphne's instead.

"No," Kit said quietly, thankful that she could answer honestly and still keep the children's identities as secret as possible. "No, Kettlewell isn't his father. Or anyone else's here."

A wry smile touched Wharton's mouth. "The boy looks just like him. I went to school with Kettlewell, and it was like looking back in time."

"I'm sure your memory has faded." At least Kit hoped it had. Here she'd been worried about Blake and John, thinking their appearances could cause them problems if their lives took them into serving aristocratic circles. She'd thought they had a few years before worrying about that, as the rest of them only bore a passing resemblance if one knew what he was looking for.

"It's possible." He pushed off the couch to cross the room and examine some of the other baubles scattered around the library. "The age would work. He would have been at Oxford at the time."

The library was the only room they hadn't emptied of its valuable treasures. Kit just hadn't been able to do it. She loved books, adored stories, which was probably why she was so captivated by Lord Wharton right now. The library had been so beautiful and glorious that they'd chosen to leave it as it was.

"You know what I haven't done in ages?" he asked as he fiddled with a wood-and-brass sextant from a shelf.

"What?" Kit tried to bring her mind around to the shift in atmosphere. Gone was the serious, dark gaze, and the light-hearted jokesmith had returned.

"A picnic." He placed the sextant back on the shelf. "The grounds here are beautiful, even if they have been left to run amok. I'm only here for another day or two. Let's have a picnic."

"Um . . . I suppose . . ." Kit stuttered, still a bit off center.

"Excellent. I'll go tell the children."

Kit snapped her mouth shut as the man nearly ran from the room. He was going to tell the children. Which meant they were now having a picnic whether she wanted one or not.

Kit sat on the sofa, staring at the globe for a long time. Thoughts whirled through her head, but she wasn't able to actually catch any of them. The same could be said for the emotions sliding through her veins. She wasn't sure what to think or feel. Eventually she shook herself free from the trance and went to the kitchen to help with dinner. As was becoming all too commonplace since Lord Wharton came to the house, none of the children were where she expected them to be. Only Jess was in the kitchen.

"Where is everyone?"

"Outside." Jess's golden eyes speared Kit. "Riding a horse."

"Riding a . . ." Kit snapped her mouth shut and swallowed. "He's letting them ride his horse?"

"That man is dangerous, Kit." Jess turned back to the food.

"I know," Kit mumbled. And she did know. She knew Jess wasn't talking about any sort of physical threat. Even knowing that every minute she spent with him made her more vulnerable, Kit pushed her way out the kitchen door and went to the lawn behind the house.

There was Wharton, and his horse, taking each child on a ride around the lawn.

Daphne stood to the side, lip between her teeth, fingers twined tightly together.

"Don't worry," Kit said as she came to stand beside Daphne. "He won't let them get hurt."

Her trust in him on this matter was solid, even if he terrified her in other ways. The way he'd been with Arthur in the garden, the careful way he'd answered questions in the library, those moments when he was more than a joke and a smile had shown her that he meant no harm to the children. Those same moments had been very dangerous to her, though, unearthing thoughts long buried, making her wonder if there were good men in the upper classes.

He kept one hand on the knee of the youngest children, holding them in the saddle as the horse ambled around the grass. The older ones were allowed to guide the reins themselves. All of them wore enormous smiles that pierced Kit's heart.

It was possibly the first and last time some of them would have the memorable experience of riding a horse.

The children were destined for lives of work. Trades or household servant positions were the best they were likely to do. Kit put aside as much money as possible from each child's support payments, but it wasn't going to get them very far. Apprenticeships could be purchased, but what then? There wouldn't be enough for them to go into business for themselves. The best they could hope for would be a modicum of comfort while they worked for a living, and that wasn't likely to include rides on horses.

Dinner was loud once more, the way it usually was, although this time all of the chatter was about what it was like to sit so high off the ground on a moving animal. Kit sat silently while the children talked. She remembered riding, remembered loving the power of a horse as she rode across the countryside to her favorite reading spot on a hill overlooking the village.

She didn't share those memories, though. She never talked to the children about her life before Haven Manor. Those memories belonged to the Honorable Katherine FitzGilbert, and she wasn't that woman anymore. Now she was simply Kit.

"Where are we going on our picnic tomorrow?" Sarah asked.

Kit winced as Jess and Daphne swung questioning looks in her direction. She probably should have mentioned the newest Lord Wharton development to them.

"I don't know," Jess said slowly, one eyebrow lifting along with one side of her mouth. "Where would you like us to go?"

"The glen by the lake!"

"The bluebell patch in the forest!"

"Mama Kit's secret tree!"

Kit let her eyes sink closed at the last suggestion. Mostly because she'd seen the brief look of triumph cross Lord Wharton's face at the mention of yet another secret of hers.

"Mama Kit has a tree?" he asked.

The children were only too happy to tumble over themselves to tell their new friend about Kit's hideaway, the tree she ran to on the few occasions when she took time for herself. It wasn't often, but sometimes she simply had to step away. And when she did, she went to her tree. She hadn't known that all the children knew about it, though. She leaned in toward young Geoffrey. "How did you know about my tree?"

"Mama Daphne told us, but no worry. We be *shhh* about it."

Kit bit her lip to keep from laughing at Geoffrey's stilted words. Looking at Lord Wharton was out of the question so she turned to Daphne instead. Her friend was finding her empty plate exceedingly interesting at the moment.

"If they don't know about it, they can't avoid it," she mumbled.

"I think the glen is a good choice," Kit said as she turned her attention to her own plate. "There's a view of the lake, and it will have been in the sun all day so it might be dry.

"But," she continued, looking from little face to little face, "if we're taking a picnic in the afternoon, it will mean everyone has to work on boxes in the morning. Mr. Banfield will be coming to collect the market goods in two weeks."

A few of the children grumbled, but most simply nodded since decorating boxes was one of the more enjoyable tasks at the manor. The paper filigree–covered boxes were one of the best sellers in the market stall Mrs. Lancaster put up on behalf of Haven Manor. They also sold goat cheese and blackberry jam, but the boxes made more for them than everything else combined.

"Evening chores and then it's time for music," Daphne announced as she rose from the table and collected her plate and one of the now-empty serving dishes. "Most helpful child gets first pick of instrument.

I'm going to teach you something new tonight."

Kit looked up from the dishes she'd been collecting. There was a hint of teasing in Daphne's tone and a faraway look in her eyes. What was she up to?

"It's time we learned one of my favorite songs." Daphne smiled at Kit, then cut her eyes toward Lord Wharton. "It's good for dancing."

The children cheered and piled out of the room, rushing to take care of their evening duties. For once, Kit was wishing they hadn't taught the children to be quite so self-sufficient. If she could claim the need to help more of them, she could put off the trip to the music room. Perhaps indefinitely.

CHAPTER SIXTEEN

Graham wasn't of much use other than a body to haul things, so he helped carry the dishes down the stairs and then hauled buckets of water in and out of the kitchen. He spent most of the time staying out of the way and anticipating possibly getting to dance with Kit.

The woods, the library, the London ballroom, there'd been so many moments with her, moments when he'd felt like his whole world was getting ready to shift, but then hadn't.

He wanted to know what was waiting for him on the other side, what would happen if he actually opened himself to the idea of a woman like Kit. Or rather, what would happen if a woman like Kit opened herself up to the idea of a man like him.

While it was true he didn't know a lot about the actual labor of an estate, he could learn. Although he'd be much more likely to hire people than do the work himself.

The setting sun was blazing through the large window, lighting the music room up in shades of red and gold as the children piled in, grabbing instruments and arguing good-naturedly over what song to sing.

Jess circled the room, lighting lamps to ward off the encroaching darkness.

Graham found a seat in the corner and settled in. His musical abilities were limited to keeping the rhythm while dancing.

It was amusing to watch the first few songs, as the children traded off instruments and Daphne went around offering instruction. Most of them were rather hopeless, even more so than Graham would have been, but they all tried.

It was another piece to the puzzle, another glimpse into the women and children. It was frustrating, having to dig and scrape and pull pieces together to form an accurate picture, but he'd pushed as much as he dared in the library earlier. Kit was a skittish filly, wanting to be near him but ready to bolt at the snap of a twig. At least, she seemed to want to be near him. It would have been easy enough to avoid him, yet she kept coming back.

Still, he wondered about her, about this house, about the children. Did they know what they could have had? The world they could have been born into? If their blood truly ran as blue as his did, what did it mean that they were destined for work as servants or tradesmen or possibly worse?

Aaron was illegitimate. It hadn't stopped him from claiming the life his birth had destined him for, but even Graham had to admit it placed restrictions on his future. Graham had never really considered that before. Aaron had always just been Aaron and his life was his life. He wasn't in line for a title, even though his father held one. If Graham's guess was correct, the same could be said for some of the children in this room.

So why them and not him? All of his life Graham had been told that his birth was a blessing from the Lord, his station a gift from God bestowed upon those who deserved it.

But that same blood was running in the veins of the children before him.

The ones who needed to be forgotten.

The idea didn't sit comfortably with Graham. Because it meant his way of thinking, of viewing the world . . . was wrong. Or at the very least, flawed.

Slowly the noise settled into something that could be described as music as one by one the children abandoned the instruments until only two remained playing.

Sarah was at the pianoforte and Reuben played the violin. The gangly, quiet boy who seemed all arms and legs had found some sort of grace with a bow in his hand, while Sarah's fingers plucked over the piano as well as any young lady Graham had ever seen exhibit in London.

And she was still a child.

Daphne went to join Sarah at the piano, and together they played a lively tune that had the children back on their feet, skipping and laughing and singing. Graham glanced around and found that Jess had slipped away at some point, and Kit was sitting in the corner, tapping her toe to the music.

With a grin, Graham made his way to a trio of potted plants in the corner and knelt to scoop one of them into his arms before crossing to Kit's side. He placed the plant in front of her and smiled.

She looked from the plant to his face and back again, confusion covering her features. Good. Kit was much more pliable when he managed to surprise her. "My friend here says you owe him a dance. You promised him one in London and never followed through."

Her lips quivered as if trying not to smile and failing. "That is hardly the same plant. My partner in London was a tree."

Graham pretended to give the plant a quizzical inspection. "Ah, so it was. I suppose this next dance will simply have to go to me, then."

He extended his hand, knowing it was a gamble, but wanting to do something to draw her further out of her shell. The more he pried away her cold and calculating outer layers, the more glimpses he managed to get of the woman beneath the prickly exterior, which only served to intrigue him more. He thought that appeasing his curiosity would be enough to make him willing to forget her, but the opposite was happening. Every answer unearthed three more questions about a girl born into his world, yet different than any other woman he'd ever met.

Graham liked different.

The song shifted until only Daphne was playing, and her abilities were impressive enough to distract Graham for a moment until he realized the song she was playing was perfect for a quadrille.

A glance at her sitting at the pianoforte revealed a wide grin. It made her plain round face almost pretty. And it was happy.

How was it that Daphne didn't seem to carry the same darkness that Kit did? It was one more secret to uncover.

But first, he wanted to get Kit to dance.

When her hand slid into his, triumph surged through him, followed quickly by a burst of attraction. The warmth of her palm sliding across his without any gloves in the way made him want to curl his fingers tightly around hers and never let go.

She stood, using her free hand to smooth the skirts of her sprigged muslin gown. "It's going to be awfully difficult to dance a quadrille with only two people."

Graham lifted a brow. "You mean you have not been teaching these children how to dance?"

Kit frowned, and Graham had a feeling she was thinking it wasn't a skill they were likely ever to need since none of them would be gracing the same ballrooms as their parents. For some reason, that was where Kit was drawing the educational line.

He knew from the books he'd seen strewn about and listening to the children talk that she was giving them a considerable education for what she expected their station in life to be, but to not be teaching them to dance?

He lowered his head toward her ear.

"Even the poorest people I've seen in my travels like to dance. It is the freest entertainment available."

Her cheeks stained pink as her blue eyes met his gaze.

Graham didn't wait for her to respond. He simply hauled her to the middle of the room and loudly asked, "Who wants to learn to dance?"

This was a bad idea. Kit could feel it in her middle as it clenched. But the sensation didn't quite feel like dread or even fear.

It felt like anticipation.

Which made this an even worse idea than she'd originally thought.

Memories and longings battered the wall behind which she'd placed everything she'd left behind. Was Daphne suffering the same pangs? Did this feel too much like old times? So many times in London Daphne would be banished to the keys so that others could dance. Every country assembly. Many of the smaller gatherings in London.

Eventually Daphne had stopped waiting to be asked, declaring that volunteering to play felt better than being told in polite, veiled terms that no one wanted to dance with her, so she might as well play for others.

But the smile on Daphne's face was genuine. There was joy in her eyes as she swayed in her chair and played. Her laughter was easy and pure as she watched the children rush forward to join Lord Wharton's lesson.

Then she caught Kit's eye. And winked.

Winked.

As if she approved of this ridiculous . . . well, flirtation, for lack of a better word. Yes, somehow in the middle of a lost estate in the middle of nowhere in the middle of a group of rowdy children, Kit was having a flirtation.

The wall in her mind cracked a little.

Lord Wharton lined up the children in rows, pairing them off by height instead of anything else. Little Pheobe kept falling on her chubby two-year-old legs and her eyes were blinking slowly, but before Kit could use it as an excuse to leave the dance, Eugenia scooped up the small child and declared that she would take her as a partner.

It was such a touching, loving, familial act that Kit almost lost her composure right then and there. That one action was more thoughtful than anything her father had ever done for her. It had been just him and her for as long as she could remember, but there had been cousins, too. Had any of them

wondered where she'd gone when she disappeared? Had any of them noticed? Or
cared?

Lord Wharton returned to his spot in front
of her, a beaming smile on his face as he
took a deep breath. "I think we're ready.
Let's keep it simple, shall we?"

Daphne began to play a tune that niggled
at more of Kit's memories, a song they'd
danced to during their days in London. She
played it as if her fingers knew the notes on
their own. But she hadn't played any music
like that in years.

Kit glanced Daphne's way. Or had she?
Had she waited until Kit was out of the
house, worried that the old tunes would
upset her?

"Kit?" Lord Wharton asked softly.

She snapped her head back around, getting snagged in his golden-brown eyes and
caught by his quizzical, teasing expression.
"Yes," she stammered out. "Simple."

Lord Wharton directed everyone in how
dances went, laughing when he had to pause
and think about how to explain things. He'd
probably learned to dance as a young boy
and hadn't really had to think through the
process much since then, certainly not to
explain it to someone else.

Kit skipped and turned and tried to

remind the children which way to go, but it quickly descended into chaos, with everyone whirling about the room, laughing, holding hands, and having a generally good time.

Alice and Henry clasped hands and swung themselves in a circle until they fell over in a fit of giggles. Benedict threw his arm over Kit's shoulder and guided her around the room, doing some sort of strange walking kick that made her laugh so hard her side hurt.

And through it all was Lord Wharton, being just as ridiculous as the children, if not more so.

When it was time to stop, the children fell into bed with exhausted smiles on their faces. When was the last time she'd seen them so happy?

No one was particularly unhappy at Haven Manor, at least she didn't think they were, but had she become so focused on survival that she'd forgotten they were children? If it hadn't been for Daphne, Kit wasn't even sure she'd have known what it was to be a child even when she had been one. She would have made it all the way to adulthood without taking her nose out of a book.

That strength had made her capable of doing what needed to be done when their world had fallen apart, what made it possible for her to keep Haven Manor going.

But now that she'd heard the house ring with laughter, she had to wonder if she'd been doing the best for everyone, after all.

Kit's head hurt with the conflicted thoughts as she made her way down the stairs after seeing the children settled for the night.

Life had been simple before Lord Wharton stumbled his way into it.

She could only hope it would return to that simplicity when he left.

With no other valid reasons to delay, Kit pushed open the rough wooden plank they'd used to replace one of the back doors and went out onto the porch. Daphne and Jess were already there, watching for her as if they knew she'd considered going straight to bed.

Neither said anything when she arrived. Jess lowered herself to the step and looked out into the night while Daphne closed her eyes and swayed back and forth, humming.

"We should do that more often," Daphne said as Kit came over to lean on the railing.

"Do what?" Kit asked.

"Dance. I'd forgotten how much fun it could be." Daphne whirled around in a circle before leaning one shoulder against the tall columns at the top of the stairs.

Kit's mouth gaped open a bit, and she dropped onto the step beside Jess, unable to trust her legs to hold her up. "Daphne, you sat at the pianoforte all night."

She shrugged. "It's fun to watch." Her mouth curved into a grin. "Especially when our visitor got you all flustered."

Jess sat up a bit straighter. "What's this?"

Daphne sat on the other side of Kit and leaned across as if she were imparting a great secret to Jess. "He brought a plant over to her, which is a story I desperately want to hear about later, and then asked her to dance."

Jess laughed. "And she agreed?"

"He didn't give me much of a choice," Kit mumbled, though she wasn't sure that was true. She'd wanted to dance with him.

"I remember watching you dance for hours before we moved to Marlborough," Daphne said with a sigh.

Kit wrapped her arms around her knees and pulled them close to her chest, hoping the pressure would still the unsettled fluttering inside. They never spoke about their life before Marlborough.

Daphne plunged on, ignorant of Kit's internal struggle. "It's so much fun to see the people whirling around, moving to whatever music I create. I could make them go faster or slower or anything I wished. I can't believe we haven't thought of dancing with the children before now."

"I told you she didn't miss it," Jess said quietly in Kit's ear.

Was that true? Did Daphne really prefer this life to her old one? Had she avoided talking about it for Kit's sake instead of her own?

"Dancing doesn't bring back bad memories for you?" Kit asked softly. She was almost afraid to know the answer. If Daphne didn't miss London, didn't miss society and the life they'd had, what did that mean? Did that mean she'd forgiven Kit?

Was that enough if she did?

Daphne lifted one shoulder. "Dancing here is so different from dancing in London. Even the country assemblies were all about who was partnered with whom and who had the prettier dress. No, I liked it much better when I would play the pianoforte at your father's house and you could make the dolls dance around."

Kit's guilt rolled over in her gut, growing and sharpening until she wouldn't have been surprised to look down and find herself bleeding. All Daphne had ever wanted was to be a country wife, to live a simple life. It was Kit who'd been drawn to the sparkle and glitter of London, to the parties and the opera. And Daphne had gone with her because that was what Daphne had always done.

"Do you know my favorite memory from London?" Daphne clasped her hands together and leaned forward onto her knees, staring out into the night. "I remember going to the park early in the morning, when the only people there were the ones exercising their horses for the joy of it. No one was looking at anyone else, no one cared who else was there. And you and I would go as deep into the park as we could and find a tree and pretend we weren't in London anymore. I would sew and you would read until we got too hungry or thirsty to stay."

Kit had forgotten those times. They'd occurred when they first went to London. As the Season had gone on, they'd happened less and less, Kit insisting on staying out so late that she had to sleep through those early-morning hours.

And Daphne had stayed out with her. Standing on the edge of ballrooms, talking to other wallflowers, watching just like she always had.

What had Kit done to her friend?

Daphne yawned. "It's been a long day. We

need sleep if we're taking these children down to the glen tomorrow." She shook her head. "I still can't believe he talked you into a picnic. I think Lord Wharton may be just what you needed, Kit."

Then Daphne rose and went inside.

Kit couldn't move.

Jess swayed, bumping her shoulder into Kit's. "I knew you were hiding something about London. What didn't you tell us about the house you took a shortcut through?"

Kit had to rather admire Jess's restraint in waiting until now to pin Kit down. "He was in the ballroom. I met him behind a potted plant. He brought me lemonade."

Jess's eyebrows rose. "You were in a ballroom? I assume this was between the garden and the back corridor?"

Kit nodded.

Jess stared out over the lake for a few silent moments. "I've learned a funny thing about the past," she finally said. "The ghosts that haunt you the most are the ones you refuse to acknowledge. The past you try to bury has the most power to hurt you."

Kit snorted. "You aren't usually so cryptic."

"I was trying to be philosophical. Like those books you're always reading."

A laugh burst out of Kit's mouth. "I hardly think plays, poetry, and novels qualify as philosophical."

Jess gave a delicate shrug. "I'll be blunt, then. Face your past. Stop trying to bury it. Or one day it's going to eat you alive."

"And what about your past, Jess?"

"Just because I'm running from it doesn't mean I haven't faced it. It just means I know how dangerous it is. There's a difference."

Then Jess rose, gave Kit's shoulder one solid pat, and followed Daphne inside.

Kit sat in the dark, watching the sliver of moonlight rippling on the lake. She had faced her past, hadn't she? Wasn't that what she did every day with the children? What was she doing if not living down her past?

The past she tried never to think about, never to talk about.

What if Jess was right?

Kit stumbled back to her room and lay on her bed, staring at the ceiling as she did every night, but this time instead of thinking about household accounts or how to fix the roof, she let her mind wander back. And she cried.

CHAPTER SEVENTEEN

13 Years Ago
London
1803

She could feel her heart pounding in her head. *Thrum, thrum, thrum.* A constant steady barrage of spears to the middle of her brain that couldn't be stopped unless she died.

Right at that moment, she thought that could perhaps be a blessing.

Katherine FitzGilbert held herself as still as possible, hoping against hope that not moving would be enough to stave off the next coughing fit. Because if her heartbeat were a spear, each cough was a bullet to the head. And if the pain weren't bad enough, the few thoughts that managed to make it through her tormented brain only inspired a groan of agony.

Which made her head hurt more in a vicious and unfair cycle.

She closed her eyes, did her best to relax into the feather pillow, and tried not to think of Maxwell Oswald.

Which meant she could think of absolutely nothing except Maxwell Oswald.

Maxwell Oswald who made all the ladies swoon. Well, perhaps not all the ladies, but all of the ladies of Katherine's station. For daughters hovering at the bottom of the aristocracy, the first son of a second son of a marquis was a catch worth setting her cap for.

Blood rushed through her head, and Katherine forced herself not to sigh, groan, or make any other noise as she wallowed in her self-pity. Would it be so bad to stop her heart just for a moment or two? Just for a second's respite? Laudanum hadn't managed to alleviate the pain, but it had made her mind a bit more muddled.

Which helped her avoid picturing the disaster that was going to happen a few streets away when she didn't show up to the masquerade ball.

Maxwell expected her to be there. He'd been smiling at her for months. He'd been smiling at a lot of other young women, too, but the past few weeks, Katherine had been special. He'd made a point of seeking her out for the first dances, fetching her glasses of punch or lemonade, meeting her gaze in a crowd. It was obvious he'd decided she was more worthy than the other young women fighting for his attention.

It had made Miss Charlotte Rhinehold particularly upset. The rumor was that she'd turned down a proposal from a country squire because she believed Maxwell would offer for her.

But Maxwell hadn't.

But then yesterday he had told Katherine that he had something very important to talk to her about tonight, something he wanted to ask her.

She'd been so happy about the prospect of his attentions at the coming masquerade ball that she'd sat up half the night in her small window seat, window thrown open so she could breathe the night air and listen to the sounds of London.

The night air, which had seemed so refreshing at the time, had attacked her lungs, leaving them pained, thick, and coughing.

There wasn't a chance she could make it to the masquerade ball tonight. Not a chance. She couldn't even make it across the room.

A light tap on her door pricked her head with so many needles she thought she might become ill. That would involve moving her head, though, so she gritted her teeth and breathed in through her nose.

The door slid open, and Katherine's dearest friend in the world walked in.

"How are you feeling?" Miss Daphne Blakemoor asked, crossing the room to smile down at Katherine. Her bright green silk gown was covered by a gauzy overdress, and she carried a feathered mask in her hand. "You look a bit peaked."

"I'm sick as a horse," Katherine groaned.

Another cough racked her body, seizing her middle until it nearly forced her to sit up in the bed. With a groan, she flopped back onto the pillow, her head lolling to the side. The elaborate Catherine the Great costume that she'd been so proud of hung outside her wardrobe, glittering blue skirts trailing to the floor, with its lowered waistline and jeweled sash lending it a distinct look. The coifed wig and feathered mask sat on the table beside the wardrobe. Everyone had been in awe when she'd tried it on in the dress shop. Her costume had been the talk of her friends for weeks. Everyone knew she was going as Catherine the Great.

Even Maxwell Oswald.

Who'd told her that he couldn't wait to come and find her.

Who'd mentioned that he particularly

wanted to see her tonight, that he'd been waiting for just the right moment to ask her something.

And she wasn't going to be there.

Another whimpering groan escaped her.

"Well," Daphne said in as decisive a tone as her soft voice ever managed, "if you aren't going to the ball tonight, I won't either. It's not like my costume was anything much to speak of anyway. I'm not even sure what I'm supposed to be. No one will know if I'm not there."

"Of course they will." Katherine would have winced if it wouldn't have hurt her head more. She'd said the sentence automatically out of loyalty, and both of them knew it. The only person who would miss Daphne was Katherine, and she was stuck in bed.

"They won't," Daphne said with a dismissive shrug. "I've never once had anyone ask me if I'm coming to an event or seek me out as soon as I walk in, unless it's to ask me if I know where you are." She plucked at the bed coverings.

The idea that bounced around Katherine's head was wrong. It had to be. At the very least it was dishonest. But it would be just for one night. And if she didn't show up . . .

If she didn't show up, Miss Rhinehold

might convince Maxwell that she was the special one, that she deserved his attentions. A few weeks ago, he'd seemed quite taken with her, so would it really take that much effort for her to win his regard again? Especially if Katherine wasn't there?

But what if she could keep that from happening and give Daphne a bit of a fairy-tale evening at the same time?

It wasn't as if he would ask her to marry him in the middle of the ball. Whatever he wanted to talk to her about was something Daphne could handle. Daphne was sure to tell Katherine everything anyway.

"Would you like to know what it's like?" Katherine croaked.

Daphne's head came up, brown eyebrows drawn tight enough to scrunch up her round face. "What do you mean?"

Katherine pointed toward the graceful costume. "Be me."

The gasp that escaped Daphne's mouth sucked enough air from the room to start Katherine coughing again. "I couldn't!"

"Why not?" Katherine asked, pleased with herself. This was the perfect solution. It almost made being sick worth it. "Who knows? You might discover a side of yourself that you didn't know before. One that will help you get off the wall and show London how wonderful you are."

Katherine loved her friend dearly, but Daphne was horribly quiet and shy, two characteristics that didn't draw the attention of many men. Or the women either. Daphne was utterly forgettable as far as their social circle was concerned.

"I'd still be me even if I wore your costume, Katherine," Daphne said with a shake of her head.

"That dress is fabulous." Katherine slid her eyes closed because just looking at the dress pained her more. It was so out of fashion, it wasn't as if she'd get another chance to wear it. And she'd spent so much time on it. "Anyone wearing such a dress will be the center of attention."

"I don't really want to be the center of attention," Daphne said softly.

A bit of panic crept into Katherine's veins, and her pounding heart made her head hurt more and sent her into another fit of coughs. If Daphne didn't go, if she didn't pretend to be Katherine, well, it didn't bear thinking about. Katherine simply had to know what Maxwell Oswald wanted to tell her, and she simply had to keep him from going back to Miss Rhinehold.

If it was anyone else, she might not have minded so much — there were other men in London, after all — but Katherine harbored a severe dislike of Miss Rhinehold. She was fairly certain the feeling was mutual, given the way she'd deliberately stepped on the hem of Katherine's dress three weeks ago. Katherine had responded by tripping and spilling an entire glass of punch down the front of Miss Rhinehold's dress. Right before she was supposed to stand up with Maxwell.

There was no question about it. If Katherine wasn't there tonight, Miss Rhinehold would do something to convince Maxwell to throw Katherine over.

"You could be me," Katherine said. "For just one night, you could be me."

Daphne bit her lip but slowly crossed the floor to run a hand over the skirt. It was finer than anything Daphne had, which made Katherine feel a little bit guilty. With a look from Katherine's gown to the spring-green ball gown that served as the base for her own costume, a peculiar light shone in Daphne's eyes.

"Do you really think I'd like being you?"

Katherine rather liked being herself, so why wouldn't Daphne? Besides, if Maxwell Oswald was going to bestow his attentions on a girl besides Katherine, she'd rather it be Daphne any day. How long would it be before Maxwell Oswald regained the courage to ask whatever he intended to ask her tonight? "There's only one way to find out."

A glimmer of excitement danced across Daphne's face along with her usual caution and trepidation, but she rang the bell for Katherine's maid.

The dress fit her perfectly, except for the height. It was a little long but not enough for anyone to notice. By the time the wig and feathered mask were in place, it was hard to tell it wasn't Katherine. The face was a different shape, but it was bordered by feathers, so no one was likely to notice.

"You're beautiful," Katherine said.

"I'm going to be you tonight," Daphne said with more conviction than her voice had possessed since coming to London for their Season. "Tonight I'm going to dance and have fun and not stand against the wall. I'm going to see what all the fuss is about."

"Good for you," Katherine said. She coughed again. "Now get out of here before I make you sick and you end up in this bed right next to me."

After Daphne left, Katherine took another dose of laudanum and managed to find sleep.

Many hours later, when the sun was creeping in her windows, her father barged into her room, slamming the door against the wall hard enough to crack the plaster.

"Stupid, stupid girl," he ranted. "Whatever possessed you to do such a thing?"

Katherine blinked and raised a hand to her pounding head. What was her father talking about? What could she possibly have done now? She hadn't moved from this bed.

"Did you think no one would see you?" He started pacing. "There was a window right there! Right beside you! Lady Beatrice had the perfect view from the garden below."

Despite the shooting pain it caused, Katherine pressed the heels of her palms into her eyes, trying to wake up, trying to understand, trying simply to think something other than *what.*

"It's all anyone can talk about. You're ruined. Completely. No one will have you now, no one. I should have known you'd mess this up, that you couldn't actually do something right and helpful for once."

As he circled the room, sleep finally fell away from Kit's brain and she pushed herself up into a sitting position. Something must have happened at the ball last night. Something horrible. Was Daphne safe? Had she been hurt? She couldn't ask, because everyone, her father included, obviously thought it had been her at the party last night. Telling him it had been Daphne would only make the situation worse. But how had he not known she was sick?

"You're not to leave this house," he grumbled, pointing one long finger in her direction. "No visitors. We'll pretend you don't exist until everyone stops talking about it."

Pretend she didn't exist? Guilt ate at her. What could possibly have happened to Daphne? Whatever it was, Katherine had sent her into it, all in the name of keeping her hold on Maxwell Oswald.

It was fairly safe to assume she'd lost her position of esteem in his eyes, though she'd never been entirely sure how she'd gained it anyway.

More importantly, she had to find a way to talk to Daphne.

Her father stormed out of the room, muttering about business contacts and political alliances and reputations. Katherine pushed the covers aside and eased her feet over the edge of the bed. She managed to stand but then collapsed into a pile of rasping coughs.

She wasn't going to be able to leave. She could only hope Daphne was able to visit, and soon.

And she did. Daphne did come, but she was a pale version of herself, even quieter than she normally was. And her tale of woe buried Katherine until she couldn't breathe.

Because Daphne had danced, she'd tried to be Katherine, and when Maxwell Oswald had taken her into a little alcove off the ballroom and kissed her — kissed her! — she'd been swept away, glorying in what it was like to have someone actually care whether you were there or not, to have someone say she was special, important.

Beautiful.

By the time Daphne's mind had dug its way out of the swirl of fantasy, by the time she'd realized that she shouldn't have left the ballroom with him after the kiss, it had been too late. She'd been ruined. And so was Katherine.

Katherine didn't know what to do. She stayed in bed, even after the illness receded. Daphne regained her composure and seemed her old self again within days, though she stayed in Katherine's room most of the time, refusing to go out without Katherine.

Maxwell Oswald announced his engagement to Miss Charlotte Rhinehold. Charlotte made a point of finding Katherine after church, whispering that it was a shame Katherine hadn't realized before that there were women who married and women who dallied. She'd made a bet with Maxwell about which one Katherine was. The way she'd run her finger around her new diamond bracelet left little question of who the victor had been in that little game.

Because it certainly hadn't been Katherine.

The life she'd always dreamed of was crumbling. She didn't see how it could possibly get worse.

Until the day Daphne arrived in her room, pale and shaking, with the news that they weren't going to be able to hide the fact that Daphne had been ruined.

Their fathers had been livid, had threatened to disown them, cast them out. It was the only way to salvage the family name. But Katherine wasn't going to let Daphne suffer for this, not when it had been Katherine's pride, Katherine's greed, Katherine's ambition that had sent her into a situation she didn't know how to cope with.

Katherine had seen her father do business for years, and she put those skills to work. She negotiated a deal. Their dowries in exchange for their disappearance. They'd leave. Never come back. London could pretend they'd never existed.

Katherine had taken the money, taken Daphne, and packed up as much as they could carry. Then they'd shaken the dust of London from their slippers and headed west.

The realization had come too late, but now Kit knew that no matter what she'd done, no matter who she would have married, she wouldn't have won her father's love and approval, because he wanted more. And so had she. If she'd only been satisfied to stay within the social sphere she'd been born to, none of this would have happened.

Their life in London, the futures they'd dreamed of, were gone forever, but Katherine was determined that Daphne not suffer for it. She would make a life for Daphne if it was the last thing she did.

CHAPTER EIGHTEEN

Kit could feel her heart pounding in her head. *Thrum, thrum, thrum.* A constant, steady barrage of spears to the middle of her brain that told her Jess was absolutely wrong on this one. Thinking about the past had only left Kit feeling wrung out and defeated. She didn't feel empowered or whatever else her friend expected to happen.

There were a dozen other women out there getting a second chance to do life right, to make a difference, but Kit hadn't managed to give the same to Daphne.

Kit went through her morning routine slowly, letting the steady movements and the calm of habitual patterns ease the pain in her head. By the time she actually made it to the dining hall, the table was already covered in wooden boxes and colored papers. Jess leaned over the shoulders of the boys, directing them which papers needed to be cut into long narrow strips.

Quills of various sizes were scattered across the table, notches cut into their ends to hold the paper strips. Daphne had one of the quills in hand, trying to show Pheobe and Sophie how to slide the paper into the notch and then roll it around the quill until it made a tight paper cylinder that could then be glued onto the box. Sophie was trying to create a coil of her own while Pheobe tried to shove one of the papers up her nose.

The older girls were rather more successful, creating short rolls of paper in sizes varying from a little larger than a pin to nearly half an inch in diameter. Some of the coils were pinched into other shapes before getting glued into the pattern forming on one of the boxes Benedict had crafted.

Kit was distracted from the paper filigree as Lord Wharton walked into the room, a smile on his face. His shirt was badly wrinkled and showing signs of having been worn for days, something a man like him had probably never experienced before. Kit couldn't think of a single article of clothing in the house that she could offer him that would be more comfortable.

Clean clothes were one of the aristocratic luxuries she'd never been able to remove from her life. She washed her shifts with a frequency that would have stunned most of the other women living in the countryside, but she couldn't help it. Just thinking of wearing the same cloth against her skin for that long made her itch.

"What's this?" The man reached over Blake's shoulder and picked up a thin strip of paper the boy had just trimmed off the larger sheet.

"Paper," Arthur piped up.

Lord Wharton grinned. "I see that."

"Boxes," the little boy added.

Lord Wharton nodded gravely, taking a moment to look at the variety of boxes spread along the table: a tea caddy with rotating bins to hold more than one type of tea, a jewelry box with hidden compartments in the back, even a small model of Brighton Palace that contained several drawers and doors. Benedict loved to craft elaborate creations with moving parts and hidden openings. There were several normal boxes on the table as well, all of them just waiting to have the recessed panels filled in by the delicate paper filigree.

"The question is," he said, "what are you doing with the boxes and papers?"

Several children started talking at once. Sarah pulled him down into a chair and shoved a quill into his hand. The feather portion was more than a bit ragged, but the slitted tip was usable.

Watching Lord Wharton try to slide the paper strip into the notch and then wind the paper into a tight coil was almost humorous enough to make Kit forget the tragic past she'd made herself relive the night before.

"I had no idea this was so difficult," Lord Wharton murmured on his third attempt at making a small paper circle.

Eugenia, who was probably the best of the girls at this work, began laying out an elaborate design on the side of one of the boxes, gluing red, brown, and blue paper coils side by side on the box's surface. Kit stepped next to her to assist with the glue, but her gaze kept straying to Lord Wharton. His clumsy attempts were drawing enough notice that the children obviously weren't going to create as many items as normal this morning.

Kit bit her tongue to keep from pointing out that fact, though. After all, wasn't it her drive for more that had sent Daphne to that ball all those years ago? Perhaps if she let life follow its course, tried to enjoy the little moments along the way, it would be better.

Lord Wharton wasn't going to be here forever, and they still had two weeks before

Nash came to pick up their items for market.

Today, she'd let the children smile and wouldn't push.

Maybe Jess's point about learning from the past hadn't been completely wrong.

After two hours of work that had been more fun than it had ever been before, Kit dismissed the children to do their other morning duties so that they could go on the picnic.

No matter what fun outing was planned, there were still goats and chickens to see to, still daily household chores that needed to be done. It was all well and good to say that her focus on goals had ruined Daphne's life, but maybe letting go of that completely wasn't the answer.

Graham had no idea his picnic plan was going to cause such a commotion. Considering that the children spent most of the time outside and saw the lake every single day, a picnic shouldn't have been so exciting. Yet there they were, practically running all over each other as soon as Kit released them from paper-rolling duty.

The table was cleared as the paper and other materials were stashed in a cabinet that stood against one wall in the room.

Then they scattered. Off to the goats and the chickens and whatever other chores had to be done around a house every day. Graham had never really thought through the necessary daily tasks before. He wandered to the kitchen where the women prepared the food.

Daphne lifted a large basket in the air to avoid one of the children as he ran through the kitchen. She was laughing as she set the basket on the large worktable. "They've never moved this fast before."

Jess slid a second basket onto the worktable. "They're afraid it's going to disappear."

The frown on Daphne's face reflected the way Graham felt about the statement. As far as he could tell, the children didn't have much, at least not much by Graham's standards. There were no horses, no tutors, no trunks full of clothing so that ruining shirts and pants weren't a worry. Yes, they had space and toys and food, but they also worked around the manor for most of the day. Was a life like that enough to make them worry that something as simple as a picnic might be too far out of their reach?

"We're not going to let that happen," Daphne said with more conviction than Graham had heard the soft-spoken woman possess in the entire time he'd been at the house. "I don't care if the sky opens up and God tells us to build an ark. We're having a picnic."

One of Jess's eyebrows lifted as she turned from where she was slicing bread at the side table. "If the skies were to open up today, I think it'd be a bit late to start building an ark."

Daphne tried to maintain her indignation, but the trembling pull on one side of her mouth gave her away. "Oh, go slice your finger off."

"Who's slicing a finger off?" Benedict said as he walked into the room to collect a basket to carry.

Graham had finally stopped jolting every time he saw the boy, but he hadn't been able to stop the emotional kick he felt. Was it because Benedict was about to leave the safety of this place?

Daphne smiled. "Jess is."

Benedict snorted. "Not likely. She trimmed the chicken feather off John's boot the other day from twenty paces."

The bundle in Daphne's hands tumbled to the table, and Benedict jerked to catch it. She swallowed hard. "He wasn't wearing them at the time, was he?"

Jess's shoulders shook as she wrapped up the sliced bread. "Yes, Daphne, I've taken to throwing knives at the children now, but only when I find them extremely vexing."

"You throw them at everything else," Daphne grumbled before reaching out and hugging the small blonde as she placed the bread in the basket.

Jess didn't look entirely comfortable with the embrace but leaned her head into it anyway, pulling away as soon as Daphne relaxed her arms.

Something about the interaction reminded Graham of how he and his friends interacted. Without a doubt, if Graham were to say something negative about Jess, Daphne would be the first in line to frown at him.

After Jess threw her knife at him, of course.

Kit charged into the kitchen. "Have we packed a blanket?"

"Yes," Daphne said, patting the basket in Graham's arms. "As well as plates and cups, and everything else."

The assurance of "everything else" didn't stop Kit from running down a list of everything they'd need for the picnic.

Graham held on to whatever they gave him but gave his attention to watching the women. There were secrets here, inside every feminine head, but it was Kit who most fascinated him. He'd never worked so hard to get to know someone in his life, not even when there'd been language barriers during his travels. His biggest effort then was having to find and hire a translator.

Unfortunately, he didn't think Kit interpreters were something that were very easily found.

The last time Graham had gone on a picnic, there'd been tables and chairs, tablecloths, fine china, and a servant making sure no one's wineglass was ever empty.

Even though this one consisted of several blankets spread across a grass carpet, he had to fill his own glass of lemonade, and most of the meal was eaten from whatever could be piled onto a slice of bread, Graham found himself having a better time.

Arranging everyone so that he had a spot beside Kit had been simple. Most of the children were running hoops up and down the glen, pausing to occasionally stop by the blanket and stuff their mouths full of whatever they could reach. Daphne had eaten and then waded into the middle of the fray to make sure no one ran into anyone else. Jess was leaned up against a tree, eyes half closed, as if contemplating taking a nap in the warm afternoon sun.

Graham nudged a tart in Kit's direction.

"Try one. They're delicious."

She picked it up and pulled a small crumb of crust off the edge. "Why were you in the forest two days ago?"

Honestly, he was surprised it had taken this long for her to ask him. As far as he'd been able to tell, there was nothing else out this way other than a few patches of farmland, likely populated by people much too busy to care about the house in the middle of the forest.

He broke off a piece of his own tart, watching her closely to see how she responded to his answer. "I was looking for Henry."

She choked on air as he popped the bite he'd broken off into his mouth, fighting a smile. He loved surprising her. The touch of color that streaked across her cheeks was adorable.

"Henry?" she gasped.

He nodded. "I met a young boy named Daniel in a shop in town. He told me about his friend Henry who lived in the trees on the north side of town." He shrugged. "Curiosity got the best of me."

"Oh Daniel." A small chuckle accompanied the shaking of Kit's head. "And that's all it took for you to strand yourself on the other side of the River Og? Curiosity over the musings of a six-year-old boy?"

"He's six?" Graham asked, avoiding mentioning that he'd been trying to connect the boy's father with the missing Priscilla. "I'd wondered. I haven't spent enough time with children to have much of a guess as to their ages."

"No children of your own?" she asked.

"I'm not married."

She cast a slow glance around the glen at the running, giggling children. "I haven't noticed that stopping everyone."

He didn't want to get pulled back into a discussion about the children. He wanted to know about her. Sadly, he was probably going to have to use the children to do that. He'd like to think that one day soon he wouldn't have to resort to such tactics, but he was running out of *one days*. "How long has Benedict been in your care?"

"Twelve years." She sighed. "He was our first. It's hard to believe that he's practically a man. The master woodworker is a friend of ours. He's helped out at the manor a time or two, so he knows Ben's situation. I trust him, but that doesn't mean I don't worry about what will happen to Benedict when he leaves here."

Twelve years. So Graham had been in school when the boy had been born. And when Kit had started taking care of other people's children.

And that was probably the strangest thing of all. What made a young woman leave society behind and bury herself in the country with children? There wasn't any roundabout way to ask. He peeked at her face, the features relaxed, a soft smile on her lips as if she were happy without even realizing it. "Why do you do it?"

Would she pretend to misunderstand? Give him some sort of vague answer?

"Because I owe it to someone," she said softly. It wasn't what Graham had expected. He had to admit, he'd wondered for a moment if it was possible Benedict was her child, if she'd been forced to run away, but something about that didn't quite sit right with him. She was too strong, too blunt to have fallen into such a situation. Of course, he had no idea what she'd been like thirteen years ago.

"Who?"

Her gaze cut across the glen and then dropped to her half-eaten tart. "It doesn't matter. The only important thing is that I made a mistake, pushed someone into a bad situation, and I had to do whatever I could to rectify it."

The result of the bad situation had to have

been Benedict. This wasn't the sort of endeavor a woman simply took up because she felt like it. "And why do you take in the others?"

She broke off another small crumb but ground the pastry between her fingers until it turned to dust. Her voice was quiet when she finally spoke. "Because my life was already ruined. There wasn't any reason for someone else's to be. I think, on some level, it was what I thought God wanted me to do. That He'd entrusted me with this idea, then this place, then these children. Day by day, He lets us keep doing it, so we do."

What could he possibly say to that? Of all the things, of all the reasons, he hadn't expected that. He'd thought she'd say something noble, something profound, maybe even something biblical since it was obvious that Bible teachings were a frequent part of their life here. But that she had also included the admission that she retreated here to get away from a ruined life, and that she wanted to save other women from a similar fate, knocked his conversation plans askew.

The argument he'd overheard in London, about her promising never to return, suddenly made a bit more sense.

Still, he didn't know what to say. So he

said nothing at all. He could see the tension in her shoulders, could feel her closing him off. If he'd had all the time in the world, he'd have made a joke, put her at ease, but he was leaving soon. If he was going to return to London with his curiosity satisfied enough to get her out of his head, he had to get his answers now. There wouldn't be another chance.

And he really didn't want her plaguing him after he returned home. The few days when he'd known her only as the lady in green had been bad enough. What would it be like now?

"Where'd you get the green dress?"

She looked up from her crumbled tart pastry and then glanced down at her rough blue calico muslin. "What green dress?"

He leaned closer, invading her space the way he had that night at the ball. "The one from the ball."

Her voice chilled, and her eyes dropped away from his. "From an old friend. I wear it to honor her. As a promise. It's needed a few alterations over the years, but I don't wear it often."

Graham tilted his head and looked at her. The dress might not have been hers originally, but there was no question it was hers now. She was the type of woman who would

309

wear green in a ballroom.

The kind of woman he'd been desperately looking for at the ball not so long ago.

He'd never dreamed it would take a friend's family crisis and a flooded river for him to find her.

CHAPTER NINETEEN

Graham felt a little panic and a lot of frustration as Kit's eyes met his and then fell away once more. He knew he was at risk of losing this conversation, of having her join Daphne in whatever game the children were playing now, but he didn't want her to go.

So he changed the subject. "It's beautiful here."

"It is. I still remember the first time I came out here. The idea of Haven Manor was nothing but that. An idea. A desire with no practicality. But this place, it was an answer to all the prayers I hadn't the courage to voice. That first night I sat on the steps up there, staring down at this lake for as long as the moon's reflection could be seen. It seemed so large then, so impossible." She reached out to snag a wayward hoop and send it back toward the playing children. "Now it's home."

So she would talk about now, talk about the children, talk about what he could see with his own eyes. But her past, the details he hadn't learned on his own, those were forbidden.

And those were what he wanted so desperately to learn.

"What's your favorite color?" he asked instead.

She blinked at him. "Green."

Like the dress. Only he wasn't going to mention the dress again. He didn't want her thinking about those things. "Best food you've ever tasted?"

"White soup."

He laughed. White soup was so common to him, it was hard to imagine it being the food that lingered in someone's memory. "Truly?"

She nodded. "I'd never had it before going into London society. But it was served at the first dinner party I went to and I loved it so much that I asked a servant for another bowl of it later in the evening." She smiled, but shadows quickly encroached upon her happy expression.

"Favorite book?"

Her bark of laughter chased the shadows away and made him feel like a conquering hero. "You can't ask a book lover such a question. It's like asking a mother who her favorite child is."

He waggled his eyebrows at her. "Who's your favorite child?"

One side of her mouth lifted in a smirk as she shook her finger in his direction. "I'm not falling for that one, Lord Wharton."

"Call me Graham," he said, surprising himself. "It feels strange being the only one in the house being formally addressed. Why, I don't even know your last name."

The offer felt right. It made them equal, somehow, which hopefully made him a little less intimidating. It was why he, Oliver, and Aaron had decided to go by given names instead of titles. Neither Graham nor Oliver had wanted Aaron feeling like he was less important.

"I'm simply Kit now," she said, instead of giving him the information he'd hoped for. "To everyone."

"Then I insist on being Graham. For you, Daphne, and Jess at least. The children have fallen into calling me Wharton already, which I've no problem with."

She winced. "I should have taken the opportunity to force more lessons on proper address."

He waved his hand. "They'll figure it out. It will be easier to learn when everyone around them is doing the same thing." At least, he hoped it would. Either way, he didn't want them practicing their formality on him.

"I suppose."

Silence fell between them, and Graham wasn't sure what to do with it. Kit pushed up from the blanket and went to join the children before he could come up with another question she would be willing to answer. He loved talking to her, wanted to talk to her more. But what could he do if she refused to tell him things? If she continued to hide everything she was?

But then again, wasn't he doing the same? What had he offered her while he dug for her secrets, while he searched for her vulnerabilities?

Nothing. He'd offered her nothing. Nothing real, anyway. Yes, he'd made her laugh and smile, and he was convinced those were important, but they wouldn't make a woman like her feel like her secrets were safe. He was going to have to give her a piece of himself.

The only question was, what? His life had been easy compared to what he knew of hers. The only secrets he had were the ones relating to Oliver's family, and he couldn't share those until he knew more about them.

And even then, those secrets weren't really his to share.

His life really hadn't been riddled with dark moments. It was something he'd never considered regretting before.

The night slid like a soft blanket over the manor house. Even after more than a dozen years, Kit still marveled at the quiet of the country. Growing up, she'd only known city life, where the nighttime was only a slightly dimmer and quieter version of the daytime.

She smiled. Of course the country hadn't been very quiet this afternoon. They'd have to remember to take picnics more often, or at least take the afternoon to play in the glen.

Of course, next time Lord Wharton — Graham — wouldn't be a part of the festivities. He wouldn't be there to haul the large baskets around, wouldn't be there to chase the children and throw them into the air or show them a better way to climb trees, wouldn't engage her in conversation over an apple tart.

There were men who came to the estate on occasion, a few trusted friends of Nash who brought their plows and donkeys to assist with the spring planting or to help replace the windowpane Blake had accidentally broken with a rounders ball. All of those men were polite to the children they happened to see, but for the most part they came, did their job, and left.

Nash would occasionally interact with the children more, but he never stayed long. He had a family to see to and a business to run, with clients who actually paid him for his services, unlike Haven Manor, which he did for free since he'd been a part of the project from the beginning.

But Graham gave the children attention they didn't know they'd been missing. They clamored for it now.

They still did their chores and tasks, although they'd all discovered how much fun it was to watch Graham bumble his way through a menial task with good-natured laughter over the past two days.

He'd done well enough when it came to hanging out the linens to dry, but folding them had been another situation entirely.

And then there was the time he'd tried to fix the stuck hinge on one of the stable doors and made a complete mess of it. Daphne and the children had fallen over laughing about it while Graham had simply stood there, holding an oil can and talking to it as if the can were at fault. They'd all laughed until they were gasping for breath, tears in their eyes.

But soon he would be leaving.

He knew it, she knew it, and yet, she didn't know how she felt about it. She liked having him here, but his presence was dangerous. He was like having a taste of her old life mixed in with her new one. He made her remember. Not just the bad and horrible circumstances that had fueled her desire to live out here away from everything she'd once known, but the good parts, too, what she'd loved about London and being the daughter of a baron.

His stay was temporary. She was afraid her yearning for what she could no longer have was going to be a bit more permanent.

She stood on the porch, waiting for Jess and Daphne, clutching a mug of tea that was quickly losing its heat to the cool of the night. Before long it wouldn't be worth drinking, though she would anyway. Tea was an indulgence, one she had tried to break herself of many years ago and failed. No matter how cold, she'd finish the cup.

A sip of the still-hot liquid slid down her throat as the door opened behind her.

"Daphne fell asleep putting Sophie to bed," Jess said as she padded quietly across the porch. "I just tucked the blankets around her and left her there."

"I suppose the picnic wore everyone out," Kit said. Her body certainly felt weary, even if her mind wasn't yet ready to succumb to sleep.

She glanced at Jess, who didn't look at all wilted from the day's activities. When did she go to bed? She was always the last of the women to retire yet never seemed to lack for energy during the day.

"It's a pleasant night," the younger woman said, stepping up to Kit's side so that the scent of the ever-present coffee overpowered the subtle aroma of Kit's tea. There was always a pot of the bitter brew simmering on the stove. Sometimes Kit thought the woman must run on coffee and sarcasm. Her quick wit was legendary around the house, though she rarely targeted the children with it. Kit was by far her favorite foil.

"I can see the stars." Kit took another large drink of her tea.

Jess nodded and took a sip of her own drink. "It's not like the city."

One of Kit's hands dropped to her skirt, sliding the folds through her fingers as she contemplated how to phrase her next question. She thought they might be continuing their earlier conversation about facing the past but in some form of code. Jess had been a spy. Wasn't talking in code something they did?

Still, Kit couldn't help but wonder if Jess felt the same way she did sometimes, a little bit trapped by the peace that surrounded them. "Do you miss it? The city?"

A slight shrug of Jess's shoulders seemed to be the only answer Kit was going to get for several moments. Then Jess started speaking. "I learned very young that where I am matters little. When all you want is to survive, the view is the least of your concerns."

Kit didn't know much about Jess before they'd met in a London alley, other than that her life had been rough enough that Jess knew how to save Kit from a group of drunken gentlemen making their way home from their club on St. James's Street. Still, there was a polish about her, a refinedness that spoke of higher birth. "And now?" Kit asked.

Jess looked at Kit over the edge of her mug. "What do you mean?"

"Well, you're safe here now, right?" Kit shifted. Jess was safe here, wasn't she? Yes, she'd been planning on fleeing London when Kit met her, or more accurately, got in a fight with her over whether or not Kit was more than a foolish nitwit of a debutante who should know better than to wander the back alleys near the clubs by herself in the middle of the night. Eventually Jess had offered to teach Kit how to defend herself, and Kit had offered Jess a refuge away from whatever she was running from in London.

Kit had just never had the courage to ask what that something was. Now that she thought about it, though, Jess usually avoided the men from town who occasionally came out to the manor. Kit cleared her throat when Jess didn't answer. "I mean, Nash, Margaretta, and Mrs. Lancaster are the only ones who know you're here."

"And our unexpected guest."

Kit winced. "Yes. But surely he gives you nothing to fear."

Jess eyed her. "There are different kinds of survival, Kit. And while yes, I've spent more than enough time running for my actual life, I've discovered that far more dangerous things exist in this world."

Like looking into one's past. Like learning to live with mistakes. Like waking up every day torn between knowing your friend wouldn't be in this place if not for you, but then again neither would the children.

"Like love," Kit murmured.

Jess smirked. "You fancying yourself infatuated with the gentleman snoring on a pallet in the pantry?"

Kit's eyes widened, and she hoped the darkness hid the sudden heat in her cheeks. "What? No. I meant . . . I meant that love makes us act on or choose what might not seem to be in our best interest, but we do it anyway because we can't help it."

That was what she'd meant, wasn't it? That she'd loved Daphne enough to make sure she didn't suffer the consequences alone? Of course, if she'd loved Daphne more to begin with, none of it would have happened. And a dozen other women and children would have been left to fend for themselves. Kit rubbed a hand over her chest as if that would settle her heartbeat and allow her to pick one single emotion to feel.

But one thing that Jess had forced her to face was that she couldn't keep pretending she'd been dropped down onto the planet at age eighteen with a mission to save the women society would rather discard, the ones with nothing to their credit except a good name and a sterling reputation that, once marred, made them worse than worthless.

Because when she thought about her life that way it seemed so noble.

And Kit was anything but noble.

Jess shrugged. "I suppose that's what I mean. Love is a weakness. It causes us to make foolish choices."

"Is that what we are?" Kit asked with a sideways smile. "A foolish choice? Is staying here a weakness?"

A half-laugh escaped Jess as she looked down into her coffee. When she looked up again, humor was evident in the soft glimmer of moonlight shining on her face. "What makes you think I care one jot about you? Could be it's just a good place to hide."

"Could be," Kit said, trying to match Jess's nonchalance. That had probably been the truth at one point. Once they'd finished yelling at each other in that alleyway, Kit had seen Jess only as a woman in trouble. Perhaps it was the fact that she'd just come from having the father of Pheobe's mother sign the payment contract, but Kit hadn't been able to leave Jess to whatever she was running from. She'd invited Jess to come with her, and they'd both been on the stage out of London within an hour.

But Kit would bet their last shilling that life had changed for the young woman. She'd tried to stay removed from Kit, Daphne, and the children, but even in a house this large it was hard to do. "But I'm not the one who takes the time to remember everyone's favorite dishes and cook them on their birthdays."

"We don't celebrate birthdays," Jess mumbled quietly.

"Which makes it all the more amazing that you make them feel special that day."

A movement to their left had both women falling into silence. A large shadow separated from the side of the house and drifted out toward the walled garden. It was far enough away that Kit knew he hadn't been listening in on their conversation, had in fact probably just exited the kitchen door from that side of the house, but it still made her breath catch and her heart pound against her ribs to know he was out there.

"It would seem someone else is having trouble sleeping," Jess murmured.

Kit lifted her mug and took two long swallows of tea, trying to settle the itch to wander across the damp grass and join him.

"Someone should see what he's up to," Jess continued. "Make sure it truly is midnight wanderings and not something more nefarious."

Kit blinked. More nefarious? Graham? Had Jess met the man? While yes, he'd spent a great deal of time prodding into matters she wished he wouldn't, he seemed much more interested in making them all laugh.

"Like what?"

"He could tamper with the livestock. Muck up the vegetable garden." Her eyes found Kit's. "Perhaps come across a stash of papers hidden beneath the floorboards of the milking stall?"

Tension raced across Kit's shoulders with such speed that she jerked her arms and sent a splash of tea to the stones at her feet. How did Jess know about the papers under the floor in the stable?

"How did you —"

"Kit." There was such derision in the single word that Kit squeezed her eyes shut. Of course Jess had found Kit's stash of insurance.

Jess sipped her coffee. "I found it the second day I was here."

And today was Graham's third. Of course, he wasn't a spy or whatever it was Jess had been. The chances of him finding the loose floorboards were incredibly low.

"I suppose we should walk with him, then," Kit said slowly.

"We?" Jess snorted. "I'm not wearing any shoes."

Kit glanced down, and sure enough, Jess's bare toes peeped out from beneath her skirts. "Why on earth aren't you wearing shoes?"

The tilt of Jess's head suggested Kit was a bit of a simpleton for asking such a question. "Because I want to save you from your boring sacrificial existence and make you go for a walk in the moonlight with a handsome gentleman."

Kit sighed. "Very subtle, Jess."

"Tact takes too long. Besides, I used up all my subtlety talking about the city earlier." She turned back toward the house and waggled her fingers in a little wave. "Have fun!"

Kit spluttered as she watched Jess disappear back into the house. Save her from a boring existence indeed. And sacrificial? Well, how else was she supposed to serve penance for the wrong she'd done to Daphne?

No, Kit didn't need saving from anything except well-to-do gentlemen with nothing to do but snoop. It didn't seem to matter that all Graham was doing right now was walking through a garden. Jess had planted the idea, and now Kit couldn't shake the thought that he was looking for her most secret secrets.

And if he found them, he'd know she had much more to do with his friend's missing sister than she'd let on.

CHAPTER TWENTY

Graham tripped over an uneven spot of ground but caught himself before he sprawled across the damp grass. That's what he got for looking at the sky instead of his feet, but he'd missed looking at the stars. During his travels, the stars had fascinated him.

He'd spent a great deal of time in the country as a boy, and the stars were probably as beautiful from his father's estate in Staffordshire as they were here, but he'd been too young then to appreciate them.

It wasn't until he'd been on a ship in the middle of the ocean that he'd learned to truly appreciate the majesty of the night sky.

A majesty that had been lost to him when he'd returned to London.

"If you keep in that direction you'll run into the wall."

The soft voice was more than enough inducement to pull his gaze from the stars and bring his feet to a halt. A glance revealed that he had been about ten paces from running into the wall, missing the entrance to the garden by a good six feet. "Lucky for me you came along, then."

"Hmm." She kept her slow pace until she'd drawn even with him, stopping at a conversable distance but keeping more than an arm's length of space between them. "Trouble sleeping?"

He laughed. "Believe it or not, I'm not quite accustomed to country hours."

She looked at him quizzically. "You're blaming the hours and not the conditions?"

"It's not the first time I've found a pallet on the floor for the night." He shrugged as if he slept in such minimal conditions on a regular basis. He hadn't. It had only happened twice that he could remember, and he hadn't slept well either time, but he wasn't about to mention that. A glance at her revealed that she didn't believe his nonchalance for a moment.

He cleared his throat and rubbed a hand along the back of his neck. Every muscle in his body was sore from two nights on the kitchen floor, and after the amount of exercise he'd gotten today chasing the children around the glen, he was afraid another night would have him hurting to the point of being unable to move. "I might have been thinking that the straw in the stable might be a little more comfortable."

An adorable wrinkle appeared across the bridge of her nose. "And considerably smellier."

He was finally getting the opportunity to have a truly private conversation with this woman, one where she'd come to him instead of trying to run away, and they were discussing the odors of a barn? Surely he could do better than that.

"I was just admiring your view of the stars. I haven't seen such a clear prospect since I was on a ship in the middle of the ocean."

"We're surrounded by heavy woods on all sides." Her head tilted back to admire the view. It exposed the long, elegant line of her throat, and Graham jerked his gaze back to the stars with an uncomfortable tightness in his chest.

He coughed to ease the constriction. "That would give you an unpolluted view."

Silence fell as they both looked at the sky, lost in their own thoughts. She could stay lost in her thoughts if she wished, but more than anything Graham wanted to be right there with her.

"You can't see the stars in London," he said gently.

When her only response was a broken sigh, he pressed on. "Do you miss the city?"

One shoulder lifted. "Not the city itself so much as —"

She cut off the words abruptly and sank her teeth into her bottom lip. Graham ached to know what she'd been about to say. What did she miss? What did she once have that she no longer did? There was a lot that Graham could give her. Maybe not right this moment because he had little more than a horse and the clothes on his back, but he could return, bring her back the ingredients for white soup or whatever else she missed.

He kept his voice soft as he slid a half step closer. "What do you miss?"

She dropped her eyes from the sky to meet his gaze. The darkness enveloped them until there was nothing else in the world but starlight and the sound of the occasional breeze through the distant trees. Did she feel it? This sense of joining? He'd felt it somewhat in the ballroom, and now it was significantly stronger.

Mystical soul mates and love connections forged through a single glance weren't anything Graham believed in, but he could recognize attraction. And for the first time in his life that attraction was growing the more he got to know the woman in question, instead of waning, suffocated by sheer boredom as the woman turned out to be exactly the same as everyone else.

If that wasn't the beginning of love, what was it? His father had once told him that love was difficult to explain but easy to recognize. Graham wasn't sure that he believed it was easy to recognize — there were too many poets who made a living off the reverse — but he could certainly agree that it was hard to explain. He couldn't explain what he was feeling right now even if he wanted to, and he didn't even think he'd truly fallen in love yet.

Still, he felt a pull to her, a craving to know her, and her past was somehow mixed up in her present.

"Just one thing you miss," he whispered. "One thing you can't find in the beauty of God's countryside."

One side of her mouth lifted in what should have been a smile but somehow ended up looking sad. "I miss dancing."

As soon as the words had crossed her lips, he saw her wince, felt her pull away and tighten her muscles even though her feet didn't move.

"We danced last night," he murmured.

Her laugh was brief, little more than an amused exhale, and she shifted her feet until they pointed back toward the house. "That wasn't dancing. That was chaos."

Desperate to keep her out in the moonlight, Graham placed his hands on his hips and gazed out at the trees surrounding the estate. "Well, given your penchant for dancing with plant life, you have only to step out of your house and find any number of suitable partners."

A short giggle was the reward for his lighthearted comment. When he turned back to her, the sadness still remained on her face but some of the wrinkles had eased from the corners of her eyes. "I'm afraid they're all a bit too tall."

"Ah, yes, the trees would be." Graham made a point of nodding his head in consideration. "The rosebushes are no doubt too thorny and the vines are simply too clingy. All hands, you know."

The giggle that escaped this time was a bit longer, a touch more solid. It made Graham feel like he'd been honored by the Prince himself.

"Have you tried the juniper? I believe I saw some along the wall of the barn. Actually, I've no idea if those shrubs are junipers. That's just the only type of shrub I know the name of."

A full laugh, though short, escaped her,

and Kit's lips curved into a genuine smile. "They're sweetbriars, I'm afraid, and they're rather prone to ripping skirts."

Graham sighed, exaggerating the rise and fall of his shoulders. "I suppose there's nothing for it, then." He swept into a bow worthy of a sixteenth-century courtier. "May I have this dance? A proper one this time, without the children underfoot."

"There's no music." Kit's words were quiet, as if she'd used too much breath to say them and the words hadn't quite known how to form around so much air.

"I'll hum."

He waited, arm extended, until the leg he was bracing most of his weight on threatened to tremble. But then she slowly, ever so slowly, reached out.

His breath stalled in his chest as her slight fingers slid against his. Never would she have accepted his invitation during the day. It was the magic of the night, the beauty of the stars, and the quiet of the hour that allowed him to slip past her defenses.

That or the fact that in another day or two he'd be out of her life. Or so she thought.

Whatever had allowed her to lower her defenses, he'd take it. Without qualm or complaint.

A simple tune vibrated through his chest as he started to hum. In one movement he straightened and pulled her into his arms.

She squealed. "I don't know how to waltz."

It startled him for a moment, the idea that a woman wouldn't know how to waltz, but then it had been many years since she'd moved through society. The last time she'd graced a dance floor, waltzing wouldn't have been considered even remotely proper. "Just hold on to me," he said. "I'll guide you."

Her waist was warm beneath his hand as he pulled her into the proper position. The music paused as he forced himself to swallow so he didn't choke on his own tongue. Then he began to hum again and guided her in a gentle arc across the lawn and into the walled garden.

Here the starlight glimmered over the crushed rock paths and reflected off the shiny leaves of the plants until the area sparkled like a fine ballroom. Still he hummed, though he'd no idea of the tune anymore and was fairly certain he was simply making it up. As he hummed, he guided her, relishing the feel of her in his arms, which he'd wanted since that very first night, but enjoying even more the look of childlike excitement on her face.

They danced until they were dizzy, until they could no longer ignore the prick of rocks under the soles of their shoes, until their breath sawed in their lungs and made it difficult for him to continue humming. He stumbled to a halt, pulling her a bit closer so she wouldn't fall from the unexpected cessation of movement. Her breathing was still rapid and her eyes shone with something he couldn't name, but he knew he wanted to make that look appear on her face again and again.

With a start, he realized he might be seeing happiness. Pure, untainted happiness. Dancing was something she didn't associate with whatever mess was in her life now. He'd been able to give her a little piece of the life she'd had . . . well, before. He still didn't know what had happened to make her leave London, but he was one step closer.

"It's late," she rasped through her calming breathing. "I should go. The children will be up early."

She pulled from his arms, and he immediately felt chilled, as if her delightful presence had been replaced by a block of ice in his hands.

"There are more blankets in the library. In a chest near the window. If you need more for your pallet." She backed two more steps away before turning and fleeing toward the house.

It was a long time before Graham followed.

The house was quiet when Graham rose the next morning. He groaned as he crawled up from his pallet. As predicted, his body was protesting his current conditions rather violently. Every part of him ached.

At least he'd had the sense to move his pallet into the dry goods storage room so that the sun's first rays didn't sear his eyes as soon as he opened them.

Stumbling into the kitchen, he found a note next to a glass jar. The note contained clear instructions for making himself a cup of willow bark tea. He was fairly certain the note had been written by Jess, since next to the line that told him hot water was in a kettle by the smoldering fire were the words *Do try not to burn yourself. We're out of plasters.*

Since he was alone, he didn't try to stop the groans as he went about fixing the tea according to the instructions. He remembered taking willow bark tea before when he'd had a headache or other pains. Hopefully, a cup or two of this and he'd be able to move without sounding like a carriage on gravel roads.

He should probably ride out to check the bridge today. Even if the water hadn't receded completely down to normal levels, it was likely crossable. But after last night, he really didn't want to leave. Not yet. And if he checked the bridge and found it passable, he had no excuse to stay.

No solution had come to mind by the time he was staring into the bottom of his second cup of tea. No noise had come his way either. Where was everyone?

The tea was still working its magic, but he wasn't going to wait around for it to finish. He could possibly find enough excuses to stay at the house today, but there'd be none tomorrow. And he wasn't going to waste his day sitting alone in the kitchen. So he pulled himself up the stairs, gritting his teeth against the urge to complain about the movement.

The main floor was quiet as well. On the first floor, though, he heard . . . singing?

He paused at the bottom of the stairs. He'd never been to the upper floors. Of all his different tasks, none of them had involved climbing these stairs.

But, as was becoming increasingly common for him, curiosity won out and he gritted his teeth to climb another flight.

At the top of the stairs, he found himself in a square upper gallery with three doors exiting from it. He poked his head in the first one and found a room lined with small beds in the style normally found in servants' chambers. Six narrow beds, three sticking out from each wall, practically filled the room.

An open door beyond the beds showed another two beds and a wardrobe.

As interesting as the room was, though, the sounds weren't coming from there.

Across the gallery, another door stood open, revealing another room full of beds, but on the third wall, a set of double doors stood closed, muffling the singing. Graham moved toward them slowly, making out words as he got closer.

"Other refuge have I none, hangs my helpless soul on Thee."

He opened the door quietly and slid into a room as large and square as the main hall below but not as tall. Rows of wooden benches faced an elaborate set of statues and carvings situated in front of a wooden table draped in embroidered cloth.

A chapel. That was actually being used.

Graham slid into the room and eased the door shut.

"Leave, ah! Leave me not alone, still support and comfort me."

He sat in the back, slumping down to avoid as much notice as possible while the children and women sang. Was it Sunday? He didn't think so, but he'd rather lost track of reality as one day blended into the next in this little bubble in the forest. But there was apparently a service going on this morning, so he could pretend it was Sunday, which would provide him all the excuse he needed not to leave.

The delay of his impending departure allowed him to fully appreciate the scene in front of him. Everyone was crowded into the first two rows of benches while Daphne faced them in a straight-backed wooden chair, looking down at a small brown book.

Sitting up a little higher, he saw several similar books scattered among the children.

Hearing them sing about Jesus with such emotion and passion made him wonder if he'd been missing something in all the years he'd sat in the pews of ornate churches and listened to the most esteemed preachers and rectors. He'd heard similar singing when he'd gone through Africa, but never could he recall hearing such a sound in England. It was beautiful.

As the song finished, he sought out Kit

among the children and found her sitting at the far end of the second row, staring straight back at him, a look of worry on her face.

Did she think he was going to stop them? Call it blasphemous that they were essentially holding a church service in their own home?

He wasn't. He might think it strange, but what about this visit hadn't been strange?

His limits were tested, though, when Daphne set the songbook aside and opened a Bible to begin teaching the story of Ruth.

Graham had attended church for as long as he could remember, had been told the importance of faith and God since he'd been born, but never had he sat and listened to a woman teach.

But as Daphne told the story of a woman who left everything behind to care for and support her mother-in-law, Graham was enthralled. He'd heard the story before, had even read it for himself at some point, but hearing it from the lips of a woman who actually had left her own life behind to care for these children brought new meaning to the words.

Geoffrey slid out of the pew and toddled in Daphne's direction. Without missing a word, she moved the Bible to one leg and scooped the child up onto the other one.

"Mama Daffy," the little boy said, head tilted up so his brown curls tumbled back off his face. "Are you my kinsman deemer?"

Daphne laughed and explained to the child that a kinsman redeemer was something they did a long time ago, but now it was the job of all God's people to care for one another. "And that is why I am here to care for you."

Graham looked at Kit in time to see her reach up and wipe her cheek.

It was obvious now why the children sprinkled Bible stories into their conversations, why they found it so easy to talk of subjects he'd once thought reserved for church.

Even Kit had made mention of God's provision with ease. But now she looked like she'd rather be anywhere but here, listening to a story of sacrifice and redemption.

Soon Daphne was asking Benedict to pray and the children ran off to their respective jobs, charging out of the chapel with the same enthusiasm he'd seen them use with everything else.

None of them left the room faster than Kit did, though.

She was scared — that much was obvious

— but of what he didn't know. And he was running out of time to find out.

CHAPTER TWENTY-ONE

"You're avoiding me."

Kit looked up from the chickens she'd claimed needed to be checked on. As if chickens needed supervision in the middle of the day when they'd already been fed and the eggs had already been collected.

Thinking of eggs made her smile. While Graham was right in that she had been avoiding him since she'd seen him in the chapel, she'd always known where he was.

From the dining room window she'd watched as he tried to help the children collect the eggs. He'd sent chickens scattering across the small, fenced-off poultry yard until the children had shown him the hinged nesting box Benedict had designed.

The birds had all settled since then, happily pecking and scratching at the ground within their fenced area, in no need of anything from Kit. Yet she stayed. It had been an excuse to come outside when he'd ventured back into the house.

And he knew it.

That didn't mean she had to actually admit it, though. "I don't know what you mean."

"Really?"

She glanced up to find his eyes opened comically wide while his mouth dropped open in exaggerated shock. The urge to smile hit her, and she forced her gaze back to the strutting chickens.

"I'd have thought," he continued, "with all that reading that you reportedly do, *avoid* would have been a word you would've come across already."

Laughter threatened, and she bit her lip to keep it in, trying to push herself closer to annoyance. "I know what the word means. It simply doesn't apply in this case."

"Ah." He strolled closer until he was shoulder to shoulder with her, looking down at the chickens scratching happily in the dirt. "They look to be in fine shape."

She couldn't suppress the smile this time. "And what do you know of chickens?"

He rubbed the back of his hand. "That their aim is impeccable." He dropped his hand and gave her a boyish grin. "And that their eggs make for a marvelous addition to breakfast." He turned toward her. "Why don't we go for a walk?"

"Why?" Surprise had her swinging side-ways until she was facing him, looking up at him, too close to him. As close as she'd been last night, only this time she couldn't blame moonlight and lack of sleep. Well, she could probably still blame lack of sleep. Even after she'd found her bed, she hadn't slept much.

"Because" — his voice held a slight roughness that raked over her skin, leaving tiny bumps in its wake — "in my world that's what a man does when he wants to know a woman better. They sip tea in the parlor, dance in the ballroom, and take a walk through the park. As I've already dined at your table and waltzed through your garden, a walk is the last weapon left in my arsenal."

Kit curled her lips between her teeth to keep from laughing. Why was she always wanting to laugh around this man? What was it that seemed to make her giddy, like a woman at least a decade younger than she was? "An arsenal, is it? Am I under attack?"

"Yes," he answered without hesitation.

Then he offered her his arm in a move she hadn't seen directed toward her in many years. There'd been a time when she ex-pected to go nearly everywhere with her hand tucked delicately in the crook of a gentleman's elbow. That had been long ago, and since then she'd had to depend only on herself for balance and security.

It was tempting to link her arm with his, but the man would be leaving. Tomorrow. Maybe even today. It was possible he could have left yesterday, but he hadn't gone back to check the bridge since that first day. Neither had she.

It was ridiculous. They were only delaying the inevitable.

By this time tomorrow, he would be out of her life. Perhaps there was some safety in that. Perhaps she could indulge herself just a little, walk with this man, talk and get to know each other as adults. She was already going to miss him when he returned to London. What was one more memory?

She would walk. But she wouldn't take his arm. It was a compromise with herself that allowed her to do something she knew to be foolish.

She linked her hands together at the small of her back and stepped past his arm and toward the wild, overgrown part of the estate's parkland. "There are some interesting views along the lake on the side opposite the glen. The former owner built a grotto on one side. It's quite remarkable."

He fell into step next to her. "A grotto?"

Kit nodded. "It's a strange little rock cave

tucked into the side of the woods, but I'm intrigued by it. Every time I go I wonder about the person who would commission such a thing."

"Does the current owner like it?"

Kit pursed her lips together in thought. "I don't think he's ever seen it. Rumor is, he won the estate in a card game and then forgot about it completely."

"Ah."

The drawn-out sound of understanding made Kit look up at him. "What do you mean, *ah*?"

"He doesn't know about the children."

Kit looked away from his knowing eyes. No, the owner didn't know about the children, didn't even know the women were the ones taking care of the house. Nash was the official caretaker on paper.

"How is it," Graham said slowly, "that three women come to raise a passel of children out in the middle of the countryside?"

"Good fortune?" she mumbled. They'd been building to this question with every conversation they'd had over the past few days. Now that he was leaving, he must have decided to push the subject since he wasn't going to get another chance. He knew bits and pieces, knew she didn't come from the type of life she was now living.

Tucked away as they were in the country, neither she nor Daphne had ever bothered to change their mannerisms or ways of talking to match that of the surrounding countryside. It had turned out to have a rather nice benefit in that all of the children sounded a bit more refined than the other village children. That would serve them well when they set out to work for a living.

He could come to those conclusions on his own, probably already had. It was something more that he wanted to know, the deeper questions that didn't quite make sense.

Silence fell as they walked. Kit watched her toes appear and disappear from beneath her skirts. Could she redirect the conversation like she had before? Now that he'd had the courage to bring it up, would he be willing to let the topic drop? Probably not. But that didn't mean she had to answer.

But then he redirected the conversation himself. "Where did you grow up? I know you're from London, at least partially, but what part?"

Was that what he wanted to know? How far from grace she'd fallen? How much would she have to tell him before he filled in the holes in her story? He'd have been at school when everything happened, when the gossip had flown around Town like the Tower of London ravens, proclaiming a death sentence on her social aspirations. But that didn't mean the stories hadn't lingered.

"My father lived in Paddington. What about you? Where did you grow up?"

"Mostly Grandridge Hall in Staffordshire. Then Harrow and Cambridge before doing a bit of traveling."

Based on his plethora of stories the other day in the library, *a bit of traveling* was not an apt description, but she forgave him the understatement.

They left behind the maintained areas of the grounds and entered the barely discernible path through the woods. Flowers and vines that had been left to their own devices bloomed around them, creating a glorious arch in a riot of color. Their sweet scent filled Kit's lungs, bringing her a measure of peace.

As much as she missed the life of the city, she also loved the peace of nature. It had been too long since she'd walked these woods just for pleasure. It had even been a long time since she'd visited her favorite tree. She'd forgotten how getting away from the house restored a measure of precious sanity.

This was a bad idea. She could already feel her guard lowering as her heart seemed to slow to a sluggish, peaceful beat. Her blood lazed through her veins until all she wanted was to find a patch of grass and rest like she'd done at the picnic. Had it really only been yesterday?

Graham kept talking about other things, like his favorite places in London. Had the Egyptian Hall been there when she'd lived in London? Had she ever eaten ices at Gunter's? Did she know that eating the head off a rose in the garden did not taste the same as eating a rose-flavored ice?

The picture of a small boy eating a rose after trying an ice made her laugh. She couldn't resist asking about it. "How old were you?"

He grinned. "Nineteen."

She laughed and couldn't find the way to shut her mouth once more. She gave in to the urge to talk and remember, unable to deny herself these last few moments before her life went back to the way it had been. Had it been a mere three days ago that her routine was solid and predictable? And now here she was going for a stroll when she should be buried in other tasks back at the house.

The trail broke out of the trees into a

clearing beside the lake, revealing the rough sides of the grotto. With a laugh, Graham jogged the last few paces to run his hand along the bumps and dips of the side. "This is amazing."

They explored the grotto, but it was too dark to see much. On a cloudless day in the midafternoon, the light would stream through the openings in the grotto, making it easy to see around. But all too soon they were back in the foliage, making their way toward the house. Kit found herself slowing her pace further, not wanting to return to the practicalities and the endless stress, the worry and constant need for vigilance.

"How did you end up here, Kit?" Graham asked softly.

Kit swallowed, knowing he wasn't going to give up the question this time, and it would either be answer or send him away with a fight. "Lord Wharton —"

"I thought we agreed you would call me Graham." He slid a hand across the back of his neck. "I'm sleeping on the floor of your kitchen, after all."

"Graham," Kit said with a small smile. She took a deep breath and decided not to insult his intelligence by skipping out on his question. She trusted Graham. She had no worries about what would happen when he finally left Haven Manor and returned to the real world. He would keep their secrets, keep them safe.

She took a deep breath and blew it out before answering. "Life doesn't always take the paths you think it will."

He sent her an inquisitive look but said nothing as they strolled forward.

"I thought my life would be fairly simple. Take my bows in society, find a suitable husband, have children, and raise them to take the same path I did."

"And what happened?"

Kit swallowed. This was the hardest part. The part she relived in nightmares, the reason she worked herself to exhaustion in the hopes that she'd be too tired to see the one time in her life that Daphne's face hadn't worn a sweet smile. "The man I chose wasn't suitable."

Graham's heart threatened to explode, but he forced himself to breathe easily and keep moving. There were so many implications to her statement, but he didn't want to draw the wrong conclusions. "Did you marry him?"

"No." She shook her head, and a few tendrils of hair escaped from the tight chignon at the base of her neck. One hand lifted to tuck the strands behind her ear, and her blue gaze drifted up to meet his for only a moment. "He wasn't actually interested in getting married."

"What was he interested in?" Graham considered all the men he knew, the nefarious and the less-than-honorable. What drove them? Power. Revenge. A ridiculous need to prove to themselves that they were better than someone else. What had been the reasoning of the man who'd sent Kit into exile?

"I don't know. Not really." She sighed. "Status? Notoriety? He wasn't in line to inherit anything of note and that made him unimportant to a lot of people."

The way she was dragging this story out was killing him, leaving him to guess and suppose and come to conclusions that left him horrified and wanting to run back to London and punch someone. He suddenly hated that he'd waited until the last possible moment to push for this answer. He was ripping down her walls and then he'd be leaving. He had to. He'd left Oliver in Marlborough with nothing but a note that he was going for a ride in the countryside. And there was still Priscilla to consider. He couldn't simply ignore that problem.

But he also couldn't leave without knowing what had happened. "Kit." He stopped and turned her to face him, leaving his hands clasped on her shoulders and lowering his face until he looked her in the eye. "What happened?"

"Daphne was ruined," she whispered.

Graham almost let her go, because bringing Daphne into the story had surprised him more than anything. It was hard to imagine Daphne getting into that sort of circumstance, but what did her apparent indiscretion have to do with Kit's choice of potential husband?

Kit swallowed, her throat jerking with the motion. "He thought she was me."

The story spilled out of her in half-formed sentences and words that ran together until they were as difficult to decipher as little Geoffrey's. He had a feeling she'd never told this story before, and as difficult as it was to decipher, he was fairly certain he got the idea.

"He seduced her?" Graham asked as his brain tried to fill in the pieces Kit was leaving out. *Dear God, please let her have been seduced.* The alternative made his stomach clench.

"Yes. She'd never gotten much attention before, didn't really know what was happening until it was all over. But everyone thought she was me. Everyone."

"The man?"

She nodded. "And the people who saw them kissing through the window and then sneaking out of the ball together. He'd planned it all. Intended to ruin me. I don't know if he hated my father or simply hated the fact that the daughter of a baron was getting so much attention. The girl he married soon after despised me, so maybe he did it out of some twisted form of caring for her. His motive doesn't really matter. The fact is that he planned to ruin my life. And he succeeded."

He noted her little slip in letting him know that she was the daughter of a baron. The confrontation in the parlor at the ball made more sense now, but he didn't care who her father was at the moment. What mattered was that she finish the story so the horrid knot in his throat could loosen, so he could try to find a way to right what had obviously been a horrible wrong.

"Gossip doesn't last forever." Graham slid one hand from her shoulder and cupped her cheek, catching a lone tear on his thumb as it slid down her face. She looked pale, fragile. As if acknowledging the past was going to be the one thing that could finally break her indomitable spirit.

"No." The word rasped out of her throat. "But children do."

Graham swallowed. Benedict. It should have been obvious, of course. Benedict was the first, he was the one who had started it all. Of course he would belong to one of the women.

Kit's shoulder shuddered beneath Graham's palm, and the tears came faster, along with shaky hitches in her breathing. "Daphne had nothing. Nowhere to go, no one to help her, and all of it was my fault." She fell into near sobs. "She didn't want to go that night and I made her. I sent her in my place because I didn't want anyone to gain something I wanted for myself. I destroyed her."

Graham's chest hurt. Physically hurt as he listened to her pour out years' worth of feelings. He was afraid to move, afraid to even breathe in case he stopped her. Somehow he knew that once she rebuilt that wall, he'd never find his way over it again. And she would rebuild it. Because he wouldn't be here to stop her.

"I remember the day she came to me. Daphne is always joyful, always smiles. But that day she was crying. She was scared. She didn't know what to do. Her father was livid. They didn't have the money to convince a man to marry her in her condition, and no one would believe it if she went to the child's father, so she came to me. I knew she was my responsibility then. It was my fault she was in this situation, my fault that her life was ruined."

Graham couldn't be silent anymore. "No, Kit, no."

"Yes. She was there because of me. He targeted her because of me. When Daphne came to me, my father was already acting as if I didn't exist, afraid of what it would do to his fledgling connections, so I convinced him to give me my dowry and I would disappear. Then Daphne and I ran."

"And you ended up here." Graham didn't know the rest of the story, how Jess and Mr. Banfield fit into the whole thing, but he was willing to bet that every last child in that house had come from a mother in as desperate a situation as Daphne. A mother with nowhere to go, nowhere to turn, riddled with the judgment and gossip that only the most powerful in England could dole out.

How many times had he heard the whispered stories and inwardly chided the women for allowing themselves to get in such a situation? How often had he shaken his head, shrugged his shoulders, and said they had to live with the consequences of their actions? Suddenly, when it was personal, when he really knew the people involved, it didn't seem so simple.

"Lord Whar—" She cleared her throat. "Graham. I hope I don't need to tell you how important it is to keep this quiet. Secret. These children . . . their very existence could ruin their mothers."

Their mothers. Not the fathers. The so-called gentlemen who had played a part in the creation of tiny human beings would suffer little to no consequences.

The women were another matter and she was right to be worried about them. It wasn't unheard of for an aristocrat's illegitimate child to take a certain place in society. People like Graham's friend Aaron. But Graham had never considered the mothers. Now that he did, shame on behalf of his peers and himself washed over him.

She took a shaky breath and swiped at her damp cheeks. "It's not just the children. Nash has put himself in danger as well. And his family. His wife . . . she was the first woman we were going to help, but she married Nash instead. When he was put in charge of finding a caretaker for the house, he made sure the owner had little to no interest in it. It wasn't in good enough condition to sell, and the owner didn't want

357

to put the work in. He just needed someone to make sure it didn't get any worse."

It bothered him that another man's name rolled off her tongue so easily when she'd stumbled over his, but Graham pushed past it and focused on what she was telling him. The image she created brought a small smile to the edge of his lips. "And he thought three women and some children were up to the task?"

"We were only two women and one child at the time, but yes. If word got out, though . . ."

She trailed off but didn't need to finish the sentence. Mr. Banfield's professional reputation would be in tatters if it became known that he was allowing so many people to live in a house entrusted to his care.

He focused on the woman before him, her strength, her character. She'd been beautiful to him before, but now he was enraptured. He saw her story differently than she did, and suddenly all he wanted was to make her see it that way, too.

"You are," he said slowly, "the most amazing woman I've ever met."

Her eyes lifted to his, water still pooled along the lashes. "Didn't you hear anything I just said?"

He nodded. "Yes. I heard the story of a

woman who wouldn't leave her friend's side, who sacrificed her future to throw their lots together. A woman like Ruth."

More tears spilled down her cheeks, and he gently caught them with his thumbs. "I heard the story of a woman who looked at life and decided that others deserved a second chance and didn't have to meet the same fate. I don't know the particulars of what you're doing here, but I can guess, and what I see can't have been easy. Never mind the fact that you're running an estate that would normally require a staff of at least thirty people."

She sniffled. "We've let a few things slide."

He grinned at her. He couldn't help it. "I am in awe of you, Kit."

There was so much more he wanted to say, so much more he wanted her to realize, but the words failed him. He looked down into her blue eyes and none of his thoughts could solidify into words.

So he told her how special she was in the only other way he knew how.

He dropped his lips lightly to hers. As the softness of her lips touched his, clarity flew through his mind. This kiss was an assurance that she was still a beautiful, desirable woman, that time and circumstances had not stolen that away from her. It was a promise that he saw her as more, that he wouldn't forget her when he rode Dogberry back into town.

Perhaps it was even a suggestion of what was to come, a promise that he would return. Because he wanted to. Here, in her, he'd found everything he hadn't even known he'd been searching for. God had put her in that ballroom to start him on this journey, and he didn't think he could go back to seeing life the way he used to.

He didn't even want to.

Very aware of the story she'd just shared, he kept the kiss light, a mere press of lips to lips, even as his heart rioted for more. His arms ached to circle her and pull her close, but he made his hands stay on her shoulders even if he couldn't stop his fingers from tightening.

Her sigh drifted across his lips, and he drank it in, tasting the tears she'd cried.

As their lips pulled apart, he rested his forehead against hers. His breathing was rough and harsh, as if he'd been running across the countryside. They touched nowhere except his hands on her shoulders and his head against hers, but he felt her in every pore of his body. She was a part of him now. He didn't know what the future held, but knowing her was going to change everything he did for the rest of his life.

"Why did you do that?" she whispered.

He swallowed. "Because you needed to know how special you are and I couldn't find the words. I still can't. But you had to know, I had to show you, how utterly captivating you are."

His eyelids fluttered open to find her staring at him, her face so close he could see the way her eyelashes clung together in wet spikes, the redness that rimmed the whites of her eyes, and irises such a beautiful expanse of blue that he'd never be able to see a cloudless sky again and not think of this moment.

"Thank you."

He'd been bracing himself for her to argue, restate again all the reasons she was at fault for what had happened to Daphne. Her simple gratitude left him at a loss.

She went up on her tiptoes and brushed her lips against his once more in a fleeting kiss that rocked him to his core. "You're special, too. I've never met a man like you, Graham."

Then she stepped back, forcing him to slide his hands from her shoulders. He searched her face, trying to decide if the small smile that curved her lips was one of resigned sadness or the beginning of healing, but before he could determine which it was, she turned and walked up the path with the quick, confident strides he'd become accustomed to seeing as she walked around the estate.

Just like the night before, she left him devastated, unsure of what to do next. And just like the night before, it was a long time before he followed her.

When he did, she was nowhere to be found. And as Graham looked around at the faces he encountered upon his return to the house, he knew that it was time.

It was time to go, at least for now, because suddenly he didn't know who he was anymore. And if he was going to make a difference here, if he was going to come back — no, *when* he came back — he needed to do so with assurance that he was doing what was right.

He put his flimsy excuses aside and saddled Dogberry slowly, hoping she'd come out as everyone else had to say good-bye. But she didn't. And soon he was riding out, but he couldn't stop himself from looking back.

CHAPTER TWENTY-TWO

He was gone.

She'd watched from the window in the girls' bedchamber as he'd ridden away with waves and hugs for all the children. He'd looked around, obviously noticing her absence, but she couldn't go down there, couldn't let them see how much his leaving hurt.

Not that he could have stayed. She knew that.

But she missed him already.

When she regained her composure and went downstairs, it was obvious that his departure had left a pall over the entire house. Everyone moved a bit slower for the afternoon, but soon routine won over the sadness and by the time they sat down to dinner, life had returned mostly to normal.

For everyone except Kit.

"Mama Kit?"

Kit blinked down at the food on her plate

before looking up at Sarah. "Yes?"

"I called your name four times. Are you well?"

Kit forced herself to smile. "Yes, of course. Just thinking. Did you finish changing the linens in the bedchambers today?"

Conversation fell back into its normal channels: discussing the daily tasks, telling funny animal stories, and trying to understand what Geoffrey was saying.

For Kit, the evening routine wasn't any better than the afternoon had been. Somehow, Graham had insinuated himself into every part of the manor, and she saw reminders everywhere that made her think of him. She felt his kiss on her lips every time she swallowed.

This wasn't any way to live her life if she wanted to move on.

So she grabbed a book from the library and slipped out the glass doors, careful to skirt far around the walled garden so none of the children working in the outbuildings or the stable yard would see her slipping away as the sun slid down the sky.

Not that any of them would say anything. Daphne and Jess were often after Kit to take more time for herself, telling her that constantly pushing herself was going to break her one day.

The truth was, though, that Kit didn't particularly like being by herself. When she was by herself, nothing was loud enough to drown out the voices of worry and guilt that plagued her endlessly. Laughter drifted over the garden wall as Kit passed the corner. Daggers of pain stabbed her heart even as the children's happiness soothed her like a balm. The constant emotional battle was one she'd become accustomed to most of the time.

Today, it felt like it was ripping her apart. The craving for what might have been clashed against the guilt for what she'd torn apart and the anger over the betrayal of the people who were supposed to protect her.

She hugged the book tighter, desperate to escape into another world.

The loud gurgling of the rushing brook announced that she was getting closer to her favorite spot. The tree trunks thickened and the carpet of plants and flowers beneath her feet thinned until she was treading on small sticks and pebbles, the ground too shielded by the canopy of intertwined limbs to grow much.

And then she was there. Her secret tree. Although apparently it wasn't as secret as she once thought. A small circle of light where the sun slid through a break in the forest roof. A patch of flowers that surrounded a tree that had grown at a peculiar angle out of the steep bank, jutting out and then curving up toward the sun, creating a perfect reading nook. Like a magical boat that would carry Kit away from real life.

It took a few wiggles and a good deal of skirt adjustment, but in moments she was settled into her personal hideaway, opening the book and drifting away.

But she didn't drift far. The hero's golden-brown locks darkened in her mind until his hair was nearly black and a bit too mussed to be fashionable. She saw golden-brown eyes and a mouth that looked constantly on the verge of a smile, even though the character's face was not described in such detail.

She slammed the book shut and rested her head against the tree. Yes, she'd spent her entire adult life exposed to the worst of London's elite. Men who claimed the title of *gentleman* only when it suited them. Fathers who thought more about their reputation and ability to use their daughter's hand in marriage as a bargaining tool than they cared about her health and happiness. A society that would trample in the dust anyone who didn't conform to their expectations and leave them there to die, possibly quite literally.

There was no question that it had made her a bit jaded, convinced her that the entirety of the aristocratic world was corrupt and horrible.

And then Graham came along.

He'd abandoned London in the height of the Season to help a friend. A friend who was apparently consumed with more concern for his sister's well-being than he was for the reputation of his family or his own amusements.

She wished she'd had the opportunity to know more men like that. It was nice to know, however, that the upper echelon of her country wasn't a complete waste of breath, that some of them were good and noble as they were supposed to be.

Yes, it was nice to know. But it hurt, too. It hurt because she would never have anything to do with the good people, the upright people. They didn't need her help or require her manipulation.

She didn't deserve to be among them anyway. She deserved to be in the shadows, cleaning up life for other people. If it hadn't been for her, Daphne would have been a nice squire's wife by now. Possibly even the wife of a clergyman. She'd be quiet and respectable, spreading her good nature to her neighbors and a houseful of children she could actually claim as her own. Instead, she was here in the backwoods of a small English town, pretending her child was just like all the others so he wouldn't feel different.

This was what Jess had been driving at. Kit may have made herself remember, but she hadn't let herself feel, hadn't let herself embrace the memories. She'd viewed them from a distance, as if they'd happened to someone else.

But now she couldn't stop them. Everything flooded her brain at once, and it felt like all of it had happened yesterday. The ball, Daphne's revelation, Graham's kiss, all of it piled into one emotional mass. It had been years since she'd let herself cry, but since Graham's arrival, the tears had pooled in her eyes as easily as laughter had come to her lips.

Salty drops of emotion spilled over her lashes for the second time that day and she couldn't do anything to stop them.

So she sat in the tree. And sobbed.

Oliver was sitting in the inn's taproom, staring into the fire and sipping on a mug of ale when Graham returned. Stopping in the doorway, Graham took a minute to compose his thoughts. What was he going to say to

Oliver? Graham had never kept a secret before, at least not a big one. He'd have to find a way to tell Oliver where he'd been for the past several days without speaking about Haven Manor, Kit, or anything else he'd actually done.

Given the current mess his thoughts and emotions were in, that was going to be a tall order.

Oliver's eyes widened when Graham stepped into his line of vision. "What happened to you? You've been gone so long I expected you decided to make the jaunt out to the white horse in Pitstone, but why take such a long journey without a change of clothes?"

Graham grimaced. Oliver didn't know the half of it. The jacket and waistcoat that he hadn't worn in the country were covering the griminess of his shirt. A bath and change of clothing were going to be his next order of business. "I thought I was just going on a ride through the countryside. The rain trapped me on the other side of the river."

They'd traveled enough that Oliver accepted that explanation without issue. Weather had hindered them more than once. He grinned over his mug of ale. "Farmer's hayloft?"

"Kitchen pallet."

Oliver winced. "For three nights? And you're still walking?"

"I'll be happy to see my bed tonight." He'd be even happier to have a bath.

"I suppose it doesn't matter much that you didn't go out to Pitstone. It's probably as much of a wild goose chase as the carvings in Pewsey and Westbury were." He offered his mug to Graham. "I'm not holding out much hope for the market tomorrow either. When I wasn't riding out to neighboring towns, I walked this one end to end. There's nothing. The solicitor is incredibly boring and annoyingly upstanding, with the exception of the chess set contract, which I can't even really blame him for. If someone's idiotic enough to sign that thing, they deserve to be fleeced."

The solicitor was craftier than Oliver knew, but Graham couldn't say anything without endangering Kit.

Being an open and honest person was certainly an easier life.

He drank the rest of Oliver's ale while the man shared everything he'd done over the past few days. Graham listened with half of his attention. The rest of his mind was mulling over the chess contracts. How did the solicitor find time to handle Haven Manor, the strange chess pieces, and his normal clients? Or was everything more connected than he'd thought?

The chess pieces had rather slipped his mind while he was at Haven Manor. It had been difficult enough to keep remembering he was supposed to be helping Oliver and Priscilla. Did Kit know Mr. Banfield was involved in getting people to pay exorbitant amounts for simple chess pieces? He wanted to throw the mug in frustration. He was missing something, but he felt like he was missing something that he already knew. He just couldn't quite solidify it into an actual thought.

"We'll leave for London on Monday," Oliver said with a sigh. "Maybe Father will be more amenable to talking since a few weeks will have passed."

Graham nodded, because there was nothing else he could do. As much as he'd like to talk to the solicitor again, he could hardly tell the other man he knew about Haven Manor. Especially since Oliver wasn't likely to let him talk to Mr. Banfield alone.

The bath and clean clothing felt as rejuvenating as Graham had expected and the night's sleep in a bed even better.

Still, he wrestled with the idea that he knew something. Never before had he felt like he didn't know his own mind.

■ ■ ■ ■

Overnight, the sleepy little town erupted. Oliver and Graham stepped out of the inn and into the colorful, noisy world of Marlborough's market.

They strolled among the selling stalls and crowds of people on High Street, looking for, though not really expecting to find, a clue as to Priscilla's whereabouts. Graham really wasn't sure what such a clue would look like unless they stumbled across Priscilla herself. And if she'd gone into hiding, she was smart enough not to come out on market day.

Graham stopped at a stall displaying boxes covered with paper filigree. Colors and patterns he recognized spread out across the table before him on tea boxes, jewelry trays, and even a chipboard reticule. One box was angled to display a hidden compartment in the back, very similar to the ones the children had been working to cover a few days ago.

He resisted the urge to buy the entire lot.

Oliver looked over Graham's shoulder. "Are you planning on buying something for your mother?"

"Yes," Graham said, partly because he

needed an excuse after being found gawking over the boxes, but mostly because it would at least give him a reason to buy one, to support the children in some small way.

He chose a tea caddy with a large flower on the front and swirling leaves extending out across the sides. The exposed wood was pale gold in color and the flower seemed to grow from within the little box. Which child had made the design? Eugenia? She'd certainly had a flair for laying the swirls and loops just right.

"That's a fine one."

Graham looked up into the smiling face of the old woman who ran the store where he'd met Daniel. Graham cleared his throat. "Yes, it is."

She named him a price, and Graham handed her a few coins that more than covered the number she listed. "Make sure the artist gets a little something extra," he said quietly. "Maybe a box of those chocolate diablotins I saw on the shelf in your store."

The old woman's eyes widened and her smile fell a bit. Her composure recovered quickly and the smile righted itself. "I'll see to it."

He nodded and tucked the tea caddy

under his arm before walking through the rest of the market.

Oliver was almost as anxious to return to London as he'd been to leave it. Then again, Oliver threw himself headlong into everything he did so it wasn't a complete surprise.

His energy had an edge to it, though, that worried Graham. A desperation. He wouldn't have understood it before, but he thought maybe he did now. He found himself fretting over what would happen to the children as they got older, particularly Benedict and Sarah.

And their future wasn't as questionable or imminent as Priscilla's possibly was.

Graham's view of nearly everything had changed.

When he arrived home, he was met by a servant who took Dogberry to the mews, where the horse was competently brushed, fed, and cared for. Never before had Graham considered where the people performing those tasks had come from or the amount of work they put into having his horse healthy and ready whenever he wanted to ride.

When he strode into the house, he was met by another servant who took his hat and luggage and promised a hot bath and tea tray would be delivered to his room shortly.

In his room was a perfectly tucked feather mattress on a perfectly strung bedframe. There would be water for a bath and delicious food that he'd more than taken for granted.

With his every need and comfort seen to, he should have finally been able to get a good night's sleep.

But he didn't.

Even when he'd returned from his unorthodox travels, he hadn't been this aware of every benefit life had given him. Today he was, though. He was aware of every blessing, every minutia that birth had bestowed upon him that made his life good.

And he was thankful in ways that he never had been before.

Because for the first time he realized that it wasn't birth, it wasn't a right, it wasn't some special ordination from God — it was a blessing. A gift. Yes, God had put him on this earth in a position of title and power, but it wasn't because Graham was special or more important. The very idea that anyone would tell Benedict or Blake or young, quiet Arthur that they were curses who never should have been born made Graham's hands curl into fists.

It could just as easily have been Graham learning to milk goats and planning on living a life in trade.

When he'd been at Haven Manor, he'd felt a bit guilty that what he'd once considered hardships were nothing more than inconvenience, but the long ride home, blocking out Oliver's constant rantings about his father, he'd had time to think about it. He didn't feel guilty anymore, but he did feel incredibly, unbelievably blessed.

The thing about living an incredibly blessed life, though, was that it gave him the means and the opportunity to do something. He could make life better for the children of Haven Manor, for the women raising them.

For Kit.

The only problem was that he didn't know how.

Chapter Twenty-Three

It took two days after Graham's departure for Kit to convince herself life had gone back to normal. On the outside, it had. The days passed like usual, though with possibly a few more opportunities taken for spontaneous fun.

Three days after that, though, their lives were back in turmoil. Mr. Leighton wanted to bring Benedict in to work on a special desk even though the boy wasn't scheduled to start his apprenticeship for another month. Desks were Benedict's joy, with all the opportunities for compartments, hinges, latches, and secret moving parts. There'd been no real reason to say no, so here Kit was, walking to Marlborough through the dew of early morning, the young man loping along at her side.

They'd left the house as the sun peeked over the trees because Kit would be making the long walk back on her own, after visiting with Mrs. Lancaster and checking in with Nash. She didn't have anything truly pressing to discuss, but they hadn't wanted to send Benedict into Marlborough on his own, not for the first days of his new life.

Daphne was originally going to walk him in, but she'd shown up in Kit's room with red-rimmed, swollen eyes, unable to do it, even though she knew it was an amazing opportunity for Ben. Though his work was still a bit rough and complicated projects took him a long time, by the time he finished his apprenticeship, he would be making cabinets, desks, and gaming tables that would be the envy of everyone in England.

It had ripped Kit's heart out. Daphne had never been able to be a mother to her little boy, not really, but she'd never stopped loving him like one.

Despite Daphne's pain, Kit believed it had been a good decision. Benedict had grown up with the other children, feeling like he was one of them. Good decision or not, though, Daphne's tears only added to Kit's guilt.

Marlborough was bustling by the time they made it to High Street. A stage was loading passengers outside The Castle Inn, deliveries were being made, and men were walking to the factories to spend their days making cheese and textiles.

Through the large office window, Kit saw Nash already sitting at the desk in his office. She swallowed. "Do you want me to —"

"I know the way to Mr. Leighton's house," Benedict said, pushing his shoulders back and standing as tall as he could.

Kit nodded and swallowed hard again. Everything in her wanted to walk him across the street, guide him to the woodworker's shop. But he wasn't a little boy anymore. He was becoming a man. "We'll see you in a few days, then."

His steady stride through town nearly made Kit break down like Daphne had. Unlike the other children, Benedict had been with Kit since he'd been born. She'd changed his diapers and walked the floor with him in her arms when he was fussy. No matter how they might have tried to pretend otherwise, that distinction made Benedict different. And it made it very difficult to let him go.

She watched him until he disappeared down a side street, turning back at the corner to give her a wave, and then she pushed her way into Nash's office. "Good morning."

Nash looked up, hair already sticking out

at odd angles even though it was only the middle of the morning. "Kit."

She took a deep breath and held up a folded piece of paper. "Will you post this to Priscilla for me?"

"Right. Yes. Of course I can do that." He shoved his hand through his hair. "Sit down."

What? He was simply agreeing? Normally he asked a dozen or more questions when Kit asked him to contact one of the women.

Something must be wrong.

Nash picked up a paper. "I got a report from my man in London."

Kit dropped into the chair across from his desk, her legs refusing to hold her a moment longer. By necessity, Nash and his wife, Margaretta, maintained contacts in London who knew a limited amount of Haven Manor's business.

Margaretta kept in touch with a small group of women they referred to as "The Committee," who helped them find women in need of their special type of assistance, and Nash had a couple of men who kept an eye on all of the people paying Haven Manor to raise their children. His own method of insurance, Kit supposed, to avoid any surprises showing up quite literally on his doorstep.

Kit nodded at the paper in Nash's hand. "What does it say?"

"Someone is trying to find you. He's not sure who. Only that there's been some whispers floating around of someone who is looking for The Governess and is willing to pay a good bit of money to anyone who helps locate her."

Kit winced at the nickname but tried to hide it by dropping her gaze to her lap and pleating her skirt with her fingers. "Is it Lord Charles?"

"Possibly," Nash said with a sigh and another pass of his hand through his hair. "I've already heard from him directly once. A rather large, menacing man delivered the first bank draft. If he intends to deliver all of them that way, I may have a nervous collapse." Nash sat back in his chair and flicked a finger across the paper. "Lord Charles isn't the most discreet of men. I'm not sure he's keeping your visit much of a secret, and it's possible that's stirred up someone else. If London is talking about you, they're going to try to figure out who all you have contracts with."

He dropped the paper and lifted his gaze to lock with Kit's. "Someone could be getting scared."

"Most of them have moved on and built

good lives, just like we hoped they would," Kit murmured.

"That's true," Nash said with a nod, "and if those good lives are threatened . . ."

"We'll have to be careful."

She should probably tell Nash about Graham. Given this concern, the fact that there was someone out there who not only knew what they were doing but how to get to the house was a potential problem. It made Kit feel vulnerable to know that, but then again everything about Graham made Kit feel vulnerable.

As soon as Nash brought up Priscilla's brother being in town, she would tell him about Graham. It would be a logical conversation and allow her to impart nothing but the most vital of details.

Only Nash wasn't saying anything about Priscilla's brother.

Kit frowned. How many other men had come to Nash for information that he'd never told her about?

Perhaps he didn't think Kit cared. "You, Margaretta, and the children are the most important concerns in this matter," she said, wanting him to know that she appreciated what he did and knew how difficult it was. "No one knows who The Governess is or where she lives. The only connection anyone has is you."

"Margaretta is keeping the children close to home for now and limiting her trips in to town."

"We'll do the same." Kit grimaced. They didn't bring the children to town often and never more than two at a time, which meant the trips they did get — an occasional attendance of Sunday services, a visit to Mrs. Lancaster — were precious. Losing those would be disappointing. "We'll distract the children from what they're giving up."

Nash laughed. "Distract them? With what?"

"I don't know. Perhaps a picnic in the glen, or we'll teach them to dance."

Pangs accompanied the memories, but gratitude overwhelmed her, too. Graham may have left her behind with conflicting emotions, but he'd also reminded her how to let her charges be children.

"You are going to take the children on a picnic?" The disbelief in Nash's voice made Kit sit up straighter.

"Why not?"

He shuffled papers around on his desk. "I can't think of a single reason why not. A picnic sounds like a wonderful idea. I'm sure the children will enjoy it."

They had. And Nash's disbelief was actually quite understandable given that Kit had needed to essentially be tricked into allowing it. Graham was quite good at maneuvering her into doing things she wouldn't have otherwise.

An icy chill of fear wound up her spine. What if Graham wasn't as good and kind as he appeared? What if he had something to do with the rumblings Nash's man was hearing?

Twelve years. They'd gone twelve years without anyone raising much of a commotion about them, mostly because revealing they knew anything about The Governess would have called their own honor into question. Their pride had been Kit's greatest safety measure. But what if that was failing?

All it would take was one man to decide that his money was worth more than his pride and that bringing her out into the light was worth any damage it would cause to his reputation.

What if Graham was part of such a thing?

Her instincts told her he wasn't, but she wasn't sure she could trust those instincts. She'd thought that Maxwell Oswald was a good sort of man all those years ago, and he'd turned out to be a cad of the highest order.

And society had done nothing to him. He'd married Miss Rhinehold, who had apparently turned into a bit of an heiress when her father's shipping venture expanded. But what if his vindictive and horrible ways were continuing? Could he possibly have discovered she was The Governess and set out to ruin this as well?

Or was it a father who didn't want to pay anymore? Perhaps even one of the mothers, concerned about her reputation with her new husband? They'd always encouraged the women to tell the men they eventually married about having a child — without mentioning the details of Haven Manor — but Kit had no way of forcing the women to do so.

It could even be her own father.

"Your man," Kit said, gesturing toward the paper on the desk. "Does he say what he's hearing or only that people are talking about me?"

Nash cleared his throat. "No one," he said with definitive emphasis, "is talking about you. They are talking about The Governess. And at the moment, everything is simply vague inquiries to see if anyone knows where she is or how to contact her."

"And no one has mentioned you yet?"

"No. But it's only a matter of time. Once

the person looking makes contact with me, we'll know more."

Kit hated that Nash was putting himself in such danger, but what else could they do?

She nodded her agreement, set the letter for Priscilla on his desk, and left the office.

Her walk down High Street wasn't as enjoyable as it normally was, the prospect of visiting with Mrs. Lancaster not as appealing. She had to speak with the woman, see how sales had been at the market Saturday and what they needed to make more of, but for the first time ever it felt like a task instead of a privilege.

All she really wanted to do was run to her special tree with a book in hand and pretend her world wasn't falling down around her.

Everyone Graham knew had somehow become more annoying while he'd been in Marlborough. That or his newfound understanding of life made the conversations feel even more vapid and empty than they had before. All he knew was that three weeks back in London had him ready to rip his hair out.

He wanted to be doing something more with his life.

One day he'd be the earl. One day he'd

have tenants and the laws of the land would be in his hands, but his father was in excellent health and the family's estates were running smoother than they ever had before. And there wasn't anything in him that wanted that to change, not even to dispel the uneasiness he was having to learn to live with.

One day.

But even then, would life as an earl be enough? Had his father found it to be enough?

Graham's valet finished creasing the cravat tied intricately at Graham's throat before declaring him ready for the night's ball. He wandered downstairs to await his parents and found his father alone in the drawing room, a book in one hand and a glass of sherry in the other.

Spectacles rode low on the straight, slim nose, and his hair, once as thick and dark as Graham's, was now more grey than black and had to be carefully styled to keep from revealing the fact that there was a bit less of it than there had been before. It was likely that Graham would look exactly like that one day. He couldn't think of anyone else he'd rather be. If he could one day resemble his father in more than just looks, all the better.

He lowered himself into a chair and waited until his father glanced up to give him a smile and a nod of acknowledgment.

"What makes a good earl?" Graham asked. It wasn't what he really wanted to know, but he couldn't think of how to phrase his real question.

The earl set his book aside and took a slow sip of sherry. "The same thing that makes a good man."

"And that is?"

"Love for country. Love for God." He set the glass on a table and leaned forward, taking off his spectacles to better look Graham in the eye. "A good man sees what he's been given and does the best he can to earn it."

"And when he's been gifted an earldom?"

Graham's father sat back with a shrug. "He makes sure he remembers that it's a responsibility as well as a blessing."

Was that what Graham's life was missing? Responsibility? A sense of purpose knowing that what he did mattered to someone else? Graham's next words slid out in a hoarse whisper. "And when he's waiting for an earldom?"

"I suppose that's a bit harder," the earl said slowly, "but what he does in that time to become a good man determines whether or not he'll be a good earl."

"What did you do?"

"Nothing I'm all too proud of." He picked up his spectacles and folded the ear pieces in and out while he stared at them with a frown. "Nothing I'm excessively ashamed of either, though. I suppose I did just what you said. I waited."

"And if I don't want to wait?"

A smile kicked up one side of the earl's mouth. "Are you planning on having me expended?"

Graham laughed and shook his head before dropping his elbows to his knees. "No. I don't want to become the earl for a very long time." He looked up, meeting a golden-brown gaze that was so very much like his own. "But I don't want to wait to become a good man."

For a long moment, the earl considered his son. It had been a while since Graham and his father had really talked. Even longer since they'd talked this baldly.

Finally the older man smiled. "Then be one. When I married your mother, she rattled around this house for months before declaring she was going to burn it down if she had to sit through one more pointless visit. She's got her charities now, like the school back in Staffordshire and the hospital. She still has as many inane teas as she ever did, but they don't bother her as much because she's got a purpose, too. When she needs something for the hospital, she has those women over for tea and plucks at their reticules until she's got the funds she needs."

The earl sat back with a shrug. "If a purpose is what you need, we'll find you one. Or you can find your own. There's nothing that says you have to wait until you're the earl to love your country and love God."

"And if my purpose isn't popular?"

Slowly, his father slid his spectacles back on and then looked over the top of them so his sparkling gaze connected with his son's. A small smile tilted the edges of the older man's lips into a confident grin. "You're going to be an earl, son. You get a little bit of say in what's popular."

CHAPTER TWENTY-FOUR

Kit had made a horrible mistake. She'd thought telling Priscilla her brother loved her enough to be concerned about her was a good thing. After all, so many of the women they helped talked about how lonely and unloved they were feeling. And if Priscilla gave Kit permission to tell Oliver what was going on, it might give Kit an excuse to see Graham again.

Which proved the idea had been foolish on more than one level.

And now she really had a problem on her hands.

"You're up late."

Kit looked up from the distressing letter sitting on her small writing desk to see Daphne standing in the doorway of Kit's bedroom. A single candle sat on the corner of the desk, throwing an eerie set of shadows across the old silk robe draped across Daphne's shoulders. It was one of the few pieces of clothing from London that Daphne still had.

"You wouldn't be able to say that if you weren't up late, too," Kit said, trying to push out a smile and a bit of levity. She would have to tell Daphne and Jess what had happened, but her first instinct was always to protect Daphne from anything unpleasant whenever possible.

A serene smile glowed across Daphne's face. "True. But I'm going to blame Sophie for that one. She fell out of the bed."

While Kit and Jess slept in the main floor apartment, Daphne had a room on the same floor as the children's bedchambers. It allowed Jess to go down to the kitchen early and let Kit stay up late to work on accounts, but it meant that Daphne got to handle any middle-of-the-night problems.

"Is Sophie hurt?"

Daphne shook her head. "She barely even woke up. By the time I got in there Sarah was already scooping her back into bed."

Kit nodded and ran a finger along the edge of the letter. She could wait until morning, but the news wasn't going to change. "I've made a bit of a tangle, Daphne." She forced her eyes to meet Daphne's soft gaze. "Priscilla's missing."

Concern and confusion chased the remaining sleepiness from Daphne's face. "Missing?"

Kit held up the letter. "It's from Mrs. Corbet."

"She's the woman housing Priscilla, isn't she? The family in Yatesbury?" Daphne perched on the edge of Kit's bed.

Kit turned in her chair and nodded. Mrs. Corbet was with child as well, only a month or two further along than Priscilla. She would give Priscilla a place to live until the baby was born and then care for both babies until Priscilla's child was ready to move to the manor. It was what Mrs. Foster was currently doing with baby Olivia. What they'd done with every child. It was a process that worked.

But only if the mother stayed put.

"I'm not sure where she's gone to," Kit said, "but she's run away. Oh, Daphne, what have I done?"

Where had she gone? Why had she gone? Was she going home? Trying to see Oliver? Coming to Haven Manor? What if she showed up at Nash's office? Kit would really be in trouble if that happened. Nash worked very hard to make sure nothing in his office reflected the true nature of Haven Manor. It was why they'd drawn up the contracts about the chess sets. It made everything simpler from a legal standpoint.

But the contracts and chess sets were the least of Kit's worries at the moment. What was she going to do about Priscilla?

"She is a grown woman, Kit. If she wants to brave the world on her own, that's her prerogative." Daphne's forehead scrunched together, and her head tilted as she looked at Kit. It was the same look she wore when one of the children got sick.

"But we had an agreement," Kit said, turning back to the desk so that she didn't have to see the concern on Daphne's face.

"And how is her breaking it your fault?"

Kit was silent for a moment and then propped her elbow on the desk and dropped her head into her hand. "Because I wrote to her and told her that her brother was worried."

"Oh." Daphne's voice was small and when she didn't say anything else, Kit dropped her head down on the desk.

A rustle of fabric preceded the light touch of Daphne's hand on Kit's shoulder. "Go to sleep."

Kit's head popped up, and she twisted to look at her friend. "What?"

"Sleep," she repeated. "You can't very well go riding off into the countryside tonight to find her, and if you don't get any sleep you'll not be able to think clearly tomorrow, so put the letter down and go to bed."

Kit looked from the bed to Daphne, then down to the letter. Daphne was right. While sleep might be hard for Kit to find, sitting up and burning through candles wasn't doing anyone any good. So she let Daphne guide her to bed and pull the covers up to her chin. Surprisingly, by the time Daphne took the candle to guide her way back up the stairs, Kit was already falling asleep.

Kit woke as the door to her room banged against the wall, possibly hard enough to break the hinges.

Daphne pushed her way into Kit's room, a firm, determined line to her lips. Jess was directly behind her, looking curious as if she'd followed Daphne through the house just to see what she was going to do.

Kit looked from one to the other as she pushed her disheveled hair out of her eyes. She'd forgotten to braid it the night before, which meant she probably looked a fright this morning.

Though not quite as frightening as the menacing look on Daphne's face — a novel experience indeed. "I need the satchel."

Kit blinked at her declaration and looked to Jess as if the blond woman could provide a bit of clarity to Daphne's cryptic comment. Jess simply leaned a shoulder against the doorframe and tilted one corner of her mouth up in a grin. She had a look of pride on her face, like a mama bird watching her babies try to fly.

"What satchel?" Kit asked, trying to push her brain into wakefulness.

Daphne fluttered one hand in front of her. "*The* satchel. The only one we have, as far as I know. It's not like we do a lot of traveling or require much luggage."

Kit sat straight up. "Are you traveling?"

She nodded. "I think The Committee needs to know Priscilla is missing. They could help us keep an eye out for her. Obviously, this entire situation is causing you a great deal of trauma." She swallowed hard and set her shoulders back. "Therefore I intend to take the meeting."

Understanding flashed through Kit, and she pushed to her feet so fast that she felt a bit dizzy. There was no way she was letting Daphne go back to London, no way she was subjecting Daphne to the myriad emotions that flooded Kit every time she returned to the city. "No."

"Oh." Daphne deflated a little bit.

Jess kicked her in the knee, making Daphne stumble forward a bit.

Her nose went back up in the air. "Yes. I've let you take that role for far too long. It's time I pulled my weight around here."

"Pull your weight?" Kit stepped forward and grabbed Daphne by the shoulders. How could she say such a thing? She worked harder than anyone. "Who put little Sophie back in bed when she fell out of it last night? Who do all the children come crying to when they get a scrape? Who teaches them how to hold a fork or tie their shoes?"

What would possibly make Daphne feel like she wasn't doing enough? Kit looked at Jess over Daphne's shoulder and then pushed around her friend to come nose to nose with Jess. "Did you put her up to this?"

Jess scoffed. "Hardly. If I had determined it was time to do something about your mood I'd have just thrown you in the lake."

The thought of an early-morning dunking in the lake had Kit wrapping the thin robe she'd fallen asleep in a bit tighter around her body. She knew she hadn't been the easiest person to live with lately — even the children were avoiding her when they could. "I'm surprised you haven't done so already."

"Me too." Jess pushed away from the wall. "But Daphne has a point. There's only so much that we can do to help Priscilla from here. We trust The Committee. If we're truly concerned, I have people I can contact to find her."

Whatever emergency contacts Jess had were sure to be fearsome, but at the moment the idea of Daphne — sweet, caring Daphne — going back to London scared Kit more.

No. No. Kit shook her head. It couldn't be Daphne. London had forgotten Daphne. The world had forgotten Daphne. Kit was The Governess, she was the one who put herself in danger. If something were to happen to her . . . well, she knew that everyone would cry and be sad, but honestly Haven Manor didn't work without Daphne. She was the mother here, the one who made sure the children knew they were special and loved. Even Jess, in her own way, was better at that than Kit. Kit got too caught up in tasks and order and she forgot simple matters like telling the children good morning. Daphne never did. The children needed her more than they needed Kit.

"And you aren't going either," Jess said, "so you can stop that thought right now."

Kit reached beneath her bed and pulled out the beaten leather satchel that they rarely had reason to use. "Why not? Maybe getting out of the house is the very thing I need."

"You need to get out of your head," Jess grumbled, stepping into the room and grabbing the bag.

Daphne put an arm around Kit's shoulders. "I know you're worried that Wharton is going to tell someone about us, but it's been three weeks. If he were going to say anything, he'd have done so by now."

Kit swallowed. It was good for Daphne to think Kit's mood had been because of worry. That was better than the thoughts that had actually been coursing through Kit's mind. All the what-ifs, all the might-have-beens, all the wonderings of how life could have been different if Kit's attention had been captured by a man like Graham all those years ago instead of a cad like Maxwell Oswald.

She glanced at Daphne and smiled, then avoided looking at Jess. That woman could see through Kit like a window.

"I'll go," Jess said.

"But The Committee doesn't know you," Kit said.

"They don't actually know you either," Daphne added, biting her lip.

"Then we're agreed. It doesn't matter which of us goes because whoever makes the trip is going to have to take Margaretta with them anyway. So I'll go." Jess stepped

399

toward the door, satchel in hand. "I'm more concerned about the whispers Nash's man keeps hearing. I'd like to know what's being said and put a stop to it."

She hugged the leather satchel to her chest and took a deep breath before lifting her eyes to meet Kit's gaze. Never before had the petite woman looked so vulnerable. "I don't want to have to run again."

Graham awoke feeling better than he had in weeks. He didn't know what his purpose was going to be yet, but just the idea of looking for one gave him a better sense of self. A vague, undirected desire to make someone's life better drove through him, leaving him unable to sit for very long.

When the butler gave him a note from Oliver letting Graham know his friend was back in town, Graham took his nervous energy and walked over to Oliver's house, landing on his doorstep a little bit before it was socially acceptable to be there.

He was shown straight to a drawing room, however, and Oliver soon joined him.

"There was nothing in Sussex," Oliver said as he came in the door. "No one there has seen her in months."

"You've had no luck with your father?"

Oliver shook his head. "I talked with him

twice before traveling to Sussex last week. I waited and picked the best possible times to approach him, trying something a little different every time. When I talked to him this morning, he finally admitted to sending her somewhere."

Graham frowned. "But he won't say where?"

"No." Oliver jumped from his seat and started to pace. "He says I should trust that he has her best interests at heart."

Perhaps Oliver wasn't the best place for Graham to start his life-enrichment goals. There wasn't really much Graham could do here unless he confronted Lord Trenting, and that wasn't likely to help anyone. "And the chess set?"

"He called it an investment. He said that I might not see it now, but buying that chess set would have a great impact on our family's future."

Graham's eyes widened. A wooden chess set was an investment? Jewels and gold might become more valuable over time, but wood?

He knew there was a process for declaring the king incompetent because they were all currently living under the rule of the Prince Regent, but was there a similar process for an earl? Because it really did sound as if

Lord Trenting had lost his mind.

Oliver dropped into a chair and slumped against the back, anguish in every line of his body and all across his face. "There's nothing I can do. I asked if he'd heard from Prissy since she went to wherever he sent her and he said yes, but he won't show me the letter. He won't even tell me what direction to send my own letter to. He assures me she's in good health and will return when she's learned a few lessons in how to handle herself in public."

Graham's brows drew together. There was certainly something strange about the way Oliver's father was wording everything. Assuming, of course, that Oliver was repeating the statements back correctly.

So if Graham couldn't solve the problem of Priscilla, was there something else he could do for Oliver? His friend looked tired, and his clothes fit him a little looser than his tailor would like. Perhaps Graham could do for Oliver what he'd tried to do for the people at Haven Manor and distract him from life for a little while.

"Fancy a visit to Fareweather's?"

Oliver grunted and nodded. "Maybe hitting and stabbing things will make me feel better."

CHAPTER TWENTY-FIVE

Even though Oliver looked haggard enough that young Arthur, who'd barely been higher than Graham's knees, could have taken him down, the man was nearly vibrating with energy. Had he slept in the five weeks since he'd learned of Priscilla's disappearance? Graham knew he'd traveled to anywhere and everywhere he could think of to look for her. It was a fine strategy, except that Oliver hadn't a clue what to do when he got there, so all he did was run around making himself exhausted.

But not, apparently, exhausted enough to actually sleep.

Perhaps a visit to their sporting club would do that.

Fareweather's was a club for all kinds, with sporting spaces on the lower level and coffee and cards on the upper. It wasn't as sophisticated as the clubs on St. James's Street, but Oliver and Graham weren't about to spend their time in a place where Aaron wasn't welcome as well. So they'd joined Fareweather's.

Oliver and Graham donned their protective gear, grabbed their foils and face masks, and went off in search of an empty practice area.

Instead they found Aaron, jabbing a foil at a hanging sandbag in the back corner. Lunge, retreat, repeat. Graham's legs were tired just watching him.

"When did you get back to London?" Graham asked.

"He left Sussex a week ago," Oliver said, dropping his mask and foil on a nearby bench before dropping onto it to lay his head back against the wall.

"That's right," Aaron said, chest pumping from his exercise. "I stopped at a few race courses on my way back and got home yesterday. How'd you know?"

"Because when I got to Sussex they said I'd just missed you."

Aaron's mouth pressed into a grim line. "You're still looking for Priscilla? What did you find in Marlborough?"

"I looked at chalk horses," Oliver said, crossing his arms over his chest, "and Graham went for a ride in the rain."

Graham chuckled, hoping it looked natural. It had been considerably more than a ride in the rain. It had been life-changing. He glanced at Aaron and reflected on how different his friend's life was from the one the Haven Manor children were experiencing. Benedict, Blake, John, any of those could easily have been Aaron. Or Aaron could have easily been one of them.

Oliver looked like his exhaustion had finally caught up with him as his head lolled back against the wall and his eyes fell halfway closed. He gave a yawn, lifting his hand in a pitiful attempt to disguise his open mouth.

"I don't think he's much use for anything," Aaron said, poking at Oliver with his foil.

With a stiff swing, Oliver used his foil to knock Aaron's aside. "He made me come," Oliver grumbled. "Fight with him."

"Fancy a duel, Graham? Loser buys Oliver a drink to drown himself in," Aaron said with a grin.

Graham slid his mask on and moved into place. "Oliver's father admitted to sending Priscilla away."

Their swords clashed as they started the battle. "That's a good thing," Aaron said. "At the very least it should ease Oliver's mind a bit to know that someone knows where she is."

A light snore drifted from the bench.

"I think it might have," Graham agreed.

Neither spoke for a while as their feet danced across the floor to the tune of steel on steel. Would Benedict have been a good fencer? The boy was bright, showed a knack for seeing things from a different angle. He could have been quite the sportsman, if he'd been born at a different time.

Graham let his guard down as he considered the man in front of him.

Aaron's sword connected with Graham's shoulder, the blade arcing with the pressure.

"What's it like for you?" Graham asked quietly.

Aaron froze with his foil still extended. Through the mask Graham saw dark eyebrows draw together over green-grey eyes. "Scoring against you? A pleasure."

"Life. What's it like being . . ." Despite the number of years he'd been friends with Aaron and despite the number of times he'd heard whispers and jibes about the other man's parentage, Graham himself had never spoken anything about it. So it was hard to make the words come out now even though he wasn't meaning anything bad by them. "Your situation. With your father."

This conversation was awkward enough without him stuttering over his words, and Graham's shoulders began to itch with the notion that this had been a poor idea. He used his own foil to knock Aaron's away before returning to his starting stance.

The other man was a bit slower to follow. He slid his mask off his face, revealing a wide, teeth-baring grin. "You mean, what's life like being a baseborn by-blow?"

How was he so comfortable saying it? Graham had heard that term and worse whispered not so quietly behind Aaron's back since they'd met at Harrow.

"Yes. That." When Aaron didn't get back into a fighting stance, Graham stood up and slid his own mask off his face.

Oliver groaned from his corner, obviously having woken enough to hear the conversation. "Why on earth would you ask such a thing, Graham? You don't just go around asking people about their legitimacy."

"I don't have to ask about his legitimacy," Graham retorted. "I already know it."

Aaron shook his head and laughed. "Everyone knows it. It's hard not to when your father introduces you to people as 'my illegitimate son, Mr. Whitworth.' Wouldn't want anyone confusing me with his true heir, after all." The smile faded as Aaron's gaze sharpened into more serious consideration. "You've never cared about it before, though. Why are you asking now?"

"It's never mattered before."

Aaron's eyes registered his shock. "And it does now?"

Graham dropped his mask and foil and threw a punch at the practice sandbag, making it swing between them. "Not like that. I've just come to realize that it might matter in ways I hadn't considered before. I had a lot of time to think when I was stuck in the farmer's kitchen."

Aaron said nothing for several moments, just stared at Graham, not flinching as the bag swung back and forth, inches from his face. "What do you want to know?"

The quiet voice, so unlike the jovial friend Graham was used to, made him thrust out a hand and bring the slowly swinging bag to a stop. "Everything."

"This is a seriously depressing conversation, Graham," Oliver mumbled.

"Of all the people in this room," Aaron said, "you're the one who appears to be suffering a fit of the blue devils at the moment. So don't go casting your gloom over mine. I'm not doing so bad." Aaron shifted until he was leaning against the wall, one ankle crossed over the other. "Something I always liked about you, Graham, was that you never saw me as different. At least you never seemed to."

Graham's eyes narrowed. The truth was, by the time he'd realized Aaron was different, they'd been too good of friends for Graham to care. "We went to the same schools. We're both members of this club. I'm fairly certain my mother likes you more than me sometimes."

A ghost of a grin flickered across Aaron's face. "I thought you were a bit touched in the upper works until I met your parents."

"He is touched," Oliver said, starting to sound a bit like his old self.

Graham was more than willing to put up with Oliver's teasing if it made him feel better, but he really wanted to have this conversation with Aaron. Besides, if he didn't give as good as he got, Oliver would know Graham felt sorry for him.

Reaching out one foot, Graham kicked Oliver's boots. "Why don't you go get us a table in the coffeehouse upstairs? But order tea for me." He couldn't drink coffee without thinking of the number of cups he'd drunk at the manor. Jess always had it ready and available, and he hadn't seen anyone else preparing tea, so he'd drunk the bitter brew.

Oliver frowned. "I don't want to miss this revealing conversation."

"You mean the one you called depressing?"

Since Graham had thrown his own words back at him, Oliver didn't have much recourse. He grumbled good-naturedly as he rose from the bench. As he walked through the club, greeting people he'd ignored as they entered, he almost looked like he did before the entire mess with Priscilla began. Whether Oliver wanted to admit it or not, having his father acknowledge that something was wrong but that Priscilla was safe had done wonders for Oliver's peace of mind.

Graham turned back to Aaron to find the larger man looking at him, face devoid of expression. "My father acknowledged me from the beginning. I guess that makes me one of the lucky ones. The only thing he really had to do was pay for my living until I was old enough to do so myself. Instead he claimed me, set me and my mother up in a cottage on the corner of one of his estates. There was a series of nannies as I got older, but none of them stayed long."

Aaron crossed his arms over his chest, still maintaining eye contact with Graham, still keeping any sign of emotion off his wide, strong face. "I saw him twice a year. When I was eight, he brought his six-year-old son to meet me. I'm pretty sure I was a lesson in responsibility or something like that. About a year after that, Mother left. I still don't know if that was her decision or his. He paid for school, brought me to London, and made sure everyone knew I was under his protection."

Graham knew what Aaron's life had been like from age ten and on, since they'd met during those early years at school, but they'd never spoken of his childhood. It wasn't often that Graham saw Aaron and his father in the same room together, but when he did the two always seemed to have a cold but cordial relationship. In many ways it seemed better than the one many legitimate sons had with their fathers.

It was certainly better than Oliver's. Graham said as much.

Aaron nodded. "It's better now that I'm older and have business interests of my own. We can meet and pretend the connection is merely superficial.

"The thing is, Graham, I'll never really be one of you. I wear the clothes, live the life, even attend some of the same parties. I get an allowance from my father, and he's assured me there will be a small settlement on his death. It's rather a lot like being a younger son. Except I'm not. And everyone knows it.

"And we all walk around smiling and pretending that it doesn't matter that my father's true heir is two years younger than me or that my birth was the result of a mistake that couldn't be swept under the rug. But we all know."

When Graham had met Aaron, his greatest concern had been the fact that Aaron had a fancy set of marbles and ran faster than the third-form boys.

He'd never given a thought to anyone else's parents before — probably because he'd never been around anyone who wasn't of impeccable breeding — and the first time he'd heard another boy call Aaron a mongrel, he'd learned the truth. He'd been too young to really understand what it meant, though, so he'd carried on being Aaron's friend like it hadn't mattered.

"Does it bother you?" Graham couldn't get the image of Benedict out of his head. When he'd gone to tell the boy good-bye, he'd shaken Graham's hand like a man. He said he didn't know much about his own father, but if he had to pick a man to grow up to be like, he wanted to be like Graham.

It had made it nearly impossible for Graham to get on his horse and leave.

Aaron's eyes narrowed. "Why do you want to know, Graham? After all these years, why now?"

"Because I'm beginning to realize that if it weren't for the grace of God, it could have been me."

Aaron tilted his head and looked at Graham for a moment before nodding and reaching for the buckles on his protective jacket. "Come along."

Graham grabbed his gear and followed Aaron up the stairs to the coffeehouse. "Where are we going?"

"To show you the life of a side slip."

"Don't call yourself that," Graham grunted.

Aaron stopped and faced Graham, getting right in his face, more serious than Graham had ever seen him. "First point, words like that can't mean anything because you're going to hear them. A lot. This society thinks nothing of airing your shortcomings quite loudly behind your back while smiling to your face.

"Second," Aaron said as they stepped out of the room, "as you've noted, my birth doesn't affect my life all that much. I've every opportunity, if not every benefit. But it's there. Always there."

"Are you glad that you know?"

"Know what?" he asked as they moved toward the table where Oliver sat with three cups of tea in front of him. "That I'm a by-blow?" He shrugged. "What would be the alternative?"

Graham pretended to think. "Thinking yourself an orphan, perhaps?"

He snorted. "And grow up in a workhouse or foundling hospital? Or perhaps as the hated poor relation of a distant relative who locked me away in a tower until his obligatory years of care were met?" He shook his head sharply. "No thank you. At least now I've the opportunity to seek a life that will actually support me and gain me respect."

That was what Graham had thought when he'd watched the children learning skills that could set them up for a life of work and potential drudgery. But even as he nodded a niggling thought hit the back of his mind. "What about your mother?"

Aaron stiffened. He glanced from Oliver back to Graham. "I don't wish to talk about my mother."

Oliver sighed. "Are you still discussing that? I thought we'd agreed to ignore the whole business. It's not like anyone cared about it when we were sailing to Jamaica."

Graham didn't acknowledge Oliver. He

just looked at Aaron, noticing the flat coldness in his eyes. What had happened to his mother? And why did Graham care? What did he hope to learn?

Already he knew that he liked Kit, that he liked the man he was when he was at Haven Manor, trying to make life better for the children and lighten the load of the women who cared for them. He knew that Kit's strength and spirit drew him more than any other woman he'd met. It didn't hurt that her dark blond hair and bright blue eyes were extremely pleasing to look at or that she fit perfectly in his arms and had a kiss that was sweeter than any confection his chef had ever produced.

What more was he wanting to know?

Aaron dropped into the seat across from Oliver. "If you really want to know, I'll tell you, just . . . not here."

Graham settled into his own seat, lost in thought as the conversation between Aaron and Oliver drifted to other things.

Aaron's life was turning out well, especially when one considered the alternative. But apparently his mother's hadn't.

What was it Kit had said? The very existence of the children could ruin their mothers?

Knowing what he knew about Daphne

and Kit and the way they'd left London, it was entirely possible that Haven Manor was more for the mothers than it was for the children. Even Kit had acknowledged that it had its flaws. And if that was the case, was it what was best for the children?

CHAPTER TWENTY-SIX

Kit was anxious as she waited for Jess to return from London, jumping every time the wind blew a bit too loudly around the corner of the house or whenever a child closed a door with a bit too much force.

And then Jess was there, striding into the kitchen and making bread as if she'd never been gone.

Kit bit her tongue between her teeth while the children filed through and scattered to their respective chores. Even Daphne hurried them along a bit more than normal, asking Sarah and Eugenia to take the littlest ones with them as they dusted the main floor.

Once the women were alone, Kit and Daphne pounced.

"What happened?"

"What did they say?"

"Did you actually get to meet The Committee?"

"What about the rumors? Did you learn anything about those?"

Jess lifted two chunks of raw bread dough and shoved them into Kit and Daphne's mouths. As they both sputtered and spit the yeasty mess onto the floor, Jess returned to calmly kneading her dough. "If you'll both hush, I'll tell you how it went."

Kit and Daphne plopped onto stools across the worktable from Jess, mouths shut.

"First of all, I wouldn't go see Nash for a while. He's rather upset at you."

Kit grimaced. She'd known he was going to be. He had every right to be.

Jess took a deep breath. "Second, there is certainly someone looking for The Governess, and they aren't being particularly quiet about it, at least not in the alleys. I doubt much is being said in the ballrooms, but it's only a matter of time before that changes. Despite all the questions, no one seems to be getting any answers."

"Well, that's good, isn't it?" Daphne asked.

Jess nodded. "What's also good is that with more people curious about it, no one is going to want to admit they know anything. Simply possessing knowledge makes you guilty, in this case."

Kit nearly fell off the stool as tension she hadn't known she'd been holding relaxed its grip on her spine. "We're fairly safe, then. As long as no one we've worked with talks, no one will know anything."

"What about Priscilla?" Daphne asked. "Is The Committee going to do anything to help us find her?"

Jess nodded. "I have to say I'm rather impressed with the group of women Margaretta works with. I knew of a few of them while I was in London. Good hearts, the lot of them."

"Of course they are," Daphne said. "Margaretta would hardly trust even part of our secret to someone unworthy. And all one has to do is look at the women they've chosen to send us. Every last one of them was lost and alone and . . . and . . ." Daphne's words trailed away as her breath shuddered in her chest. A few tears leaked out, but then she took a deep breath and held her hands out. "No. I'm well. Please continue, Jess."

Jess pounded the bread dough for a few moments while Daphne took another deep breath or two. "The Committee will let us know if Priscilla's name is spoken anywhere in London, even if the rumor doesn't appear to have anything to do with the situation. She's nearly five months along, but it's possible her dresses will still hide the change in her figure. If they hear of anyone seeing her, they'll let us know."

"That's something at least," Kit said. "I don't suppose there's much else they could do."

"We could contact Graham." Daphne looked carefully at something beyond Kit's shoulder, her eyes wide in innocence. "He'd be able to tell us if she contacts Lord Farnsworth."

"Oh, there's no need for that," Jess said with an impish grin aimed straight at Kit. "One of The Committee members assured me she'd know if Lord Farnsworth heard anything. She seemed to be the one in charge of the group, actually. It was her house where Margaretta and I met with everyone."

Kit's last hope that she would somehow find an excuse to seek out Graham faded away, which was probably for the best in spite of how she missed him. The dream of him joining their work at the manor and courting her in earnest was simply going to have to remain a scenario she imagined in her weakest moments.

It wasn't as if it could have ever come true, anyway. The man was an aristocrat, a peer, one of the blessed few who made up the cream of London society. He was handsome, had a title, would one day be required to take his place in Parliament. He couldn't hide away in the woods with her.

"I suppose it would make sense for The Committee to be somewhat connected to the families," Kit said, proud that there was no tremble in her words to betray her fading hopes. "I mean, they'd have to hear about the girls in trouble somehow, right?"

"They are most certainly connected," Jess said as she molded the bread into a ball and dropped it into a bowl, a grin still creasing one cheek. "Lord Farnsworth is in her house several times a week."

"Is she his aunt or something?" Daphne asked.

"No. . . ." Jess drew out the word, sounding as if she were on the verge of laughter. "Lord Farnsworth is *very* good friends with her son."

Fire and ice raced through Kit's body as she felt herself start to shake. "No," she whispered.

"Oh yes," Jess said with a laugh. "Our dear friend Lord Wharton's mother is on The Committee, and she's storing her tea in a paper filigree box her son brought home from a recent trip."

A little giggle burst out of Daphne followed by a wave of panicked laughter. "Oh no!" She heaved a deep breath. "Was he there? What did he say? What did *you* say?"

"We managed to avoid seeing him, but I heard him in the hall." Jess draped a towel over the bowl of bread dough. "And I heard enough to know that Lord Farnsworth still knows nothing about why his sister left London."

Kit winced. She'd never told Nash about Graham. "What did Margaretta say?"

"Nothing." Jess carried the bowl to the side table. "Which is the exact same thing that I said. If she knows anything about Graham, it didn't come from me. I'm going out to check the garden."

Kit sighed. Checking the garden was Kit's way to avoid everyone. Either Jess didn't want to talk about her trip to London or she didn't want Kit to hide herself in the sweet peas, which meant Kit was stuck looking for other tasks that kept her out of everyone's way. At least out of Daphne's way. The woman giggled every time she looked at Kit.

An hour later, a wagon pulled out of the trees in front of the house. It was easy enough to recognize Nash's wagon and his donkey, Balaam. But what was he doing here? He'd seen Jess only that morning. If he'd had something to send them, he could have sent it with her. Kit stepped out onto the front porch and shielded her eyes with her hand.

The wagon was full of people. Margaretta was recognizable, sitting on the seat beside Nash, but the back was full of squirming bodies as well. Nash had brought his entire family. Why would he do that?

Unless he needed to hide Margaretta and the children. Had someone come to him in Marlborough? Was something happening?

Kit rushed down the stairs to meet the wagon in the front drive.

As it came closer, she saw there was another adult in the back of the wagon with the children. Hope unfurled in her chest before Kit could stop it. She knew it wasn't Graham. What reason would he have to return? Besides, if she ever caught him wearing a flower-bedecked bonnet, she'd have to rethink her opinion of him.

Actually, she wouldn't. Because if wearing a flowered bonnet was what it took to bring a smile to the faces around him, she had no doubt that Graham would plop it on his head without a moment's hesitation.

Still, she recognized that particular bonnet, so unless Graham had taken to stealing hats from little old women, Mrs. Lancaster had decided to join the day's excursion.

Either Nash was coming with extraordinarily good news or something truly horrible had happened.

People were still piling out of the wagon when Daphne and most of the children swarmed out to greet everyone. Margaretta's children were soon swallowed into the ranks, and the entire lot ran off to play a game on the lawn behind the house.

Mrs. Lancaster shuffled her way over to Kit and Daphne with an exaggeratedly fierce scowl on her face, her right foot dragging a bit as she walked. "Where's the blond one?"

Kit bit her cheek to keep from laughing, but Daphne released her giggles without a qualm. Mrs. Lancaster didn't believe in giving Jess her own space like Kit, Daphne, and the children did, and there was something about the shopkeeper that terrified the otherwise fearless and feisty former spy.

"Kitchen," Daphne said with a grin. "She's working on cheese."

Mrs. Lancaster nodded and started up the stairs into the house, taking them with more speed than Kit would have expected, given the woman's slow gait. "I'll just sneak through the house so she doesn't know I'm coming."

This time Kit couldn't control her laughter. Wellington himself probably wouldn't be able to sneak up on Jess, but that wasn't going to stop Mrs. Lancaster from trying. Kit expected to see Jess flying out the side door of the house within minutes.

"To what do we owe this visit?" Kit asked.

Nash's mouth pressed into a grim line, and his wife clasped her hands in front of her.

"We'll talk about what you told Priscilla later. We've something else to discuss now." He reached into his coat and pulled out a sheaf of papers. "I received a letter this morning. It isn't signed. The messenger who delivered it stood in my office waiting for an answer."

He handed the top paper to Kit. "Based on the way the letter is written, I'm guessing it's a parent of one of the children, but I don't know which one. Someone definitely wants the location of the manor, though."

Kit's gaze flew over the letter. The person was requesting to meet with the recipient of the funds sent to purchase his chess pieces. It was carefully worded so that it wouldn't have allowed Nash to simply direct the man to Mr. Leighton, who made all the chess sets for them.

The letter went on to say that while the gentleman had agreed to the extended delivery at first, he was changing his mind and wanted to talk directly to the organizer of the deal. Which would have been The Governess.

Kit had to applaud the person. The letter was written in such a way that if Nash had been simply a solicitor and not known about the children, he would still be in the dark.

Daphne read the letter over Kit's shoulder and her coloring faded until she was as white as the paper.

"What did you say?" Kit asked.

"I told him no. I added something about the craftsman not being interested in meeting his clients. I don't expect it to be the last I hear, though."

Kit sank onto the steps behind her, letting the letter fall to the ground as she placed her head in her hands. "And we don't know who is writing?"

"No. Though I'd bet it was one of the fathers. I can't see one of the mothers writing in such a tone."

"And the mothers' fathers have nothing to gain by locating an illegitimate grandchild," Kit murmured. No, chances were it was one of the men she'd stood in front of and threatened to ruin. She never thought she'd have to consider actually going through with it. She wasn't sure she actually could. Could she deliberately set out to ruin someone's life?

A glance at the grim, serious faces around her told her that she was most likely going to find out.

CHAPTER TWENTY-SEVEN

Graham wanted to go back to Marlborough, to return to Kit and the children and do something for them. But until he could figure out what that something should be, he focused on helping Oliver.

He arrived at Oliver's house to discover that a solid night's sleep and a couple of meals had revived his friend — at least revived him enough to have him yelling at his father and nearly threatening the earl.

The servant who let Graham in scurried out of the way as soon as the door was closed behind him.

"She's safe, Oliver, and that's all I can tell you. I promised her, I promised . . . well, I promised not to say anything. She wants time to herself for a while. The Season didn't . . ." The earl paused, and Graham heard his sigh all the way in the corridor. "It didn't go well for her during the winter and that wasn't even a full Season. It was a party here and there and an ice-skating outing."

Graham knocked on the door to the study. The earl gestured him in, and Graham almost stumbled as he noticed that the earl looked nearly as haggard as his son had.

"Wharton," Lord Trenting said, slumping in the chair behind his desk. "Would you please convince Oliver to think about something else? Anything else? If he keeps going around London and yelling about Priscilla, he'll ruin everything. She just wants some time, and I'm giving that to her."

Graham looked from father to son and back again. What the earl said made sense, and it was a reasonable request to keep family business in the family. But Graham really wanted to be on Oliver's side in this. But then again, wouldn't it do Oliver good to have something else to do with his time, especially since he wasn't actually getting anywhere with his searching? "Why don't we meet Aaron at Fareweather's?"

"Yes, yes!" The earl waved his hands toward the door. "Go meet Mr. Whitworth."

Both Graham and Oliver raised their eyebrows at that. Lord Trenting had never particularly liked that Oliver was friends with Aaron. "Right," Graham said. "Let's go, Oliver."

Graham had to practically drag Oliver out of the house, and since he wasn't about to drag him all the way through the streets of London, he hailed a hack to take them to the club.

Oliver slumped in the seat. "What am I supposed to do now?"

"Well," Graham asked, "what did you do before Priscilla, er, took her time?"

"Went to Fareweather's," Oliver said with a grumble.

That wasn't all Oliver did, but it was something. "Good thing we're going there, then."

Graham hauled Oliver into the club and up the stairs where he all but dumped him into one of the leather chairs in the seating area.

Aaron walked over to them, laughing. "Well, you look in better spirits today. Grumpy, but better."

Oliver grunted.

Aaron shook his head but clapped a hand on his friend's shoulder in silent support.

Graham looked around the room to see who else was at the club. Lord Marwick sat in a chair on the other side of the room, slumped down until his head barely topped the edge. His hair was mussed and one arm draped over the chair's side, with a glass of

430

amber liquid held lightly in his fingers.

Graham slid around Oliver's chair until he stood next to Aaron. "What's wrong with Marwick?"

"His wife discovered he'd been visited by The Governess."

Graham's brows lowered. "I didn't realize they had children yet."

Aaron looked at Graham like he was a simpleton. "Not *his* governess. *The* Governess."

Now Graham felt like a simpleton. Well, if there was one thing he'd learned in London society, it was that you were better off pretending you knew something than admitting you didn't, even though he hadn't a clue what Aaron meant by his deeply voiced intoning of *The* Governess. Weren't there hundreds of governesses in London? How was anyone supposed to know which one was being referred to just by placing an emphasis on *the*? "Ah," Graham murmured. "Poor fellow."

"That would have been bad enough, but he came here last night, got drunk, and then told everyone else about the ensuing fight. Now everyone knows he's been caught by The Governess and that his wife isn't happy about it." Aaron nodded toward the cluster of men in the corner. "They've been talking about The Governess for weeks, but it's always vague, a bit like a fairy tale, since until now, no one had admitted being visited by her."

"But Marwick has?" Graham was more confused than ever. Apparently there was a woman known as The Governess — stupid title, that. Why would a mysterious woman name herself after the person who minds the children? Was she wrangling the men of London like they were toddlers or something?

Of course, there were times when the men acted like toddlers, so that might not be such a bad idea, but it didn't seem like something that would strike such terror that a man would keep it a secret.

Aaron nodded. "Now they're all panting for information, but he sobered up enough to learn he said too much last night. According to them" — he nodded to the men in the corner once more — "Marwick cursed himself and went right back to the bottle. As if talking about The Governess was as bad as getting visited by her."

Graham sighed. "I concede. I'm ignorant. Why is everyone afraid of The Governess?"

Aaron chuckled. "She digs up your darkest secrets and threatens to expose you if you don't pay."

Graham's stomach curdled at the description. A blackmailer? Marwick had always seemed like a good man.

Curiosity drove Graham across the floor. Whether he wanted more information or to give the man a bit of encouragement he wasn't sure, because when he got there he saw Marwick's other hand. It was loosely curled around a pale wooden chess piece. The pawn was beveled and carved in beautiful simplicity.

Familiar simplicity.

Ice rolled through Graham's veins. He felt like he was just a little bit closer to something he knew but couldn't quite put into words. It was like another piece of the puzzle falling into place, but it was revealing a grim image indeed.

Graham had an almost certain guess that Lord Marwick, like Lord Trenting, was paying exorbitant sums for the slow delivery of a chess set.

It was an ingenious way to blackmail, really. It was legal. It could be discussed openly, the contract had no need to be hidden, and the blackmailer would be guaranteed a certain amount of income spread over several years.

And all of that money was going to Nash Banfield.

A man Kit and Daphne trusted completely.

No. No. If what he was considering were true, then that meant . . .

He walked back over to Aaron, being careful to keep his gait steady and not draw anyone's notice. He had Aaron's, though, and Oliver's. They were both watching him like he might lose his grip on sanity.

"Who is The Governess?" he asked quietly.

"No one knows," Aaron said slowly. "Until now I really thought she was a myth. No one knows the first time they heard about her, and no one can describe anyone's encounter with her. By now the rumors have grown to the point that she breathes fire and carries a scythe, like the dark spectre of Death or something."

Well, that certainly wasn't helpful. Graham dropped his head back on his shoulders, trying to decide how to rephrase the question, but Aaron wasn't finished talking.

"To be honest, I'm not surprised you've never heard of her. Until the last few weeks, she wasn't spoken about in polite circles. It's more whispers on the street corner than anything else." Aaron paused. "I don't think I believed she was real until lately, when the whispers got louder and they went from the street to the ballroom. I wanted her to be real, though."

Graham slowly brought his head up to look at his friend. "Why?"

Aaron shook his head. "Man, look at me. We have one conversation about my life and suddenly I'm spilling my guts to you like a fribble."

Graham's eyebrows rose. "What —"

"Rumor is that she swoops in like an avenging angel, cornering men who refuse to do the right thing, those who turn their back on . . ."

"On?" Graham whispered quietly.

Aaron crossed his arms over his chest and glared across the room, looking at Marwick with something Graham would have almost labeled as hatred.

"Men who turn their back on people like my mother."

And there it was. The last piece of information. The fact that he'd thought so impossible that he'd never even allowed it to fully form in his mind.

An unknown woman swooping in as an avenging angel for the mothers who found themselves with child.

With children who needed to be forgotten.

A house with an owner who didn't care about its upkeep and so wouldn't be paying the caretaker much. Certainly wouldn't be paying enough to support a house full of children.

A woman in London. Hiding. Being chased by thugs who wanted something very particular from her.

The Kit he thought he knew, the Kit he had been trying to find an excuse to go back to, wasn't real. No wonder he'd been obsessed with her. It was easy to fall in love with a fantasy.

He'd thought her noble. He'd thought she cared. How many times had she listened to him comment on his concern for Oliver, his worry over Priscilla? She had patted his hand and told him she hoped he found her, and all the while . . .

The shaking eased as a sense of purpose pushed Graham's rioting emotions out of the way. "I think I know where Priscilla is."

Oliver sprang from his chair. "What?"

His voice was a little too loud, a little too harsh, and it drew too much attention. "Your house. We need to get that contract."

It was a testament to friendship and years of traveling together that Oliver and Aaron packed bags quickly and without question.

Graham borrowed his father's coach but instructed the coachman to hire horses so they would be easier to trade out at the posting inns. It wouldn't be quite as fast as taking the mail, but if they did find Priscilla, as he was almost positive they would, they'd need a way to bring her home discreetly.

As the carriage drove out of London, Graham ignored the small corner of his heart that held out hope. It was possible the contracts were just protection, a way of allowing people to support their children without anyone being able to find out what was going on.

It was possible.

But an arrangement like that didn't fuel stories of a fire-breathing dragon or inspire someone to send violent footmen to accost a woman. Those were the types of arrangements honorable men made, and Kit didn't deal with honorable men.

Still, the glimmer burned, causing an ache in Graham's chest that he tried to rub out. Continued hope was only going to make the inevitable revelation of truth hurt that much more.

Graham pulled out the contract he'd taken from Lord Trenting's office. He'd read it before, but now he read it with new eyes. The wording that implied grave consequences for breaking the agreement had sounded overly harsh when discussing a parlor game. It made absolute sense if referring to a child.

The contract ending on delivery of the chessboard suddenly made sense as well. Something could happen. Children died in England every day. They had accidents. They got sick. And there was no reason for anyone to keep paying for a child who was no longer alive.

Which would be another reason to keep them hidden in the woods. To keep them safe. To make sure a father who didn't want to pay anymore didn't decide to remove the need to do so.

Everything made sense now. Everything, that is, except the way she'd managed to make Graham care. Everything except the way she'd managed to teach him about himself and the man God had made him to be while being duplicitous and corrupt.

"He's sleeping."

Graham looked up from the contract at Aaron and then over to Oliver, who was indeed snoring, head lolling against the side of the carriage.

"Are you going to tell me what's going on?"

How to tell them what he was thinking? Some part of him still felt loyal to Kit, or at least to the children. He understood their secrecy now. Could he betray it? Even to the men he trusted with his life?

"What happened to your mother?" he asked instead.

Aaron sighed. "My mother was the daughter of the village cobbler. Not a position of great importance but one that got her invited to assemblies and things. There weren't an awful lot of gentry in the area, so boundaries were a bit blurred, I suppose. She told me once that she'd been the envy of every girl in the county when my father asked her to dance not once, but twice. She got caught up in everything and, unfortunately, the story is easy enough to surmise from there."

Graham turned to look out the window. "And your father wouldn't marry her."

"Of course not," Aaron said with a humorless laugh. "He couldn't sully the family name with someone so far beneath him. But he wasn't going to turn his back on me, the proof of his weakness and indiscretion, because he had a responsibility to see to the consequences of his mistakes." A wry smile twisted Aaron's lips. "His words."

"So he put you both up in a cottage?" Graham asked.

Aaron nodded. "Before I was born, she'd

had a fairly prominent place in the village. But after, that stopped. She went to work in my father's estate, the big house that sat empty most of the time except for the staff. She worked in the laundry. She'd bring home mending at night and work by the fireside while I told her what the current nanny and I had done that day."

Aaron rubbed his rough hands over his face. When they fell away, his eyes looked tortured. "Her own father wouldn't acknowledge her. Whenever she took me in for shoes, he'd fit me, give me licorice, but never say a word to her. That was my mother's life. Because of me."

And if there'd been someone like Kit? Someone like this Governess? What would Aaron's life have been? "How did you end up at Harrow?"

"Father acknowledged me. Always. When I turned seven, she received notice that I was now in the custody of my father and he would be making all the decisions about my care. She didn't tell me. I found the note stuffed under her mattress. It said she had no further obligation to me.

"She didn't leave then. She waited two more years, and to be honest I'm not entirely sure why. Maybe she knew he intended to send me to school. I don't blame her for leaving. I suppose I was upset at the time, but now I don't have any resentment at all. Without me, there was a chance she could make a life elsewhere."

Graham couldn't remember the last time he'd cried, but he was very afraid he might do so now. "Do you know what happened to her?" he whispered.

A shake of Aaron's head cut through Graham's heart, as he imagined the fate that could have befallen Kit and Daphne — the fate that had befallen them. It was enough to make anyone bitter, to make them lash out.

But did it excuse blackmail?

It was easy to see why Kit and Daphne did what they did, but there had to be a better way. His hand fisted on the contract. One that didn't involve this. Compounding the wrong by doing it to someone else couldn't be the way God wanted this handled.

Silence fell, and eventually Graham found his own sleep, though it was in fits and bursts. They made stops, and the men stretched their legs and ate before moving on.

Occasionally Oliver and Aaron tried to get Graham to speak, but he only said he needed a few more answers first.

And he did. One or two holes had to be filled. And he had to learn exactly where Priscilla was.

Hurt and anger shored up his energy the closer they got to Marlborough. Once his feet were on High Street's cobblestones again, he nearly vibrated with the emotions.

How much had he wanted to come back? How many times had he sought out an excuse?

Now that he had one, he wished he didn't. He slid his hand in his pocket and rolled a thumb across the edge of the chess piece he'd taken from Oliver's father's study. The weight of the small wooden figure reminded him that everything he'd learned was real.

"Get a room at the same inn," Graham told Oliver. "I've got to see someone."

"If you're going to see Priscilla, I'm going along." Oliver balled up his hands and looked ready to punch Graham if he suggested otherwise.

"I don't know where Priscilla is exactly, but I know who does."

Graham stared him down until Oliver spun on his heel and walked away, taking Aaron and the baggage with him.

The sun glinted off the window to Nash's office and Graham considered starting there, but he really didn't care what part the solicitor played in the scheme. He was little more than a pawn, as far as Graham was concerned.

Instead, he walked toward the inn's stable to see about renting a horse. Why waste time talking to the pawn when he knew how to get to the queen?

Chapter Twenty-Eight

Kit slid her finger down the edge of the ledger, adding up the numbers so she could put the totals at the bottom. Her mind wasn't on the task, though, and after three attempts she gave up and put her head in her hands.

There'd been no word from The Committee, no news from Mrs. Corbet. Nash had sent his man from London to Yatesbury, but if they didn't find something soon she was going to have to contact Priscilla's father and tell him what had happened.

Suddenly, a masculine hand smacked a piece of paper onto the desk in front of her.

"Please tell me this isn't what I think it is."

She lifted her eyes to see Graham staring down at her. His mouth was tight, with the corners pulled in until they turned white. Red slashed across his cheekbones, dark brows arrowed in until they nearly touched, and his eyes were hard. With anger? Hurt? Both? It was hard to tell what emotion was spread across his face when her only experience of him was a charming, happy, and caring man.

She swallowed hard as she carefully pulled the paper from beneath his hand. One glance showed her it was one of the contracts, but she made a point of looking over it as if she hadn't a clue what it was. She flipped the page to see the signature of Priscilla's father. Had the man confessed to his son? If so, why wasn't Oliver here alongside his friend? Perhaps Graham didn't really know anything.

Kit cleared her throat and kept her voice quiet. "It would appear to be a contract for the purchase of a chess set."

Graham straightened to his full height and crossed his arms over his chest. "My father bought a new chess set last year. It was a funny thing, though, because he purchased the entire set at once. One piece every so often seems a bit slow, don't you think? No wonder the man has to charge so much per piece if it takes him that long to carve them."

Kit's hands danced across the desk, and her eyes stayed lowered. She had to say something, had to do something. Cutting it off with Graham was something she couldn't bear to do, but losing this place, putting the women and children at risk, was something she couldn't allow. At any cost. No matter how much it hurt her. But what could she say to protect them?

As soon as she lifted her head, though, Graham continued.

"I won't let you lie to me anymore, Kit. You'll never convince me that selling cheese and trinkets is enough to feed all these people. It wouldn't be enough to buy Benedict an apprenticeship with even the most generous of master craftsmen." He laughed, but it wasn't humorous and it wasn't uplifting. "Did you get a good laugh from fooling me? When I rode out of here, did you think me a fool for not considering how much money it would take to care for all of these children?"

He stepped forward and planted a finger on the desk. "Because this is how you pay for it, isn't it?"

Kit lifted her chin. She would not break in front of him. She had to give at least the illusion of strength so he wouldn't think she would crumble under his attack. And it was an attack. Whether he meant to or not, he was attacking the only thing that kept her from being a horrid shell of a human being.

"Yes," she said. "The money from the chess sets is used for the children. Coal, food, clothing. Apprenticeships."

"These contracts . . ." Graham seemed to deflate as he walked a few steps away from the desk and braced his hands on a sofa. "Are they signed voluntarily?"

She could say yes. If she said yes now, it would smooth over a lot of whatever was between them now. But it would be a lie. A lie that was bound to be uncovered, if it hadn't been already. "No."

How she hated the softness of her voice as she said that word. Hurt ran through her, sparking every indignation she possessed, and she pushed to her feet in a surge of anger. "No," she repeated forcefully. "No, they aren't, and do you want to know why? Because these men would rather push the problem aside, leave their daughters and lovers to die socially and possibly even physically. They have to be forced to care instead of shoving the problem aside and moving on as if it had never existed."

"Illegitimacy is not a death sentence, Kit." He didn't move from his position hunched over the edge of the sofa, and his voice sounded tired. "There are laws in place to make fathers support the children until they can make their way in the world. Plenty of by-blows survive that way without ridiculous contracts and fear-inducing code names."

"And what about the mothers?"

Graham lifted his head until he was looking her in the eye, but he said nothing.

She crossed her arms and continued. "What do they do? You can't come back from a ruined reputation. Everywhere those women go, their ruin would be thrown in their face. They certainly wouldn't find a husband unless they were rich enough to buy one. And what sort of employer wants to hire a woman without skills who also has a newborn baby to care for while she works?"

The more she thought about it, the angrier she got. She saw the face of every man she'd ever faced, from the one who'd threatened her with a fireplace poker to the one who'd curled up on the ground, sobbing at the idea of having his secrets revealed to the world. She saw the face of every woman who'd gotten in Nash's wagon to ride home, leaving her baby in the arms of someone else because it was the only way to provide a future for the both of them.

She saw them all, and she was livid. Her anger drove her right up to Graham until she leaned up on her toes to whisper into his face. "Where does that leave them, Graham?" Where did that leave her? Where did that leave Daphne? "If men were honorable, women wouldn't need me."

"All men, Kit? Is that why you didn't trust me? Why you felt free to lie to me?" He waved a hand through the air and then pinched his nose. "Don't tell me. I don't want to know. Just tell me how you get the men to sign." His voice was quiet. Not a whisper, but soft. As if she were a wild animal and he simply wanted to get out of here alive.

The idea that he was trying to calm her only upset her more. "Fathers who think they can cast out their daughters and men who have no care for the consequences of their actions have to be made to do what's right. It isn't hard to make it happen, though. Men who think like that in one area of their life are unscrupulous in other areas as well."

He dropped his hand, and his face fell flat, expressionless. "You blackmail them."

"I suppose you could call it that."

Graham swallowed hard enough that Kit watched the neck muscles move. The flatness dropped from his expression and a bit of an angry growl crawled into his voice. "And what would *you* call it?"

She gritted her teeth and fisted her hands.

He would not make her feel guilty for doing what had to be done. "Vengeance."

Graham walked around her and moved the desk, picking up the mangled contract. "And what of trust?"

She hadn't been expecting that question, and she nearly tripped as she turned to face him. "What do you mean? I can't trust someone so completely without honor that he would turn his back on a woman just because she is the one who can't pretend an indiscretion didn't happen."

Graham said nothing for a moment. When he lifted his head, he looked defeated. "What of trust in God? Isn't that what you told me? That you were trusting God to keep you day to day? To protect the innocence of children who didn't ask to be born but came into this world anyway? How is this" — he jabbed one finger against the contract — "trusting Him?"

"It's doing what needs to be done."

She. Would. Not. Be. Made. To. Feel. Guilty. Those men were the guilty ones. The society that turned their backs, too. Maybe even the women who fell into indiscretion, but not Kit. Not on account of this.

"It's trying to control the situation," Graham countered.

"And what is so wrong about that? What

is wrong with wanting to be sure everything turns out the way it should?"

Graham stepped back from the desk. "Because that's not trust. It's hard to believe at this moment, but you're the one who taught me that. Trust means letting someone else have a bit of control over the outcome of your life. The fact that you trusted me with the knowledge of this place, of what you were doing. That you trusted I would be able to return to London and rub shoulders with the very people who turned you away, the very people trusting you to help them through their mistakes. The fact that you trusted me that much was humbling."

"I do trust you, Graham."

Graham swallowed. "I know. And that may be the saddest part in all of this. You are trusting me more than you trust God."

Kit wrapped her arms around her middle. "That's not fair."

Graham wondered if the pain that threatened to bring him to his knees was for himself or for her. How did a woman — how did anyone — get to a place where they believed what Kit was saying? "Isn't it? You're telling these children something you don't believe yourself. Telling them to trust and believe in a God you can't bring yourself to depend on. You think they won't ever see that? You think they won't grow up and wonder why their parents were willing to send money but not acknowledge them?"

"They will never know. I will never let them know." Kit's hands fisted again as she hugged herself tighter.

And Graham knew the sorrow coursing through his veins was for both of them. For what might have been. For the crumbling of the pedestal he'd foolishly put her on. He'd thought they'd broken down so many walls. She'd told him so much, but then she hadn't told him what really mattered. The one thing she could have told him that would let him stay, or at least allow him to return quickly, she'd kept to herself.

He didn't know if he was more angry or hurt or if the two emotions were somehow feeding each other. What they had wasn't real, just as the woman he'd believed her to be wasn't real, but he couldn't simply walk away. Some part of her had inspired the woman he'd created in his head, and it was that woman that he was now fighting for. "And that should be enough to tell you this is wrong."

"And what would you have me do, Graham? Prayers don't burn well in the fireplaces. Hymns don't fill empty bellies and sermons can't be worn."

"And faith can't be limited." The words surprised Graham even as he said them. As if the more he talked, the more he understood himself. He'd been limiting his own faith in God, floating through life on what was expected and what was normal. But no more. "Have you even listened to the Bible verses you've been teaching the children?"

"Daphne does the Bible lessons," Kit murmured.

"Because you can't say the words? Does reading the verses make you feel guilty, Kit?" He knew they had to, because he knew how convicted he'd been when Daphne was telling the children about God's care and provision. When the children talked about the different ways God's care looked, Graham had been grateful he was sitting down.

When Graham thought of Aaron, Daphne, the children of this house, even Oliver, who would never have the paternal relationship Graham had, he knew that his father was right. *A good man sees what he's been given and does the best he can to earn it.*

He'd always assumed he had God's favor because he'd been born to privilege. That those who found themselves in dire straits were there because they'd disappointed God. But life wasn't like that. Misfortune fell on the righteous as well as the unrighteous. It was what they did that proved whether or not they were faithful.

"I have to make it right, Graham."

His name on her lips made him wince.

She continued, as if she could convince him that she was right. "I've looked in the eyes of women who don't know what they're going to do, who know that life will never be the same and they are afraid."

She started to cry, and Graham was thankful the desk was between them, keeping him from wrapping her in his arms.

"She was afraid."

The change in sentence made Graham focus more, stop listening to the words and search for the meaning.

"I held her while she cried, and I watched her father throw her away. And the whole time I died inside because I knew it should have been me."

Daphne. She was talking about Daphne. She'd told him she carried blame for the night Daphne had gotten pregnant, but he hadn't realized how deep it ran.

"It should have been me, and I couldn't save her. But I can save them. And with every girl I save, I hope God sees it and forgives me for sending Daphne to a fate that ruined her life. I sent her right into a trap that was supposed to have been mine. If not for me, she'd have married a little country clergyman or something, and all of her brightness wouldn't be buried out here in the woods."

Graham couldn't stop himself. He rounded the desk. "Grace doesn't work like that, Kit. I know my life's been pretty easy, and my list of sins wouldn't make anyone blush, but I'm not perfect and I've read the Bible enough to know that grace doesn't come because of anything you can do. Jesus didn't die and rise again so you could crucify yourself with guilt."

"I know," she whispered, slashing her hands across her cheeks to wipe the tears away. "Because I don't feel any better about what happened to Daphne. Thirteen women hasn't been enough. I don't know how many it will take."

Graham didn't know what to say. She was wrong. So wrong. About so many things.

Didn't she see that life couldn't continue like this? That everything was going to fall apart? Even if no one else figured it out, even if no one ever started talking openly about The Governess, Kit couldn't continue as she was. As these children aged, as they went into the world, all of this was going to catch up with her. And these unscrupulous men she was blackmailing? What happened when one of them finally decided to fight back? Did she have any idea the number of threats Nash had probably already received because of his part in the process? He was the only contact they had. No wonder he'd been so cold when Graham and Oliver had visited him.

It was going to fall apart, and as much as Graham wanted to catch her when it did, he couldn't be a part of this. He was too involved now, too attached to walk away from her mission, from the children who really were going to need protection soon, but he was going to have to stay away from Kit. Seeing her again would weaken his resolve until he excused her actions so he could be with her.

He may have only just realized what faith and trust really meant, what being a man of honor truly meant, but he was going to hold fast to those lessons.

"I want to see Priscilla." Graham swallowed. "Oliver wants to see Priscilla. He will be one of those honorable men you claim aren't there."

"She isn't here." Kit's chin lifted a bit more, and her face hardened until Graham saw the woman the underside of London knew as The Governess.

"But you know where she is. And it isn't right that she's hiding out wherever you've put her, thinking that her worth is only there because of your ridiculous contract. Oliver loves his sister. He'd never turn his back on her."

Anger burned in Kit's face, and Graham felt his own angry fire burn away the hurt, at least temporarily. He couldn't stop her from what she was doing, but he could get his friend out from under her control.

"What would you have her do?" Kit asked. "Expose herself to the world's ridicule? They won't accept her, you know. Even if the father steps forward and acknowledges the child, they won't accept the mother."

"And what would you have her do?" Graham stepped in. "She made a poor choice. Perhaps she was coerced, perhaps she wasn't. Perhaps there's no need for the whole world to know about it. But you've already condemned the men in her life as dishonorable and worthless. Did you even give them a chance?"

"Her father was all too happy to sign the contract. I didn't even have to blackmail him."

"Well, her brother isn't." Graham turned

and walked toward the door but paused at the threshold, his back to Kit, afraid to look at her. Though whether he was afraid to see her grow even colder or afraid he'd see her harsh veneer crack he wasn't sure. "Make the arrangements for Oliver to see Priscilla or I will put everything I have into looking for her myself. I know enough now to be dangerous, Kit. I won't mess this up for you on purpose, but Oliver will know where Priscilla is."

"I don't know where she is," Kit said quietly, bringing Graham to a stop in the doorway.

"What?"

Her head dropped forward. "I sent her a letter telling her that Oliver was looking for her. She was living with the Corbets in Yatesbury, but then she left and we don't know where she went. We're looking for her."

A herd of footsteps echoed through the passageway leading to the library. Small voices soon followed. "Mama Kit! Mama Kit! There's a horse tied up at the side of the house!"

Five children ran into the room, nearly knocking Graham off his feet.

Their concerned cries turned instantly joyous as they started climbing all over him and telling him everything they'd done since he left. There were baby birds in the nest in the stable now, and Alice had lost another tooth.

Graham made himself smile, forced his voice to sound the same, and eventually the innocence of the children soothed him like a balm. He looked over his shoulder at Kit, and the anger fizzled out, leaving an enormous wave of hurt in its wake.

She wiped one last tear away before turning and going out the glass doors of the library, shutting them quietly behind her. He watched her through the glass as she cut across the lawn and disappeared into the woods.

Alone.

He tore his gaze away from her retreating figure and turned his attention to the children. He wanted to give in to their pleas that he stay, to chase them around the large room when it rained, to hoist them on his shoulders once more and hear the squeals of delight. He wanted to take the boys out into the woods and talk to them more about honor and fortitude and all the ideals they were starved to hear.

But he couldn't.

He couldn't stay.

So he said good-bye.
And he left.

CHAPTER TWENTY-NINE

The wood of the finely carved chess piece was smooth against her hand. Kit rolled it between her fingers, remembering the first time she'd made the deal. The first time she and Daphne had concocted the scheme of selling chess pieces to the parents of the children they were helping.

It had started simply as a way to handle the transaction and protect everyone involved.

When had it become something else?

She couldn't deny the moment of power she felt when confronting a man who realized his unscrupulous behavior wasn't going unnoticed this time. Their emotions varied as they signed the papers. Often angry, sometimes panicked over where they would get the funds or how they would explain the expenditure. The memorable time one man had cried. He hadn't offered to marry the girl, though, or do anything else to rectify the situation, so Kit's pity had been short-lived.

Somewhere along the way, for Kit, it had become more about the men than about the children or even the women they were helping. And she hadn't even realized it. When? When had she become driven more by making them pay? Was it the first time she'd had to push to get someone to sign the contract? When she'd been able to punish one of the men who'd done business with her father? She'd known him. Danced with him on occasion.

She'd come home from that particular encounter to Daphne and little Benedict, who'd just started to walk. The first woman they'd given refuge to was about to give birth any day, and Kit had felt flush with the power of knowing she knew how to care for all of them.

She was too late to save Daphne, but she could earn her redemption by helping others, by saving the women who'd stumbled into a bad decision from having it ruin their lives forever.

"That's not the way grace works."

Maybe not, but the men she visited didn't see her as an avenging angel, as a caretaker of problems. They saw her as a threat. So she became what they feared and threatened them.

They signed.

They paid.

And the children's futures were secured.

Kit ran a finger over the smooth edge of the chess piece. What did the men do with the pieces when they were delivered? Throw them in the fire? Hide them in a desk somewhere? Sarah's father had to be nearing a complete set by now.

With a sigh, Kit set the carefully crafted bishop back in his spot on their own chess set.

"That's not the way grace works."

Her hands trembled in her lap.

Graham was right.

God wouldn't be happy with the way Kit was doing things. A light knock drew Kit's gaze away from the pieces to see Daphne and Jess standing side by side in the library doorway.

"All the children have gone up to bed," Daphne said quietly.

Kit sat forward and picked up the queen, twirling it in her fingers. "Are we doing the right thing?"

"Of course!" Daphne surged across the room and dropped to her knees at Kit's side. "All the women we've helped. Do you know what would have become of them? Of the children? Kit, what would I have done if you hadn't run away with me? Assuming I could have even survived on my own after my father disowned me, I'd have had to leave Benedict somewhere and never see him again. I'd have had to find work as a maid or some other sort of menial labor, assuming they would even hire me with my reputation. I could have ended up down at the docks just to survive."

Daphne gripped Kit's hand hard enough that the round prongs of the queen's crown pressed painfully into her palm.

"We are providing a way out. Not everyone has a Kit to come to their rescue."

"I don't think she's talking about the children," Jess said softly, still leaning against the doorjamb.

Kit glanced up at Jess and nodded. "I'm not."

"Oh." Daphne sat back on her heels and let her hands drift away from Kit. "What are we talking about, then?"

"The chess sets," Kit said quietly.

Daphne blinked down at the piece in Kit's hand and licked her lips. "They're a business transaction."

"They're blackmail." It was the first time Kit had ever said it out loud. She'd called it by so many other names but never what it truly was. "I have been finding out horrible details about the men and threatening to expose them if they don't sign."

It was several minutes before Kit was able to look up. She didn't look at Daphne, knowing that Daphne's heart was too forgiving, too loving. Instead, Kit looked to Jess. Jess had seen the darker side of the world. She knew what life was really like, how people took advantage of those who were weaker. If anyone in this room was going to soothe Kit's ruffled conscience, it would be the former spy.

Jess's eyes met Kit's and didn't drop. Her expression was blank, giving Kit no indication what the other woman was thinking.

"Jess?" Kit finally asked.

"When you think about the men," Jess said, "you get angry. Why?"

"They're dishonorable and unscrupulous. Unwilling to do what's right even if it means they might have to take a knock or two from life."

"And how are we different?"

Kit fell back into her chair. It had been nice of Jess to try to lump herself and Daphne in with Kit's decision, but the truth couldn't be denied any longer. *Dear God,* she pled in a prayer more genuine than any she'd said in a long time, *please have mercy on me.*

She'd become the very thing she hated.

To call Yatesbury a village was generous.

Oliver rubbed a hand down his face. He'd been doing that an awful lot since Graham had broken the news of Priscilla's condition on the ride from Marlborough to Yatesbury. "Prissy was here?"

Graham had to agree it was hard to imagine. He'd known the girl most of her life, and while she'd certainly been more at home in the country than the city, it had more to do with the enormous library and experimental greenhouse she kept there and the fact that she could conduct as many experiments as she wanted and no one cared.

The staff had spent years stepping around her as she examined the way sound traveled through the different areas of the house. It wasn't unheard of to find Priscilla sprawled on her stomach on the marble floor, ear pressed to it, trying to see if she could determine where people were in the house by the sound of their feet on the floor.

And now he was supposed to believe that she'd spent nearly two months in this small community where there were certainly no marble floors hiding in any of the modest dwellings he could see from his position.

"This would be a lot easier if we had more to go on than a name and a village," Aaron pointed out. "We should have asked the solicitor."

Graham had wanted to. But he was afraid if he'd gone in that office he'd have yelled at the man, berated him for his part in Kit's dangerous scheme. What needed to happen was for Graham to get himself and everyone he cared about away from this mess.

Everyone he cared about.

He wasn't going to be able to get everyone he cared about out of this mess because Kit stood at the very center, and now that he'd had time to cool off, the boiling anger that had taken him by such surprise had fallen victim to his normally calm nature. He still cared about her. He still believed everything he'd said, still knew he couldn't be a part of her life anymore, but he still cared.

And it hurt.

He liked who he'd been with her. He liked the man she'd inspired him to be, and now that all of that had crashed down around his ears, he felt a little bit lost. Did he go back to the way he was? Try to move forward with this new idea of who he should be without her? It would take a while to separate what he wanted from what he thought he wanted, but maybe it was worth it.

"Look around," Graham said. "It can't be that hard to find where the Corbets live. There's only six or seven options."

The village wasn't quite that small, but it was small enough that anyone would be able to point them in the right direction.

In the end, it took them an hour to find accurate directions to the cottage, and that was mostly because the man they'd asked insisted on telling them the family history of everyone they passed on their way to the Corbet home.

Eventually, the carriage pulled up in front of a little farm. The house was small and tidy, with ivy growing up the brick two-story front and cheerful flowers carpeting the ground in front of one of the windows. It was an odd look, but not an unpleasant one.

Graham's cravat suddenly felt tight. Were the other men as nervous as he was? Even knowing Priscilla wasn't here, this was where she had been. It was closer than they'd been in over a month.

A glance at Oliver proved he was thinking similarly.

The men climbed out of the carriage and knocked.

The woman who opened the door was tall, with medium brown hair pulled into a low bun and intelligent light brown eyes. Her dress rounded out in the front, indicating that she was clearly expecting a child soon. Was she one of Kit's women, too?

Graham cleared his throat. "I'm sorry to bother you. My name is Lord Wharton, this is Lord Farnsworth, and this is Mr. Whitworth. We're looking —"

"You're here to see Priscilla." The lady smiled. "She's mentioned you."

Her smile fell as she wrapped her hands in her apron. "I'm afraid she's not here. I was hoping she'd gone to you after receiving that letter, but I'm guessing she didn't. Please, come in."

The door opened into a drawing room that took up the entire front of the ground floor. Through an open doorway he could see a kitchen and the bottom of a set of stairs. In the middle of the drawing room sat a young girl, about the age of Sophie, if he were guessing.

A variety of items were scattered on the floor around her, and she was carefully selecting two of them, banging them together several times, and then selecting two more.

"You'll have to ignore Gillian. When Priscilla was here, she taught Gillian that different materials make different sounds when knocked together, and she's been fascinated by it ever since." The woman lowered herself into a wooden chair with a sigh. "Mr. Porter has already been here, of course, and I told him everything I'd already told Mr. Banfield, which wasn't much. One day she was here, the next she wasn't."

Graham wasn't sure who Mr. Porter was, but he was guessing it was the man hired by the solicitor to find Priscilla.

At least they really were doing something to try to find her.

"Where could she have gone?" Aaron asked, turning toward Graham and Oliver.

"We don't have property near here," Graham said.

"Neither do we." Oliver rubbed a hand over his face. "She didn't mention any friends who would be in this area either."

"You said she mentioned us?" Graham asked.

The woman nodded. "Oh yes, she spoke of you often. Told stories about your travels." Suddenly the woman's eyes widened. "Oh my, I'm so sorry! I forgot to introduce myself to you. Mrs. Francis Corbet."

She laughed and patted her rounded front. "I'm afraid I can't quite keep my wits about me with this one. I'd forget my feet if they weren't attached. At least, I think they're still attached. I can't really see them anymore."

Graham grinned in spite of himself. He could see why Kit had chosen this woman. She was spirited while still being easygoing. Probably the perfect woman to help with a girl in Priscilla's situation.

"Did she mention anyone else? Anywhere she might have gone?"

Mrs. Corbet shook her head. "No. Well, of course she mentioned other people, but none with the same esteem as she mentioned her brothers." The woman grinned. "She called you that, you know. Her other brothers."

As an only child, Graham had never thought to be anyone's brother and it was nice to know Priscilla thought of him that way, even if she hadn't felt close enough to him to tell him her problem.

Of course, a few months ago, Graham couldn't say for sure how he would have reacted. If nothing else, his conversations with Kit, his interactions with the children, and Aaron's story had forever changed the way he looked at people suffering the consequences of their actions.

"I'll tell you what I told Mr. Porter,

though. The first place I would check is Calne. Of course, that's not the first place she'd have gone. More than likely she went to Hilmarton because the only person who left the village that day was Mr. Charters, and he went to visit his sister in Hilmarton. But Hilmarton isn't very large. She'd not be able to catch the proper stage to anywhere from there. And I do hope she took the stage because she gets a pain in her hip and can't walk very far."

Graham's mind was swimming with the abundance of information, but he was suddenly thankful for small villages.

They discussed Priscilla's stay a bit more, though the discussion was interrupted by the racket Gillian was making. Mr. Corbet came through and commented on how interesting it had been having Priscilla stay with them and that she was welcome to return if she wanted.

Finally, the men went back to the carriage.

Calne was less than ten miles away. They'd be able to make it before nightfall.

Oliver was pressed up against the carriage window as if he could will it to go faster, will it to get to Calne before Prissy went anywhere else.

Aaron was unusually quiet, though, staring out the other window, looking thoughtful. "She called me her brother."

"What?" Oliver asked, turning briefly from the window.

"I'm not missing much in my life," Aaron said softly. "I have friends, a source of income, a home. But that's the one thing I always wished for when I was young but never got."

"What?" Graham asked softly.

"Family." Aaron turned his light, piercing gaze to the other two men in the coach. "We're going to Calne. We're going to find Priscilla. And we're going to bring her home. Because she's family. She called me a brother. She's stuck with me now."

No one said anything as the carriage rolled on. What more could they say? Aaron had said it all. But Graham hadn't a clue what they were going to do when they reached Calne. He could hardly stop people on the street and ask if they'd seen a young lady walking around by herself in a delicate condition. He didn't even know if Priscilla's condition was obvious yet.

Still, they were doing something.

He leaned his head back on the carriage seat and began to pray. God knew where Priscilla was, knew what she was doing and where she was going. He also knew how desperate the men in this carriage were to find her and bring her home.

Graham closed his eyes, doing his best to trust God with Priscilla, her child, everything.

It wasn't easy, but with every mile he felt a little better. He was turning Priscilla over to God's care and that was better than anything he, Aaron, or Oliver would ever be able to do.

CHAPTER THIRTY

Daphne brought tea with her to the back porch that night. She sat on the steps next to Kit and offered a mug before sipping her own drink in quiet serenity.

Kit drank the tea. Silent. Tired. Empty. She wasn't sure what she was anymore. Didn't know what she felt. Didn't even know who to be.

After several minutes, Daphne set her drink to the side and clasped her hands around her knees. "I'm happy."

What? Had Daphne just said she was happy? Kit set her own tea down and turned to her friend. "What?"

"I'm happy," Daphne repeated. "Here. With the children, the house, the trees. I'm happy. I have a feeling you don't know that."

She didn't. And she still found it hard to believe. "But . . ." Kit swallowed. "If it hadn't been for me, you could have married a clergyman or a country squire."

"Hadn't been for you?" Daphne laughed. "Kit, you've never been anything but my friend."

"No," Kit said with a shake of her head. "That night —"

"That night you wanted me to be you so that Maxwell Oswald wouldn't pay attention to Miss Rhinehold. I already knew that, Kit. It's why I agreed to go. I didn't really want to be you for a night. Being you terrified me. But I wanted you to have what you wanted. So I went." Daphne shrugged.

Kit groaned and dropped her forehead to her raised knees. "It's even more my fault than I realized."

"No." Daphne wrapped her hand in Kit's hair and lifted her head out of her skirts. "No, it isn't. No more than it's Jess's fault if John burns his tongue on his favorite soup or my fault when Eugenia glues her hair to her paper filigree coils. We make our own choices. If we're going to place blame on anyone, we can put it squarely on Mr. Oswald and myself. Because we were the only two people in the room." Daphne smoothed a finger along Kit's frown. "Have you been blaming yourself all these years? Is that why you do it?"

Kit nodded, hating the choking feeling rising up in her throat. She was going to cry again. She was so tired of crying. Why did growing and changing have to require so many tears?

"Well. I have very high hopes for our future, then."

The urge to cry faded under Kit's sudden confusion. "What?"

"If you could do all this" — she waved a hand at the grounds and the house — "by being fired up with anger and guilt, imagine what you could do if it was actually about helping God give those women another chance at life. If it wasn't about your penance or even me, but about them." She shook her head. "We'd be able to move mountains."

"But . . ." Kit wasn't quite ready to let go of all that guilt. It had been a defining part of her for so long. Who would she be without it? "You had all those dreams, those fantasies of the life you wanted, the romance, the love."

Daphne nodded. "I did. I still do. I think that's what happened that night, if I'm honest. I forgot I was you and I got caught up in the idea that someone saw me. Wanted me. I imagined us leaving the ball and flying up to Scotland or tracking down my father right then and there. He never promised me those things, but I imagined he had."

Kit blubbered her way through a watery laugh. "Remember when you imagined yourself running away with that cheese factory owner we saw at the market?"

"Of course. He was a very nice man who gave me a free bite of cheese." She smiled. "And he was very handsome. But that's just the thing, Kit, I came home, dunked my hands in the dishwater, and imagined he came to sweep me away to a place where my most difficult decision was what sort of cheese I wanted. The dishes got done, I came back to reality, and no one got hurt. That's why being here suits me. The perfect blend of fantasy and reality."

Kit didn't know about it being perfect, but there was no denying that Daphne believed she wasn't missing out on life. All of Kit's guilt had been just that. Kit's.

"I'm so sorry," Kit whispered.

"I know." Daphne wrapped her arm around Kit. "I forgive you. I forgave you a long time ago, because in my mind you'd done nothing wrong. So I think, right now, it's about forgiving yourself."

"Maybe."

They sat in silence for a long time, listening to the wind and the animals.

The door behind them squeaked open and light footsteps crossed the porch. "We'll need to oil that tomorrow."

Kit laughed. Trust Jess to be practical in the middle of an emotional crisis.

Jess leaned against the column and looked down at Kit and Daphne, huddled together in a salty, snively mess. "Have you set her straight yet?"

"I think so," Daphne said, giving Kit's shoulders a squeeze. "It may take her a while to believe it, but she's getting there."

"Good." Jess dropped down on the steps beside Daphne. "Because we need to decide what to do."

"About what?" Kit asked, dropping her head onto Daphne's lap. She simply couldn't take another surprise, another change, another decision.

"The contracts." Jess clasped her hands together. "The chess sets."

"We end them," Daphne said immediately and with conviction.

Kit raised her head. "We can't do that."

"Why not? All we have to do is send them chessboards, right? So we do that, including a note that says the remainder of the set may be purchased if wished but the obligation to buy has ended."

"But what if no one pays?" Kit asked even

as she heard the answer in her head.

Trust God.

She looked from Daphne to Jess, feeling a renewed strength. "No, you're right." With these two women and God, she could take on the world. "If we're all in agreement, I'll take the chessboards to Nash tomorrow and tell him."

Daphne groaned. "He's going to be so very angry at us."

Jess snorted. "He'll be relieved. We've probably aged that man twenty years having to deal with these contracts."

Kit had to agree. Guilt started to creep in on her, but she quashed it. It was time to start over. That was what Haven Manor was about, wasn't it? A fresh start? A life where your mistakes didn't define you? It was time she took that for herself.

The box of chessboards was heavy, but Kit needed to be the one to do this. She needed to feel the pull of the weight on her arms, the pain in her shoulders from lugging the box all the way from Mr. Leighton's workshop.

He hadn't liked letting her carry it herself. Neither had Benedict, but she'd been adamant, and both man and boy had finally given in, even though Benedict was trailing five steps behind her in case she changed her mind.

That boy might have gotten his face from his father, but his heart was a complete copy of his mother's. If only she could tell him so.

But that was a decision to reconsider on another day. Right now, she had to get Nash to help her right this wrong before she lost her nerve.

She was terrified.

What would they do if God didn't fill the holes created by releasing the men from their contracts? Would any of them continue to support the children simply because they should? Daphne had written the note and Kit had so badly wanted to reword it, using harder language, telling the men it would be in their best interest to continue.

But no. She was going to do what she should have done from the beginning — what she'd claimed she'd been doing all along — and trust that God would provide a way for them to continue to help women who had no way of helping themselves.

She was huffing by the time she reached Nash's office. Holding the crate and opening the door at the same time was an impossible task.

Kit sighed in resignation. So much for trying to do it all herself.

Of course, that was what had gotten her into this mess in the first place, wasn't it? Jess might have said *we* when she asked her incriminating question, but Kit knew the decision to start blackmailing had been hers and hers alone.

Kit grunted and shifted the crate. "Ben, please open the door."

The wiry young man, whose shoulders were starting to show signs of broadening, jumped in front of her and swung the door open.

"Thank you." Kit surged through the door, worried that her arms were going to give out on her at any moment.

Thankfully, no one besides Nash was in his office as she nearly ran to one of his chairs and plopped the crate in the seat.

"Kit?" Nash rose but didn't make it far because Kit began unloading the chessboards onto his desk.

One by one she took the finely crafted boards and set them on top of each other, making herself think of every person she'd pushed to sign a commitment, making herself recall every face. With every board, her heart shattered a bit more.

If there was anything she knew how to do well, it was to feel guilt.

"Benedict, I think there should be more chessboards back at the shop."

"More, Mama Kit? What do you need this many chessboards for, anyway?" Benedict scratched his head.

"Mr. Leighton gave us some chess sets to sell to support the manor," Kit said. "I'm completing the transactions."

Ben nodded, happy with the explanation. "I'll go get the rest of them for you."

"Kit?" Nash asked again as Benedict left the office.

Kit watched him go. He was growing up.

And Graham was right.

She hadn't really thought about the long-term implications of everything she'd set up all those years ago. When there was nothing but little children running around it hadn't mattered. Now that it did, she could see how many ways they'd gone wrong.

"What's going on, Kit?" Nash asked. He didn't seem ruffled, didn't seem worried. The man wasn't normal, but that was what made him so perfect for Haven Manor. Even after she ended the contracts, she was going to need him. Possibly even more. Who knew how they were going to manage Haven Manor's finances without a reliable, steady income?

Kit took a deep breath and laid a hand on

the boards, feeling a calm peace run through her that was so foreign she considered running away from it. "We're canceling the contracts. They're worded as such that the payments must continue until the chessboard is received. Here they are. I want you to send them back along with the contracts. And these."

She took a pile of papers from the bottom of the crate and set them on Nash's desk. File upon file of reputation-destroying information. She didn't want to keep it. Didn't want access to it. Didn't want to be tempted to go back to her old ways when her current resolve wore off. And she knew it would. Tomorrow morning she would probably be sick with fear and panic, but that didn't mean this wasn't right.

Nash speared his hands through his hair. "Are you sure, Kit?"

No. "Yes."

"Why? Those contracts are solid. They're working."

She took a breath. "Because it's the right thing to do." One hand tapped the papers she'd placed on top of the boards. "I forced these men to sign the contracts, Nash. I'm not proud of it. The very fact that I was keeping my methods from you should have told me it was wrong, but I did it because I didn't see any other way. But recently someone pointed out to me that God doesn't always work in ways we can foresee. That's why He asks us to trust."

Nash pulled the papers toward him and glanced through them.

Kit swallowed. "You, er, might not want to look at that too closely. I wouldn't want you to feel the need to report anyone."

Nash's eyebrows lifted. "You've proof of illegal dealings?"

"Proof?" Kit shook her head. "Not enough for you to do anything with. I was more concerned with the threat of social ruination than with taking them to court."

"What are you going to do now?" Nash asked.

She took a deep breath. "I suppose I'm going to go home and learn how to trust the Lord."

Chapter Thirty-One

Kit felt lighter when she left Nash's office. He would make the arrangements to accept voluntary donations on behalf of Haven Manor and bring Margaretta with him the next time he came to the house so they could discuss what to tell The Committee.

What to tell Graham's mother.

Dread dropped like a rock into the peace that had flooded her as she pushed the chessboards toward Nash.

Suddenly all she felt was exhausted. So much so that the idea of going to sleep right there on the pavement wasn't necessarily out of the question. The last thing she wanted to do was make the trek back to the manor. Perhaps it wouldn't be a bad idea to stay with Mrs. Lancaster tonight and walk home in the morning.

It would be easy enough for Daphne and Jess to handle her evening tasks. She didn't do much with the children in the evenings anyway, because the more she'd mired herself in the darkness of blackmail and the worry of logistics, the less she'd involved herself in the part of their mission that truly mattered. She'd left nearly all of it to Daphne.

Despite the tiredness and the worry lurking on the edges of her mind she felt . . . happy. Strange, because it seemed like so much had been going wrong in her life lately, but maybe this was God's consolation prize for her doing the right thing.

She closed her eyes and took a deep breath. When she opened them again, she saw a man.

He was standing on the other side of High Street, which should have made him completely unremarkable. Marlborough's main street was a busy place. There were at least a dozen other men she could see from her current position.

But only one of them wasn't moving.

He simply stood.

And stared.

At her.

At Nash's office.

Kit glanced over her shoulder to see what was visible through Nash's large window. With the sun angling its way down the sky, there wasn't a hint of glare on the large glass window. The stack of chessboards sitting on Nash's desk was easily identified.

She should walk away, act like there was absolutely nothing anyone would find interesting going on behind her. But she couldn't move. She wanted, needed to know who the man across the street was. Was he the one who had been stirring up trouble in London? She'd been foolish to bring the boards here.

It was possible she was worrying over nothing. Perhaps the man was waiting on someone or simply lost in his own thoughts. After all, hundreds of people passed through Marlborough every day without any knowledge of Haven Manor and the children they were raising.

But then he shifted. Just enough for Kit to see his face beneath the brim of his hat.

It was a face she knew.

It was a man she'd threatened.

And he was looking straight at her. With no disguise. No carefully utilized shadows. No protection.

Lord Eversly knew she was The Governess.

She wanted to run. She wanted to hike up her skirts and race toward Mrs. Lancaster's as if rabid dogs were nipping at her heels.

But she couldn't do that, couldn't risk the

slim chance that he wasn't suspicious of her. So she walked. Slowly and sedately.

"Well, this is a nice surprise." Mrs. Lancaster bustled around her counter and gave Kit a hug. "I have to say it's nice to have Benedict stop in more often."

Kit forced a smile. "You're not still slipping him free candies every time he comes in, are you?"

"And what if I am?" The old woman sniffed and then grinned. "No such thing as too much spoiling when it comes to that boy."

There wasn't a very good argument for that, so Kit let it pass. "Could I stay in your room upstairs tonight? I don't quite feel up to the walk back home."

"Of course. You know you're welcome to anything that can be of use to you and your brood." Mrs. Lancaster shooed Kit toward the back of the store, where another door led out to a set of stairs that went up to a few small rooms. "You go settle in. I'll have some dinner sent up in a while."

Kit smiled gratefully. She climbed the stairs, flopped on the bed, and fell asleep with her boots on.

Kit woke early. She'd managed to stir herself enough last night to eat dinner and remove her clothes, but then she'd gone right back to sleep. It was morning now, though, and she felt more energetic than she had in a very long time.

She glanced out the window as she coiled her hair into a bun. Would Lord Eversly be asleep or would he be watching for her to leave town? Did he plan to follow her? Even if she lost him in the woods, that would be too close. Graham had been able to find them based on the ramblings of a small child.

Kit rested her forehead against the cool glass. What was she going to do? She'd lost Graham, her source of income, her sense of right and wrong, everything.

Although, it probably wasn't fair to say she'd lost Graham when she'd never truly had him to begin with. It was probably more accurate to say that she'd lost the idea of Graham.

And her source of income wasn't ever something she should have had in the first place, at least not the way she'd done it.

Her sense of right and wrong had apparently left her years ago, so the loss of that wasn't really new — just the revelation of it was.

Which was worse? To think she'd lost everything or to learn there wasn't much she'd really had to begin with?

No. She couldn't let herself think that way. She needed to think in terms of what she did have. She needed to be like Daphne and think positively.

Apparently that was something else she'd lost over the years. While her view of life had never been as rosy as her friend's, she'd certainly become more pessimistic.

She took a deep breath and blew it out through pursed lips. This was an absolutely pathetic attempt at counting her blessings.

"One," she said, holding up a finger. "We still have the house."

That was probably most important. It was coming on summer, even if the air didn't feel like it yet, so they didn't have to worry about the cold for several months. Nash already had a man lined up to come fix the roof.

Another rush of air expanded her chest. The breath came a bit easier this time.

"Two." She held up a second finger. "We have the goods we sell at market."

Paper filigree boxes and wheels of goat cheese wouldn't bring in enough to pay for apprenticeships, but they would allow them all to survive. And if she gave up the idea of apprenticeships and the like, they could tap into money stored away over the years, if needed.

She didn't like the idea, but it was good to know it was an option.

"Three" — she pushed up another finger — "we have the garden. Four, the library has enough books to teach the children practically anything." Another finger. One more and she'd have an entire hand to raise in thankful praise.

She walked away from the window and sat down to tie up her boots, all the while trying to come up with a fifth item for her list.

All she kept running into, though, was wondering what Lord Eversly wanted with Nash. There had to be something Kit could do. She could set up some sort of decoy location, maybe, and draw him out there, away from town, and once he was there she could . . .

But that was exactly what Graham had been talking about. Nowhere in her plans had she allowed room for God to do anything. It was all about what she could do, all about controlling the situation herself.

Daphne may have been the one telling the children the Bible stories, but Kit had listened to them. And she'd heard enough to know that God didn't work under her control. He wasn't confined by the solutions she could conceive.

So maybe all she needed to do this morning was pray, take practical and sensible precautions, and then trust God to keep them safe.

The idea of praying on her own, without Daphne or the children, almost made her panic. She'd been doing life on her own so long that letting go enough to speak out loud to an empty room and trust that the God of the world thought her important enough to listen to was more than a little daunting.

"Oh, Father, er, Lord, God." She stumbled over the words as she fell backward to flop on the narrow bed in the small bedchamber. "I'd like to get home today. Preferably without any scary men following me. That is, if you agree with that. I suppose you might want the scary man to find me, in which case I have to ever so humbly ask for you to change your mind."

As awkward and difficult as it was, once the words started coming they didn't seem to stop. Kit had no idea how long she prayed, but when she said *Amen* the sun was blazing through the window and she felt like curling into a ball and going back to sleep.

That wasn't going to get her home, though. God was all-powerful, and she was working on trusting Him, but she was pretty sure He wasn't going to magically fly her home on the wings of a sparrow.

It took Kit half the day to get home because stopping at every crossroads and watching the path behind to make sure no one was following took a great deal of time. The fact that she hadn't even seen another person since crossing the bridge made it feel ridiculous, but Kit hadn't felt like she could take the chance. They needed to be prepared.

When she arrived home, the children were everywhere, so Kit couldn't find a single moment alone with Daphne and Jess to tell them what had happened. Her news had to wait until they were on the porch that evening.

And Daphne didn't seem to be taking it well.

"Are you sure it was Lord Eversly?" she asked quietly.

Kit leaned against the balustrade. "Yes, it was him. Without a doubt. When I confronted him eight years ago, he'd held just as still as he was yesterday. He stared at me in silence for what felt like hours before simply signing the papers and telling me the bank drafts would be arranged. Then he left the room and the butler showed me out. Believe me, I'd never forget him." Kit shivered. Over the years she'd had men yell and threaten and cajole, but nothing had scared her as much as Lord Eversly's complete stillness and silence.

"I'll go into town tomorrow," Jess said, tapping one finger against the rail in front of her. "I'll find out what he knows and why he's here."

"How will you do that?" Daphne asked.

Jess simply cocked her head.

"Right." Daphne's mouth twisted as if she were trying to swallow her reaction. "You do that sort of thing."

Kit laughed. She couldn't help it. What a combination the three of them were. It didn't make sense that they should be on this porch together, yet here they were. Brought together by life and circumstances, three dissimilar individuals who'd practically become sisters.

"I've missed that," Daphne said with a soft smile.

"What?" Kit asked.

"Your laugh. It hasn't come out much lately."

Kit sobered, realizing just how much her

taking the world upon her shoulders had weighed her down. She really ought to be in the library tonight, bent over the ledger books to see where they could economize now that they had no idea how much money would be available to them, but she wasn't. She wasn't worried.

She'd done more praying as she walked today, and with every step it had gotten a little easier, the words had come a little faster. She told God what He already knew but what she hadn't admitted in a really long time. It had felt good to talk to Him.

Kit looked at her friends, her sisters, and extended a hand out to each of them. They smiled and clasped hands until they formed a circle, a sisterhood, a bond only God could bring together.

"You're both ridiculous," Jess muttered, but she didn't let go of their hands.

The happy calm was broken by the sound of horse hooves pounding down the drive.

It was late and they were in the middle of nowhere.

Had Lord Eversly found them? Had he decided to attack? What would they do? They didn't have anything to give him. All of the papers were in Nash's office.

Jess broke away first, darting back into the house. Kit and Daphne followed a few steps behind her, but by the time they got in the house Jess had already fetched a gun from the cabinet by the stairs. She handed it to Daphne, who squealed.

"I can't shoot anyone!" Daphne's grip on the gun tightened until her knuckles whitened.

"Then give it to Kit," Jess said calmly with a roll of her eyes as she lifted her skirt to slide out a knife that had been strapped to her calf. "But one of you cover the kitchen door while I wait in the hall in case whoever it is comes in the front."

With shaky hands, Kit took the gun. She left Daphne at the base of the stairs while she moved into the kitchen to position herself in front of the door. How could Jess be so calm right now? Whatever life she'd led that had her hiding here in Haven Manor, Kit was grateful. She didn't know what would've happened if she and Daphne had been facing an invasion alone.

As the beat of the horse's hooves grew louder, all Kit could think about was the fact that there were at least two doors in the house no one was watching. Not to mention the windows and the outbuildings . . .

The rider came around the side of the house without stopping. Kit's hand tightened on the butt of the large gun until her fingers cramped. Could she really shoot someone who came bursting through the door? She flexed her fingers. Well, she certainly couldn't if she lost the feeling in her fingers.

At least Jess was between the intruder and the children. She wouldn't let anyone get up the stairs.

Daphne had eased her way into the kitchen and stood a few feet behind Kit, sniffling and murmuring. Kit caught a word every now and then, enough to tell her friend was praying.

Guilt knocked against Kit's heart. She hadn't even considered praying. All that talk about trusting God from now on, and here at the first test she'd relied on her own abilities without calling on God. That was going to take a while to unlearn.

The horse came to a stop outside the kitchen door.

Kit raised the gun to her shoulder and waited.

A sharp knock echoed through the kitchen.

Someone intent on attacking them wouldn't knock, would they?

"Kit? Daphne? Jess? There's light coming through the kitchen window so I came down here. Open up. It's important."

Recognizing the voice, Kit sagged with relief and went to open the door. "Nash?"

The man pushed his way in, dark hair sticking up in every direction. He paced the kitchen, taking five long strides before turning and going the other way. "Where's Jess?"

"Upstairs," Daphne said in a shaky voice. "I'll go get her."

"I'm here," the woman said as she returned to the kitchen.

With a shake of her head, Jess crossed the room and gently extracted the gun Kit was now hugging to her chest. "Starting tomorrow we're adding guns to the defense lessons."

If Jess could teach Kit how to be so calm in the middle of a scary situation, Kit would take those lessons happily. Harsh breathing rattled from Kit, Daphne, and even Nash, while Jess didn't even look like she'd made an extra blink.

After she'd stored the gun, she put her hands on her hips and looked at Nash. "Well?"

"I probably should have waited until morning, but when I got this with the evening post I had to come tell you right away," he said.

He pulled a crumpled letter from the pocket of his waistcoat.

Kit was really beginning to hate the papers that man pulled out of his pockets. "What does it say?"

"The owner of Haven Manor died a few weeks ago. Since all I do is manage this property for him, they didn't see a need to contact me right away. It didn't affect my job unless his heir decided to handle it differently." Nash swallowed and looked from woman to woman. "And he has. The heir has decided he wants to live here."

CHAPTER THIRTY-TWO

Was it only last night that utter peace had swamped her to the point of allowing her to sleep in her clothing? How had it gone so quickly? As Kit lay in her bed, staring at the ceiling, she couldn't even stand to close her eyes.

It was Nash sleeping on a pallet in the kitchen now. They were going to need to install a bed in their larder.

Of course, it wouldn't be their larder much longer, would it?

Kit huffed out a groan and gave up on sleeping. She crawled out of the bed and threw on a dress and shoes before grabbing a lantern and letting herself out the back door. How long did they have before the heir arrived? Days? Months? Possibly even years, depending on how serious the man was about fixing up the place and making it his main residence.

The night air was cool, but not enough to

make Kit shiver as she walked the path to her tree. Like the larder, it wouldn't be hers much longer. They'd have to find somewhere to live. Something permanent this time, because she was never risking this feeling of utter loss ever again.

She set the lantern on the ground and nestled into the crook of the tree. The night was quiet, the only noise the water rushing below.

Everything she'd counted as blessings this morning was gone. Why would God pull her toward Him only to knock her down again? What purpose did He have letting loss after loss pile upon her this way? Was it punishment for waiting too late to come to Him?

She knew it wasn't, but it felt a bit like that.

"Why?" she cried into the darkness. "Why would you let this happen? Why this way?"

She called into the night, pouring her heart out in sentences that repeated themselves over and over because she couldn't think of anything else to say, couldn't move past the single thought of *why.* There was something more behind her words, but she couldn't figure out what it was. She could only hope that Daphne was right and God listened to the heart and not the words. Because Kit's words were a jumbled mess of accusations and pleadings, even though her heart desperately wanted to trust that God had some sort of plan in all of this.

Eventually the words ran out and that strange peace she'd felt earlier in the day returned. She climbed out of her tree, picked up her lantern, and trudged her way back to the house.

While she was finding the strength to trust God right now, she needed to make sure she helped everyone else find it, too. They'd looked to her for years, some of them more than a decade, and that wasn't about to stop simply because Kit had a revelation. All that had changed was the direction she was leading them in.

This was the only home the children had ever known, and soon the women were going to have to tell them they were going to have to leave, that the home had, in truth, never really been theirs to start with.

Two figures were sitting on the steps to the porch as Kit approached.

Kit bit her lip. Would Jess stay? When everything happened, when they figured out where to go, would Jess stay with them? She'd become family, and the idea of her leaving made Kit's heart hurt.

But she could only handle one thing at a time. Jess would make her own decision when the time came.

Kit walked up to her friends, waiting for them to say something, anything. But they didn't. They simply came to her, one standing on each side with an arm around her shoulders. And together they walked back into the house.

But Kit was still too restless to sleep, so she took her lantern to the library. It was quiet and dark, but that didn't make it any less beautiful to Kit. She stood in the middle, looking around at the one and only room in the house that hadn't been touched, the only one that truly looked the way a room in an aristocrat's country manor should look.

The owner, the heir, would expect the entire house to look like this when he arrived. They had to put an entire house back to rights, to replace all the furniture and paintings that had been stored in the caretaker's cottage. To extract everything a decade of children had tucked away in corners and cabinets.

Kit moved to the desk and sat, her movements slow and measured. She would trust.

She would not panic, she would not give in to the need to frantically pull everything that mattered close to her. She would put one foot in front of the other, make the best decisions she could with the information she had, and trust that God had a plan, that He was in control.

After all, He cared more about these children than she ever could. Somewhere along the way, Kit had forgotten that.

She prepared a quill and took out a clean sheet of paper. After taking a deep breath, she dipped the quill in the ink and began to write. The longer the list got, the more inclined she was to panic, but she staved it off with deep breaths. Better to get the list down tonight so that tomorrow, when hopefully everything looked and felt a bit better, they could get on with the business of doing what needed to be done, of putting one foot in front of the other, of moving forward to see where God was going to take them.

Twelve years ago, when she and Daphne had moved in to this house, she'd refused to think about the fact that this day was coming, that one day the house would be sold or inherited and eventually someone was going to want to do something with it. She'd pushed it away then because to think about it would mean that she couldn't have what she so desperately wanted.

She wasn't going to do that this time; she couldn't do that this time. Whatever solution they came up with needed to be permanent, needed to last. And that went for more than just the house.

While Yatesbury didn't have a whole lot of transportation options, Calne was a different matter entirely. The stagecoach schedule was a bit sparse, but there were plenty of options Priscilla could have taken, depending on where she'd decided to go.

Porter, Nash's man from London, had apparently decided she was going south, though Graham had no idea how the man had come to that conclusion. He only knew that a very helpful innkeeper had told them he'd sold a ticket to the man.

No one remembered seeing Priscilla, however, which was odd because normally Priscilla was so memorable.

It wasn't her appearance, which was admittedly rather nondescript and average. It had much more to do with what happened when she opened her mouth. Regular social discourse wasn't Priscilla's finest gift. It wasn't unusual for her to start a conversation with an observation about how sound travels through water differently than it does the air.

Which meant that if Priscilla had gone through Calne, she'd done so quietly.

That, more than anything, worried Graham. He was so tired of people feeling like they had to hide themselves away from the world. A voice in the back of his mind tried to remind him that he'd never really known what it felt like to be ashamed. Deeply ashamed. With the sort of guilt that rode a person for the rest of their life. But he couldn't accept that any shame was worth cutting the ones you loved out of your life with a knife of secrets.

"What are we going to do?" Oliver said, tapping his fingers against his thigh.

"Get some tea," Aaron said, pointing to a local teahouse across the street from the inn they'd just exited after another unsuccessful round of questions.

"How is that going to help find Priscilla?" Oliver asked.

"It won't." Graham clapped a hand on Oliver's shoulder and directed him across the street. "But we might as well have something to drink while we mull over our next options."

They sat in silence at a table in the back corner of the teahouse. Graham didn't know what anyone else was thinking, but he was struggling with the fact that his resolve to become helpful hadn't seemed to last very long. So far he hadn't been able to make a whit of difference anywhere.

Why had God put such a desire in him only to let him falter so miserably?

A body in dark green muslin dropped into the chair in front of him, banging against the table so that his tea sloshed in its cup.

"Please tell me you came in a carriage."

All three men looked up and blinked. "Priscilla?" Oliver choked out.

"I'm glad I found you, because I'm not quite sure how to get back to Yatesbury. I know you three usually travel on horseback, but is it possible you brought a carriage this time?"

She was here. In a teahouse. Mere miles away from where she'd started days ago. Her brown hair was pulled back and curled, but the coiffure looked the slightest bit crooked. Otherwise, she looked like she could have stepped out of her room in London. Graham blinked again. "Priscilla?"

"I suppose I could hire a conveyance, but I haven't that much more money on me. I could have stretched it further if I'd ridden on the top or held on to the side, but I couldn't quite bring myself to do that. I'm not sure anyone has studied the numbers, but I have to think that the chances of getting injured or killed increase considerably if one is clinging to the outside of the vehicle rather than sitting on the inside."

She frowned. "I find my current condition makes me uncomfortable enough without adding injury to the mix. Of course, if I died I wouldn't be uncomfortable at all, but injury occurs far more often than death so I wasn't going to risk it."

Yes, it was definitely Priscilla.

Aaron chuckled. "I don't suppose you'd like to tell us where you've been?"

"Traveling the stage halfway to Sussex and back." She pointed to Oliver's tea. "Are you going to drink that?"

Slowly Oliver pushed his tea across the table. "What . . . why . . ."

"I also spent a great deal of money on meat pies. More than I should have. My appetite simply hasn't been controllable with the baby and all. You did know I was with child, didn't you? That's why you're here?" Priscilla cupped both hands around Oliver's teacup and lifted it to her lips. She set it back down with a frown. "It needs more cream."

Graham watched, bemused, as she poured more white liquid into the tea. He loved Priscilla. She was his strange, adorable pseudo-sister, but as a man he really couldn't fathom how in the world she'd managed to get in this condition. Who had braved the verbal onslaught to even try?

"Yes," Oliver said, gently brushing a curl back from her face. "I know."

Priscilla's thin eyebrows scrunched together as her lips pushed out. Graham had seen this look many times before. Priscilla was thinking. It might take minutes or it might take days, but she'd let them know when she was finished.

While they were waiting, he ordered Oliver another cup of tea.

Finally, Priscilla sighed. "I'd rather you didn't know, but since you're here now, I don't suppose there's any way of convincing you to forget it."

Oliver turned sideways in his chair and gripped Priscilla by the shoulders. "Why would you have me forget such a thing? I want to help you, Priscilla. I'd never make you hide in some cottage while you dealt with this on your own."

"I know. I just didn't want to be the reason that you and Father finally stopped speaking entirely."

Graham rather thought her disappearance had the opposite effect. Oliver had talked to his father more in the past month than he had in years.

Her gaze dropped to the tea as if she wanted to drown herself in the cup. "I didn't want to worry you."

Aaron coughed. "Have you met your brother? What made you think he'd be perfectly happy not seeing or hearing from you for seven months?"

Oliver's face scrunched up as he snuck a glance toward Priscilla's middle. "Is that how long it takes?"

"No," Priscilla groaned. "It takes longer. Mrs. Corbet says she thinks I have another four months or so. She should know. She acts as the village midwife sometimes. Not officially or anything, but sometimes it takes a while for the one in Avesbury to arrive."

Graham's head spun with the extra information. It didn't matter if there were three of them and one of Prissy. If they didn't get a handle on this conversation she'd soon have them making all sorts of promises they had no intention of keeping. So he cut through the chatter and got to the heart of the matter. "Who's the father, Prissy?"

"I know I'm not the best at dealing with people, Wharton, but I do know better than to tell you that. It's taken care of." She frowned. "At least I think it is. She said it would be when she dropped me off with those charming people in Yatesbury. The Corbets. Have you met them? They're lovely."

"Yes, I have and they are, but Prissy, the

511

man —"

"Mrs. Corbet is going to take care of the baby for the first year or so. She's having one of her own, so she'll be producing milk. I think that's fascinating how the body only makes milk when it's had a baby. That's probably why men don't produce milk even though they're similarly built in the torso. Well, not completely, but enough that it's curious. I wish I knew how that worked. Mrs. Corbet assures me her body will adjust to feed both the babies, which I find remarkable. I considered staying around just to see it happen, but that would defeat the purpose."

"Is there a magic word to make you stop talking?" Aaron asked as he dropped his head forward until it rested on the table.

"If there is I don't know it," Priscilla said with a shrug. But she didn't immediately start talking again either. Instead, she spun the teacup around in circles, watching the swirls of liquid inside.

"I don't like the idea of leaving the baby behind, but I don't know that I'd be a very good mother."

Oliver wrapped his hand over hers. "You could be a wonderful mother. I have that little estate, you know, the one from Mother. It doesn't produce much income, but it's small and out of the way. I can take you there. You don't have to do this."

"He won't marry me, you know."

Oliver swallowed and glanced at Graham and Aaron as if they would be able to help him out of this situation.

Given the fact that Graham was considering running from the teahouse, he wasn't going to be much help.

Aaron, on the other hand, didn't seem uncomfortable, now that the rattling stream of words had slowed to a normal speed. He leaned his elbows on the table. "The father?"

She nodded. "I think he kissed me that first time just to make me stop talking. Then I kept him there because I'd never felt that way before. I wanted to . . ." She sighed again. "Well, I suppose I wanted to experiment, and I didn't think it through completely."

Graham ran a finger around his neck under his cravat. He did not want to have this conversation, wasn't even sure he should be here for it. Wasn't this something she and Oliver should discuss elsewhere?

But Priscilla wasn't done talking. "It was interesting at first, observing people and learning the easiest ways to slip off alone." She glanced around at the three men. "In

case you were wondering, the second drawing room in Mrs. Blanchard's house has a
strange little nook to the right of the second
set of windows. Two people can fit in there
quite easily and, er, converse without being
seen."

"I don't —" Graham started to speak and
then thought better of it, particularly since
Priscilla hadn't actually stopped.

"But I don't want to ever hear of any of
you using it. Even if you find a curious idiot
like me." Her gaze dropped back to her
teacup. "I know I shouldn't have done it,
but . . . I, well, I'm not very good at social
interactions but Ch— er, he didn't seem to
mind my awkwardness, and I suppose I
wanted to not feel so alone. And then all I
felt like was a fool."

"You're not a fool," Aaron said gruffly.

She shrugged. "I suppose not. If I were a
man, I'd probably be considered a genius,
but as a woman I'm simply odd. But I
wasn't smart this time, and I got myself into
rather a lot of trouble."

"You didn't do this to yourself, Prissy. I
want to know who the father is." Oliver's
hand curled into a fist.

"Why?" Priscilla said with a roll of her
eyes. "So you can get yourself shot at dawn?
No, this was my fault. I was hardly the first

514

woman he, er, experimented with, but I am the one with child. As the variable in the situation, it's my fault."

There was so much wrong with Prissy's statement Graham didn't know where to start. He did know they really needed to make this a bit more private. "Let's go back to the inn, shall we? Perhaps have this conversation elsewhere?" Preferably without Graham being a part of it. Priscilla might be the closest thing to a sister he would ever have, but this was all a bit much for him.

Then again, it was probably a bit much for Priscilla, and she didn't have the choice to walk away.

They escorted Priscilla into a private dining room at the inn they'd chosen earlier. Then Oliver went to see about securing her a room for the night while Aaron went to arrange for dinner.

Priscilla twiddled her fingers together as she leaned against the table. "How did you find me anyway? How did you even know to come looking?"

Graham wasn't sure how to explain it so he kept his answer simple. "The woman told me you were missing."

Priscilla's eyes widened. "You know The Governess?"

Everything on her face narrowed until she

seemed to be piercing Graham with her eyes.

Was she angry? Why was she angry?

One of her long, thin fingers poked him hard in the middle of the chest, and she stepped as close as her rounded front allowed, which was fairly close since she wasn't really all that large yet. "Everyone has told me that curiosity was going to get me in trouble. I've been stuck in bed with a cold for weeks, broken my arm, and suffered enough bee stings to make me look like a spotted laurel plant. All of those were temporary and rather minor and entirely my own fault because I can't seem to stop until a question is answered.

"This time the fact that another party was involved, one who knew more than I did, knew the answers, knew the risks, and participated in my experiment anyway without any intention of being around for the possible ramifications, well, let's just say I have decided I don't like him very much. I've enough obstacles stacked against my chances of marriage. Throwing an illegitimate child in makes it fairly impossible. But he didn't care."

She jabbed her finger repeatedly into Graham's chest. "I don't like him, Graham. He is not a nice man. The Governess doesn't deal with nice men. She's the last hope for people like me. So to find out that you are one of those men makes me very sad indeed. So whoever she was, you find her and you marry her right now, or I will follow you around telling you the most disgusting facts I've ever learned until your ears bleed."

Graham's mouth dropped open. She thought . . . Now it was Graham's turn to be angry. "I am not one of 'those men.' I can't believe you would think that of me. And I didn't know she was The Governess — really ridiculous name, by the way — until a few days ago. I knew her simply as Kit."

Priscilla's expression cleared instantly into her vague, simple smile, and she stepped back. "Oh. Well, that's good, then, isn't it?"

Graham was still standing there with his mouth slightly agape when Aaron and Oliver returned.

"I'm taking you home," Oliver announced as he guided Priscilla to a chair at the dining table.

"That's not going to solve the problem," Priscilla said with a sigh.

No, it wouldn't. Graham dropped into a chair himself, quietly contemplating. It was becoming easier to understand why there were women who desperately needed Kit's sort of assistance. But Priscilla had Oliver, and she had Aaron and Graham. Which meant there had to be another way, had to be some means to keep Priscilla's baby with the family.

There was one option, of course, one thing that would make all of the problems go away. He could marry Priscilla himself. The fact that he wasn't the least bit attracted to her and really didn't want to marry her was part of the reason he didn't voice such an idea. The other part was because he hadn't quite gotten rid of the fantasy of sharing his life with a certain woman who had dark blond hair and bright blue eyes.

He'd never follow through on that dream. It had been a little too damaged by reality. But as long as it still lingered, he couldn't imagine marrying anyone else.

He would protect Priscilla, support her, make sure she and the baby never wanted for anything, but he couldn't marry her. He wasn't noble enough to sacrifice himself to a life like that.

Priscilla probably wouldn't accept him anyway, but he wasn't sure enough of that to ease his conscience and risk the offer.

Chapter Thirty-Three

If Oliver and Aaron thought it strange when Graham sent them and Priscilla home in his coach while he rented a horse to ride to Marlborough, they didn't say anything. Eventually they would both demand answers, but handling Priscilla was probably enough for them right now.

But Graham needed to go back one more time. If nothing else, Kit and the others deserved to know that Priscilla was safe. And there were the children to consider. Benedict should have started his apprenticeship by now. He might need something Kit couldn't provide for him.

And Graham desperately wanted to see Kit one more time. He wanted to replace the final image in his mind with one that was softer, sweeter, stronger. He wanted to think of her standing tall without him, not broken and crushed. Not crying.

And maybe, just maybe, he wanted to

know which image he had of her was correct. Which was the real Kit?

He was going to have to walk away from her either way, he knew that. But, one day, he hoped he'd be able to stop thinking about her as well.

The last thing Graham expected to find when he came out of the trees onto the manor's front lawn was a scattering of furniture.

Small tables and chairs dotted the grass in front of the house.

Paintings leaned against the wall on either side of the grand front door.

Near the front steps, Benedict and a tall, thin man with shocks of red hair sticking out at odd angles from beneath his cap were busy building some sort of frame. Ropes and hooks and wooden blocks dangled from the top crossbeam.

Alice and Sophie exited the front door, carrying crates of toys Graham recognized from the large room in the west wing.

A group of people, including Kit, Daphne, Jess, Mr. Banfield, the two oldest girls, and all the boys aside from Ben, came around the corner of the house. They were dragging a large ornate cabinet across the lawn, large logs beneath it allowing them to roll the furniture forward. The children were busy moving the logs from the back to the front as the cabinet rolled along. More ropes wound around the cabinet, and the adults pulled steadily and slowly, easing the cabinet forward.

Graham watched, fascinated, as they maneuvered the cabinet to the contraption Benedict and the thin man had built.

The large piece of furniture rolled to a stop, and Kit placed her hands on her hips before looking up at the hook and ropes above her head. Even at this distance, he could see how hard she was breathing, see the curling tendrils of dark blond hair that had escaped the knot at the back of her head. "Are you sure this is going to work?"

"Absolutely." Benedict nodded and began darting around the cabinet, threading ropes and tying knots.

"It's how they load the ships at the docks," Jess said as she came to stand next to Kit.

Benedict paused and popped his head over the side of the cabinet. Graham had never seen the boy look this excited. "It is?"

Jess nodded and proceeded to tell him stories about heavy crates nearly falling from their moorings, men who slipped on the water-soaked decks and nearly lost hold of their ropes, and the terrifying creak of a rope that had been used one too many times. By the time she finished talking, all of the children were staring at her with enormous eyes while Kit and Daphne looked like they were about to explode from restrained laughter. Mr. Banfield simply shook his head as he checked the tightness of the rope.

"I think," he said slowly, looking around at the children now taking huge steps away from the rope-encased cabinet, "that those stories could possibly have waited until we were trying to lift the last piece of furniture instead of the first."

Jess made her way to one of the ropes dangling from the top of the frame. "At least they'll stay out of the way now."

Graham had to applaud her methods. There was a danger in lifting a piece of furniture that big, and she had effectively kept all the children from gathering underfoot.

Mr. Banfield took the rope from Jess with a quiet statement that Graham couldn't hear. She didn't look happy about it, but she joined the other women around the edges of the cabinet. Slowly and somewhat evenly, the men and Benedict pulled down on the ropes that threaded through the complicated system of wooden blocks, and the cabinet eased off its resting spot on the logs. The women kept a hand on it, and it was all Graham could do not to rush forward and push them all away. Yes, Jess had gotten the children clear, but what if it fell on top of Kit?

Graham held his breath, knowing that distracting them at this point would increase the chances that one of the men would lose his grip on the rope and send the cabinet tumbling down.

Up and up it rose until it swung freely between the posts, the ropes creaking just as Jess had said they would. Carefully they pushed the suspended furniture forward until it was above another, smaller set of logs. Then the men lowered it down and everyone breathed again.

Graham strode forward, walking across the lawn as everyone scrambled into position to start rolling the cabinet toward the front door.

"This is all very well and good," Mr. Banfield grunted as he leaned into one corner of the cabinet, trying to help it turn on its rolling logs. "But how are we going to get the beds up the inside stairs? We can hardly build one of these inside."

"We've got a great deal of main-floor furniture to move," Kit grunted back. "That gives us lots of time to figure out how to get the beds back upstairs."

They'd gotten the cabinet to the door when someone finally spotted Graham.

"Wharton!" Arthur called and bounded off the portico to meet Graham on the lawn.

Graham caught the boy and swung him onto his shoulders. "What's happening here?"

"We're 'placing furn-ture." Pheobe grinned at him before turning to one of the crates and pulling toys out.

Graham looked helplessly in the direction of the adults because he hadn't yet learned how to interpret Pheobe.

"We're replacing the furniture," Kit said quietly. "The house has changed ownership and the new owner wishes to be his own caretaker, so we have to put everything back the way it was."

They were losing the house? What would Kit do? What would the children do? The questions sat on Graham's tongue, but the look Kit gave him was pleading. He wasn't sure what that look meant, but it was better to stay silent until he knew. Maybe his silence was all he could give until he had a chance to talk to her. Well, that and his ability to push around a piece of furniture. He'd moved many a sofa for impromptu drawing-room dancing. Moving it from one house to another couldn't be that different.

He put Arthur back on the ground and climbed the stairs. His gaze met Kit's at the top. It was painful and soothing at the same time. Somehow this woman had crawled beneath his skin until he felt like he wasn't complete without her, yet he knew she was wrong for him. It was like trying to rip away his own leg.

"Priscilla is with her brother," he said quietly as he placed his hands on the same corner Mr. Banfield was pushing on. "He's going to take her to one of their country estates until they can decide what to do."

Color spread across Kit's cheeks as her eyes lowered. He could feel her sadness, knew enough about her to know that losing the care of Priscilla must feel like something of a failure for her.

"I'm glad she's safe," she said softly. Then she put her shoulder to the cabinet and pushed.

"Why is he here?" Kit whispered in Daphne's ear through gritted teeth.

Daphne shrugged and picked up a framed painting. "I don't know. But I'm not about to complain about it."

Kit knew she shouldn't either. The looks he'd sent her were filled with questions, but he'd thrown himself into hefting furniture around without voicing any of them. With his added strength, they'd been able to move twice the amount of furniture they'd hoped to. Their first priority was to get the house back in order. Without knowing when the new owner planned to arrive, they couldn't waste any time.

Once they put the large beds and other furniture back in the bedchambers, though, bedding the children down properly would be more than a little difficult. Considering that they soon wouldn't have the bed-chambers at all meant this was a problem she'd have to solve anyway.

Grabbing another framed painting from the front portico, Kit followed Daphne into the portrait gallery. What had once been the space where the children played in bad weather was slowly being returned to its state of refined glory. Kit rather preferred the jumble of toys and games to the portraits of unknown people and the stiff, uncomfortable chairs. When she'd lived in London, she'd never thought to consider the portrait galleries of grand country houses a waste, but now, looking around at a space that was virtually unusable, she couldn't help but feel like it was all a bit unnecessary. Did the new owner even know who any of the people staring down from the wall were?

The sun shot in the westward-facing windows, sending squares of light across the green and gold carpet they'd rolled out across the floor. It was the same place she'd stood their first night in the house, surrounded by the splendor she'd left behind, wondering if she was capable of the task she'd assured Daphne they could do.

Back then, she'd had so many worries, so many concerns. Over the years she convinced herself they were unfounded, but now they'd come to fruition. Daphne came up beside her, just as she had that night. Her arm around Kit's shoulders was strong, though, as if this time Daphne was ready to hold up Kit, instead of the other way around.

"I'm sorry," Kit said quietly.

Daphne gave a short laugh. "For what? It's not like you went and killed the man so his son, who apparently dreams of being a recluse, could inherit."

Even Kit, in the middle of her morose ponderings, had to laugh at the image Daphne created. "No," Kit said as her laugh settled into a smile. "I'm sorry I couldn't deliver on those promises I made. I promised you we'd make it, that we'd change our little part of the world."

"And you don't think we have?"

Kit shrugged, but it didn't dislodge Daphne's arm. "I think, at best, we just delayed it. We've no money, no home. What sort of life are these children going to have now? What will Margaretta tell the next girl who comes looking for The Governess to save her?"

"Wasn't it you who told me we couldn't save them all? That saving one had to be enough, because to think about them all would turn our brains into bacon?" Daphne laid her head on Kit's shoulder. "We've saved one. We've saved more than one. And I don't think we're done. I think we're just going to have to do things differently."

"Different how?" Kit choked out. It had taken them so long to put what they had now into place. How long would it be to come up with something new?

"I don't know," Daphne said with a gentle squeeze. "But as long as we keep trying, we'll think of something. God will provide a way for us to do whatever He wants us to do. We just have to go where He leads."

For a moment they stood that way, Daphne's head on Kit's shoulder providing strength and comfort. When had Daphne become the strong one? Somehow Kit had always assumed her happy smiles and content attitude covered the same timidity she'd shown in London. But now Kit wasn't so sure.

Daphne's head popped up, and she stiffened a bit before giving Kit's shoulders another squeeze. "I'm really proud of you," she said considerably louder than her earlier statements. "Canceling all the contracts because it was the right thing to do. I know we might have some tough days ahead, but we'll weather it. We have each other."

After one more squeeze, she dropped her arm. Then the warmth of her body stepped away, and she was gone.

"You canceled the contracts?"

The deep voice that she'd thought to hear only in her memory slid into her ears with the warmth of a cup of steaming tea on a freezing winter's day.

She didn't turn around, though, knowing that if she saw that distance in his eyes one more time she'd lose what little control she had on the tears trembling around the edges of her eyes. And she was ever so tired of crying.

"Kit?" he repeated, and she heard his steps as he walked farther into the room. "Did you cancel the contracts?"

"Yes. Nash sent the chessboards out three days ago along with any evidence I had on the men I was . . . was . . ." She swallowed. It was time she called it what it was, or at least what it had been. "On the men I was blackmailing."

Silence fell between them until Kit wasn't sure if he was still there or not. Her own breathing was too harsh in her ears for her to know if she could hear his or not.

"Mr. Leighton and I are going back to town now," Nash said, his footsteps pounding into the room and then stumbling to a halt.

What was he seeing? What was he thinking?

His voice turned hesitant. "It might be a few days before I return. The, er, the man left town, but I have a feeling he'll be back. I don't want to leave the office empty too long."

"What man?" Graham asked with obvious concern.

"One of the fathers," Kit said dully. "Did you keep his chessboard?"

"I did at first, but when he left without actually coming in to the office, I had it sent to him." There were a few moments of silence until Nash spoke again. "We're leaving Benedict here. I know it's not much, but . . ."

"I'll stay."

Graham's voice made Kit wince. Of course he would stay. Even though he hated her now, he would stay. Because he was honorable and nice and so ridiculously perfect it made her teeth ache. Actually it made her heart ache because she wanted so badly to be a woman he could love.

Kit could be strong in this, too. "There's no need —"

"Actually," Nash interrupted, "it would ease my mind if Lord Wharton stayed for a day or two. Just as a precaution."

"We have Jess," Kit said, in an attempt to free both men from obligation.

"She can only be in one place at a time, though." Graham laughed. "I'll admit that I'd probably want Jess protecting my back instead of me, too, but I can help. At least if he manages to find you, he'll know you aren't unprotected."

Kit nodded, knowing there was nothing else she could say.

"Thanks," Nash said with a sigh. "I'll feel better knowing you're here."

And then he left, bootheels echoing off the polished floor as he stepped off the carpet.

Once again, Kit and Graham were alone.

CHAPTER THIRTY-FOUR

They stood in silence as the sun began to fade from the room. Disconnected from the main part of the house as they were, the noises of children going about their evening routines were muffled and easily ignored.

Graham wanted to say something, but he wasn't sure what to say. He wasn't even sure what to think. She'd canceled the contracts. What did that mean? Did it mean anything? Did it mean she'd changed or just that she got scared because he'd found out?

In the end, Kit broke the silence first. "I'm glad you found Priscilla."

Graham leaned against the wall near one of the windows so the fading sunlight streaming in the uncovered window would illuminate her features, hopefully allowing him to see something of the Kit he thought was there. "Actually," he said with a grin, "she found us. We followed the one and only clue Mrs. Corbet was able to give us and then we stumbled around until we couldn't think of anything else to do, so we sat down for a cup of tea. She decided to join us."

A small grin emerged from Kit. "That sounds like Priscilla. I was surprised when Margaretta brought her to us. She wasn't like most of the women we helped. She was upset and scared, certainly, but the fact that she had nowhere to go and that her father was sending her away didn't seem to devastate her."

"Is that how you find the women you help? Through the solicitor's wife?"

Kit bit her lip and looked away. "Er, yes. Margaretta keeps in contact with a select group of women in London. They know the gossip and the people involved. They're the type of women who somehow know what's going on before everyone else does."

Why was she suddenly uncomfortable about this? He smiled, trying to comfort her. "That sounds like my mother. She never seems surprised by a scandal."

His comment didn't seem to set her at ease. If anything, she looked a bit more sickly.

"Care for a cup of tea?" he asked. Perhaps if they both had something to do, something to look at, this conversation would be easier.

She nodded and followed him down the

stairs. The kitchen was empty when they got down there, but Graham's pallet had reappeared and the fire was still burning low. Graham set about heating water for tea while Kit sat on a stool by the worktable, watching him with a lopsided grin. "How very domestic of you."

Graham grinned as he gathered two teacups. "It's one of the only chores in this house I actually know how to do. And that's only because I've seen it done so many times."

They fell into silence again as the water boiled, but this time it felt a bit more comfortable.

"Oliver wouldn't have let her go, you know," Graham said quietly as steam started to rise from the kettle. "If she'd come to him instead of her father. Oliver would have helped her — is helping her now."

Kit nodded. "We didn't know that when we talked to her, although I'm surprised the — er, Margaretta's connections didn't think about it. I suppose we're all guilty sometimes of assuming our problems are too big for those around us to handle."

She continued talking as she scooped the tea into the cups while Graham retrieved the kettle. "Most of our girls are broken. We set them up in homes with women willing to nurse the baby when it's born, and they're usually too sad and disturbed to do anything else but wait until the baby is born. I try to stay aware of what happens to them, but it's difficult because we don't have any communication. In some ways that makes it harder, but in other ways, a complete break has been easier for both the child and the mother. The child can grow up without any false expectations, and the mother can find a way to salvage her future."

Graham took a sip of tea, wishing there were sugar to put in but knowing they couldn't afford it. "What about your future, Kit?"

"This is my future." She drank deeply of the tea. "You were right, you know. God wasn't impressed with my attempts to earn forgiveness. Daphne forgave me a long time ago. I don't think she ever even blamed me. And even if God was interested in my penance, well, I don't think He approved of the method.

"Still, I can't leave Daphne. I can't abandon these children to work in the same poorhouses I saved them from. Even if we never take in another child, it will be years before the ones we have are old enough to be on their own. By then . . ." She shrugged. "By then my best future would probably be me and Daphne finding a way to move into a little cottage in a small village, selling paper boxes and goat cheese."

Graham bit his tongue to keep from saying she could have a better future with him. He might be able to forgive her one day — maybe sooner than he would have imagined — but he wasn't ready to go back to where they were, to the thoughts he'd had when he kissed her in the woods. He was sure she wasn't ready either. Might never be.

So he changed the subject. "What is your favorite picture from the portrait room?"

She laughed and ducked her head as a slight blush crept over her cheeks. "You'll laugh at me. I actually liked it so much that I put it elsewhere in the house when we moved the paintings out to protect them."

Graham grinned and leaned forward. "What is it?"

"A dog." She smiled. "I'm telling you, it looks like he's grinning at you. It's the most ridiculous portrait ever, especially nestled among all the somber faces."

From there the conversation flowed freely. They talked about silly things, occasionally venturing into the serious but never far enough to break the mood. They talked about food and dances, about which children had a knack for musical instruments and which ones were confined to playing the triangle. They talked about everything in a way they hadn't managed to do when he'd been here before. Was it the lack of secrets between them?

When she was blinking slowly and nodding her head, he guided her up the stairs to her bedchamber. He planted a kiss on the top of her head before pushing her toward her room.

"Sleep well, Kit."

Her smile was soft and her eyes droopy as she looked back at him. "You, too, Graham. And thank you."

He retreated to his pallet and was surprised by how easily his own eyes slid closed.

As the house got put back to rights, Kit marveled at the small treasures she'd forgotten about, like ornately carved boxes and gilded vases. The sorts of things she never looked twice at in London and had put away when they cleaned out the house. Seeing the items that were so similar to her old life taking up space in the home where she lived her new life threw Kit a little off balance.

Seeing Graham didn't help matters. The kitchen door was propped open as she worked with Jess to prepare food for the day, and every time he walked by with a piece of furniture, he'd smile and nod. The four oldest boys trotted after him with arms similarly laden down, like a strange game of Follow the Leader.

Daphne bustled into the kitchen with the eggs, and Kit decided to take the moment to talk, since finding any time where it was only the three of them had become nearly impossible. "I've been thinking." Kit took a deep breath and then plunged on. "We'll have to move to the caretaker's cottage as soon as may be."

Jess crossed her arms. "The building's not that large. If we cram all the children in there, we won't last a week before it becomes unbearable."

"I know." Kit swallowed. "Which is why I think, for at least a time, we're going to need to split up. Daphne can take the cottage with half the children. Benedict was set to move in with Mr. Leighton full time in a month anyway, so that should be easy enough to move ahead.

"I'm sure Mrs. Lancaster would let one of us stay in her upper rooms with two of the children. That means we only have one adult and three children left to find space for. I can take three of the boys and bunk up in the barn for a little while. It shouldn't be too bad in the summer. That'd be a bit tight, but doable."

"As miserable as that sounds," said Jess dryly, "with the exception of Mrs. Lancaster's rooms, that only works until the new owner is on the premises. We could keep a few children at the cottage after he's here, but he'd notice three cherubim living in his barn."

Kit sighed, knowing what Jess said was true. "We'll have to come up with somewhere else, then. Unfortunately we can't use the attic until we get the roof repaired. In the meantime, we've got the cottage and the downstairs servant rooms. It will be a bit cramped, but we can manage for now."

The other women nodded.

Inside, Kit gave a quiet sigh of relief. Jess wasn't saying she intended to leave.

Graham poked his head in the door, his arms now emptied. The smile he gave Kit reminded her of the way he'd smiled at her those first days he'd been trapped here by the rain, before it had all fallen apart between them. "Where do you want the bedframes?"

Kit rose to join Graham and the boys in their endeavors. "We'll talk more about it later," she said to Daphne and Jess.

Working side by side, without secrets and worries between them, Kit found herself craving the teasing, the closeness, the anticipation that had been between her and Graham during his first visit. Even if nothing ever came of it — and realistically, nothing ever could — she wanted that light back in their relationship.

But since she was the one who had broken his trust, she was probably going to need to be the first to reach out.

She needed to do something fun. Not just for her and Graham, but for the children. They knew that this furniture wasn't for them, and while they'd tried to pretend everything was the same, everyone knew it wasn't.

The only problem was, she didn't have any idea what to do.

Graham slowly set the chair he was carrying down in the front hall. What was going on? The ropes they'd been using to haul the furniture were strung everywhere: twisted around furniture and around each other, slinking along the floor through doorways. There were even a couple draped through an open window.

The children each had their hand on a rope and were giggling as they worked their way around and between each other and the furniture to follow their rope.

Blake got to the end of his rope first and found a piece of candy attached to the end.

He gave a loud whoop and then ran around the house showing everyone his prize. The children renewed their efforts to follow their own ropes to the end.

Graham couldn't help but smile at the scene.

On the other side of the front hall stood Kit, smiling and laughing along with the children, tickling the little ones as they went by. She looked like the woman in the green dress again, who teased him about plants and names. No, she looked more alive than the woman in the green dress he'd met that first night. She looked free.

"We made you one, too, Wharton." Graham dropped his gaze to see Alice holding up a rope. "You have to keep one hand on the rope at all times and then you get a treat at the end."

"Is that right?" Graham asked as he took the rope. "What happens if I let go?"

She frowned. "I don't know. Mama Kit didn't tell us that. We just all kept our hands on the rope."

So it had been Kit who threw together this impromptu little game. "I think that sounds like an excellent plan."

Graham wrapped one hand around the rope and began to follow it. It got a little tricky to keep his hand on the rope when it went under a chair, but he managed. Across the room, he saw two other children handing Kit a rope as well.

It was so much fun watching Kit follow her rope that he almost forgot to follow his own.

But then his hand met Kit's.

They stood in the middle of the front hall, a mass of chaos around them, hands touching as they held the same length of rope.

"I suppose you are my treat," Graham said with a smile, enjoying the blush that crept across her cheeks.

The children around them dissolved into giggles.

Graham gave them his widest grin. "What exactly am I supposed to do with her?"

"Tickle her!"

"Tie her up!"

"Kiss her!"

"Make her do your chores!"

Graham slid a hand over his mouth to hide his smile as his gaze met Kit's. He didn't really have any chores, and while kissing her was certainly appealing, the state of their relationship wasn't such that he could really consider doing such a thing. Tickling was rather the same problem. Tying her up it was, then. "The little pirates have spoken," Graham said. "You're going to have to walk the plank."

He grabbed the rope and wrapped it around her several times before taking both ends in one hand and leading her across the floor, laughing the entire way.

"What do you say, mateys?" Graham asked the crew of children pressed in around him. "Shall we toss her overboard?"

"Yes!" the children cried before running out to the front porch.

Graham hauled Kit out to the low balustrade surrounding the raised front porch. "Up you go."

Kit's eyes widened as she looked over the side. "You can't be serious."

He leaned close until his nose almost touched hers. It was a bad idea. It made him think about claiming little Sophie's suggestion that he kiss her. Instead, he asked, "Do you trust me?"

She stared at him for less than a second before turning and stepping up onto the low stone wall.

Graham's heart pounded in his chest. He had to clear his throat twice before he could speak. "On the count of three, mateys!"

The children cheered mightily. A few of them ran down the steps to stand on the ground below her.

"One! Two! Three!"

Graham grabbed Kit around the waist with one hand and lowered her over the railing until she was dangling from the ropes he'd wrapped around his other arm. Then he let her go and lowered her the rest of the way to the ground, where she was met by a swarm of children who tackled her and did the tickling for him. The laughter was glorious and infectious.

A little piece of Graham's resolve melted away.

CHAPTER THIRTY-FIVE

For the rest of that day and all of the next, Kit sought out every opportunity to add a bit of fun to the enormous amount of cleaning and rearranging. The children held races to see who could dust to the end of a table first, made up stories about the paintings they uncovered, and tried to tie back the bed-curtains using only their toes.

Through it all was Graham, encouraging them, giving them ideas, pulling Kit into one ridiculous situation after another.

It had been a rather wonderful two days, and she would treasure them forever. When they left this place and Graham left their lives, she would always remember that, for a while, she'd known a good man.

Kit walked out onto the back porch, cup of tea in her hand. How many more evenings did she, Jess, and Daphne have with this view? How much longer would they gather to watch the moon on the lake and the breeze in the shifting shadows of the dark trees?

The door behind her opened and she looked over her shoulder, not very surprised to see that it was Graham joining her instead of Daphne. It had been a strange two days, and ever since the rope incident, it seemed everyone had been conspiring to put them in the same room together.

"Have you decided what you're going to do?" he asked gently.

Kit shook her head. She'd gone over and over the options. There were places they could live temporarily, but the truth was that not only were they losing the place to live, they would be losing the income and allowances that taking care of the house came with. The money they made at the markets wasn't enough to live on by itself, especially as they were soon to lose the goats and the garden, because finding a place for the children to live was difficult enough. They certainly weren't going to find a place that would accommodate livestock and a large plot of vegetables.

"I have a house," Graham murmured, coming to stand shoulder to shoulder with her. "It's bigger than Haven Manor, though I don't think my mother would understand stripping the house of all the furniture, so we may have to teach the children not to knock over the tables."

Kit laughed. The delicate and beautiful furniture hadn't been in the house for an entire day before one of the tables had been knocked over by three children racing through the front hall. Fortunately, it hadn't broken, but it was still evidence that they'd been right to store the furniture in the first place.

Graham continued speaking, quietly, almost hesitantly. "You wouldn't be isolated like you are here, but there could be advantages to that. More exposure to life and the different types of people in it. It'd be different —"

"We can't live in your house," Kit said, breaking into Graham's sentence. "Can you imagine? A future earl with a house full of illegitimate children? They slaughtered me for far less, and I was only the daughter of a baron."

It was a valid argument, and one that Kit believed in strongly. She couldn't see Graham as having anything but a charmed life. Most of his stories had happy middles as well as happy endings. Publicly aligning himself with Kit and the children could ruin that. "Besides," Kit said, "living in your house wouldn't allow Daphne and me to remain hidden."

"That's important to you?" he asked. "That you remain hidden away from the world?"

She picked at a rough spot on the stone railing. "It was the agreement we made with our fathers. That all association would end, and we'd give no one reason to remember the story and talk about it again."

"Your father has never been invited to Grandridge Hall, so the chances of you encountering him are extremely low."

Kit looked at her fingers and then lifted her gaze to his. She might as well tell him the real reason she couldn't consider moving the children to his estate, even if it would seemingly solve all of their problems. She would tell him why she couldn't, and she would look him in the face while she did it. It was fear that had driven her to hide like a coward and confront men from the shadows.

She couldn't do the same to him.

"What happens when you marry?" The words nearly choked her because they flooded her mind with images of him smiling at another woman the way he smiled at her, kissing another woman the way he'd kissed her, making another woman laugh. It hurt because that woman wouldn't be —

couldn't be — Kit. "Your wife won't want a dozen children she didn't birth underfoot. She won't want to have to explain to her friends why she can't hold a country house party because it would raise too many questions."

Instead of nodding sagely at the wisdom of Kit's point, Graham grinned at her. "I know the perfect solution."

Kit couldn't help but smile back. There was something about the way Graham looked at her that pulled a bit of joy from the depths of a soul she thought was too tired to feel that lightness anymore. "What?"

He leaned in close and whispered, "I could marry you."

Hearts weren't supposed to pound as hard as Kit's was just then, especially not when she was doing nothing but standing still. He looked as surprised by the statement as she was. As if he hadn't meant to toss that idea out there, but now that it had been spoken, he couldn't help but think about what it would mean.

Neither could she. The images she'd had in her head shifted, and it was Kit growing old with him. Kit making him smile.

Kit showing up at his side in London and bringing all the rumors back to life.

Kit looking over her shoulder, terrified

that someone would put the pieces together and figure out what she'd done.

Kit turning Graham into a recluse because he loved her too much to put her through the terror of being recognized. He would lose a part of himself that mattered so much. Graham craved people. He was good with people. God had gifted him with the ability to relate to people of every walk and station, and such a gift shouldn't be hidden away and shared with a select few.

She swallowed and forced herself to look at him. "I can't marry you."

"I know." His smile drooped. "On second thought, no, I don't. I thought I could walk away from you and not look back, but life brought me right back here. And I can see you're different, Kit. I know I've changed. I'm not in the habit of turning God down when He gives me a second chance."

One side of Kit's mouth quirked up. "And how often has that happened?"

He shrugged. "This is the first that I've truly noticed, but I think it's a good principle."

The other side of her lips lifted until she was wearing a full smile, even as tears pricked at the corners of her eyes. "You deserve someone who can stand by your side without looking over her shoulder." She took a deep breath. "These children . . . I realize I can't earn grace and forgiveness, but caring for them, helping them, allows me to be a better person, the person God would want me to be. He's giving me a second chance. This time I'm going to think of someone else's needs before I consider my own.

"And Graham," she said quietly as tears pooled onto her lashes and a single tear escaped from each eye, "I'm not what you need."

He swallowed and braced his hands, not turning his face or letting his gaze drop. "And if you're what I want?"

"Then I'll protect you from yourself. Because I love you too much to do anything else." She hadn't meant to tell him that she loved him. That had been a secret she was going to carry with her, knowing he would feel the heaviness of her love even as she felt the lightness.

His mouth pressed into a thin line and wrinkles appeared at the corners of his beautiful eyes as pain etched across his face.

But he didn't say anything. He didn't try to change her mind, which she was grateful for, because he would have been able to. With a few well-placed words, she would have fallen at his feet, claiming love could conquer all and they could forge through life together, but the truth was, Kit didn't want to stop helping women. She didn't want these children to be the last. She wasn't sure how they would support the women and children from here on out, but she knew she wanted to.

One thing was certain, though — she was hanging up her deep-hooded grey cloak for good. No more Governess roaming the streets of London like a menace. She would find another way, because standing with her shoulders back and her head tall as she faced a problem felt good. It felt brave.

She thought about that as she turned and walked away before he could say anything. She would be brave and not wait for him to convince her to claim what she wanted instead of what he needed.

She crawled into bed and fell asleep thinking of bravery and pondering the rest of her life.

What did she want to teach the women she was helping? What did she want to show the children she was raising? Was she really doing them a favor by hiding them out here in the woods?

Kit didn't have all the answers — didn't even possess half of them — but she did know one thing. She wanted to move forward with the past in the past. Which meant she had a few more demons to face.

She was up and dressed and already on the road to Marlborough when the first slashes of pink crossed the sky.

She was so early, in fact, that Nash hadn't yet gotten to his office.

The stage from London had come in, though, and it seemed God was guiding her timing without her knowing. Because getting off the stage and walking into The Castle Inn was the very man she'd come to town to talk to Nash about.

Nash paused as he came around the corner. "I was planning on coming out to the manor today."

Kit nodded. "Lord Eversly is back."

Keys jangled as Nash spun his body around to look up and down the street. "How do you know?"

"Because I saw him get off the stage fifteen minutes ago." Kit couldn't help but grin along with the matter-of-fact statement. Then her grin fell as she continued. "He's at the inn across the street. I want to go see him."

Nash sighed and opened the lock on his office door. "Twelve years," he mumbled. "We made it twelve years without drawing the slightest bit of attention. Why now?"

"If I had to guess, Lord Eversly is a bit more determined to keep his money than others were. He's probably made a bit more of a disturbance. It doesn't really matter. To be honest, the secret has held longer than it should. We're going to keep helping children and women, but we've all decided to do it a bit differently. But moving forward means tying up the loose ends of the past."

Nash looked at her for a moment before nodding and pulling the door closed once more. "I'm going with you."

She had been preparing herself to go alone, but she had to admit to feeling a certain relief that Nash would be there with her.

"One last run for The Governess, hmm?" she asked as she wiped suddenly sweaty palms on her skirt. She wished she had her cloak, wished she could protect her identity so that whatever they chose to do in the future wouldn't be marred by her mistakes. But he'd already seen her, likely already suspected who she was. If he knew who she'd been, there was nothing Kit could do about it except hope and pray that he kept the knowledge to himself.

Crossing the street to The Castle Inn, her boots dragged like when she had to walk through the mud and rain to tend the chickens and goats. The fact that the sun was shining and she was treading on firm cobblestones mattered little. The voice that had told her to be brave the night before was now screaming through her head that this was too scary. She should start with something smaller.

But this was what needed to be done.

Lord Eversly must have been watching because he was waiting at the door to his room when Kit and Nash got to the top of the stairs and rounded the corner. He was silent and brooding, just as he'd been the last time she saw him, and Kit almost turned and ran. One step at a time, though, she made her way to the door.

"I'm assuming you're here to talk," she said in a low voice as she stopped in front of him.

Lord Eversly stepped back into his room, leaving the door open for Kit and Nash to follow. This was it, then. They were going to step into that room and see what they were dealing with.

The first thing Kit noticed when she stepped inside was the chessboard sitting on a table in the corner of the room.

"I see you received the chessboard," Kit said, clasping her hands in front of her.

"You've been released from your contract. It's not because you came here, but using your past against you is the very thing I wanted to save women from. Doing it to you, well" — Kit took a deep breath — "it was wrong. And I'm sorry and —"

"I don't want the chessboard," he said in a low, rough tone, his voice rumbling like a rarely opened drawer that grinds over its slides.

Kit blinked. "I'm sorry? Of course, if you want to keep supporting your child, we'll accept the money. We just don't want you under the forced obligation to do so."

"I don't want the chessboard," he said again. "I want my son. Or daughter. I don't even know which my child is, but I've come to claim him."

Shock made Kit's limbs freeze. He could have run at her with a knife raised, and she wouldn't have been able to move. "Claim him?"

He nodded. "Like you, I've had some time to think about the way I've done things, the way I've lived my life. I'm not proud of it, but I'm ready to take responsibility for it. Including the care of my child. Lady Caroline married, but I'm sure you know that. I wrote to her, telling her what I intended to do and that she had nothing to fear. I wouldn't name her, wouldn't tell the child."

Nash stepped forward and stood shoulder to shoulder with Kit. "You want to raise your child? Claim your child?"

He nodded. "I have an estate in Kent. There's a governess already stationed there, ready and waiting for me to return with my son. Or daughter. I think in my mind it's always been a son, but I've no idea why. I've no reason to think that."

"Son," Kit croaked out. "You have a son."

Through the buzz in her head, she heard Graham telling her that she hadn't given the men a chance to do the right thing, feeding on their panic of the moment and making the decisions for them.

Yes, it had been eight years, but would Lord Eversly have made the decision sooner if he could have? Would he even have decided to marry the mother and make the child a true son?

She would never know.

He tapped a finger against the chessboard. "Giving this to me now means I don't have a complete set."

Kit's mouth fell open.

"I'd like to buy the rest of the set." A wry smile flashed on his face before it fell back into its stoic lines. "Maybe not at the price I was paying for each piece before, but I'd like the set."

"Your son . . ." Kit swallowed, not sure what to feel about a change of events that she'd never seen coming. "I don't know. . . . He doesn't know you."

Lord Eversly nodded. "I'll stay here for as long as I have to. You've taken care of my son his entire life, and I thank you for that, but it's time I did what I should have done earlier. I don't want to cause problems for you, Miss, well, whatever your name is, but the boy's past the age of seven. As I'm sure Mr. Banfield here can tell you, I have every right to claim custody of him."

Kit didn't need to ask Nash. She knew the law. It was the very same one she had threatened putative fathers with to get them to support the child.

The panic Kit thought she should feel didn't materialize. Instead, there was a sense of rightness to the idea. Blake was going to live his entire life with the stigma of illegitimacy no matter what Kit did. But she couldn't deny him the opportunity for a life like this man could give him.

"I'll bring Blake to meet you," she said after they stared at each other for several moments.

His breath seemed to deflate from his chest and the first flicker of emotion crossed his face. "Blake? His name is Blake?"

"Yes. We allow the mothers to name the child if they wish, and Lady Caroline chose to do so. Is it a significant name to you?"

He shook his head. "No. It's just that for all the time I've been thinking about him he didn't have a name. I could only call him my child because I didn't even know if he was a boy. But I have a name now. Blake."

"We'll choose somewhere the boy is comfortable for the meeting." Kit racked her brain for somewhere she could take Blake, somewhere safe for him and her and everyone involved, somewhere Lord Eversly couldn't grab him and run. "I'll send you word with a time and location."

He nodded, the emotion deepening across his face but not in any way that Kit could identify. It was as if he felt so much that it leaked out between the cracks of his normally serious expression. "Please," he said quietly, "make it soon. I've waited so long to meet my son."

Kit nodded, but as she and Nash left, her mind was buzzing with the implications. How was she going to explain this to Blake? And what were the others going to think? Would it give them a baseless hope or leave them stricken with doubt? Because the question was going to arise: If one parent had come looking, why hadn't any of the others?

CHAPTER THIRTY-SIX

Graham hadn't seen Kit all day, and it worried him. There wasn't much else that could be moved until another man or two arrived. He hadn't wanted to move anything at all until the men arrived, but Jess had simply glared at him and set about tying ropes around a heavy armoire. He and the women had managed to move that and most of the bedframes, which now stood side by side in the front hall because they hadn't decided yet how to get them up the stairs. They'd gotten them down by laying a piece of wood over the stairs and letting gravity do the hard part. The force would be working against them this time.

The sound of a wagon signaled Nash had finally arrived, and Graham hoped Kit was with him. He'd already walked out to her special tree, but she hadn't been there. He'd even taken a quick walk to the grotto, following the path on which they'd shared that glorious kiss, but Kit hadn't been there either.

As the wagon came into view, he sighed in relief that Kit sat on the wagon bench beside Nash. Whatever she'd felt the need to go do, it hadn't been to run away, which was all Graham cared about. If she ran away, he couldn't persuade her that he didn't need a wife with a perfect past.

Her face was ashen, pale to the point of frightening him as he rushed forward to help her down from the wagon.

"Blake," she breathed out. "I need Blake. An-and Daphne and Jess."

"I'll get them, but let me help you to the kitchen, get you some tea or something."

She nodded and went to take a step, but her leg didn't hold her and she stumbled.

Sweat broke out on Graham's forehead. What had happened? He scooped her up and glared at Nash, who was coming around the wagon.

Nash simply shook his head. "I'm still in shock myself, so I can't really blame her."

Graham carried her to the kitchen, feeling a bit guilty at how much he enjoyed having her in his arms, her head resting softly on his shoulder. Her breathing was even as it brushed his neck, so he didn't think she was hurt physically.

He sat her at the worktable in the kitchen and prepared tea from the water that had been kept on the fire all day.

"Blake," she said again. "Daphne, Jess."

Graham glanced at Nash. "They're all up in the bedchambers."

The solicitor nodded and left the kitchen.

Kit drank tea and nibbled on whatever Graham forced into her fingers, but she didn't say anything. Her movements were careful, as if she were terrified that one wrong move would break her.

"Are you hurt?" Graham asked, gently running his hand across her hair.

She shook her head. "No, I" — she swallowed more tea — "I'm well. I just . . . you were right." She looked up at Graham, blue eyes wet with tears that had yet to fall. "I took away their chance to do the right thing."

A bit of Graham relaxed. Whatever had happened today had shaken Kit terribly, but at least it sounded like it might not be all bad.

Footsteps echoed down the stone stairs and suddenly everyone was rushing into the kitchen.

If possible, Kit turned whiter. "Blake."

The young boy stepped forward, shaking his straight black hair out of his eyes. He

563

put his shoulders back and stuck his chin up before straightening his shirt collar in a gesture that was all too familiar because Graham had been doing it his entire life. Was it just coincidence that the boy did it, too, or had he picked up the habit from Graham?

"I need to talk to Blake," Kit said quietly.

"I'm here," the boy said.

"We should probably have this discussion alone." Kit wrapped her hands around the teacup.

Benedict stepped forward and wrapped an arm around Blake's shoulders. "We're here for you, Blake. Whatever Mama Kit needs to tell you, it won't matter to us. This is our family."

"Right," the boy whispered. Then his voice came out stronger. "Right. This is family. So, if you don't mind, Mama Kit, we'll hear it together."

"I . . . I . . ." Kit's gaze flew around the room, resting on faces until Graham worried she'd get dizzy. Daphne stepped forward to stand on Blake's other side while Jess came and sat across the table from Kit, reaching one hand out to wrap their fingers together.

The boys were right. This was family. And Graham wanted to be a part of it.

"Your father wants to meet you," Kit said quietly. "And, if you want, he's going to take you to live with him. He wants to claim you as his son."

No one made a sound. The silence was so complete Graham wasn't even sure anyone was breathing. He knew he wasn't. He didn't know what to do, didn't know where to look, and certainly didn't know what to say.

"The only thing I've promised is that he'll get to meet you, but" — Kit paused to take a deep breath that shuddered through her — "he'll be able to give you a life unlike anything we can provide. You should know that."

Daphne guided Blake to one of the empty stools and then sank onto one herself.

All of the women were focused on Blake, but when Graham glanced at the other children, his heart broke. What was it Aaron had said he wanted more than anything? A family? Yes, this was a family, here in this room, but every last one of them was aware that it was a family they'd had to create, a family of necessity. It wasn't the same as a family with parents and siblings and a future that extended beyond preparing them to work for a living.

There was happiness on behalf of Blake,

565

that his father wanted him at all, but also a lonely sadness on all the faces. The older ones held the mix better than the younger, probably able to decipher what they were feeling and understand. The younger they were, the more another emotion mixed into their faces, one that took Graham a while to identify.

Hope.

If someone came back for Blake, was someone coming back for them?

Graham almost fell to his knees because he knew Blake's situation was the exception. No one was coming for these other children.

The look on their faces was so similar to the one Aaron had worn when he told Graham about his childhood. When he'd said that the one thing he wanted more than anything else in the world was a family.

An idea sprouted in the back of Graham's mind. He couldn't give it too much attention right now, had to make sure everything was safe here, but it was hard to push it away. If he could make it work, if it was possible, he could give these children everything they'd ever dreamed of. And maybe even fulfill his and Kit's dreams in the process.

They'd chosen the rooms above Mrs. Lancaster's shop for the meeting because it felt more private and intimate than Nash's office, and Kit wasn't about to take anyone to Nash and Margaretta's home.

She, Daphne, and Blake had arrived in the morning, escorted by Nash and Graham. Kit had sent the men away, though. Blake needed to do this, needed to face his father, on his own. Even Kit and Daphne planned to wait in the other room . . . with the door open, and ears pressed to the gap, of course.

Graham had brought his bag into town with him, so Kit had to assume that he'd found whatever he needed and was going home. At least they were parting with some strange sort of friendship rather than in a flurry of tears and accusations. Still, it hurt knowing she'd likely never see Graham again. Nash had mentioned there was a small farm for sale on the edge of Marlborough. It would take all of their saved-up money to purchase it, so they'd have to make new plans for the oldest children, but it would be theirs.

And Graham wouldn't know how to get to it.

That knowledge was sure to hurt more eventually, when she found the time to really think about it, but it was the right thing to do, and that was what she was set on doing from now on.

Kit held her breath when the knock finally came.

Blake stared at the door, shaking.

"Do you want me to open it?" Kit asked. The plan had been for Blake to do the honors, but the boy couldn't move. He was in the best clothes Haven Manor had to offer. Extra linen was stuffed in the toes of his shoes because Reuben had the newest pair and had insisted that Blake wear them.

They'd pinned the waistcoat at the back because Benedict was the only boy with such an item in his wardrobe. It hung too long on Blake, but it had given him confidence, so Kit hadn't said anything as Daphne adjusted and pinned the best she could.

At that moment he looked exactly like what he was. A poor boy trying to make a good impression on someone very important. If Lord Eversly crushed his spirit, Kit didn't know what she would do. It certainly wouldn't be anything pretty.

Another knock echoed through the room, and Blake pressed a hand to his middle.

Kit crossed the floor and lifted the latch on the door.

Lord Eversly nodded to her and stepped

into the room, his gaze immediately searching out Blake.

They stood there. Staring at each other. Neither moved.

Kit knew she should step into the other room but she couldn't. The stillness in the room felt fragile, and walking would only disturb it.

Finally, the man spoke. "My name is Richard, Lord Eversly."

"Bla—er, Mr. Blake Harrison." The boy's voice trembled slightly and Kit wanted to run and hug him. If she was having this much trouble, Daphne was probably a ball of trembling mush on the other side of the door.

Lord Eversly reached into his pocket and pulled out a brown paper sack. "I saw licorice in the store downstairs. I used to like them when I was a boy." He pulled one out and popped it in his mouth before extending the bag to Blake. "Have you ever tried one?"

Blake's eyes were wide as he looked at it. Of course he'd tried licorice before. Mrs. Lancaster was always sneaking the children candy, but an entire bag had never been presented to him like this.

He carefully slid his hand in and took one. The man nodded and rolled the bag closed. "We can have another later, if you want."

Blake nodded and shifted his weight from foot to foot. "We can sit."

They crossed the floor and sank into the chairs near the fireplace. Neither seemed to remember that Kit was in the room. She slid along the wall until she reached the door to the bedchamber. She slipped in and then closed the door partway, leaving her head hanging around the edge so she could see. She felt pressure behind her knees and looked down to see Daphne had crawled over to look through the opening as well.

Boy and man said nothing, and Kit's heart threatened to explode. Should she go in? Tell Lord Eversly this wasn't working?

Blake scuffed a toe along the floor. "Did you ever eat boiled turnips as a kid?"

"Probably," Lord Eversly answered. "But I'm an adult now, and I don't have to eat the disgusting things unless I want to, so it's been a while."

"When I'm an adult, I'll never eat turnips again!" Blake crossed his arms over his chest and stuck out his tongue.

Lord Eversly chuckled. The laugh sounded much smoother than Kit would have imagined. "They're not too bad if cooked in butter. What games do you like to play?"

And that was the only opening Blake needed.

He started talking and, in the way of a child who had always had to share everything, including attention, and who suddenly found himself with a captive audience, the talking never stopped. After exhausting his list of favorite games, all it took was an encouraging nod for him to talk about what he liked about the goats and how to avoid being pecked by chickens. He talked about learning to throw knives and play the pianoforte, about attending chapel and lessons in the big house. Everything.

Kit's legs grew tired so she sank onto the floor next to Daphne, swinging the door open wider, as neither Lord Eversly nor Blake seemed to remember they were there.

Whenever Blake started to slow down, Lord Eversly would ask a question. A real question. The kind people ask when they're really listening.

Finally, Blake stopped to breathe. Lord Eversly asked, "Would you like to hear about where I live?"

If Kit had expected him to try to win Blake over with riches and grandeur — and she had expected him to do just that — she was bound for disappointment.

Lord Eversly told Blake about the way the

house was situated so that the morning sun hit the stained-glass window in the front hall, making it a welcome sight when he came down to start his day. He shared about the lake he liked to swim in and his favorite place to ride, past the tree he'd loved to climb as a boy and down to the cliffs where he could hear the ocean crashing far below. He talked about his dog and the way the animal liked to curl up in front of the fireplace when Lord Eversly sat reading in the evening.

There was no doubt that the life Lord Eversly was sharing about was more than enough to tempt a little boy, but Kit was surprised that what he'd mentioned, what Blake was likely to dream about tonight, was real. It was about life and living. Lord Eversly had money and connections, but he either knew those weren't what was important in life or he was trying to impress Kit and Daphne.

Given that the man had made his way to a small-town inn twice in one week for the express purpose of arranging this meeting, Kit didn't think the man cared whether he impressed her or not.

An hour later, they had finally lapsed into silence. Blake had definitely talked more of the two, but the man had said more words than Kit thought possible.

"I'd like to see you again," Lord Eversly said.

Blake, who had been bouncing in his seat while talking about the table Benedict had made that held all the boys' shoes in racks underneath, dropped his gaze back to the floor and scuffed it again with his toe. "Mama Kit says you want me to live with you."

The man sighed, and Kit's hand found Daphne's and gripped it tight. "I do want that. But I want you to want that, too. So, I thought we could meet again. Maybe eat dinner or whatever else there is to do. I go to the menagerie in London sometimes, and I enjoy the theater, but I'm afraid I don't know what's around Marlborough."

"There's the white horse. If you've never seen it, you should."

Kit winced. An aristocrat from London wasn't going to want to —

"Perfect. Why don't we let your, er, the ladies come out of the other room and discuss a time?"

Blake bounced up, excitement having returned. "Should I get them?"

The man smiled and cast a glance toward Kit and Daphne, acknowledging them for the first time. "I think they're listening.

These are good women who've taken care of you, Blake. I couldn't have asked for better."

His praise stabbed Kit in the heart. Daphne was good, but Kit knew she'd been forgiven too much to hold such a label.

Her legs protested their prolonged stillness as she rose to her feet and went to discuss the next time Blake could see his father. If the meetings continued to go like this one did, she had a feeling they'd soon be waving good-bye to Blake permanently.

CHAPTER THIRTY-SEVEN

"Please explain to me why I'm in your coach again?" Aaron grumbled from his position facing Graham as the traveling coach rolled north out of London. Graham had taken the mail stage to London, stopped by his house to change clothes and repack his bag, then driven to Aaron's rooms to convince him to throw a bag together as well.

Now they were on their way to Staffordshire.

"I have a goal to achieve, and bringing you along is the fastest way I can make it happen." Graham's plan was still more of an idea than an actual plan, but once he got a better grasp on it, there would be no one better than Aaron to help him finalize it. "We're going to Grandridge Hall. I'll have to meet with a few people there first. It'll possibly take a day or two, but then I need you with me."

Aaron crossed his arms over his chest and grumbled incoherently. "If you need me, I'll stay. But you're going to owe me for this one."

If everything went the way Graham thought it might, he was going to owe Aaron more than he expected.

Two days later, they were back in the carriage. Graham had met with the estate manager, a local solicitor he trusted, and the local clergyman, and he was now armed with a bit of knowledge and a list.

The carriage rolled to a stop, and Graham opened the door to see a plain, sturdy cottage. He dropped to the ground, a flare of excitement in his middle. This was going to work. And he was going to make all those little faces light up with smiles, and Kit was going to see there was another way to do things, a way to be together that didn't involve avoiding societal rumors for the rest of their lives.

Everyone was going to be better off if Graham could make this work.

"What are we doing here?" Aaron asked as he climbed out behind Graham.

"Come along," Graham said cheerfully.

Aaron followed slowly as they walked up to the door. It opened before they got there.

Graham smiled at the woman, whose eyes

widened. "Lord Wharton!"

"Yes." He gestured to Aaron beside him. "Have you met my friend, Mr. Whitworth? He's illegitimate."

"What?" Aaron spun to Graham, but Graham ignored him, watching the woman closely as her lip curled for a moment.

No. She wouldn't do at all.

"We're just stopping by to see how you like living here," Graham said, keeping his smile firmly in place.

The woman turned back to him and smiled. "We love it, of course. Living in the shadow of such a great estate is a joy in itself. Would you —"

"Wonderful." Graham spun on his heel. "Enjoy your day."

Graham nearly jogged back to the coach, Aaron close on his heels. Graham beat on the ceiling for the driver to move on before he and Aaron were truly settled in the seats.

Aaron glared at Graham and talked through gritted teeth. "What. Was. That?"

With eyebrows raised, Graham tried to look innocent. Even as serious as his current mission was, he couldn't pass up the opportunity to tease his friend. "What was what? I introduced you to someone who already knew me. It's proper etiquette."

Twenty minutes later, the coach stopped

at another house. This one was a bit larger, with ivy crawling toward the windows and chickens scratching in the yard. "Now this looks promising," Graham said as he climbed out. "Come along, Aaron."

Hesitantly, Aaron climbed out of the carriage.

Again the door was opened before they could get there, this time by a girl of about eight. At least that was Graham's best guess. She looked about the same height as Blake. Then again, did boys and girls grow at the same rate?

"Can I help you?" the girl asked.

"Is your mother or father home?" Graham asked.

A man came around the side of the house as a woman came from the back, cradling a baby.

"Lord Wharton?" the man asked.

"Yes." Graham smiled. "You are Mr. Pierce, correct?"

The man nodded, looking a bit nervous.

"Allow me to introduce my illegitimate friend, Mr. Whitworth."

Graham nearly chuckled as Aaron started mumbling under his breath.

The man and woman looked at Graham as if he'd lost his mind, but they made no reaction otherwise.

"Would you like to come in?" The woman and girl stepped aside. "I've made fresh biscuits, but they're ginger. I've heard you don't care for those, Lord Wharton. Do you like ginger, Mr. Whitworth?"

"Actually, they're our favorite," Aaron said.

Graham nearly chuckled. They weren't. Aaron hated ginger as much as Graham did, but he was determined to make life difficult for Graham. Not that he blamed him. He probably should have told his friend what they were doing today, but he'd been too focused on moving forward.

They entered the house and sat down to tea, asking the Pierces about their life and their children. Graham was particularly interested in the children, and he tried to ask questions without seeming too obvious.

As he left, though, his heart was happy. This plan was going to work.

Two houses and one hour later, he was a bit more discouraged. The reactions had been much like the first house, with all of them immediately showing a bit of distaste over Aaron's presence.

As Graham threw himself into the coach once more he looked up to see Aaron glaring at him. Frankly, Graham was surprised the man was still getting in and out of the coach.

"No more." Aaron crossed his arms over his chest. "I know I told you my parentage was always there, but it's usually not something I knock on people's doors to announce."

Graham nodded. "Let's get something to eat." He ran his tongue over his teeth. "My mouth still tastes like ginger."

Once they were in a tavern, plates of food in front of them, Graham looked up at Aaron. "I suppose I should tell you what I'm doing."

"That would be nice," Aaron said blandly.

Graham took a deep breath. He trusted Aaron completely or he wouldn't be about to tell him about Haven Manor, about Kit and Daphne, about the children. Still, it felt like a betrayal since he hadn't asked Kit about it first. He threw all of it out there in a rush. "I'm in love with a woman who has spent the last twelve years caring for illegitimate children."

Aaron stopped eating and slowly put his bread down. "This woman. She's the one who told you Priscilla's location?"

Graham nodded and explained how the process had worked, at least until recently. He left out the blackmail and the connection to The Governess. They weren't particularly relevant now, and Aaron would eventually put all of those pieces together anyway.

Once he'd finished explaining, Graham gave Aaron time to think, making himself eat food he didn't really want anymore.

"That doesn't explain what we're doing," Aaron finally said.

"I thought about what you said. About how what you wanted most was a family, and the more time I spent with the children, the more I wanted them to have it, too. All of them have aristocratic blood, but that's not going to get them far."

"Of that, I am aware."

Graham fiddled with his fork. "I want more for those children than a life of drudgery and survival. I thought it might be possible for the initial idea, living with a family, to become a more permanent thing. If someone were to take them in like they were their own children, raise them. With the really young ones, they could grow up with no one even remembering they weren't originally part of the family. I talked to a solicitor who said it wouldn't cause much of a ripple, legally speaking, as long as I looked to non-titled families."

The more Graham thought about the

idea, the more excited he became, but he made himself sit quietly and let Aaron soak in what he'd just heard.

"Do you think people would do that?" Aaron asked quietly.

"Not many, but it doesn't have to be many. Kit has twelve children including Prissy's baby." He didn't count Benedict. Daphne would never part with her son even if she couldn't claim him as her own. "That's twelve families. I don't need a hundred. Though if I could find a hundred, we could help more women."

"And if you get the children out of the way," Aaron said slowly, "Kit would be free to marry you?"

"Yes." Then Graham understood what Aaron was implying. "No! I hope she will, but if she doesn't . . ." Graham sighed and shoved his plate away. "I feel like I spend half the year traveling to house parties all over the country. It would be simple enough to visit families in those areas, find more that are willing to take in a child. Kit could keep doing what she's doing, but instead of raising the children herself, they'd be getting a family. She'd only be limited by the number of families we can find instead of how many she's able to raise herself. So I suppose freeing Kit so I can convince her to marry me is part of it, but it's certainly not all of it. Possibly even not what's most important."

That was hard for him to admit. He knew Kit was who he wanted to be with, knew he wanted these children to be his purpose, knew they made him a better man. With or without Kit, those children and others like them had become important. If that joined up with Kit's passion to save the mothers, well, it seemed like a rather unstoppable combination.

Aaron was quiet for a very long time, and Graham began to wonder if his idea was ludicrous. Saying it out loud had made him feel a bit silly.

"You want her to keep doing this? Even if you're married?"

Graham nodded and pushed his food around. "It's important. More important than I ever realized."

"And the reason I have to be here?"

Graham pressed his mouth into a thin line. "I don't want anyone to ever make a child feel bad for being born on the wrong side of the blanket. It wasn't your fault and it's not their fault, and the last thing I want is to put them in a home where they're constantly made to feel like they're less."

"So you want to see people's reaction to

me, to finding out I'm illegitimate," Aaron said.

Graham nodded.

Both men fell silent, and Graham couldn't bring himself to look up.

The barmaid stopped by the table to see if they needed more ale or food. Graham shook his head but looked up when he felt Aaron shifting toward the woman.

Aaron was smiling for the first time all day. "I'm Mr. Whitworth," he said, "and I'm illegitimate."

The barmaid stepped back like Aaron had a disease and rushed off.

Graham's eyes were wide as Aaron turned back to him and shrugged. "I don't think she's a good candidate."

Kit missed Graham. She missed the way he made her think and the way he made her smile.

She also missed his ability to haul heavy furniture.

"One, two, three!" With a grunt, she and Jess pushed the last heavy bed into place.

That did it. The house had been set back to the way it was when Daphne and Kit had moved in all those years ago.

There was still work to do, though, ledgers and papers to clean out of the library, chandeliers and windows to clean, small decorations and artwork to place around the house. How much of this would the new owner even keep? In his mind it had been sitting here unused for nearly twenty years, with a caretaker in place to make sure it didn't fall apart. What sort of condition would he expect the house to be in?

Kit looked around. The views from the window were the same, the walls were the same, even some of the artwork gracing the walls was the same, but it didn't feel like home to her anymore. She felt like she had to be careful everywhere she went.

"Is Blake staying with Nash and Margaretta tonight?" Jess asked as they walked down the stairs. Kit nodded. The conversations with Lord Eversly were going well. Much better than Kit had ever expected. "I don't know if Blake feels comfortable leaving with his father, but I don't know how much longer he'll be able to maintain this. As nice as The Castle Inn is, Lord Eversly isn't going to want to live there for much longer."

Jess nodded. "It's a good sign that he's stayed this long. He could simply take the boy and leave and we couldn't do anything about it."

Kit hated that Jess was right. She'd been

looking, hoping for some sign that Lord Eversly was not a good man, that something would happen to make this situation horrible. But each time Blake returned to Haven Manor he was happier, more hopeful. It wasn't hard to see what that was doing to the rest of the children. As difficult as it would be, it was time for Blake to go make a new life, a better life than Kit could have ever provided.

As they walked toward the caretaker's cottage, tension knotted across Kit's shoulders. After a lot of thought, they'd decided to try moving everyone to the smaller house. The narrow servants' beds from the house were tucked into every conceivable place in the cottage, edge to edge and nearly wall to wall in the three upstairs bedchambers, tucked in the corners of what was supposed to be the dressing room and the downstairs parlor. Jess was sleeping on a pallet in the kitchen.

The children were bearing up under the misery, but it couldn't last. Kit wished she'd dared stay in the big house longer, but she couldn't risk what the new owner would do if he found them there, if the house wasn't the way he expected it to be. And there would be no reason for him to send advance warning.

Margaretta was contacting The Committee to see if funds could be gathered to purchase the farm. Even if the women spent all of their money on the land, they'd be living a step above squalor until they could figure out how to buy the needed furniture and make some necessary repairs.

Until they had that figured out, they were living in a home that would have been more than adequate for a normal-sized family.

It was a bit small for a family of fifteen.

It was just one more thing to make Kit sad, and that was not what she needed right now.

She opened one of the trunks they'd layered clothes in and shifted aside a few garments to pull out her night rail. A splash of green underneath it made her eyes prick with tears. Daphne's evening gown — well, sort of hers now — peeked up at her. The one that had first drawn Graham's notice. He'd thought her to be a woman she wasn't.

But she wanted to be. She wanted to be that confident, honorable woman, and that was why she'd sent him away. To have kept him would have been selfish. She would have slowly ruined him. Their relationship would never have survived waiting for the axe to fall on their heads, waiting for someone to figure out her secret life.

She didn't know how Daphne, Jess, the children, and she would continue from here, but she'd find a way. She trusted God to find a way. Already He was opening doors she would've never thought to consider, such as the option of becoming a sponsored charity. They were still discussing that one, though. Would Haven Manor work if more people knew about it? Or would it become like the foundling hospital where the most desperate women left their babies? Over-worked and overcrowded.

Kit sighed as noise emanated from the small caretaker's cottage. Of course, without a manor house, Haven Manor was rather overcrowded as it was.

CHAPTER THIRTY-EIGHT

Kit was milking the goats when she heard it. Horses coming down the lane, the jangle of their harnesses, and the rattle of large wheels, but without the telltale creak of an old wooden wagon. A carriage had come to Haven Manor.

Was it Lord Eversly bringing Blake back after having had full care of him for a mere two days? Would Blake really have told him how to get to the house?

Or was it the new owner?

Kit cast a look back at the caretaker's cottage. Some of the boys had chosen to take their pallets out next to the house since the nights were so mild right now. It had helped ease the crowding in the cottage, but spirits were certainly low. They had to find somewhere to go soon. She hoped Margaretta was having some luck making discreet inquiries in London. It was the only chance they had.

With a whistle, Kit caught the attention of the children and waved her arm in the air, indicating they needed to set the pallets inside.

The carriage that rolled out of the woods was indeed fine. Even from this distance, Kit saw the golden trim gleaming in the light, despite the road dust that covered the underside of the carriage. A liveried driver drove the horses down the lane, coming to a stop where the drive met the corner of the house instead of continuing on to the front steps.

It was almost as if he knew no one would actually be in the house.

Kit frowned as a very tall, broad gentleman she'd never seen before climbed out of the carriage. She sucked in a sharp breath and smoothed her dress. The new owner was a bit younger than she'd expected.

But then Graham climbed out next, and Kit's mind whirled with confusion. Did Graham know the owner of the house?

She walked quickly from the barnyard toward the house.

As she got closer, she saw that Graham was smiling. A wide smile without any trace of the sad resignation he'd left here with before.

When she was in arm's reach, he wrapped

his arms around her, drawing a squeak from her lips as she was hauled close in an embrace she'd thought never to feel again. And then he was kissing her.

It wasn't a long kiss, but it was enough to addle her brain.

"Wha . . ." The partial question was all she could get out because she couldn't think of anything else, couldn't even mentally form the rest of the sentence.

His smile faltered a bit and uncertainty filled his eyes. "Kit," he said softly. "I love you. And I'm sorry."

What was he doing to her? Why was he doing this? "Graham —"

"No," he said, putting one finger across her lips. "Just listen for a moment. I'm sorry for the way I yelled at you and shut you out. I've never been desperate until I didn't know how to keep you in my life. There's more, but for right now, please, don't tell me all the reasons you're afraid, don't give me logistics. Just tell me how you feel."

She should lie. She could lie right now and save him from a mistake he seemed determined to make. But she'd promised herself and him there'd be no more lies, that she wouldn't control the situation but trust God to work it out. The pain of saying the words almost choked her, but she said them anyway because he'd asked for them. "I love you, too."

The questions left his eyes and his smile relaxed, though it remained large. "Excellent. That's going to make my announcement a great deal more enjoyable."

"Announcement?" Kit asked, blinking up at him.

He nodded. "Gather everyone together, because I've done something."

The tall man behind Graham barked out a short laugh. "You've done something, all right."

Alarm ran through Kit. What had Graham done?

Graham waved a hand in the other man's direction. "Pay Mr. Whitworth no mind. He's still smarting over the fact that I've embarrassed him quite continually for the past week in my efforts to solve our problem."

Our problem? Haven Manor wasn't Graham's problem. He could walk away without any repercussions.

Did he really love her enough to fully claim it? Did he not just want to marry her and let her keep running it in secret on the side? Or did he expect her to move it to his estate?

"Embarrass him?" Kit looked the man

over. He looked strong and confident, despite the wry, resigned smirk he wore.

"My name is Aaron Whitworth, and I'm illegitimate."

Her eyes widened. "Graham, what did you do?"

"Ignore his bluster. He was a willing participant." Graham winced as Mr. Whitworth gave him a pointed look. "Well, most of the time."

"Graham," Kit said, finally pulling herself out of his arms. "What did you do?"

"Let's get everyone together, and I'll tell you all at once. I've already visited Nash and gotten him in contact with my solicitor in Staffordshire. We're going to need a trusted fellow in Derbyshire, too, which might take a bit more time, but I've only been at this a week, so I'm not too worried about it."

Graham grabbed her hand and started off down the side lawn toward the outbuildings. He'd been recognized, and the children were spilling out of the cottage.

Kit glanced at Mr. Whitworth, unsurprised to see a look of shock on his face.

"You've saved all those children?" he asked quietly. "You've saved their mothers?"

The awe in his voice was enough to make Kit wonder what Mr. Whitworth's life had been. What had happened to his own mother? It was a story that would have to wait for later because her entire family, with the exception of Blake and Benedict, was swarming around them.

Graham looked a bit uncertain suddenly as he pulled a sheaf of papers from his jacket. He looked around at the smiling young faces, at Daphne and Jess, at Kit, and then back at the papers, his brow furrowed.

Mr. Whitworth stepped forward and clapped a hand on Graham's shoulder. "This is a good thing, Graham."

Kit's worry increased.

Graham took a deep breath and then sent his words out in a slurred rush. "I found families."

Families? Kit looked around to see if Graham's sentence made sense to anyone else. Even Jess blinked in confusion. "Families for what?"

Graham swallowed. "For the children. Well, not all of them, not yet." He winced and looked at his toes. "There's more concerns when it comes to the older children, but" — he looked back up with a small grin in place — "I've got seven families ready and waiting to grow their family by one. They find the idea of having another child without the pain of childbirth rather appealing."

Kit's eyes widened. Was such a thing possible? She'd never heard of it. "Can they do that?"

"They're not aristocratic. Not a title in sight." He rolled up the papers and knocked them against his leg. "Working families, mostly. With farms and such. I thought that would be best since the children are used to animals and gardening and the work involved. Most of them are from the villages around my family's estate, but we also went to where Whitworth grew up."

Graham looked around, twitching and fidgeting.

Kit wanted to reassure him, wanted to help him feel better, but she was frozen. She didn't know what to do or what to say.

"A real family?" came a lone little voice. It trembled so much that it was hard to identify as Arthur, but then the little boy stepped up and gave Graham a wide-eyed look. "You found me a real family? I'm going to have a father?"

Kit fell to her knees and wrapped an arm around Arthur, both of them looking up to Graham for his answer. She and Daphne had done everything they could, and Kit still believed, would always believe, that they'd done right by these children.

Kit's methods of support might have been suspect, but the life the children had was a good one and they'd been raised well. But that didn't mean the children hadn't missed having a father, having a real family.

Graham knelt beside them, his own gaze looking a little wet as he swallowed hard. "Yes, Arthur, a father. He's choosing you to be his son."

And then Arthur was throwing himself at Graham. The rest of the children followed. Even the oldest ones, who had done the math and realized they weren't among the lucky seven, joined the massive hug.

When the crying eventually subsided, Graham turned back to Kit. "I haven't given up on families for the rest of them, and there's two that are ready to take in babies as soon as they're weaned. If the timing is right, they'll even take them as babies."

He took her hand and pulled her out of the crush of children. "I want to keep doing this, Kit, but I'd like to do it with you at my side. We could marry and then travel around the country finding more families. I won't lie — they aren't as plentiful as I'd hoped, and it might take us longer because I'm not going to drag Whitworth around with us everywhere."

"I appreciate that," the other man said flatly.

Graham took a deep breath and took Kit's hand. "I've been wondering for so long what I was supposed to do with my life, thinking there had to be more to it than sitting around waiting for my father to die and make me an earl. That's a rather depressing life. No wonder so many of my friends turn to drinking and gambling. But I wanted something else, and you've shown it to me.

"I love you, Kit, and together we can do this. We can keep helping women, but we can help the children, too. We can find them families that will raise them and love them even if they were born to other people." He took a deep breath and cast a nervous glance at the smiling faces surrounding them. "Marry me, Kit. Together I'll help you save them all."

She reached out a hand and cupped his cheek. "We can't save them all. We can only save one at a time."

"Then start with me," he said. "Save me. Because without you, my life is going to be dark and sad. I can't do this without you."

Kit nodded. "Yes. Yes, I'll marry you."

The idea terrified her. She'd be going back to London, back into her father's world. Someone would revive the rumors, but she'd be married. To a man who would one day be an earl. And she'd be able to help more people than she and Daphne had ever dreamed of.

Another mass hug ensued, and Daphne declared they were having a celebratory picnic, right on the house lawn.

There was a great deal of laughter as the food was prepared, as Graham was told everything that had happened in the week he'd been gone, as Mr. Whitworth was introduced to the goats and chickens.

After the meal, Kit and Graham reclined on a blanket while the children played. They talked quietly, mostly of all her concerns about her father and the rumors, and Graham telling her that he didn't care, that his life was due a little scandal.

Sarah came over and sat by them, smiling but serious. "I don't want you to find me a family," she said softly.

Graham sat up, but Sarah rushed on before he could say anything.

"Hear me out. My life, well, it's about to start. I've never planned on doing anything but working. I hope to find a position that lets me play a bit of music, but I've never expected anything else. I don't blame those families for wanting the younger ones, the ones who will grow up with them. I've got a life waiting for me, Lord Wharton, and I want you to keep finding families for those who don't have that."

Kit reached out and wrapped her fingers around Sarah's. "That's brave of you."

"This house, this life, it's all I've known." Her grin turned a bit impish. "And besides, with all the younger ones out of the cottage, I'll actually have room to sleep in a bedchamber."

Kit laughed along with Sarah, but her heart hurt a bit, too. There were going to be a considerable number of luxuries available to Kit once she married Graham. And here Sarah was just excited to not sleep in the drawing room. Life wasn't fair.

But Sarah, for all her young, tender years, was content. And that was really all Kit could hope for. Life hadn't been fair to these children. But Sarah looked at her life and knew she could make it good.

To think that Kit had even a small part of building that contentment made her want to throw herself facedown before God in gratitude. Because the truth was, Kit had complained, even if only in her mind, about the lot in life she'd been given as well. But now, she was thankful. So thankful. Because without it, she wouldn't have learned what it meant to love someone, wouldn't have learned how to give like she could now.

She glanced at the man beside her. She wouldn't have been the woman he needed in his life. If she'd met Graham in a London ballroom, well, if she'd met him under more traditional ballroom circumstances, she wouldn't have been ready and able to help him find purpose in his life, to do something that fulfilled the great desire God had given him to make a difference.

Now, with her own life stretching before her in ways she'd never expected, she was glad for the bumpy road she'd taken. Because it had led her here.

And here was a wonderful place to be.

EPILOGUE

Kit stood at the window, London stretched out before her, glistening like the polished jewel she was. Along those streets and in those houses still lay the greed and deceit that had long disgusted her, disillusioned her, colored her perceptions until she'd believed one wrong could right another.

But now she also knew that good people walked those streets and danced through those ballrooms. Good people who wanted to love the world the best they could, wanted to be the powerful change that brought God's love and forgiveness. Shadows and grime stretched from the corners of the streets, but sunlight glinted off windows, and bejeweled carriages rolled along, providing a sense of balance she hadn't seen before.

And maybe that was what God wanted her to remember. That there was good and bad in this world, and she could choose which she focused on, which she wanted to be a part of. She could push back the shadows without living in them herself.

If she was honest, and she was trying awfully hard to always be that now, she liked being back in London. It was nice to be here without the guilt.

Daphne and Jess were still at Haven Manor in the official capacity of housekeeper and cook. As long as the two of them stayed employed by the new owner, those roles should make a way for the older children to stay in the caretaker's cottage a few more years, surrounded by the area they'd grown to love. Kit really couldn't have asked for it all to work out any better.

"My mother is insisting that you wear this tonight," a disgruntled voice sounded from behind her.

Kit turned from the window to grin at her new husband. "Is she?"

"Yes." His sigh was an over-exaggerated expulsion of air that let her know he was about to tease her without mercy.

He held the glittering emeralds and diamonds aloft. The necklace was intricate and beautiful, a kind of glorious splendor often reserved for royalty, but without the gaudy ostentatiousness so often held in the jewels of the aristocracy. Delicate strands of jewels dripped from the double-tiered necklace. They swayed and caught the light, sending sparkles across the room from ceiling to floor.

"Well, if your mother is insisting . . ." Kit let her sentence fall off, swallowed by the wide smile she couldn't contain.

Lady Grableton had been far more excited about Graham's plans and Kit's presence than Kit could ever have expected. Kit had been more than a bit chagrined that she'd assumed a woman who worked with Margaretta as a member of The Committee would hold Kit's past against her.

Of course, it was anyone's guess which man was more astonished to learn that Lady Grableton was on The Committee, Graham or his father. When the countess had revealed that Haven Manor was one of the charities she spent her time on, Lord Grableton had beamed with pride.

Kit had never been happier to join a group of people in her life.

And now she'd be with them in a London ballroom. And this time she wouldn't be slinking in the back door to hide behind a potted palm. Instead, she'd be gliding into the ballroom on the arm of a man she wasn't sure she'd have believed existed if she hadn't met him herself.

Yet here he was.

He draped the cool jewels around her neck and fastened the clasp. "There's matching earrings, you know. And a bracelet. But I told her one thing at a time."

Kit ran a hand along the necklace, shivering as the metal and stones warmed to her touch. "You can get the rest of the set."

Sudden stillness filled the room at her whispered words and then a rush of movement as Graham moved until he stood in front of her. One hand reached up to cup her cheek and the other slid down her arm until he could lock his fingers with hers. "Kit, I'm proud to walk into this ballroom tonight with you on my arm, jewelry or no jewelry. You've shown me how much more there is to life. What the rest of them think, well, it's not as important as it used to be."

"I know." Kit leaned her head into his palm and gripped his fingers tighter. "But you've shown me there's more to life, too. Life that I haven't been living because I've been waiting for it to turn sour."

She freed her hand so that she could frame his face and pull him close, close enough that she could see the flecks of gold in his deep brown eyes. "I love you. All of you. The title, the family, the jewels, but most of all the heart. I love the man you are, and whatever comes with you, I'm happy to accept, because it means I can give you all that I am in return."

Strong arms wrapped around her back and pulled her tightly to his chest before his lips closed the gap between them and fused with her own. The kiss was glorious and wonderful, a beautiful representation of love that chased the last of the shadows from Kit's mind.

The past would always be there, its scars a part of her, but at this moment, with this man, she felt beautiful and knew that God could bring something beautiful from her pain.

Graham let out a breath he hadn't known he'd been holding as he and Kit made their way through the crowd mingling near the entrance of the ballroom. There'd been more than one curious glance and a few furtive whispers, but nothing like what Kit had likely feared. Eventually they'd have to talk with her father, but the baron wasn't likely to cause a commotion in the middle of the ballroom, not when Kit was now so closely connected to an earl.

"Ah, this looks like a good spot." Graham grinned as he directed Kit to the side of the ballroom. The scattering of plants wasn't as grand as the trees they'd met behind, but it would do nicely for his plan. "Stand right here and don't move."

She glanced at her feet and then sent him an impish grin. His heart turned over, knowing he'd brought the fun light back into her eyes. "Right here?"

"Precisely here." Graham stepped back, holding his hands out as if he was stopping her from following. "I'll be back in a moment."

Her only answer was another grin, and Graham sauntered away, smiling, to retrieve two glasses of lemonade.

"She's beautiful, Wharton. Wherever did you find her?" Mr. Sherrington nudged Graham's shoulder.

Lord Maddingly chuckled and slapped Graham's other shoulder. "Even more so if she brought a handsome sum with her."

Graham shook his head as he scooped up the glasses. "She only brought herself, gentlemen, and that's more than enough for me."

The two men looked a bit slack-jawed at the announcement. "You didn't marry a country bumpkin, did you? I mean, the rumors are flying about who she could be, but I assured everyone you had a better head on your shoulders than that."

Graham wasn't about to get into Kit's family history with this group of gossipers, but he wasn't going to let her be maligned either. "Take a look, gentlemen. Does that look like a girl of country manners to you?"

All three men looked across the ballroom to where Kit stood, the picture of refined grace even as she stayed precisely where he'd left her, swaying gently with the music.

Graham didn't wait for an answer before breaking away from the men and making his way back to his wife.

"Lemonade?" he asked, extending one of the cups. "I assure you it's harmless."

Recognition lit her smile as she took the cup carefully and made a show of looking at it askance. "You'll have to try it first and show me."

He took a small sip and toasted her with the remains. "See?"

"I see." She took a delicate sip and nodded.

Graham took another sip. "I'm sure you're having a grand time with your friend here," he said, nodding to the squat potted plant beside her, "but I was hoping you'd agree to break away and take a turn with me on the dance floor."

"And if I've already committed the next two to him?" She tried to hide her smile behind the lemonade cup, but Graham could see her white teeth through the wavy glass.

"I'm afraid I'd have to break his heart. And his limbs." He took one last drink and emptied his glass. "Husbandly privilege, you know."

She finished her lemonade and set her glass and his on a nearby window ledge. "I suppose I'll have to dance with you, then. Wouldn't want you causing harm to an innocent plant."

Graham grinned as he escorted her to the floor. A waltz was just starting, and he swept her along into the circling couples. Kit's head jerked as they rounded one couple in particular.

"Kit?" Graham asked.

"I-I know her. I didn't think about that." Kit pressed closer to Graham's side. Was she trying to hide? He spun her around, and the couple they'd been circling looked over.

Surprise made the woman stumble before she gave Kit a small smile and a nod.

"Lady Godfrey," Graham whispered.

Kit jerked her gaze back to his. "Who?"

"Lady Godfrey. She married three years ago. They've a son and she sponsors one of the finest charity hospitals in Leicestershire." Graham squeezed her fingers.

Kit glanced at the woman. Graham's heart pounded. Could Kit see that she had allowed Lady Godfrey to be the woman she'd become? That Kit had a hand in the huge number of people the aristocratic couple had been able to help?

A wet glimmer appeared in Kit's eyes before she whispered, "She's beautiful."

"Yes." Graham released her waist to nudge her chin up. "And so are you. Beautiful in a way that others can't begin to touch." His hand skimmed down to graze the jewels at her throat, ones that had been in his family for generations. "The most precious gems are forged from pressure. God brings beauty from adversity, when you let Him."

Kit's smile glowed brighter than the jewels even as a single tear slid down her cheek. "Then let us forge ahead, dear husband." She swallowed and set her shoulders, looking as if she were ready to go to war even as they swirled across the ballroom. "Let us find the diamonds among the dust."

Graham pulled her close, not caring about the scandal that such an act would cause. He lifted her off her feet and held her tight as he spun her to the edge of the floor and out the door. They had the rest of their lives to show London what a beautiful person Kit had become, both inside and out, but

right then Graham was of a mind to remind
Kit that he'd seen it first.

ACKNOWLEDGMENTS

This is the book that almost wasn't.

The concept was complicated and difficult, the subject matter potentially divisive. But it was a book I desperately wanted to write and I can't say enough about the people who came around me and encouraged me and helped me make it happen.

First, thanks always goes to God, who shows up and shows out and makes words appear that strike me so deep in the heart that I don't know how I managed to type them. It would be so much easier if He would just spit out the whole book for me that way.

And then to Jacob, who always has my back and will always love me no matter how well my books are reviewed or how many lovely readers I have.

To my amazing agent, Natasha Kern, who saw the importance of this story right away and helped me rework and massage the idea

611

until it was cohesive.

To the team at Bethany House that took a chance on this series, but not until it was right. Thank you for your courage and discernment.

Huge thanks also goes to the people from various pregnancy care centers who talked to me and helped me understand more about unwed mothers and fathers and their children than I ever have before. What you do every day is so important.

Writing can sometimes feel like a very solitary thing. Most days it is me and my computer and my Post-it notes. Occasionally words from another enter the arena, but usually in the form of things I need to change (thank you, editors and beta readers!). But that loneliness is temporary because right now you, the reader, are completing the circle and you are joining with others doing the same thing. I am no longer alone.

You are not alone.

So thank you, dear reader, for joining me on this journey, for visiting Haven Manor and seeing yourself, your friend, your neighbor in the pages. We are all a family of sorts now, and I've always loved family. Thank you for joining mine.

Oh, and big smooches to the Bethany

House design team because that cover . . .
Seriously. Gorgeous. The bar has been
raised, and I now expect nothing but perfec-
tion from you amazing people.

ABOUT THE AUTHOR

Kristi Ann Hunter graduated from Georgia Tech with a degree in computer science but always knew she wanted to write. Kristi is a RITA Award winner, an ACFW Genesis contest winner, and a Georgia Romance Writers Maggie Award for Excellence winner. She lives with her husband and three children in Georgia. Find her online at www.kristiannhunter.com.

The employees of Thorndike Press hope you have enjoyed this Large Print book. All our Thorndike, Wheeler, and Kennebec Large Print titles are designed for easy reading, and all our books are made to last. Other Thorndike Press Large Print books are available at your library, through selected bookstores, or directly from us.

For information about titles, please call:
(800) 223-1244

or visit our website at:
gale.com/thorndike

To share your comments, please write:
Publisher
Thorndike Press
10 Water St., Suite 310
Waterville, ME 04901